WILLOWTREE PRESS, L.L.C.

A ROWAN GANT INVESTIGATION

A Novel of Suspense and Magick

By

M. R. Sellars

E.M.A. Mysteries

LOVE IS THE BOND: A Rowan Gant Investigation
A WillowTree Press Book
E.M.A. Mysteries is an imprint of WillowTree Press

PRINTING HISTORY
WillowTree Press First Trade Paper Edition / October 2005

For information, contact WillowTree Press on the World Wide Web:
http://www.willowtreepress.com

ISBN: 0-9678221-2-2

Cover Design Copyright © 2005 Johnathan Minton

Cover Photography: Johnathan Minton

Cover Model: Ms. Gwendolin "Wendi" O'Brien

Author Photo Copyright © 2004 K. J. Epps

10   9   8   7   6   5   4   3   2   1

PRINTED IN THE U.S.A.
by
TCS Printing
North Kansas City, Missouri

Books By M. R. Sellars

The RGI Series

HARM NONE
NEVER BURN A WITCH
PERFECT TRUST
THE LAW OF THREE
CRONE'S MOON
LOVE IS THE BOND

Forthcoming in the RGI Series

ALL ACTS OF PLEASURE

ACKNOWLEDGEMENTS

Once again I find myself with the monumental task of thanking those who made this installment—and in some cases even the entire RGI series—possible. As I have said before, with each book I write, the list of people I feel compelled to thank grows, and eventually, this roll call will take up an entire volume in itself. Still, my good and true friends are very important to me, so this list of "thank you's" has become like a moral imperative. That said, if I happen to miss someone, I hope you understand that it was unintentional, so please accept my apologies in advance.

Finally, while I may simply run down this list like an *Oscar* winner getting the "wind it up" signal, please know that you all made this possible through your love and support (and in more than one instance, your abject lunacy)—

Dorothy Morrison: Two words—Dunkin' Donuts.

Officer Scott Ruddle, SLPD: Two words—Scotch and Cigars.

Roy Osbourn: I concur! See you at the buffet.

Trish Telesco: Thanks for being a friend.

Ann Moura: Thanks for the title!

A.J Drew, Aimee, and Aubrey: Y'all are extended family. I'm sorry I only get to see you once each year.

As always, my ever-expanding, long distance families: *Mystic Moon Coven* and *Dragon Clan Circle*.

Duane & Chell: Words still cannot express my love for you two.

Angel & Randal: Ditto.

Scott & Andrea: Ditto again.

All of my good friends from the various acronyms: F.O.C.A.S.M.I., H.S.A., M.E.C., S.I.P.A, etc. (And even the acronyms that have since disappeared...)

Patrick Owen: I'm running low on MX2's... And, pass the Rye.

Tish Owen: Love ya' hon! Tell your husband I need MX2's!

Lori, Beth, Jim, Dave, Rachel, Doug, Duncan, Kitti, Edain, Boom-Boom, Kevin, David, Bella, Shannon, Denessa, Annette, Boudica, Imajicka, Owl, Breanna, Anne, Maggie, Gail, Phyllis, Zita, Heather, Kathy, Lin, Jerry, Mark, Christine, Kristin, Velvet, Rollie, Hardee, Z, and probably twenty or thirty more...

My parents: You know... I wish you were here.

"Chunkee": Two words—Angry Squirrel.

Johnathan Minton: Are we there yet?

My daughter: Yes, tomorrow is after "this day."

My wife Kat: Sorry, I have to be serious for a moment...You are my one, my all, my everything. I love you more than you will ever know.

Firestorm Publicity Services for making me look good.

The gang at CAO for the *MX2* and entire *Brazilia* line of cigars...

Coffee, Wendi, E.K., *The Bobblehead Lady,* Little Green Men, dancing hamsters, the makers of hard salami...

And, as always, everyone who takes the time to pick up one of my novels, read it, and then recommends it to a friend.

For E.K.

Don't stop until you hear, *"Ushmuff!"*

AUTHOR'S NOTE:

While the city of St. Louis and its various notable landmarks are certainly real, many names have been changed and liberties taken with some of the details in this book. They are fabrications. They are pieces of fiction within fiction to create an illusion of reality to be experienced and enjoyed.

In short, I made them up because it helped me make the story more entertaining—or in some cases, just because I wanted to do so.

Note also that this book is a first-person narrative. You are seeing this story through the eyes of Rowan Gant. The words you are reading are his thoughts. In first person writing, the narrative should match the dialogue of the character telling the story. Since Rowan (and anyone else that I know of for that matter) does not speak in perfect, unblemished English throughout his dialogue, he will not do so throughout his narrative. Therefore, you will notice that some grammatical anomalies have been retained (under protest from editors) in order to support this illusion of reality.

Let me repeat something—I DID IT ON PURPOSE. Do NOT send me an email complaining about my grammar. It is a rude thing to do, and it does nothing more than waste your valuable time. If you find a typo, that is a different story. Even editors miss a few now and then. They are no more perfect that you or me.

Finally, this book is not intended as a primer for WitchCraft, Wicca, or any Pagan path. However, please note that the rituals, spells, and explanations of these religious/magickal practices are accurate. Some of my explanations may not fit your particular tradition, but you should remember that your explanations might not fit mine either.

And, yes, some of the Magick is "over the top." But, like I said in the first paragraph, this is fiction...

When the wind comes from the South,
Love will kiss thee on the mouth.

Couplet #11
The Wiccan Rede
Lady Gwen Thompson,
First Printing, Green Egg #69, Circa 1975

Friday, December 3
7:23 P.M.
Room 7, Satin Tide Motel
Myrtle Beach, South Carolina

PROLOGUE:

S he could feel the tickle rising in her belly. It had been there ever since they walked into the room together. It was faint and fleeting, in the background but always there. Now it was getting stronger.

Steady.

Even.

And, it was crawling upward in an ever-increasing ripple of internal pleasure. At this particular moment, the level was comfortable.

More than comfortable, really, it was desirable and almost hypnotically rhythmic.

She knew from experience that as the rhythm of the tickle increased so would the pleasure—and with it the hypnotic trance. And, with that trance would come yet another step in her journey toward an ultimate goal; of course, that was what this was all about, *her* objective.

Her needs.

Her wants.

She took in a deep breath and closed her eyes, focusing on that which she desired. As she allowed the breath to slowly escape between pursed, red-glossed lips, she could feel the surge beginning. What was at this moment in time merely titillating would very soon push beyond that fragile envelope, exploding forth with untamed fury.

But, not until *she* was ready…

Absolutely not until *she* was ready…

It simply wouldn't be allowed to happen until *she* deemed it time. This may only be a game to him, but for her the game was a ritual—and so much more. And, after all, *she* was the one in control.

She opened her eyes slowly, feeling the rush as her pulse quickened and her breaths became shallow pants.

"Kneel," she commanded, her voice alluringly hoarse but authoritative nonetheless.

The man was facing away from her just as she had instructed him to do. In response, he uttered a simple, "Yes, Mistress," thus finally breaking the silence she had imposed on him fully fifteen minutes before. He set about complying with the order, struggling to keep his balance as he began lowering himself.

He was completely nude with only a few minor exceptions. His hands were tightly bound behind his back; a beige athletic bandage stretched securely in a figure eight about his wrists. A nylon dog collar encircled his neck, and attached to the chromed D-ring was a matched training lead. The tough strip of webbing made a straight line down the center of his back where it eventually looped beneath his restrained arms and trailed off at an upward angle through the space between the two of them, finally ending where it was held in a loose grip by his Mistress' leather-gloved hand.

His right knee hit the floor with a hard thud, and he rocked forward as he fought for the equilibrium necessary to keep from slamming face first into the motel room's thin carpet. Even so, Mistress didn't yield her grip on the leash; instead, much more than simply allowing it to pull taught, she tugged hard on the end, levering his arms backward and straining the collar against his throat with delicious agony.

He gurgled for a moment as he choked then thudded his other knee against the floor as well, still reveling in the pain that brought him such pleasure. He felt his own tickle between his thighs and knew without looking that he had begun to stiffen. Whether the euphoria came from the lack of oxygen to his brain, the curious bent of being tortured by a beautiful woman, or both, he couldn't say. All he knew was that his entire body was beginning to tingle, and he relished its off-kilter pleasure.

A rush of blood was beginning to roar in his ears, and bright spots of color flickered before him as the room began shifting out of focus. His nerve endings were tingling with what he perceived as pure ecstasy, but he knew also that there was a danger zone quickly approaching. Reluctantly, he began to shift his weight back to relieve the strain on the collar that was choking him into his personal bliss. The resistance he met was wholly unexpected.

His pathetic gagging was fueling the tickle in her belly, pushing it up to her solar plexus and out through her extremities, setting each individual cell in her body alight with a smoldering pleasure. Her breaths became shallower and quicker still as she listened to him, twisting the end of the leash in her hand to pull it even tighter. She could tell by the way he was beginning to shift that he was reaching his threshold, but she was not yet ready for it to end. The tickle was still growing, and it had now become a not-so-singular tingle. It needed to be nurtured, and she knew just exactly what would feed its hunger.

As he began to lean back, she maintained tension on the leash and quickly lifted her foot, placing the sole of her stiletto-heeled pump against his spine. She pushed him back forward, and though she was shorter and far lighter than he, she was in full command of the physical laws of leverage.

His gagging and gurgling continued unabated, and she began to almost tremble as the tingle skipped up the scale several notches to become a more than pleasurable full-body itch. She looked up toward the ceiling then closed her eyes yet again, stretching her milky-skinned form toward something unseen. She took in a sudden, deep breath out of autonomic reflex and let it go with an almost imperceptible moan. Opening her eyes she let her gaze fall back down to her slave then clenched her teeth as she slitted her cold stare. With a heaving sigh she released her grip on the leash and gave him a shove with the foot she held planted against his back. He fell forward into a heap, sputtering and gasping as he struck the floor. She watched him slowly roll over, his naked chest rising and falling as he sucked hungrily at the charged air in the room. Her gaze continued to roam his form, falling momentarily between his legs. It was obvious that he had been on the verge of release, and he was still throbbing as he lay there.

"Good," she thought to herself. "He's ready, and so are we. Almost..."

She moved forward, slowly stepping over his prone body but not without dragging the toe of her shoe hard across his heaving chest, taking a moment to relish the sudden yelp the scrape elicited from her slave. She then continued on with a high-heeled swagger that bordered on obscene then strode over to the bureau and stood with her back to him.

An airline bottle of a popular brand of rum was all she had on hand; she hadn't had time to purchase any of the really good stuff. This session had come about far too quickly. The man on the floor behind her wasn't even the real reason she was here. He was serendipity incarnate, spur of the moment and a fully unexpected bonus. Even more—dare she even *think* the cliché pun—almost literally "right out of the blue." But, still, he was one she couldn't pass up; *they* needed to be fed—all of them, including her. And, at least she *did* have rum, so she was certain that *Papa* would understand. He always did.

She looked down and opened the aluminum attaché that adorned the scuffed top of the bureau. Latching the lid upright, she proceeded to arrange the contents within, just as she had done countless times before. But even with her practiced ease, there was still an absolute reverence in the solemn task.

The sweet itch was all but ravaging her now, morphing into a luscious burn that couldn't be quenched, and she knew it was only going to quicken. She reached to the surface of the bureau and retrieved the man's pilot's wings. She had taken them from his uniform earlier while he was dutifully prostrate before her, face down in the carpet and begging pathetically for her sadistic attentions. She laid the prize amidst the other items in the attaché—money clips, rings, watches, and even some things that defied description; those were the most frightening. Some of them actually looked vaguely organic; some appeared as though at one time they should have repulsed the casual observer, even if they did not do so now.

She carefully thumbed through a small stack of photographs, propping them around the items so that she could inspect the images at her leisure. They were simply more mementos of her conquests, but looking at them made the itch swell yet again.

She felt her hand slipping between her thighs as if by its own volition, and she knew it was time. Consciously stopping the hand before it could go any farther, she allowed herself an anticipatory sigh.

She reached up to the bureau and picked up the miniature bottle of rum. With a flourish she twisted the cap from it then pressed the opening against her lips and tilted her head back. She quickly swished the caramel-colored liquor around in her mouth, letting its alcohol-burn tingle for a brief moment, and then carefully spit it into a shot glass. She gently placed the glass jigger directly in the center of the assorted items. With a soft touch she fingered a partially smoked cigar, which still possessed a band proclaiming *Cohiba* and that was underscored by the word *Habana*—true Cuban contraband. She rolled it back to rest against the measure of rum and then allowed herself a fleeting, girlish smile.

As she looked up, she listened intently to the room. She could hear her slave's breathing from his position on the floor behind her. He was finally settling into an even rhythm as he continued to come down from the rapid sexual high she'd inflicted. She looked straight into the mirror and flipped a shock of her waist-length auburn hair back over her shoulder then carefully turned her head side to side, checking her makeup. With the tip of her finger, she made a practiced swipe against the corner of her lower lip, blending a spot she felt needed attention. Then, she inspected it again before letting out a satisfied sigh.

"So," she purred as she turned and began slowly sauntering forward until she stood over the man. "You weren't lying, were you? Asphyxiation really is your kink, isn't it, worm?"

"Yes," he muttered as he tried to give her a nod.

"Yessss?" she questioned with a raised eyebrow, allowing the word to hiss between her teeth.

"Yes, Mistress," he replied.

"Yes, Mistresssss…?"

"Yes, Mistress Miranda."

"You like being choked by women, don't you?"

"Yes, Mistress Miranda."

"Especially beautiful women."

"Yes, Mistress Miranda."

"Tell me I'm beautiful."

"You're beautiful, Mistress Miranda."

"Yes, I am… Aren't I." She uttered the words as a statement of fact.

She squatted next to him with fluid grace, displaying exquisite balance on the teetering heels, and ran her gloved fingertip along his chest, down his abdomen, stopping just before the upper reaches of his pubic hair.

"Then…" she began, pausing as she eyed him seductively. "Since you like it so much, maybe you would want me to do it again?"

"Oh, yes, Mistress," he answered, an excited catch in his throat.

"Then… Beg me to love you," she ordered quietly.

"Mistress?"

"Beg me to love you," she demanded again.

"Please, Mistress," he murmured. "Love me."

"Excellent," she trilled softly as she smiled. "We do love you."

"We, Mistress?"

She didn't answer. In fact, she didn't say another word. She simply scooped the end of the leash into her hand and stood. Taking a stance that would ensure her steadiness, she then lifted one foot and placed the sole of her shoe against his throat as she began bearing down. She watched his face as he fought for air, yet in the midst of it all, he curled the corners of his mouth into what could almost be a smile. She more than sensed the sexual energy pulsating outward from him as he began to gurgle once again, and she let it join with the insane burn that was racking her own body. Immediately, it began feeding on the intensity and sent her inner fire flaring to near ecstasy.

In that moment, she knew she commanded his absolute devotion.

Looking to the side, she could see that he had stiffened yet again and was now throbbing in time with her own racing heartbeat.

In *that* moment, she knew she held captive his innermost desire.

But, for *her*, that simply wasn't going to be enough.

She continued to lean forward, placing all but the smallest amount of her weight onto the one foot, all the while twisting the sole of her shoe against his throat. It didn't take long before he gurgled a barely intelligible utterance that resembled more than just random sounds but a group of deliberate syllables—a phonetic string that sounded like it might possibly be his "safe word."

She knew it was meant to be her cue to cease the torture. But, it was a cue that would go unheeded. She simply smiled down at him and continued to inflict the deliberate cruelty with renewed fervor.

A flicker of realization lit behind his eyes, and he began to struggle, but she had him pinned—held fast and completely at her mercy. There was no way he could break free of the bonds she had so carefully applied. He tried to buck against her, but it was obvious that he was already growing weak from the lack of oxygen. She now brought her full weight to bear on his collapsing windpipe, laying her gloved hand against the nearby wall for support.

In that final moment, she knew she had his fear, and it was delicious.

During the quiet minutes after that, as his eyes turned glassy, staring sightlessly upward to the stained ceiling, she knew she had the last thing she—and they—needed from him.

When she felt the very essence of his terrifying death seep into her own soul, satisfying the gnawing hunger for a time, she stepped down and slowly lifted her foot from his throat. She barely heard the quiet hiss of his trapped breath as it quietly escaped his lifeless form.

Then, and only then, did she receive her reward.

She now allowed the fury to run rampant through her body as she stepped forward and collapsed on the bed, writhing with an ecstasy not entirely of this earth.

11 Months Later
Thursday, November 3
7:23 A.M.
St. Louis, Missouri

CHAPTER 1:

"You knew I was taking these classes, Rowan." My petite, Irish-American wife made the statement and then paused to poke her head through the neckline of a sleeveless, pullover sweater then tug it down over her blouse. Quickly sliding her thumbs along either side of her jaw, she gathered her recently shower-dampened spirals of auburn hair and pulled them from the back of the garment then allowed them to spill over her shoulders, falling almost to her waist. She looked back at me and gave her head an exaggerated shake. "So what's the problem?"

"I never said there was a problem," I replied.

"You didn't have to," Felicity stated.

Her normally soft, Celtic lilt was taking on a far more discernable edge, and the colloquial speech of her heritage was starting to add itself to the mix. While the undertone was always there, it didn't usually present itself so clearly except under particular circumstances—such as being overtired, inebriated, or surrounded by her relatives. Since I knew she was none of the above, it could only mean one thing. She was getting perturbed.

"I'd call it more of a concern," I told her.

"Semantics," she chided.

"Not really."

"So, you don't have a problem with this then?"

"No… Yes…" I almost stuttered, fighting for some middle ground with regard to my feelings. "I don't know. I just wish you'd said something earlier instead of springing it on me like this."

"I'm not springing anything on you, Rowan," she returned. "I just took some photography classes, that's all."

"You're the most sought after freelance photographer in Saint Louis, Felicity," I objected. "You don't *just* take some photography classes."

"If I'm going to maintain that reputation, then I have to keep up on new techniques now, don't I?"

"Quit dancing around it. You specifically took certification courses on crime scene photography."

"Fine," she spat. "Yes. I took classes on forensic, crime scene, and evidence photography to be exact. And, yes, I'm certified now."

"Why?"

"Because I passed the final exam."

"You know what I mean."

"Because it's an aspect of the business I wasn't familiar with."

"And it doesn't have anything to do with Ben mentioning the freelance consultant program for the police department?"

She tried to sidestep the question. "You were sitting right there when he asked me if I was interested, and you didn't object then."

"No, I didn't." I gave a slight nod. "But, that was what? Seven, maybe eight months ago? As I recall, you said you were going to think about it."

"Aye, I *did* think about it," she shot back. She fixed her jade-green eyes on me and arched her eyebrow, daring me to challenge her response.

"And, apparently you came to a decision," I said with a half-hearted shrug.

"Aye, that I did."

"And now you've taken these classes, which tells me your decision is that you're going to sign up for the consultant gig."

She nodded. "Probably."

"Probably?"

"Okay then. Yes. I am."

"Felicity, it's not like we need the money. Between my business and yours, we're in great shape. The house is paid for, our investments are stable, we've..."

She didn't let me finish. "Money isn't the point, Row. It's something I want to do."

"You WANT to take pictures of dead bodies? Victims of violent murders? Suicides?" I asked with more than a note of incredulity in my voice.

"It's not likely to even come to that," she explained. "The freelance program is for specialized photographic techniques that the regular crime scene unit doesn't do. Infrared, ultraviolet, painting with light, and that sort of thing. Primarily for evidence."

"So you would never be photographing dead bodies?"

"Well, maybe not *never*." She shrugged. "I suppose it all depends on what they need then."

"Well, don't you think you should give this a little more thought?"

"Why?"

"Maybe because when you look through a camera lens, you see things most people don't."

"Then I should be pretty good at it, shouldn't I." She was telling, not asking.

"Probably too good. That's what I mean... Think about who you are for a minute."

"Who I am? What do you mean by that?"

"Come on, you're a Witch."

"So are you. What's that got to do with anything?"

"Gods, Felicity!" I exclaimed. "Are you trying to tell me the last few years have only been my imagination? Because if you are, I'm not buying it."

"You're the one who carries on conversations with the dead, Row, not me."

"Excuse me?" It was my turn to raise an eyebrow. "What do you think I meant about looking through a camera? Besides, have you forgotten your last little brush with the ethereal?"

"That was different."

"Really? Do tell."

"Kimberly was my friend. We had a connection. And, besides, that was more than two years ago."

"Twenty-five months, today," I offered. "And don't tell me you didn't know that. The two year anniversary was marked on your friggin' calendar. That's how *I* knew."

"What were you doing looking at my calendar?" she barked.

"Checking to see if you were free so I could surprise you with a night out," I shot back. "You know, dinner. Symphony. Maybe even a hotel room just to be different…"

She closed her eyes and gave her head a quick shake. "I'm sorry. I was out of line."

"You were evading the subject is what you were doing," I replied.

"Yes, well, Kimberly's death has nothing to do with this."

"Yeah… Right…" I nodded as I paused, then fixed her with a serious stare. "You know, I thought the same thing after the first time it happened to me… Ariel Tanner was my friend, and I figured that pretty much had to be the reason for all the ethereal bullshit I was dealing with… I spent a lot of time trying to convince myself of that… You know that… But then… Well, we both know how that worked out, don't we?"

Her gaze softened a bit. I could tell by the look on her face that my reference had hit home. The first homicide case I'd ever been dragged into by the spirit of the victim had affected her as well. Ariel had been my student of The Craft as well as a good friend to both of us. And, unfortunately, she was but one of a series of victims who were brutally tortured and murdered by a serial killer bent on a misguided quest that I still didn't understand. I didn't know that I ever would, but it haunted me on a daily basis, and that was bad enough.

Finding and stopping her killer hadn't really brought me the peace I so desperately sought. In fact, it seemed more as if it had created a permanent connection between the other side of the veil and me, and ever since then the voices of the dead had become a constant din in my ears.

A few years later when Felicity's friend, Kimberly Forest, was murdered, my wife ventured down that very same path with the same devastating results. I knew it was taking a toll, even now after all this time.

"Aye, but even you haven't had anything major happen since Kimberly either," Felicity countered. "Maybe it's over, Rowan. Maybe we can finally get back to a normal life."

I closed my eyes then reached up and pinched the bridge of my nose between my thumb and forefinger. I could feel a headache coming on. It was hovering directly between my eyes, but unlike some of the ethereally induced pains I'd faced over the years, I was pretty sure this one could be easily addressed with a fistful of aspirin. At least I hoped it could.

"I wish I could believe that, honey," I finally muttered. "But, I still hear them."

"But..."

I didn't let her finish. "Felicity... Sweetheart... It's been a nice reprieve, but I think we both know this is probably just the calm before the storm."

"Aye, maybe so," she muttered. "But I'm still going to do this."

"Why?" I pressed.

"Because I want to, then."

"Okay, but why? Why do you want to?"

"Because I find it interesting," she stated with an unconvincing shrug, once again trying to sidestep the issue. She turned her back to me and picked up a wide-toothed comb from her dressing table. Gathering a handful of her hair, she began intently working at detangling a section.

I watched her for a moment, silently mulling over my impending choice of words. I had been exactly where she was now, and I understood far better how she felt than anyone else possibly could. What I was about to say to her was something she had said to me more than once, and I didn't want to come off as if I were feeding her own words back to her—even though that was exactly what I was about to do. After a measured beat I responded. "Because you find it interesting, or because you have something to prove?"

"What would I have to prove, then?" she asked, shifting her gaze slightly to look at my reflection in the mirror.

I took in a breath and with my words laid open the wound. "Maybe you feel guilty because you couldn't save Kimberly Forest."

She wheeled back around to face me and thrust the comb in my direction. "Don't..." The word caught in her throat, and I thought I could hear her voice crack slightly. "Don't... Just don't go there."

I nodded. "I thought so."

"Damn your eyes, Rowan Linden Gant!" she admonished.

"Yeah, damn my eyes."

I stepped forward and pulled her close, wrapping her in a tight hug. She melted into me as she rested her cheek against my shoulder. I knew she was harboring a desire to cry, but at the same time I was all too aware that she wouldn't. We stood there for quite awhile, neither of us saying a thing but still communicating with clarity unmatched by simple words.

She finally pulled away then turned back to the mirror without comment and began working at her hair again. Her darkened mood was obvious from the vicious strokes she was making with the comb.

"Aye, I'm still going to do this, you know," she eventually announced.

"Yeah," I answered softly, placing my hand on her shoulder and giving it a light squeeze. "Yeah, I know you are."

There are certain inalienable truths.

We're born. We grow old. We die. And, somewhere within that span we live our lives. If we're lucky, we find someone to live that life with. If we're very lucky, we find that particular someone who makes us whole.

That was one of my personal truths.

In Felicity, I had found just exactly that person who made me whole. I suppose that would explain why I was so adamant about protecting her from those horrors I had already experienced—and would surely experience many more times before reaching that final truth.

At this particular moment, however, the biggest conflict in my mind was the fact that she was, for the most part, correct.

I was the one who talked to the dead.

It was *me* who had this preternatural connection with the Otherworld that brought unimaginable agonies to my life, both mental and physical. Felicity had only been dragged into the fray because she was desperately trying to protect me, even if it meant sacrificing herself. After repeatedly watching me go through ethereal visions so intense that bloody stigmata mimicking a victim's wounds had appeared on my own body, she had seen more than enough. From her side of the fence, it had been a wholly different kind of torture, and when the tables were turned and I witnessed her going through the same things over Kimberly Forest, I gained a healthy respect for her feelings. I guess I couldn't blame her. She was only doing exactly what I would do.

Still, I was just as stubborn as she, and when it came to being the protector, I felt it my place to assume that role. It was the very meaning behind the name Rowan, after all.

I plunged the tip of a shovel down into the soft earth and used my foot to shove it deeper still. Pulling back on the wooden handle, I levered a sizeable chunk of dirt upward and plopped it off to the side then repeated the process as I continued mulling over the events of the morning thus far.

We had reached an impasse. Felicity had it in her head that she was going to add herself to the list of freelance crime scene photographers used by the local police departments. As a matter of fact, at this very moment she was literally on her way to fill out the necessary paperwork.

The plain truth was that I was most likely worrying myself over nothing. Ben had told us that the local departments rarely used the freelancers. They were primarily there for the specialized photos just as Felicity had said. The only reason she'd had to go through the crime scene technician certification courses was to meet the requirements set forth by the city police department. What it really came down to was that the freelance program was really nothing more than a contingency plan born of an anal retentive bureaucracy.

So, as it stood, the likelihood of needing them was minimal, much less Felicity having her name drawn from the pool. Still, anyone can tell you that Murphy's law will invoke itself without warning, and I just had a bad feeling that if her name was on the list, she was going to end up in the middle of something. What's more, I feared that since she had been fully across the veil once, it would only take a single, highly charged experience to drag her under in an ethereal riptide. That was how it happened with me, so I had to figure it could happen with her—unless of course, I had any say in the matter.

And, that was the very reason why I was standing in our back yard on a chilly November morning, digging a hole in the rock garden.

It was cold enough to cause my breath to condense in rapidly dissipating clouds of steam yet still far enough above the freezing mark that the somewhat soggy ground was soft and easy to penetrate. My most laborious task so far had been moving the small boulder from the spot where I wanted to dig.

I had waited until I was certain Felicity was well on her way so that I would have ample time to complete my project. It was a task that was a long time coming. Something I'd started better than two years ago and now felt compelled to finish without delay.

I struck the point of the shovel into the hole with a repeated chopping motion, widening the small excavation to suit my purpose. I only stopped for a brief moment when my heart skipped a beat upon hearing our English setter and Australian cattle dog yelping at the gate. But, I immediately breathed a sigh of relief when I caught a glimpse of someone walking past the house on the sidewalk out front. For a frightening instant, I feared Felicity had returned too soon.

I finished squaring up the hole, which now looked to be better than a foot deep, then set the shovel aside. Kneeling next to it, I opened a small, metal toolbox I had set off to the side before starting the manual labor portion of this job. Inside the shallow container, pristine as when I had placed it there, was what would at first glance be considered a toy. It was a fashion doll to be exact, complete with long red hair and a smooth, ivory-tinted complexion. If ever there was a perfect representation of my ethnically stereotypical wife, this was it. The doll was wrapped securely in clear cellophane and trussed with a criss-crossed purple ribbon. It was a piece of SpellCraft commonly known as a binding. A powerful act of magick with, in this case, one purpose—to keep Felicity safe from harm. It was something I had worked immediately following my wife's experience with Kimberly Forest's kidnapping and eventual death.

Unfortunately, the day I had set about casting the spell, she had come home unexpectedly, and I'd had to hide the box before I could bury it. Soon after that, everything in our lives had calmed. It had been so quiet for the past two plus years that I had never seen the need to fully complete the spell. Still, I had kept the old metal box in the back of my desk's file drawer all this time, hidden but not forgotten. I knew, as it sat now, in some sense it was working its intended magick. However, placing the poppet into the earth would bring the spell completely to fruition beyond any doubt—as long as Felicity didn't know about it.

And, right now, something was telling me that it was imperative for the spell to be finished. I tried not to dismiss those "somethings" when they talked to me. Because, even though they usually got me in trouble, ignoring them just made the trouble that much worse.

I finally realized I was staring blankly at the doll and broke myself out of the shallow trance. I closed the lid and snapped the latch shut then nestled the box snugly at the bottom of the hole. I stood and with almost mechanical repetition, scooped the loose dirt in on top of it then tamped it down with the back of the shovel. After rolling the decorative boulder back into place—as well as muscling it around to make sure it looked close as possible to its original position—I scattered some of the fallen leaves around it in an attempt to hide any evidence that it had been disturbed.

I stood there staring at the rock for a long while, leaning on the shovel handle as I pondered the magnitude of what I had just done. A spell was supposed to be cast in perfect love and perfect trust. I could easily claim perfect love, but the issue of perfect trust was another story entirely. I was inflicting my will upon my wife without her knowledge, much less her blessing, and I knew for that I would eventually pay. Even so, if it kept her safe, the debt was one upon which I would gladly make good.

Finally, even though there was no one there to hear the words but me, I simply said, "Not on my watch, Felicity Caitlin O'Brien. Not on my watch."

A few minutes later, I stowed the tools back in the shed then went inside to clean up and get down to work. I had a client with a system crash and two more with remote updates scheduled for installation this afternoon.

It was going to be a full day. Had I realized how full the days beyond this one were about to become, I would have considered it a vacation.

Tuesday, November 8
12:27 A.M.
Suite 1233, Concourse Suites
St. Louis, Missouri

CHAPTER 2:

She couldn't remember the last time she had been this frustrated. Even the bath hadn't helped, and she'd even used six cans of milk instead of four.

Of course, maybe milk wasn't what she needed to use. Perhaps purity wasn't the remedy she needed to seek.

She should know by now that purity couldn't satisfy the hunger.

She finished closing her garment bag and tugged on the zipper. When it didn't immediately yield to her pull, she gave it a violent jerk then shrieked at it. "Dammit!"

"Dammit…" She muttered the word again, her angry voice held low under her breath. "That fat bastard just had to ruin it…"

It was entirely his fault. She would be fine right now if it wasn't for him.

She couldn't believe it. The sensory deprivation, smothering, the razor; shit, even the gun didn't make him afraid. And, he had known it was the real thing, it was *his own goddamned* gun! He just kept getting more excited no matter what she did to him. No matter what she threatened, there was no fear. Even after she would carry out a torture and follow it with psychological intimidation, implying that worse was to come, he would just get that much more aroused.

What a complete pervert he was! He was even so wrapped up in the game that he didn't need manual stimulation. He just got off right there on the bathroom floor.

Damn the premature fucker.

She hadn't been ready. Not yet.

None of them were ready. Especially *her*.

She hadn't even had a chance to open her attaché, much less do the ritual.

Damn him!

And, if that wasn't enough, when he had blown his load, it got all over one of her shoes. Good damn thing he was carrying a healthy wad of cash. Her fees didn't include having a three hundred dollar pair of suede pumps ruined by the likes of him.

But, even though he had the cash, it still made her angry.

And, when she got angry, she made mistakes. Mistakes like the one she made last night when she pulled the trigger.

No, she hadn't been ready.

Dammit, dammit, dammit, she just wasn't ready yet! And it was his fault! A few more minutes and maybe it would have been the right time. Maybe she could have evoked some fear, and then they would have been satiated. And if they were satiated, then she could have taken him quietly, and she would have had her reward.

But not this time…

Now, they were turning their backs on her.

She was ignoring her.

She was going to let her suffer.

She was being punished because of him.

She finished snapping the closures on the garment bag and hefted it from the bed then placed it near the door with her laptop and makeup case.

As she stood there, the word "no" suddenly rang through her head born of an ethereal voice.

She didn't move. She simply continued staring at the luggage, trying to ignore the command.

The hunger continued deep within, hunger that went far beyond the physical. She closed her eyes, waiting for the gnawing sensation to pass, but as she feared it only grew stronger.

They needed to be fed. No… *She* needed to be fed.

She opened her eyes then stepped over to the window and absently peered through at the sparkling downtown Saint Louis skyline. Crossing her arms, she hugged herself tightly as if steeling against the chilly darkness.

"Not yet," she murmured. "Not here. It's too soon."

The hunger didn't listen. She could hear the response echoing in her ears with an unnatural hiss, "Yeesssss… Nowwwww…"

"No," she objected quietly, her voice almost a whimper.

"Yeesssss," the voice returned. "Ssssheee demandssss a ssssacrificsssssse forrr yourrrr failurrrrrreeee…"

She allowed her head to hang forward, squeezing her eyes tightly shut once more. What had she done? What pact had she made that now brought her to this point of addiction?

The voice echoed again, "Yeesssss… Nowwwww… Ssssheeee demandssss theeeee ssssacrificssssse…"

Slowly, she reached to the desk and picked up the phone then reluctantly tapped in a number with a lacquered nail.

"Yes," she said after listening to an overly cheerful greeting from the concierge. "Suite 1233. Could you let the front desk know in the morning that I am going to need the room for an extra day, perhaps two… Yes… No, I would really prefer to keep the same room… Yes… No, just some fresh towels… Yes… Thank you."

After she nestled the handset back into the cradle, she looked over at her luggage, all packed and ready to go. She hadn't planned for this, and she would be needing a few things. She then glanced over to the aluminum attaché sitting on the desk next to her purse.

With a resigned sigh, she stalked over to the baggage, retrieved her computer case and began unzipping it as she made her way to the desk. She might as well get started.

She needed someone to have for dinner, and it couldn't be just anyone. No, the demand had been too specific. *She* wanted *the* sacrifice, and for this occasion, it needed to be someone very special.

Fortunately, she wouldn't have to go far. She already knew him very well.

Tuesday, November 8
3:07 A.M.

CHAPTER 3:

A completely unexpected pain bit into my side. It was sharp and unpleasant but not what one would call agonizing. In fact, it was really just more along the lines of "insistently uncomfortable." Still, whether agonizing or not, I rolled over out of reflex, moving in what my muddied brain perceived to be the opposite direction of the vexation.

My head was buzzing as an obnoxious clamor droned in my ears, and I might have focused in on that disquiet were it not for the fact that it suddenly, and thankfully, fell silent. I started to dwell on it anyway, or at least I think that's what I was doing. I couldn't be sure because the dwelling didn't last very long. Apparently, my sleepiness-reduced serotonin levels were more than enough to convince me it wasn't worth the time. In what was probably a span of no more than a second, I started drifting back into the comfortable darkness of sleep.

Of course, it was at about this point in time that the pain returned, just as sharp and even more unpleasant than before. This time it arrived in conjunction with a repeat of the raucous droning followed by a string of unintelligible speech. Neurons dutifully awakened inside my head, hurried through their electrochemical greetings with one another, then informed me that the elbow of the woman beside me in the bed was the instrument of my torture. Next, I was made privy to the fact that the droning noise had most assuredly been the ringer on the telephone.

However, my brain still couldn't interpret the muddled string of syllables. A full translation being unlikely, and not being satisfied with simply getting two out of the three, it did the next best thing and gave me a short list of possibilities. The top pick among them was something akin to my wife telling me to answer the phone. Of course, after all of that thinking being foisted upon me, I was actually awake enough to lay money down that said pick was dead on the mark.

I groaned and sent my hand searching for the telephone on the nightstand. As I groped in the dark, using only one barely open eye for guidance, a passing thought rolled through my brain: If the thing had a longer cord, I could move it to Felicity's side of the bed. It sounded like a good solution at the moment, but I knew she would probably just move it back. I tried to dismiss the idea, but something in the mind-fog kept reminding me that this was the reason she was still sleeping and I wasn't.

I managed to wrap my hand around the receiver and yank it from the base just as it started its annoying clamor once again. Unfortunately, I was a split second too late to avoid a third purposeful jab and annoyed burst of gibberish from my grumbling wife.

I winced and tried to roll out of her reach without falling off the side of the bed. I wasn't overjoyed about a phone call in the middle of the night to begin with. Getting physically abused over it definitely wasn't helping my mood. Right about then, another thought shot rapidly through my grey matter: Was this just going to be a hang-up? We'd had more than our share of those, at all hours, over the past few years. So many, in fact, that we'd had our number changed several times. All had been quiet for a while now, so it actually wouldn't be a big surprise for the prank calls to be starting up again.

"This had better be good," I muttered as I pushed the handset up next to my ear. At least, that was what I thought I said. Judging from the response I received, apparently what I was thinking and what was coming out of my mouth were mutually exclusive.

"What?" Detective Benjamin Storm's somewhat confused sounding voice filtered into my ear. "That you, white man?"

My heretofore-sluggish synapses instantly began arcing at full speed as I pushed myself upright and fought to disentangle my lower half from the bedding. A sickening feeling of déjà vu was setting in, and I didn't like it one bit.

Next to Felicity, Ben Storm was undoubtedly my best friend in the world. He was exactly the kind of friend for whom you would do just about anything without question and knew beyond any doubt he would do the same for you. However, as close as we were, neither of us were in the habit of calling the other in the middle of the night just to socialize.

No, we had been down this road far too many times in the past few years. If he was calling at an odd hour, it was guaranteed not to be pleasant news, and more often than not, I had a pounding headache of ethereal origin to prove it. This time, however, my head felt just fine. Maybe still a bit groggy but completely devoid of pain. Given the circumstances, that just piqued my curiosity even more.

"Ben?" I replied, this time managing to keep my tongue from wrapping around my teeth.

"Yeah," he replied. "Woke ya' up, didn't I?"

I cast an eye at the glowing numbers on the bedside clock. When I replied I couldn't keep the sarcasm out of my voice. "What do *you* think?"

"Uh-huh, well ya' can go back ta' sleep in a minute, Kemosabe. So listen, can ya' put Felicity on the phone?"

"What's wrong?"

"I'm a homicide cop, and it's three in the fuckin' mornin', Row. Whaddaya think's wrong?" he retorted, his own snippet of sarcasm underlining the words. "Lemme talk ta' your wife."

"Ben..." I allowed my questioning voice to trail off.

"Row," he replied succinctly then fell silent.

After an extended verbal staring contest, I spoke. "Tell me what's up, Ben."

"You got some *Twilight Zone* goin' on?" he asked, using his favorite turn of phrase for my supernatural visions.

"No."

"Good."

"Well, should I?"

"No, so put yer wife on the phone."

"But..."

He cut me off. "Listen, Row, chill out. For once it's not all about you, okay? Now, lemme talk to Felicity."

Even though he wasn't willing to give me the details, his comment about being a homicide cop spoke volumes. The fact that he was calling for Felicity also told me that I had been correct about Murphy and his damnable law. I obviously wouldn't be going back to sleep anytime soon.

I conceded. "Hold on…"

Out of reflex, I sent my free hand searching through the darkness and switched on my reading lamp then mutely cursed myself for the action as I squinted against the sudden influx of light. With a groan I reached over and gave my slumbering wife a far gentler nudge than she had previously afforded me. She shrugged, grumbled something just as unintelligible as her earlier string of syllables and then tried to roll away as she pulled the comforter up over her face. I hooked my hand into the bedding and tossed it back with a quick yank, unceremoniously exposing her to the cool air in the room. This time I had no trouble understanding the Gaelic curse that flew from her lips.

"*Damnú ort!*" she yelped as she flailed an arm about in search of the blanket.

Leaning back, I gently caught her wrist mid-grope then stretched the telephone receiver across the bed. I stuffed the device into her hand and carefully pushed it toward her ear.

"It's for you" was all I said before laying back against my pillow.

I didn't know why I was even bothering. I was fully awake now.

I listened to the one-sided conversation as she answered with "uh-huh's" and "umm, yeah's" for a moment then finally pushed herself up on an elbow and asked, "Are you sure?… But I thought… Yeah… Okay then, just a second, let me find a pen…"

What I was hearing from this side didn't sound good at all. I gave in and pushed myself into a sitting position then swung my legs over the side of the bed. Felicity was still searching for something to write with when I stood up and headed for the bathroom.

If my wife was about to apply her warm, artistic talent to the face of cold, brutal reality, I was going to be there to make sure she stayed *behind* the camera.

"You just filled out the paperwork a few days ago." I called into the dining room from the kitchen. "Have they even had time to get you on the list?"

I was already dressed and was brewing a fresh pot of coffee by the time Felicity had taken down the address of the scene and started slipping into some clothes herself. Now, I was removing the lids from a pair of oversized travel mugs while my wife gathered together the photographic equipment she thought she might need.

"Aye, would seem so," Felicity replied, her words were forced squeakily through a deep yawn.

"Tired?"

"I've only had about an hour of sleep. What do you think?"

"What time did you get in?"

"I didn't get here until almost one forty-five," she replied.

"Why so late?"

"The shoot ran late, then I took a wrong turn getting back to the highway, so that took forever. It was a bad night all around."

"Sorry to hear that."

"How about yours?"

"Uneventful. Took the dogs to the park, answered some email then looked at the news."

"You seemed pretty zonked when I came to bed. I tried not to wake you."

"You didn't," I called back to her. "I was going to wait up but finally called it a night around eleven-fifteen or so."

"You..." the rest of the sentence was nothing more than a squeaky garble as she yawned again.

"What?"

"You didn't have to wait up," she said in a far more intelligible fashion.

"I missed you."

"How sweet."

"Okay, it's a little early, so before this gets any mushier, what's up with this call?"

"What do you mean?"

"I mean I thought this whole thing was supposed to be for the specialized stuff."

"Or emergencies."

"You never told me that part."

"I didn't?"

"No."

"Must have slipped my mind then."

"Yeah," I grunted. "So this is an emergency?"

"Apparently."

"How so?"

"Flu epidemic."

"Yeah, that's old news. What does it have to do with this?"

"Crime scene technicians get the flu too."

"All of them?" I asked with a note of disbelief.

"The ones who know how to use a camera it seems. There's a bit more to it than taking a few point-and-shoot snapshots you know."

"Yeah, I know."

"Anyway, Ben said they were short-staffed across the board."

"But, still, it's a bit quick to be calling you out, don't you think?" I pressed. "Didn't they have anyone more experienced on the list?"

"Aye, this is really getting under your skin, isn't it then?"

"No."

"*Cac capaill,*" she mumbled.

"I heard that," I said in reply to her under-the-breath Gaelic epithet. "And, where I come from we say 'bullshit'."

"Horse shit works too."

"Okay. Yeah, so I'm not excited about it. But you already knew that. Even so, that didn't answer my question."

"You mean about experience? I guess. Maybe," she replied, and I could almost hear the shrug in her voice. "Ben said he called four others before he got to me. I can't help it that I'm the only one who answered the phone."

"You didn't." I corrected her over my shoulder as I carefully filled the travel mugs. "I did."

"Minor detail."

"Oh yeah? Next time I'll just let the machine get it."

"I'll only hit you harder."

"Yeah, you would, wouldn't you?"

"Aye."

I plopped a trio of raw sugar cubes into one of the mugs then screwed the lid tightly onto it before continuing. "So you're telling me no one else answered?"

"That's what Ben said."

"Lucky you."

"Aye. Lucky me."

I stepped through the doorway and nudged Felicity's arm with the metal and plastic vessel. She looked up from the street guide she was intently studying and turned her head toward me.

"Here," I said. "This might help get rid of the accent."

She looked at me and simply shook her head then accepted the proffered mug and immediately took a swig. In a quick motion, she held it back toward me at arm's length. "Needs sugar."

"It's in there," I told her as I turned and headed back into the kitchen. "Just give it a good swirl."

"You didn't stir it?" she called after me.

"No."

"Why not?"

"You're in a hurry, right? Besides, why dirty up a spoon?"

I heard her let out a heavy sigh. "How many then?"

"Three."

"This is a big cup. It needs at least five. Maybe six or seven."

"You're sweet enough already. You got three."

"Hah hah" was her exaggerated reply.

"So, do you have everything you need?" I asked, coming back out of the kitchen with my own mug of the brew. I had already donned my coat, and now I peered at her over the rim of my cup as I took a drink.

"Where are *you* going?" she asked after sizing me up.

"With you."

"Why?"

"Because I 'find it interesting'."

"Rowan..." she huffed. "I'll be fine. I can do this without you."

I reached down to pick up the larger of the two camera cases she had sitting on the table then slung it over my shoulder and headed for the door.

"I know you will, and I never said you couldn't." I stopped in the living room and turned back toward her. "So... Are you driving or am I?"

My wife rolled her eyes at me then muttered, "Damned Pisces."

"Damned Taurus," I replied with a grin.

She simply sighed again and shook her head. A moment later she took hold of the other equipment bag, hefted it onto her own shoulder, then started forward and brushed past me while saying, "Aye, we'll take my Jeep. I think I've got some sugar packets in the glove box."

CHAPTER 4:

"Heya, Felicity," Ben called out, nodding toward my wife as he put himself through the excessive gyrations necessary to slip his bulk beneath a bright yellow strip of crime scene tape. "Sorry I had ta' call ya' out like this."

"It's no problem, then," she returned.

Once he'd unfolded his frame, he continued walking toward us. "Jeez," he continued. "We've never had anything like this happen before. I had ta' make five calls just ta' get the okay ta' bring in a freelancer."

"That bad, huh?" she queried as he came to a stop in front of us.

"Yeah. We're so fuckin' short-staffed it's a wonder some asshole hasn't stolen the entire city," he grumbled. "And now this. Shit, if this whole scene wasn't such a cluster, I'd just stick a camera in someone's hands and have 'em take snapshots. I'm really sorry I had ta' call ya' out on this."

"Aye, Ben, it's okay. Not a problem," Felicity repeated.

He abandoned seriousness for a moment and allowed his face to spread into a slight grin. "Damn, I love it when ya' do the accent."

"How many times do I have to tell you, Ben," my wife quipped. "I don't have an accent. You do."

He chuckled and then leveled his gaze on me. "So, what the hell are YOU doin' here, white man?"

"Nice to see you too," I replied.

Homicide Detective Benjamin Storm stood six-foot-six, and a quick glance at him was enough to show he was no stranger to the weight room. He was casually dressed as usual, clad in a pair of faded denim jeans and a loose-fitting, charcoal grey, fisherman's sweater. His gold shield was hanging around his neck on a thick cord, and his nine-millimeter Beretta was nestled beneath his left arm in a worn, leather shoulder rig.

Now that he was close enough for us to see his face, it was obvious that he'd probably been dragged out of his own slumber just as unceremoniously as had we. Still, even with his rumpled appearance, he made an altogether imposing figure. Of course, it probably didn't help that at this particular moment the three of us were standing here in the oblique shadows of a motel parking lot watching our breath condense on the chilly breeze.

Harsh red and white splashes of brightness flickered across the scene from active light bars atop emergency vehicles, their on and off glare lending a patina of chaos to what would seem an otherwise somber night. The familiar background din of static and tinny voices prevailed from police radios, running the gamut of low range volumes.

Although Ben had recently begun to show a minor bit of greying, he still possessed a collar length helm of almost completely jet-black hair. That, his complexion, and his dark eyes combined with his rugged features to leave no doubt as to his full-blooded Native American heritage. If any doubt still existed, however, the nickname he had just tagged me with was a direct product of that history as well.

We'd been friends longer than I cared to remember, and the tongue-in-cheek banter had been a part of our dynamic almost from the word go. I would call him "Chief", "Tonto", or even "Injun". He would counter with "Kemosabe", "white man", or "paleface". He even went so far as to give Hollywoodesque Indian names to Felicity such as "Firehair" or "Red Squaw".

We were both perfectly aware that people around us could be so caught up in runaway political correctness that they would visibly cringe when they heard us. Of course, if we happened to notice their discomfort, we would both be so amused that we would exaggerate the repartee for nothing more than our own entertainment.

However, at this very moment, the most important thing about the moniker was that it told that he wasn't angered about me tagging along. He was merely giving me grief just for the sake of it. Considering his earlier tone, I hadn't been sure what his reaction was going to be. His eventual reply to my non-answer simply perpetuated the chaff.

"Didn't say it wasn't nice ta' see ya'," he said. "I just don't remember invitin' you to our little rendezvous."

"You woke me up," I told him. "That's invitation enough for me."

My friend grunted then gave his head an exaggerated shake and parked his hands on his hips. Looking over at my wife with a flirtatious grin, he exclaimed, "Well damn, sweetheart! Guess we're gonna have ta' find a different place ta' meet now."

She quickly picked up on the joke and nodded. "Aye. I suppose you're right, pookums."

"Go ahead," I offered with a shake of my head. "She'd just hurt you."

"Yeah, you're prob'ly right 'bout that," he agreed with a chuckle.

"So, you're in an awfully good mood considering the circumstances," I said. "You didn't sound this chipper on the phone."

"Prob'ly lack of sleep," he replied, rubbing a large hand across his chin. "That, or just tryin' ta' stay sane, take your pick."

"Knowing you? All of the above," I returned.

"Uh-huh," he grunted then added with a note of seriousness slipping into his voice, "Yeah, well, you got no idea, Row."

"Is it really that bad in there?" Felicity asked.

My friend reflexively brought his hand back up to smooth his hair, something he always did when he was carefully mulling over a crucial thought. "If you're talkin' like real gory, yes and no," he finally said. "It sure's hell ain't pretty, that's a fact... Guess it depends on your stomach, but I know you've both seen worse."

"So not very high on the gore-meter?" she returned.

"Oh, I dunno. 'Bout a six or seven, I guess… But that's not really what I'm talkin' about. The bad is gonna happen soon as the TV people get here."

"I'm surprised they aren't already," I observed.

"Yeah, me too," he agreed then suddenly gave his head a quick jerk and exclaimed, "Jeezus, this is gonna be fucked up!"

I shrugged. "You mean the press? So what? That's not unusual."

"Yeah, I know, but I'm tellin' ya' this is worse. It's gonna be capital F-U-C-K-E-D fucked with an underline this time."

"Okay, I give. Why?"

He looked me square in the eyes and sighed. "Well, you're gonna know soon enough anyway."

"Okay, so now I'm getting curious," Felicity announced. "What in the world has you so wrapped, then?"

"Jeezus…" he muttered then cast a glance quickly between us. "So look, we're tryin' ta' keep a lid on this for as long as we can, so what I'm gonna tell ya' doesn't go any further, 'kay?"

I nodded. "Yeah, okay."

"Of course," my wife answered.

He looked off into space for a second then back to us. "Either of you ever heard the name Hammond K. Wentworth?"

I nodded. "Sounds familiar. He's a judge or something, isn't he?"

"District court judge," Felicity piped up. "Isn't he the one who presided over the big racketeering case with that construction company earlier… Wait a minute, you're not saying…"

"Yeah, I'm sayin'…" Ben affirmed as he nodded. "He's the stiff yer gettin' ready ta' immortalize."

"A federal judge?" my wife almost yelped the question.

"Yeah. That's why we had ta' have a decent photographer on the scene and not just have someone do the 'point, snap, okay I got the picture' thing."

The magnitude of the victim's identity struck home, and my brain immediately seized on the most obvious scenario. "So do you think this was some kind of a contract killing?" I asked. "Organized crime, all that?"

"Who the fuck knows?" he replied. "Maybe. Maybe not. We gotta figure all the angles, and we definitely ain't rulin' that one out."

"But is that how it looks?" Felicity asked.

"Let's put it this way: The back of his goddamn head and most of his brain is all over the wall, but... Well..." he verbally stumbled, searching for words.

"Something's not right?" I offered.

"'Zactly," he said with a nod. "Somethin's hinky... I dunno what it is, but it just doesn't look right.

"Why a motel room?" Felicity asked. "Are you thinking maybe suicide instead?"

He shook his head. "No. Prob'ly not suicide. Not unless the gun grew legs and walked off. Maybe robbery..."

As his last words trailed off, I started making my own connection with what I believed he was implying, so I asked, "Robbery as in a personal services transaction gone wrong, you mean?"

"Personal services transaction?" He wrinkled his forehead at me as he spoke. "When the hell did you get all PC?"

"Like you said," I returned. "Lack of sleep."

"Uh-huh. Well yeah, it's a real possibility. Word is Wentworth had a thing for hookers... He's been popped with 'em more'n once, and the department looked the other way. Buried the whole thing so the press couldn't jump on it."

"Good to have friends in high places," Felicity jibed. "I'll bet the woman didn't get the same treatment."

Ben shot her a glance. "Got a soft spot for whores, do ya'?"

"I'd really prefer you didn't use that term," she returned coldly.

Ben paused for a moment, giving her a surprised look. "Well... Okay... Yeah, ummmm... Listen..." he finally stammered.

"So you think he might have been with a woman, and she robbed him?" Felicity suggested.

"Or her pimp," he offered as he shot her a questioning glance. "Can I say pimp?"

She simply looked back at him without a word.

"Well, yeah, like I said it kinda looks that way." He nodded then continued, "And that's just a whole 'nother reason this is gonna be a clusterfuck when the media jumps on it."

"But you have doubts," I offered.

"Shit, Rowan," he spat. "I've always got doubts, but yeah, somethin' just ain't right in there."

"Not right how?" Felicity asked.

"It just doesn't look like... Well, you'll see it when ya' get in there. Maybe I'm just chasin' my tail."

"Detective Storm," a uniformed officer called to Ben from behind the barrier tape. "Circus just came to town."

We all looked up to see a pair of news vans pulling into the parking lot. My friend shook his head again and muttered, "Fuck me. Just fuuu-cck me." Looking back to us he said, "Let's get you signed in and workin' before they start makin' movies. Last thing I need is for Bible Barb ta' see yer smilin' face on the mornin' news."

My friend held out his arm and quickly ushered us toward the barrier tape and the waiting officer who was manning the clipboard.

This was the first time I'd heard him mention Barbara Albright's name in several months. At one time, she'd been a constant vexation to him, even banning him for better than a year from serving on the Major Case Squad. Since the MCS was her command, he'd had little recourse and had spent that time more or less pushing paper around the city homicide division.

Her reasoning for his exile was primarily based on the fact that he was my friend, and she absolutely despised me. On the surface, the naked derision she displayed, even publicly, would have seemed unusual. However, when you considered all the facts, it instantly made sense. She was a fundamentalist Christian with a badge, and I was an out-of-the-broom-closet Witch who had been instrumental in solving more than one series of serial homicides. Not exactly what you would call a perfect match.

I'd made no secret of the fact that I blamed myself for Ben's career derailment, even if he didn't. And, while to this day I still felt guilty over it, ever since Albright's promotion, things had gotten much better for him including being re-assigned back to the Major Case Squad.

"I thought you said Albright hadn't been causing you any trouble since she made captain," I commented as I waited my turn to autograph the crime scene log.

"Bee-bee?" the uniformed officer chuckled, overhearing me, then he muttered as he shook his head. "What a piece of work."

"Yeah," Ben answered me. "Well, not much anyway. She still gets her kicks in. But, you're right. It's been manageable. She's been fast trackin', and lately she's climbin' the ladder and bein' a bureaucrat. Rubbin' elbows just like she wanted."

"So," I asked as I scribbled my signature on the log and then handed the pen back to the officer. "What are you worried about?"

Felicity had already slipped beneath the crime scene tape and was photographing the exterior of the motel, approaching the task by-the-book, working her way inward on the actual scene.

My friend was holding the yellow barrier up for me as he answered my query with his own biting rhetorical question. "Like I said, she's climbin' the ladder, and there's a dead federal judge in that room over there. You're not gonna get much more high profile than this. Jeezus H. Christ, gimme a break. You really think she's not gonna make for damn sure she's up to her scrawny ass in it?"

CHAPTER 5:

The Chippewa Courts Inn was your typical no-tell-motel. The building itself was an unremarkable, twenty-four unit, one-story structure in the shape of a lopsided, block-style letter "U". At the truncated end, which was farthest from us at the moment, was the office. Behind that there were four rooms. The two longer expanses housed the remaining eighteen less-than-spacious accommodations, ten in one section and eight in the other. Each had a double window, exterior door, and a single parking space in front of it.

Across the almost deserted expanse of the parking lot, a timeworn marquee stood in front of the office, near the street. Its mismatched backlit letters proclaimed "FREE IN-ROOM ADULT MOVIES." Beneath that bit of visceral marketing, a pinkish neon pretzel struggled to announce "VACANCY," occasionally blinking into darkness, only to eventually issue a loud buzz and snap back to something less than brilliance before flickering off yet again.

Room seven, where we were now entering, was itself your typical hourly-rate special—rectangular, not quite clean, and poorly lit. The streaked windows next to the weather-beaten door were covered inside by heavy drapes, which were themselves a good decade out of style, if not more. In keeping with a basic configuration, there was a dressing area and sink at the back of the room. Over the basin sat a large mirror that was now reflecting the flicker of lights from outside as they bounced in through the open doorway. To the right of that area appeared to be a smaller room, most likely the bathroom and shower.

Ben pointed to the smaller room as if he'd been reading my mind. "Body's back there in the john," he offered, thereby confirming the suspicion.

Wafting on the chilled atmosphere was the usual unsavory blend of odors one encountered in such a room—stale smoke, musty carpet, and old intimacy. However, in this case the olfactory aura of bygone lovemaking was merely a subtle backdrop to the unmistakable odor of recent, unbridled sex. In fact, the very charge of extreme passion hanging in the air would have been enough to provoke arousal were it not underscored by the less than commonplace, but just as palpable, funk of death. As if that weren't enough, pulling the unlikely mélange together was a cloying watermelon-like scent.

"TV assholes are here," Ben called out to the lone crime scene technician inhabiting the room. My friend swung the door closed behind us then stabbed a finger toward the silvery back wall as he instructed, "We better keep the door shut, or one of the fuckers'll be bright enough ta' try pointin' a camera into that mirror."

The dust-mask-wearing technician gave a nod as he took a few steps toward us. "What about the plate on the car?"

"Covered," Ben replied. "Got a squad parked behind it."

From all indications, the tech had simply been milling about and leaving the scene untouched, presumably waiting for us to arrive and create the visual record that was the next step in the chain of evidence. I was getting ready to ask about the mask when he quickly turned away and pulled it down. Slapping a handkerchief up to his face, he broke the near serenity of the interior with a resounding sneeze.

"Jeezus, Murv," Ben said. "You really that sick?"

"What the hell gave ya' that idea?" he replied, a slight Southern drawl affecting his raw voice. Still, even his obviously heavy congestion didn't hide the sarcasm tainting the words.

"Well why didn't ya' stay home then?" Ben asked.

"Oh, maybe 'cause you told 'em ta' get me outta bed."

He finished wiping his reddened nose then pulled the mask back up to cover the lower half of his face.

"You shoulda said you were sick."

"I did," he returned through the disposable cup-shaped shield. "But, then I got told, 'Storm says don't be such a wuss'."

"Yeah, well…"

"Yeah, well my ass. You're gonna owe me for this one."

My friend nodded. "Yeah. Okay. Booze or cigars?"

"The way I feel right now? Booze."

"Bottle of Jack?"

"Screw that," Murv huffed. "This is worth *Maker's Mark*. The big bottle, not the little one."

"Yeah, okay," Ben agreed. "So, listen, this is Felicity and…"

"Yeah, we've met. It's been…" he interrupted then abruptly ended his own sentence with a repeat of the earlier sneeze. "Look, no offense," he finally continued, gazing back at all of us with bleary eyes as he repositioned the mask once again. "But all I wanna do right now is go home. Can we just do this so I can get a team in here to work the scene?"

"You got a team? I thought everyone was out sick?"

"I've got three techs," he replied. "And two of them are as bad off as I am, so can we get moving on this?"

"Yeah." Ben nodded.

"Can you smell that?" I asked, grabbing at the opportunity to interject the question.

"I couldn't smell shit if I was neck deep in it," Murv replied, shaking his head.

"Yeah. Ya' talkin' 'bout the sickly gag-a-maggot reek?" Ben asked.

"Yeah."

He pointed to a nightstand next to the twin bed. "There's a tube'a crap over there. Some kinda novelty eat-me gel or somethin'. Smells like a whor…" He caught himself mid-sentence, casting a quick glance at Felicity. "…Reeks don't it?"

"That's an understatement."

"Is there anything in particular you want me to concentrate on, then?" my wife asked.

"You get the outside already?" Murv asked.

"The door and a few shots of the lot leading up to the entrance. I didn't see any markers, so I just shot mid-range."

"Yeah, nothin' out there in the way of evidence we could see," he agreed. "Except the car. It's the victim's, so we'll want it covered in and out before we start tearin' it apart."

"No problem. I still need some overalls of the lot and sign too," Felicity offered. "But I thought I might wait for daybreak since it's not far off."

"Makes sense," Murv told her with a nod. "Then just play it by the book. I've got a few markers down in here. Not much, but go ahead and shoot every angle just to be safe. We'll sort it out later."

"Yeah," Ben agreed. "Cover all the bases. Two of everything."

"Aye," she returned. "No problem. Digital okay?"

"Hi-res?" Murv asked.

"Six megapixel, raw."

He nodded. "Go for it."

"You got gloves for 'em?" Ben asked.

"Yeah," he replied, rummaging around in his coat pockets for a second then extracting a wad of latex. Just as he was handing them to us, he let loose with a third explosive sneeze. This time, however, it exited well ahead of his reflexes, containing itself within the mask.

"Crap," he exclaimed then shoved the gloves into Felicity's hand as he headed out the door muttering, "If y'all 'll excuse me for a minute."

"You couldn't get someone else, Ben?" Felicity admonished as she picked a pair of gloves from the wad then handed the rest to me. "That man should be in bed."

"Don't let 'im fool ya', Felicity," he returned. "He runs the CSU. He would've insisted on being here anyway. Besides, he's the best there is."

"Aye, well I still say he needs a tottie and a good night's rest."

"I'll tell 'im you said that."

She cast a quick glance between us then handed me the camera bag she had been carrying slung over her shoulder.

"All right," she announced, moving on to the business at hand. "We'll work the main room clockwise, including the dressing area, then we'll do that bathroom separate. Row, there's a logbook in that bag. Just stay behind me and write down whatever I tell you. Ben, I hate to tell you this, but you need to be somewhere else. Because, right now, you're in my way."

A blinding flash of illumination burst forth, painting the corner in its harsh glow, then dissipated almost as quickly as it had presented itself. The steady whistle of the thyristor on the flash unit started squealing through the otherwise quiet room, rising in pitch until it was almost imperceptible.

The owner of the motel had arrived just after we began working through the main room and per one of the uniformed officers, was asking to speak to the person in charge. Ben staved him off for a few minutes, but as soon as Murv had returned from replacing his ruined dust mask, my friend had left to address the situation. The flu-stricken crime scene tech walked the room with us, only once interjecting a question about a particular angle, but other than that he left Felicity alone to do her job. I assumed that was a good sign.

"That was forty-eight, correct?" my wife asked without turning.

"Yeah. Forty-eight," I replied.

I watched over her shoulder as she peered at the miniature LCD on the back of the camera.

"Evidence marker B," she called out as she kneeled down and put the viewfinder back to her eye. "Men's wallet, floor, mid-range. Fifty millimeter, strobe." The flash popped again, and she continued. "And, forty-nine. Marker B, wallet, floor, close-up. Fifty millimeter, strobe."

I backed out of her way as she stood, but I continued scribbling the notes she had dictated.

"Got it," I finally said.

"All right then," she replied absently as she inspected the top display on the camera then deftly ejected the flash memory card and handed it to me. Once she had popped in a fresh card, she looked up and handed me the small protective case. "That's it for the main room. Let's move to the back."

Thus far, the process had been nothing more than routine. Admittedly, since this was a homicide crime scene, and with knowing that the victim's body was awaiting us in the next room, it lent a surreal quality to each shot taken; but even that didn't prevent it from approaching abject boredom.

Still, I had to say I was more than just slightly impressed by my wife. With every passing moment, she was demonstrating just exactly how much of a pro she truly was. Even though she had never said exactly how well she did in the courses she had taken, I was willing to bet she had aced them. Watching her now, if I didn't know better, I would have sworn she'd been doing this job for years.

"Rowan," she asked, looking up at me. "Are you okay?"

"Yeah, I'm fine," I returned with a shrug. "Why?"

"You're kind of quiet."

"Just tired," I replied, not wanting to embarrass her here with a gush of praise. I'd wait until we were alone for that.

"No headaches then?"

Her query suddenly made more sense. "No. Nothing to worry about," I answered then added as an afterthought, "Yet."

"Aye, yet. That's what I'm afraid of," she replied with a sigh then after a brief pause, cocked her head toward the back of the room. "Come on, then."

"I'm gonna go ahead and get a coupl'a guys started on this stuff out here," Murv told us.

"Sounds good," Felicity replied. "We'll be another half hour, maybe forty-five minutes, back here."

"That'll work," he answered. "Take all the time ya' need. By the way, rumor has it the Feebs are on their way."

"That was quick," I offered.

"Storm wanted 'em in the loop," he replied to my unasked question. "Federal judge, all that jazz."

As crime scenes go, Ben's assessment had been for the most part correct, up to and including the fact that Felicity and I had both seen much worse. For instance, when you've viewed the remains of one of your friends who'd been eviscerated by a madman, you've pretty much pushed the envelope.

Still, even though the horrific visions of that, and other things I'd witnessed, would never be completely erased from my mind, they had at least dulled with time. Unfortunately, that familiarity had also served to desensitize me to the offensive sights, or so I had come to believe. The simple fact was that there were even times when I found myself wondering about my own capacity for compassion after everything I'd seen.

On this particular morning, however, upon reaching the doorway of the bathroom, it became painfully apparent that not stopping and grabbing a quick bite for breakfast had been a wise choice.

As we had worked the main portion of the room, moving systematically around the clock face just as Felicity had prescribed, we had made sure to include the dressing area just outside the bathroom door. But my wife had been doing the actual shooting, not me. Since the area was too small for the both of us, I had remained back and out of the way in order to allow her ample space to work. Because of that, I was only just now witnessing the abomination that had been patiently waiting.

Maybe it was the fact that it had been two years since I'd been directly involved with a homicide investigation. Maybe I had finally managed to simply forget. Whatever the reason, I had been forced back across the line between callousness and humanity. I had been living in a calm, safe world long enough now that in a single instant I discovered I wasn't nearly as jaded as I had once feared.

Unfortunately, that realization was forced completely out of my mind by the acrid tang of bile on the back of my tongue. I heard

Felicity call out a description followed by a focal length and light source just as she'd been doing earlier. However, I was completely unable to write it down, especially not now that I had my head hanging almost between my knees, and I was struggling to control my breathing. The bright stab of the strobe flash flickered red through my tightly shut eyelids, and I heard my wife saying something again, but I was still unable to respond.

In some small way, I suppose I should have found it comforting that the reason for my preoccupation was the fact that, at the moment, I was desperately trying not to involuntarily expel my morning coffee.

CHAPTER 6:

My mouth was still somewhat watering from the nausea, but the major wave seemed to have passed for the most part; at least I hoped that it had. I was still keeping my eyes closed, but the image I'd seen was freshly imprinted on my retinas, so I suppose it didn't really matter. I was going to see it one way or the other, and I suspected that my rampant imagination was probably coloring my memory of the sight to appear much worse than it actually was.

"Rowan?" Felicity's worried voice filtered into my ears, and I felt her hand softly pressing against my back.

"I'm okay," I mumbled after puffing out a heavy breath.

"Keep yourself grounded," she told me, her tone wavering as I heard the note of concern begin to rise.

"No," I slowly shook my head. "That's not it. Don't worry."

"What is it then?"

I swallowed hard and opened my eyes, then as I slowly brought myself upright, I pointed past her through the doorway. "Just a little queasy, that's all."

The first thing that had caught my eyes was the very point that now had me transfixed. A large splotch of blood intermixed with what was presumably brain tissue and bone fragments formed a hideous blot against the dingy tile of the bathroom's back wall. My suspicion, in this case, had been dead wrong. My imagination hadn't even begun to do justice to the horror that now fell directly in my line of sight. It was all I could do to keep from staring at it, and truth be told, even that wasn't enough. I was losing the battle with each passing second.

I tried to calm my churning stomach by forcing myself to detach from the reality of what I was seeing and view it from an analytical standpoint. It wasn't easy, considering the circumstances, but after a moment I managed to invoke the thin delusion out of self-defense. It was no panacea, but it helped, even if only a little.

Judging from the density of the smear along with the shattered tile, the point of the matter's impact appeared to have been just over halfway up the wall. From there, it continued to spread heavily along its vertical path. Above that, the splatter arced outward in a wide pattern, eventually becoming a light spray of rusty red upon the dull surface. Below the broken squares, blood and bits of flesh trickled downward, streaking the ceramic and eventually pooling on the bathtub ledge. I finally allowed my gaze to roam as I followed the drizzles of crimson downward, inevitably coming to rest on the victim himself.

Wentworth, or what was left of him, was a gross adornment to the already dirty floor. He wasn't what you would call a small man, but he also wasn't exactly enormous either. Still, his bulk went a long way toward filling the tile floor of the small bathroom. He was visibly overweight by a good margin and certainly out of shape, both facts that couldn't be missed because he was completely nude.

Based on his current position, he probably would have been facing outward through the doorway were it not for the fact that he was pitched back against the side of the bathtub. He appeared to have been kneeling at the time of death, and that was pretty much his position now, albeit canted backward and slightly to one side where gravity had forced him to slip. He hadn't gone far, however, as his shift to the right had been halted early on by the unaccommodating narrowness of the gap between the toilet and the tub.

What remained of his head was lolled to the side, face slack and jaw hanging open with bright blood dribbling across his chin, dripping down onto his chest. A wide strip of silver-grey duct tape was positioned firmly over his eyes. The left side of his skull, from just above and behind the ear on up to the crown, was all but completely missing and of course, now formed the sickening mosaic behind him. It didn't take much to figure out that someone had shoved a gun into his mouth and then pulled the trigger.

Even though his body had gone limp in death, his shoulders appeared strained, and upon second glance one noticed that his arms disappeared behind his back as if bound there.

In front of him was a multi-hued puddle, ranging from yellow to an orangish-pink. Amid it all was a stream of something whitish and viscous looking. The bulk of the liquid was obviously a mixture of blood and what was probably his own urine. I wasn't certain, but I suspected the white substance was seminal fluid.

There was no real way to tell for a fact if the urine had been the product of fear or simply muscles relaxing once his life had fled. My guess, however, was that it had occurred after death. I couldn't prove it, of course, but I felt no fear in the room, only the buzz of heightened passion. Even now, standing in this doorway and looking at this macabre scene, sex came to the forefront. Those physically intangible facts weren't helping me deal with this at all. When you added the suspected ejaculate to the list of oddities, I was even more unnerved.

Up to this point the scene looked much like I had voiced earlier—a contract killing. It had all the hallmarks of an execution style murder. However, as I took in the raw tableau, I continued to have even more of the "not quite right" sensation tickling my brain—as had Ben. I knew that what I was feeling didn't fit the scene, and I couldn't yet put my finger on it, but something I was seeing, other than just the semen, didn't belong either.

"Are you going to be okay?" Felicity asked me.

I realized that I was still staring past her and gave my head a quick shake then focused on her face. "Yeah... Yeah, I'll be all right. What about you?"

"Aye, me?" she asked. "I'm fine."

"This doesn't affect you?"

"Yes... and no," she replied almost apologetically. "I'm afraid perhaps I'm a bit indifferent right now. I've seen this sort of thing quite a bit because of the classes. And... much more recently than you as well."

"Yeah. Probably so." I gave her a nod then fell silent again, shifting my gaze to stare back over her shoulder at Wentworth's corpse.

"Do you want to go outside then?" she asked after a moment. "It's okay. I can finish up here."

I shook my head.

"What is it?" she asked.

"What do you mean?"

"You've got that look on your face, Row," she pressed. "What are you thinking?"

"What Ben said..." I answered as I returned my eyes to meet hers. "You know, about something not being right. Do you get that too?"

She gave a quick nod in the affirmative. "But I'm not sure what."

"Well, if the white stuff is what I think it is..." I offered.

"Aye, I noticed that... And... and..." She allowed her voice to trail off.

"And what?"

"Gods, Row," she almost whispered, her tone disturbed. She looked away for a second then back to me with a tortured embarrassment in her eyes. When she started speaking again, she kept her voice low but stammered through the sentences as if trying to confess a mortal sin. "There's something about this room... Ever since we came through the door... It sounds crazy... No, more like sick... No, it IS sick... But if... If we were alone right now, I'd... Right now, I want to..."

I gave her a knowing nod, and when I spoke I kept my voice down as well. "I know, hon, I can feel it too. There's a residual sexual energy in this room that's beyond..." I stammered myself, searching for the right words. "...Intense, is the only way I can explain it."

She nodded back in agreement. "And it feels far too singular and recent, then. Not like something built up over time."

"Yeah, I got that too," I returned. "And did you notice there's no fear?"

She gave me a quick nod. "Aye. I did. And, I really don't know what to make of that."

"Me either," I huffed. "But something is definitely odd here."

"Is everything okay back there?" Murv called out from the front of the room.

"Fine," I replied, looking up with a quick wave. "Just took me by surprise is all."

"Yeah," he replied, continuing about his business with the other tech he'd brought in. "It's a friggin' mess."

"Are you sure you're okay?" Felicity asked me when I turned back to her. "Are you certain you don't want to wait outside?"

"No, I'll be okay. Really. It was just the initial shock."

"If you're sure."

"I'm sure. Let's get this done."

"All right then." She gave me a nod. "There is a set of photoevidence scales in the bag. I'm going to need them."

Even though I was more than ready to put distance between this scene and me, my stomach had calmed considerably. I knew there was a time when it would have taken much longer for me to get over something like this, but my own learned indifference was starting to return, much to my disappointment.

We had already shot the wide angle and mid-range photos of the scene proper then moved immediately into the close-ups. We ran into a problem positioning a photoevidence scale near the exit wound, so since I had the free hands, I had been charged with the duty of reaching in and carefully holding it in place. Felicity didn't really have it any easier as she was forced to contort herself into a position where she could shoot the picture and not disturb any potential evidence. Still, it wasn't the most pleasant task I'd ever performed.

I was certain that the medical examiner would be taking far more detailed photos and even made mention of it aloud. However, my wife informed me that this was standard operating procedure, and she was going to follow it to the letter. I couldn't disagree.

I stepped back out of the way and watched on as she steadied herself in the doorway while snapping off a series of pictures to show the location of a bed pillow, which had been haphazardly tossed into the bathtub. It bore its own velocity-patterned bloodstains, as did the translucent plastic shower curtain. Both spatters had their own stories to tell. One said that the pillow had probably been used to muffle the gun's report; the other hinted that perhaps the shower curtain had been used to shield the killer from the spray. Still, even as Felicity called out the particulars of the shots for me to record, my gaze kept being drawn back to the victim.

Wentworth's chest and protruding belly were flaccid and pale, making the red spatters and trickles of blood stand out in stark contrast beneath each harsh white burst from the camera's flash unit. I lowered my eyes to make sure I was writing in a straight line as I filled the logbook with the details I'd been given but almost unconsciously returned my gaze to his lifeless torso.

The niggling "something not right" feeling grew into a full-fledged itch at the base of my skull as I stared. The brilliant glow of the strobe painted his form once again, and I heard my wife call out another set of notes. This time, however, I didn't look away.

Instead, I asked, "Are you going to do close-ups of his chest?"

"No," she replied. "That will be in the mid-range shots. You only do close-ups of wounds or anomalies."

"Okay, but look at his chest," I told her, pointing.

The streaks of blood, which at first had appeared to be merely a by-product of the head wound were beginning to reveal much more. Upon close scrutiny, a few of the trickles followed an opposing pattern to that which had dripped from above. It wasn't readily obvious, primarily due to the amount of collateral spattering, but if you looked hard enough, you could see it. On top of that, they looked as though they formed some kind of pattern.

Felicity cocked her head to the side and concentrated on the area I indicated. Finally, she leaned in at the threshold and peered through the viewfinder of the camera. That didn't surprise me, as the lens always seemed to act as an amplifier for her. It was a focal point of sorts and one that often caused her to transcend the physical, allowing second-sight to take hold. And, through it she could see things even I could not.

After a moment she snapped a series of pictures then turned back to me. "I think they're shallow cuts. Like from a razor."

"Like maybe he was tortured?"

"Maybe." She shook her head. "I don't know. They aren't very deep. In fact, there are several of them that are almost completely superficial. They don't even look as though they actually bled. But, there might be a pattern there. I'm not sure."

"Bizarre," I mumbled.

"Aye, that's for sure. Either way, the medical examiner will be able to get better pics once he's cleaned up."

Whether it was an effect of the flash, prolonged staring, or just luck, I couldn't say. At any rate the equation suddenly changed. It wasn't solved, but there was definitely a new value to assign to one of the variables. Of course, new values sometimes do nothing more than beget new unknowns, and that didn't always make solving the equation any easier.

I kept telling myself that we were just here to take the crime scene photos, but in the back of my head I knew better. There was a reason for the flu epidemic and rash of no-answers from the other photographers on the list. I might not be having one of my customary headaches or visions just yet, but they were probably just around the corner. There was something ethereal at work here, and it had brought us to this particular scene for a purpose; of that I had no doubt.

I could feel the muscles in the back of my neck tighten as my hair prickled upward. A tired bromide that I'd spouted to my wife only a few days before popped into my head, and I suddenly realized just how foretelling it had been.

The calm was over and a violent storm front was fast approaching. What's more, Felicity and I were standing directly in its path.

CHAPTER 7:

"I already told you I don't work for you," Felicity spat angrily while remaining fully engaged in a "stare down" confrontation with a young, overly groomed, FBI agent.

The sun had been up for almost an hour now, and we had only just finished shooting the exterior of the motel, the parking lot, and Wentworth's car when he had stopped us and quickly displayed his badge.

"That is not an issue," he replied, his own gaze not wavering from the face of the petite redhead in front of him.

"It is for me."

"Get over it."

"All right then, who's going to pay for the flash cards?"

"You'll get them back when we're finished," he told her.

"Yeah, right," she snipped.

Ben walked over to where we were standing, coming within earshot just in time to catch my wife's adamant commentary. "What's goin' on here?" he asked. "Pay for what?"

"Flash memory cards," I explained. "The FBI wants us to hand over the crime scene photos. We were just…"

"Bullshit!" my friend interjected without letting me finish. Even though his voice climbed a pair of notches in volume, he was still maintaining far more composure than I was used to seeing from him when dealing with most federal law enforcement. He shook his head and looked over at my wife. "Felicity, you got the film or whatever it is with ya'?"

"Aye," she replied, not taking her heated stare off the agent.

"Givit here," my friend said, holding out his hand and gesturing with a wag of his fingers.

She reached into her pocket and extracted the two compact flash cards then dropped them into Ben's palm.

"That all of it?"

"Detective Storm," the agent spoke up.

"Just a minute," he snapped in return. "Felicity?"

"Yes, that's all of it," she replied. "Rowan, give him the log."

I handed over the small notebook but kept my mouth shut.

Ben stepped back and scanned the activity on the parking lot then yelled, "Yo! Harrison. Over here."

Across the way, a tousle of blonde hair poked up from beneath a trunk lid. The young woman was turned away from us and was wearing a jacket emblazoned with the words "CRIME SCENE UNIT" across the back. She turned around, and with a confused expression creasing her face, she pointed at herself and mouthed the word "me."

"Yeah, you," Ben yelled. "C'mere."

"Detective Storm," the FBI agent started in again. "You need to consider…"

"Fuck that," he spat. "What I need ta' consider is that I called ya' in as a courtesy since the stiff is a federal judge. Other than that, it's still a homicide that falls under local jurisdiction, and right now Major Case is gonna handle it. You wanna help, great. You wanna take over, fuck off."

"Yes, sir?" the young woman spoke up at Ben's side, interrupting before the agent could respond.

He turned to her immediately. "Yeah, look, Harrison…"

"Detective Storm!" the agent demanded.

Ben glared back and held up a finger as he declared, "I'm talkin' ta' Harrison right now."

"Huddleston, sir," the woman offered.

My friend looked back to the woman, creased his brow, shook his head, and then said, "What?"

"My name is Huddleston, sir. Not Harrison."

"Yeah, okay, whatever," he replied with a dismissive wave. "I need ya' ta' take these to Murv. Tell 'im to bag 'em and process 'em."

"Yes, sir," she replied as he handed the cards and log to her.

"…And stop callin' me sir. You're makin' me feel old."

As she hurried off we heard her reply, "Yes, sir."

"Now," Ben continued, turning back to the FBI agent. "You were sayin'?"

"Detective Storm, we assumed that since you called us, we could count on your cooperation."

My friend planted his hands on his hips and gave a quick nod. "Cooperation, yeah. Rollin' over and playin' dead, fuck no. Once we get the pictures processed out, you want copies, no problem.

"Now if you wanna go in there right now and make your own scrapbook, have at it, but ya' better get a move on before the coroner pulls the body."

"Detective," the agent attempted to reason with him, "As you said, you are dealing with a federal judge here. Hammond Wentworth is a very influential individual, and there are circumstances here that should remain confidential."

"Listen, Agent...?"

"Drew."

"Agent Drew, what ya' got here ain't circumstances, it's a DEAD federal judge. He's not gonna influence anybody anymore."

"There is still the matter of how and where he was found," Drew objected.

Ben was starting to get angry now. "This ain't like sweepin' another vice bust under the rug. This is a homicide."

"I'm aware of that, but I've been in there. I know what the situation is. Those photographs could be very embarrassing..."

"Is that all you're worried about?" Ben snapped.

"No, not entirely, but they are definitely an issue."

"Well, don't get all worked up about it," my friend replied, sarcasm dripping from his words. "I'll make sure we wait a few days before we put 'em out on the fuckin' internet, now why don'tcha go chase a terrorist or somethin'."

"Thanks for not handin' over the pictures to the Feebs," Ben said to Felicity.

"Aye, no problem," she replied. "I wasn't about to."

"Where's Constance anyway?" I asked. "She wouldn't have dreamed of getting pushy like that."

I was referring to Constance Mandalay, an FBI special agent we had worked with several times in the past. Upon our first encounter, she had been much like Agent Drew. In fact, she was even worse. Within the course of that first investigation, however, she had done a complete about-face. She went from being a hard-nosed femme fatale out to prove herself to being a good and trusted friend. And in Ben's case, ever since his divorce, she had become something even more.

"Talked to her last night. She's still in D.C. Will be till the end of the week prob'ly." He let out a harrumph before saying, "Yeah, I'd sure as hell rather be workin' with *her* on this. But even if she was here right now, they'd most likely assign someone else."

"So that means you two are still seeing each other then?" Felicity asked.

"Off and on, yeah," he shrugged. "Right now. Kinda on. She's been in D.C. for damn near a month though, so it makes it kinda hard."

"Sorry."

He shrugged again. "Nothin' ta' be sorry 'bout."

We were standing next to my friend's Chevrolet van, keeping out of the way while waiting for the medical examiner to clear the scene. The vehicle was in far better shape than it looked from the outside, and he went to great pains to keep it that way. The side door was presently locked in the open position, and Felicity was perched just inside on the floorboard, putting away her camera equipment.

After a brief quiet I switched the subject. "So, you were right, Ben. Something's definitely off kilter in there."

"You go *Twilight Zone*?" he asked.

I shook my head. "No, but that didn't keep me from feeling some things. Felicity too."

"Yeah, I keep forgettin' that you get all freakazoid on me now, too," he said, looking over at my wife.

"Once, Ben. Just one time," she stressed without looking away from the task at hand.

"That's enough for me," he replied. "So whatcha get?"

"There was definitely sex involved," I offered.

"Well yeah," he grunted. "That was kinda obvious. Wentworth, or somebody, shot his wad all over the floor looked like."

"There's more than that," Felicity interjected, looking up. "It's something palpable... Still."

I knew what she was implying with that last word, even if Ben didn't.

"I hate to tell you two this, but if ya' walk in any one of these rooms, it just plain smells like sex. That's nothin' new. They don't rent rooms by the hour here for corporate conferences if ya' know what I mean."

"Aye, but this is different," my wife added.

"Different how?" he asked.

"Intensity. Urgency." Felicity shook her head.

He shrugged. "Okay. But like I said, that's all kinda obvious just from lookin' at the scene. Got anything else?"

"Fear," I offered. "Or lack thereof, I should say."

"Come again?"

"From the looks of things, he was executed, right?" I asked.

"Yeah, that's how it looks."

"Well, if someone had me bound, blindfolded, and a gun in my mouth, I'd be terrified," I offered.

"Join the club," he said.

"That's just it, Ben," Felicity told him. "There was no fear in that room. Only arousal."

"How do ya'..." He shook his head as he caught himself and allowed the rest of the sentence to fade away. "Forget it. So there was no fear, eh?"

"None," I confirmed.

"And that tells us what?"

"I don't know for sure," I answered with a shrug.

"Yeah, well no offense, but I think ya' know what I'm gonna say ta' that."

I nodded. "Uh-huh. It doesn't help."

"Ding-ding," he returned. "Give the man a cigar."

"Well, there did seem to be something physical that was a bit odd," I offered.

"What's that?"

"Some kind of lacerations on his torso."

"Whaddaya mean 'some kind of lacerations'?"

"Felicity had a better look than I did," I replied.

He looked over at her and raised a questioning eyebrow. "Whatcha got?"

"I can't be sure," she replied with a shake of her head. "There's quite a bit of blood obscuring it, but there definitely seemed to be a pattern to the lacerations."

"What kinda pattern?"

"Sectional. Almost like a checkerboard from what I could see. I took a couple of shots, but I don't think they'll show much. Once he's cleaned up, I suspect it will be a bit more pronounced."

"Okay. I'll give the coroner a heads up. So what do YOU two think it means?"

"Maybe that he was tortured?" she said with a shrug. "Although, honestly, they really looked superficial. But like I said. There was a lot of blood obscuring them."

"Same here," I offered. "Just not sure. But it did seem a bit strange to me, so take that for what it's worth."

"With you?" he harrumphed. "If YOU think somethin's strange, it's usually not good."

"Sorry."

My friend reached up and smoothed back his hair then stood there massaging his neck in silence. Finally he said, "The number seven mean anything to you two?"

"Most consider seven to be a lucky number," Felicity offered.

"Reward, money, payoff," I ticked off some of the possibilities then added, "There are seven days in a week."

"There are seven continents," my wife continued. "Seven seas, the dance of the seven veils, seven deadly sins... Some prophecies speak of seven archangels."

I nodded and continued her thread. "They also mention the seven plagues, the seven seals, and..."

"Okay, okay," he interrupted, holding up a hand and waving me off. "It's probably just the luck thing. That's what I kinda figured anyway."

"What is?" I asked.

"Desk clerk said Wentworth specifically requested room seven," he replied.

"Was it him or his companion making the request?"

"Dunno at this point." He shook his head. "The clerk said he's the only one that came in, but we're thinkin' it coulda been whoever he was with."

"Sounds like a setup to me," I offered. "That sort of thing would fit with a contract killing. Right?"

"Yeah, way ahead of ya' on that one, Row," he replied. "Problem is the clerk didn't see anyone in or outta the place."

"So she didn't see whoever he was with leaving either?"

"Nope. Matter of fact, she says she can't remember seein' anybody else in the car at all when he checked in, and he pulled up right out front. Big help, huh?"

"Well, he had to have been here with someone."

"No shit," my friend huffed, an overtone of halfway jovial sarcasm in his voice. "I think we kinda established that already."

"Just thinking out loud, Ben."

"Yeah," he grunted. "Guess we all are. Anyway, we're gonna shake down some of the local hoo... uh, working girls, and see what we can find out."

"Let me ask you something," Felicity interjected.

He glanced over at my wife. "What? 'Working girls' is out too?"

She ignored the sardonic query and launched into a question of her own. "I've been wondering this ever since you called, and what you just said reminded me of it. How did the body get found at such an odd hour? I mean there wouldn't be any maid service this time of night, and if he hadn't checked out..."

"Clerk heard the shot and called nine-one-one."

"So the killer didn't have very long to get away," she mused.

"Somewhere between ten and fifteen minutes, best guess," he explained. "She hesitated to make the call for something like five to ten minutes, she's not for sure. Then response for a unit was right at six minutes."

"Not much time," I mused.

My friend grunted then reached up to massage his neck as he said, "Yeah, well, apparently it was enough."

CHAPTER 8:

"**D**o you want to grab some breakfast?" I asked.

"What?" Felicity replied, looking over at me as she downshifted the Jeep.

We were only a few blocks from home at this point. Ben was still wrapping things up back at the crime scene, but for the time being, my wife's part in the investigation was done—her official involvement anyway.

There was no doubt that something unnatural was already hard at work, and it had every intention of dragging both of us back into the middle of the entire mess. The intensity of the feeling was actually enough to make one feel claustrophobic, and that made me more than just a little nervous.

I had no choice but to wonder what, or who, was pulling the strings. Especially when my friend finally sent us on our way, and it became obvious that we weren't the only ones who could feel it. He had gone so far as to hedge the dismissal with a promise to contact us later in the day if he had any questions. I wouldn't have thought anything of the comment if it weren't for the fact that I could tell simply by the way he spoke the words that even he wasn't sure why he'd said them. That in itself told me he knew something was going on as well, even if only subconsciously.

Still, the aberration thus far was that there were none of the usual signs. No psychic flashes, no preternatural headaches, and not even a hint of ethereal contact from the victim. There was no apparent reason for us to be involved other than the emergency photographic services Felicity had provided. Even so, it felt like a foregone conclusion that we were now connected to this crime in some vastly deeper way. For the life of me though, I had absolutely no clue what that connection could be.

"Breakfast," I repeated. "We could hit the Corner Coffee House. I'll buy."

She gave her head a slight shake. "Maybe later. Aren't you still queasy?"

"Unfortunately, no," I replied, sincere in my words. "I'm afraid my tolerance for the horrific is back in full. I *am* a little tired though. What about you?"

"No."

"No what?"

She shook her head again and spoke absently, "No. Not queasy then."

"Well, you've got to be tired. You're running on only about an hours sleep."

"Hmmmm?"

"Tired. You've got to be tired."

"Not really."

"Okay," I replied, giving a nod in her direction. "So what's on your mind?"

"What?"

"Yo, Earth to Felicity," I said, reaching over and poking her in the shoulder with my index finger. "Would you like to fill me in on what's going on here? You're completely scattered, and I find it really hard to believe you aren't tired. Is something wrong?"

"No... I don't think..." she replied hesitantly. "Oh, I don't know."

"Now you're sounding like me," I told her. "What is it?"

I twisted in my seat and watched her through a long pause. I could see that she was struggling with something, and the aura surrounding her was one of intense frustration.

"That room..." she finally said after finishing the turn onto our street and accelerating down the block.

"What about it?"

"The feeling..." she murmured. "I... I just can't shake it."

"You mean the lack of fear?"

"No, not that. The sex."

"Oh," I replied, slightly taken aback.

I had been affected by that aura myself but for the most part, only while inside the room. Once outside the feeling had rapidly diminished, and after we had left the premises, it had disappeared entirely. But, apparently the same wasn't so for my wife, and that worried me.

For a moment I started wondering if my earlier SpellCraft simply wasn't good enough to keep her from harm. But, that tinge of panic didn't last long. I knew full well that I'd gone to great lengths constructing the spell, weaving it only to keep her safe, not to cut her off from the ethereal entirely. So, it stood to reason that she could still be overly sensitive to myriad other energies. Besides, sensing and channeling positive energies shouldn't be harmful. And, sexual arousal probably qualified as positive, or at least that's what one would think.

I immediately abandoned my mental analysis and grabbed for the dashboard out of self-preservation as my wife whipped the vehicle into a hard right, squealing the tires and tearing into our driveway at a higher rate of speed than I considered advisable. She immediately accelerated out of the rapid turn and barreled up the concrete expanse through the open gate and brought us to a sudden halt directly in front of the garage. The Jeep lurched as she jammed the gearshift into first and let the clutch out even before she managed to switch off the engine.

I eyed her wordlessly for a second then opened my mouth briefly before deciding not to chance a comment on the fact that I knew she was a far better driver than she'd just demonstrated. Of course, all I saw was the back of her head as she was climbing out of the vehicle, almost before she'd extracted the key from the ignition. I simply gave a mental shrug then twisted around in my seat to reach for the camera bags. She turned back to close her door and looked at me with an intense fire behind her green eyes.

"Aye, leave them," she instructed, her tone harbored no room for negotiation. "Just go inside and get undressed."

When I stared back at her, almost dumbfounded, she added, "Right now."

I wasn't entirely sure if what I was hearing was a demand, a plea, or something born of both.

The door chime rang out for the second time, setting the dogs into a repeat of the frenzy it had brought about on the first go around. The deep-throated woof of our aging English setter again formed a bass backdrop to the snarling bark of our Australian cattle dog as they vociferously stood watch over their territory. Whoever was out there, however, wasn't easily frightened away it seemed, and that told me it was probably Ben.

"We need to answer the door," I told my wife.

"No we don't," she breathed into my ear. "Whoever it is will go away."

"They haven't yet," I replied.

"They will," she purred.

She was astride me in the bed, body pressing down against mine as she continued to nuzzle at my neck. Her dainty hands encircled my wrist, and she held my arms in place over my head and down against the pillow. Of course, she wasn't strong enough to actually keep me pinned without quite a bit more leverage than her current position offered. Even so, she was demonstrating more strength than I expected, and she was definitely making it difficult for me to move. That simple fact seemed to delight her in ways I couldn't begin to describe. Apparently, something about exercising dominance and control had become a focal point for her arousal, and she wasn't about to let it go.

She'd been all over me the moment we got into the house. I hadn't even had the chance to "get undressed" as she had told me to do, and in fact, I wasn't certain I would be able to find all of the buttons she'd managed to rip from my shirt when she'd descended upon me. That had been sometime around eight-thirty this morning, and she hadn't let up since—not that I'd been able to keep up with her by any stretch of the imagination. Truth be told, what was certainly an adolescent boy's dream come true, was for me rapidly becoming a real problem.

I had never seen my wife act like this, even during the times of passionate discovery in our early courtship. I hated to resort to the overused term "nymphomaniac," but at this point I couldn't think of anything else that would accurately describe the visceral intensity of her physical desire.

Whatever it was that had gone on in that motel room, Felicity was tapped directly into some portion of it. I was actually beginning to wonder if it was she who was in control, or something else. In any event, she was insatiable, and I was just plain exhausted. How she was still even awake, I had no clue.

I tried to reason with her. "Honey, it's probably Ben."

"Can't be," she whispered. "He's supposed to call."

"Yeah, but something tells me that's him at the door."

Her reply came in another breathy murmur. "Then he can just go away."

I forced my arms upward and began levering my body to the side, actually finding myself needing to struggle in order to push her off my torso without hurting her. She wasn't going to give up easily, and in fact, me resisting only seemed to inflame her libidinous mood further.

"Aye, where do you think you're going?" she giggled as she pushed herself into a half sitting position, still straddling me. Then she proceeded to wrestle my arms back into place as she wriggled forward and dropped her knees across my elbows before beginning to slowly rock her hips.

"To get the door," I told her flatly. "Let me up."

"Aye, how about if we just borrow his handcuffs and send him on his way, then?" she murmured.

I was beginning to get concerned. I managed to pull my arms free after a healthy struggle and then tried to shift her off my chest. She immediately took hold of my wrists again, trying to force my arms back down, but I twisted my hands from her grasp and quickly took hold of hers.

"Oh, but I'm not finished with you yet," she purred, then without warning she dug her fingernails into the backs of my hands and drew them across my flesh.

I yelped then called her name with more than a hint of sharpness. "Ouch! What the?! Felicity!"

"Hmmmmm?" she murmured as she continued to rock, seeming not only pleased with, but also intensely aroused by, what she had just done to me.

"Honey, get a grip here," I told her, tightening my hold on her wrists.

The look she gave me was almost a glare as she snapped, "Aye, I knew I should have just tied you up like I wanted to do in the first place."

"You wanted to what?" I asked.

"Make you my love slave," she purred mischievously.

I simply didn't have an immediate answer for that. I stared up at her for a moment before I finally forced my shoulder back then quickly forward, rolling with her and using the momentum to break free as I slid from the side of the bed.

"Honey, you need to ground and center, right now," I told her.

"I'm grounded," she replied. "Come back here and I'll show you."

"No you aren't," I said as I started quickly slipping into my clothes. "I don't think you're even *you* right now."

She rolled to her side and grabbed the belt of my jeans as I pulled them on, engaging me in a tug of war with my own clothes. I stumbled back out of her reach, and she giggled again.

"Come back here, little man," she ordered. "You need to kneel down and worship me."

Now, I was really starting to worry. She was definitely channeling something, and while it may have started out as a neutral force, it was starting to become something that was not so benign.

"Stop it! Felicity, you need to ground. Whatever has got hold of you needs to go. Now."

She ignored me, asking instead, "Where do you think you're going?"

As she spoke, she took a quick swipe at me again, but I was already far enough away to easily sidestep the grab.

"I'm going to answer the door. If it's Ben then it's probably important," I told her. "You know that."

She rolled back and tossed her head against the pillow then let out a disappointed sigh before pouting at me and saying, "You're no fun."

I stopped in the middle of pulling a fresh t-shirt over my head and stared back at her. After a wordless moment, I proceeded to push my head through the neck hole in a quick motion and pulled the shirt on then regarded her seriously. I held out my hand and showed her the bright scratches where she had dug her nails into it.

"Okay," I said. "While I'm certainly not opposed to spicing things up, this is a bit far, and I think you would have to agree. If you were yourself right now, that is."

I watched her face as she looked at the deep marks she had gouged into the back of my hand. At first I feared that I might only be enticing her, but there was definitely a flicker of realization in her eyes, so I continued. "Look, we both know something ethereal is driving this, and…"

I looked up with a start as the sound of a fist pounding heavily against our front door set the dogs off once again. The raucous clamor served as a fresh reminder that I needed to get out there and answer it.

I looked back to my wife and appended my prematurely truncated sentence. "…The problem is that I just didn't realize how far it had gotten into you, or I would have stopped this a lot sooner.

Anyway, look, I need to go get the door. You stay in here and ground yourself, okay?"

The flicker had grown into a full-fledged glimmer, and she gave me a quick nod, which went a long way toward allaying my earlier fears.

"I'll be back to check on you in a minute," I told her as I started out of the bedroom then stopped and looked back, adding as an afterthought, "You might want to consider putting some clothes on."

I pulled the door shut behind me then headed up the hallway and out into the living room. I stumbled around the dogs, commanding them to sit as I put my eye to the peephole on the front door. As I suspected, I caught the back of Ben's head as he was starting down the stairs with a cell phone up to his ear. I shushed the dogs again then twisted the deadbolt and pulled the door open just as the phone began to ring.

My friend stopped and turned at the sound then thumbed off the cell phone and stuffed it back into his pocket. As he did so the ringing phone across the room cut off mid-peal. He started back up the stairs and pulled open the storm door as he gave me the once over. "I was startin' ta' get worried. I get ya' outta bed or somethin'?"

I stepped to the side so he could enter, and as he moved past me, I noticed a manila envelope tucked under his arm.

"Actually, yeah," I answered, punctuating my words with a nod.

"You sleepin'?" His tone was surprised.

"Not exactly."

"Oh," he replied, seizing immediately on the implication. "Sorry 'bout that, white man. Uh, so you an' Firehair were... Uh... Um, look, I can run down the street for coffee and maybe..."

"Don't apologize," I told him with a shake of my head, cutting him off as I pushed the door shut and motioned for him to have a seat. "You actually did me a favor."

"Yeah? How's that?"

I paused then said, "It's kind of a long story."

"I don't wanna hear it, do I?"

"Probably not."

"Then don't tell it."

"I'll try not to," I replied. "Besides, I have a feeling you've got a story I don't want to hear either."

"What makes ya' say that?"

"You told us earlier this morning you'd be calling this afternoon."

"Yeah, so?"

"Yeah, so, you didn't call. You showed up at the door instead. That always means something quite a bit more serious is happening... Or is going to soon enough."

"I'm that predictable, eh?" he huffed.

"Let's just say I've grown accustomed to the warning signs."

"Well, speakin' of signs," he said, waving the manila envelope in the air. "Got some here I want ya' ta' look at. Might wanna get Firehair in here so she can check 'em out too."

I glanced down the hallway toward the bedroom then down at the back of my hand. A thin trickle of blood was seeping through my skin from one of the deeper scratches. "Don't tell me," I said without turning. "The coroner determined that several of the injuries on Wentworth's body were consistent with intense sadomasochistic sex play."

"Yeah," my friend grunted. "How'd ya' know?"

"Like I said," I replied, a sullen melancholy taking over my voice. "I've seen the signs."

CHAPTER 9:

"**L**ooks like Wentworth was definitely a sick puppy," Ben announced as he emptied the envelope of autopsy photos he had brought from the coroner's office. As they spilled onto the table, he began systematically shuffling through them. After extracting several he felt would support his conclusion, he offered them to us. "Have a look at these."

The three of us were gathered around the breakfast nook in the kitchen. I had started a fresh pot of coffee several minutes ago, and the maker was presently sputtering and steaming as it neared the end of the brew cycle. The strong aroma was filling the room, and it reminded me that I could really use a jolt of caffeine right about now.

"Maybe not sick," Felicity countered, taking the 8-by-10's from his hand as she slipped her reading glasses onto her face. "Just different."

"Yeah, well, you say different, I say sicko."

I glanced over at my wife and watched her furrow her brow as she began carefully scanning the images. That countenance was a drastic contrast to the one that had been staring back at me earlier, but it was welcome nonetheless.

As it turned out, she had been on her way out of the bedroom at almost the same instant I had started down the hall to check on her. She was already dressed and to my great relief, very much herself once again, albeit wearing a somewhat chagrined frown. Of course, such an expression was something you didn't see very often where she was concerned, and in keeping with par, this one didn't hang around for very long either.

The fact that she had brought herself under control so quickly had quelled some of my unease over what had happened earlier. I knew all too well that emotions pretty much always cloud judgment, and in the heat of lovemaking, passionate feelings run very high. In the final analysis, it appeared that this was exactly the case with Felicity. She had allowed herself to open up to the ethereal energy simply because it had been heightening her physical pleasure. Unfortunately, as that pleasure increased, so did her lack of control over the stimulus. In essence, it had become like an addictive drug, and she rapidly gave herself over to it.

While opening herself to an unknown energy certainly hadn't been a wise choice on her part, given the circumstances, it was completely understandable. Besides, I was the last person with any right to pass judgment in that department.

In any case, what was most important was that the actual circumstances turned out to be far less heinous than the alternative I had originally feared, which was that something had forced its way past her defenses and taken over.

"Are these the marks we saw at the scene," I asked, looking at the photo I had just been handed.

"No," Ben replied. "That picture is of his back. But there's a picture of his chest in here too. I want ya' ta' look at that one for sure."

A group of lacerations were the focus of the particular shot I was currently perusing. A plastic photoevidence scale similar to Felicity's was pictured along the rightmost side, showing the marks to be anywhere from three to five inches in length. The incisions were straight and somewhat evenly spaced. While they were thin, they were also deep enough to have drawn what must have been more than just a trickle of blood.

"Doc says they were prob'ly made with a straight razor," he replied, reaching over and pulling down the corner of the photo with his finger so he could see it. Then he indicated an area above the wounds. "Look here though."

I followed his fingertip to the edge of the picture. I could just barely make out three thin lines intersecting the corner of the image.

"What's that?"

"Scars," he replied. "There's actually a better picture here somewhere."

"Here," Felicity interjected, sliding one toward me without looking up, as she was already engrossed in a different image.

"Yeah," Ben said with a nod. "That's it."

Even though they were still faint, the lighting on this particular photograph was more conducive to showing the marks. There were, in fact, far more than just three of the lines creasing Wentworth's pallid skin. I stopped counting at seventeen. Some were starker in appearance than others, a telltale sign that they were more recent.

"Most of 'em are on his back," Ben explained. "But he's got 'em on his buttocks and thighs, and what ya' saw on his chest too. Basically he's been down this road before, which is why I'm sayin' he was a sicko."

"He got off on being cut," I mused.

"Yeah, that's how it looks. Doc Sanders called it zero-phobia, or somethin' like that." My friend pulled a small notebook from his hip pocket and began thumbing through the pages. "Got it here somewhere..."

"Xyrophilia," Felicity said aloud, still studying the images.

"Yeah, that's it," he agreed.

"A love or obsession with razors and knives," my wife continued. "Combined with some kind of self or reverse piquerism apparently."

My friend looked over at me with a puzzled expression. "Peekawho? Sounds like that friggin' cartoon character."

I simply shrugged and nodded toward my wife as I tossed the photo onto the pile and pushed away from the table. "You'll have to ask her. I'm going to get a cup of coffee, you want some?"

He nodded. "Yeah, why not."

"Felicity?"

"With lots of sugar this time" was her response.

"Okay," Ben started in on my wife as I retrieved a trio of mugs from the cabinet. "So what's with the 'ism'?"

After a short pause, Felicity set aside the photo she'd been inspecting then looked up at Ben. "Piquerism is a condition whereby you become aroused by stabbing or cutting another person. In his case, it appears that Judge Wentworth became aroused by *being* cut or stabbed. I don't know if there is an actual word for that, other than masochist."

"Ya'know, Firehair, it fuckin' scares the shit outta me that you know that stuff."

"Aye, I bet I know some other things that would scare you even more."

"Yeah, well between the two of ya' I'm not takin' that bet. Let's just not go there."

"Well, if this was his kink," I offered, sliding a steaming mug in front of Ben. "Then you're right, Felicity. He was definitely a masochist."

"Like I said. Sick fuckin' puppy." Ben gave a quick nod then nudged my arm with the back of his hand. "By the way, I meant ta' ask ya' earlier. What happened to your hands?"

I looked quickly at the welted scratches that raked across my flesh then started to offer an excuse. Felicity, however, was faster with the explanation, and what she gave him was the unadulterated truth.

"A sudden attack of piquerism on my part," she interjected.

"Come again?"

"You don't want to…" I started, but again I was too late, as my wife was already serving up the gory details.

"I sexually dominated and physically abused my husband for several hours this morning," she announced with calm poise. Displaying her hands, she wriggled her fingers in an animated fashion while adding, "And I got just a bit overzealous with the fingernails."

"Awwww, Jeez…" Ben mumbled in an embarrassed tone. "I knew I shouldn't've fuckin' asked. Just forget it."

As if she hadn't even heard him, my wife continued her unabashed disclosure of how we'd spent our morning. "Of course, since I was sitting on top of him, holding him down, and…"

"Jeez, Row, I said I didn't wanna know this stuff," Ben appealed to me, cutting her off.

"I tried to stop you," I told him.

"Well, ya' didn't try to stop *her*."

"Aye, like he could," Felicity replied. "Now, can I finish the story?"

"I wish you wouldn't," my friend said.

"It's just sex, Ben," she stated.

He shook his head. "Apparently not, if you were... If it was..."

"Kinky?" she asked.

"Jeezus fuckin' Christ, yeah... 'Zactly... Besides, with you two... It's like... Like... I dunno, like hearin' your parents talk about doin' it."

"Come on. We aren't that old, Ben," she admonished. "At least, I'm not. You're both older than me, then."

"That's not what I mean and you know it... Shit. Can we just move on ta' somethin' else, please?"

"You're embarrassed," Felicity stated with a grin as she took her glasses off and cocked her head to the side. She was thoroughly enjoying the fact that she had him squirming. Maybe even a little too much.

"So what if I am?" he replied.

"It's funny."

"No it ain't."

She nodded vigorously. "Aye, but it is."

"Listen, does this even have anything at all to do with what I came here ta' show you?"

"Actually, I think it does."

"How?"

"Well, when I think about it, it all makes perfect sense."

He looked over at me as if seeking help. I just shook my head as I set a full coffee mug and the sugar bowl in front of my wife then said, "Leave me out of it."

I was pretty sure I knew where she was headed, and she was correct, it did make perfect sense. Still, I wasn't about to get in the middle the conversation. Not yet, anyway.

"Jeezzzz... I know I'm gonna regret this..." he began as he looked back at her. "Damn... Okay, what makes sense?"

"Why I connected so easily with the sexual energy in that room," she replied.

"Well yeah, it's 'cause you're a *Twilight Zone* freakazoid just like Rowan," he told her.

"Not funny."

"It wasn't a joke," he said. "Besides, it's just about as funny as me bein' embarrassed. Anyway, what's the big deal? I thought Row felt it too."

"I did," I offered. "But, that's just it. I felt it. Felicity, on the other hand, really connected. Up to and including channeling it."

"You felt it yourself," Felicity told him flatly.

"I dunno about that," he replied. "Like I said, it's pretty obvious what goes on in a place like that."

"That's beside the point," she returned. "You felt it whether you realized it or not."

"Okay, I give. How do ya' know that?"

"You were flirting with me when we arrived," she returned.

"I've flirted with ya' before," he huffed. "It's just, ya'know, friendly... Well, you know what I mean."

"Aye, but you were flirting with me at a crime scene, Ben. Heavily."

"Jeez," he mumbled. She had him more flustered than I'd ever seen. "Listen, I'm not doin' the hocus-pocus, that's you two, so give it a rest. Now let's get back ta' what you were originally sayin'... If I'm understandin' the deal here, you mean because you're female and the killer is prob'ly a whor... hook... Fuckit... a prostitute, you tapped into this shit?" His words were half-statement, half-question.

"That aspect of her profession has nothing to do with it," she replied. "But yes, I think the killer was a woman."

"Lemme ask ya' this, how'd'ya know it wasn't some kinda gay thing?" He waggled his fingers before her to represent something mystical. "Wouldn't that make for some girly *Twilight Zone* shit too?"

"Ben," she snipped. "That's simply rude."

"I'm just askin'," he replied.

"Did Wentworth have a history of bisexual activity?" I asked.

"Not that we're aware of." He shrugged. "Just coverin' the angles."

"Your killer is a woman," Felicity stated with unshakeable determination.

"So she's prob'ly a hooker then." Ben wasn't asking, he was telling.

"Actually, she may be a professional dominatrix," she replied.

"Yeah, okay, and the difference is?"

"Professional domination is just that, Ben. Domination. It's not prostitution."

"Tell that to a judge."

She reached out and tapped the photos. "It looks as if someone already did."

"Yeah, right," he returned. "So what makes ya' think she's a pro dominatrix?"

"Because I'm no stranger to the scene."

"The scene?"

"Yes," she said with a nod again. "Fem Dom."

Ben began shaking his head and waving his hands vigorously as he spoke, "Awwww, Jeez, I already told ya' I don't wanna know what you two do when…"

"Whoa… Hold up." I cut him off then added, "This isn't a 'you two' thing."

My stint of neutrality had been immediately ended by her comment as my curiosity piqued. Now I was going to get into the middle of things. I looked over at my wife. "So, do you think you might want to expand on that a bit?"

"Not much to tell really," she said with a shrug. "Quite awhile before I met you, I dated a guy for a couple of years who was heavily into submissive role play. I used to dominate him all the time."

"Really," I replied, surprised but not really shocked. "You never mentioned that before."

"It never came up," she said, shaking her head. "Does it bother you?"

"No. Just a little surprised, that's all... Of course, given your personality I guess I shouldn't be."

"Aye. I do have a dominant personality. And I must admit, I thoroughly enjoyed playing the role."

Ben groaned as if he had just been struck square between the eyes and reached up to massage the bridge of his nose. He started to speak, hesitated, then shook his head and groaned again. It was obvious that a question was rattling inside his head, and a large part of him wanted it to remain unspoken.

"What is it, Ben?" Felicity asked.

Her prompting fueled his curiosity, and the words came tumbling out before he could stop them. "So you're actually sayin' you're into like whips 'n chains and all that?"

"Whips, every now and then," she replied. "Actually, it was a leather flogger and a belt. Chains, not so much. Quite a bit of bondage, superior attitude, some verbal humiliation... But, his real turn on was trampling."

"What's a trampoline got ta' do with it?" he asked with a puzzled shake of his head.

"Not a trampoline," she replied. "Trample-*ing*. He got off from me walking on him in high heels."

"Awww, Jeezus..." My friend held up his hands again. "Stop. I don't wanna hear any more."

"Why?" Felicity pressed. "Are *you* getting turned on?"

"Do what?" he spat, staring back at her with an incredulous gaze.

"Well, you put on a good front, Ben, but deep down I think you would probably enjoy submitting to a woman." She stated the observation without apology.

"Excuse me?" he almost yelped.

"And, you do have a thing for women's legs," she continued. "You've said so yourself. Bob did too, so it stands to reason that you might very well have the same kind of kink that he had."

Felicity was obviously taking more than just a bit of pleasure from his discomfort. In fact, there was a recognizable glint in her eye that told me she might even be getting turned on again. However, I wasn't entirely sure if it was sexual arousal or merely giddiness over antagonizing Ben. Considering what had happened earlier, if it weren't for the fact that I'd seen them interact this way before, I would have been worried. However, they had a tendency to pick at one another on a regular basis. It was just how they were. Still, I kept an eye on her just in case.

"That's different," Ben said, shaking his head.

"Different how?"

"You're supposed ta' be lookin' at these autopsy photos," he said in an attempt to divert the conversation. "Not psychoanalyzin' me."

"Tell me how it's different then," she pushed.

"Well, ya'know... It's just different."

She was unrelenting. "It's still a fetish. And it's called crurophilia, by the way. You know, Ben, the first step here is just admitting it. I can help. I'd be more than happy to walk on you."

"What?!"

"Sure, I'd love to do it. It would be fun. I can go put on some heels for you, and I'm certain Rowan won't..."

"Felicity!" he objected.

"Really, Ben. You just lay down on the floor, and I'll go change shoes. I've got this really sexy pair of blue pumps, and I could..."

"Dammit, Felicity!" he barked.

"Oh. Would you prefer black or red? I have those too."

"Stop it! Just stop!"

"It's okay. I understand," she replied with a wicked grin.

"Jeezus…" my friend muttered, letting his forehead fall into his hand.

My wife still wasn't finished. "It's okay. Really. I do understand. Constance and I wear the same size. I'll just loan them to her."

"Felicity, goddammit!" Ben snapped. "Will ya' just knock it off?!"

She shrugged. "Okay, if it makes you uncomfortable."

"Thank you," he spat.

"No. That should be, 'Thank you, Mistress'."

My friend sighed and looked over at me. "Jeeezus… Row… I dunno how you do it."

I leaned back against the counter and took a sip from my own cup of coffee. I couldn't help but be somewhat amused by their exchange, especially since it didn't take the turn I had feared.

"Actually, she's not usually as mean to me as she is to you," I replied.

"I can be if you'd like," she offered.

"We'll discuss that later."

"Fuckin' wunnerful," Ben spat then started shuffling through the pile of photos once again until he found the shot he was looking for and pulled it out with a quick jerk. Holding it up, he continued, "So, you two clowns wanna get serious for a minute and have a look at this one? Believe it or not, the reason I came here is 'cause I've got some police work to do."

CHAPTER 10:

"This is what I really wanted you two ta' check out," Ben offered, handing a picture to Felicity.

I stepped toward the table and peered at it over her shoulder.

The image we were staring at was that of the quadrant on Wentworth's chest where the series of shallow cuts had been scored into his flesh. These had been the lacerations I had first noticed when we were at the crime scene, and they were also what had sparked that foreboding tickle in the back of my skull. Now that I was standing here looking at the close-up photograph, and I could see the wounds in all their unconcealed glory, that feeling was returning as a full-blown aggravation.

I continued staring at the glossy color page following the thin, and sometimes faint, marks with my eyes. As I had suspected earlier, they seemed to form a pattern. At the time, all I had been able to see was an almost random checkerboard, but now more detail had been revealed. What I was seeing certainly wasn't symmetrical, and was far from perfect, but upon close inspection it appeared to be the outline of a heart within the crosshatched slashes.

"A heart?" I said aloud.

"That's what we thought it looked like," Ben replied. "Mean anything to you?"

"Other than the obvious, 'I heart this' or 'I heart that' bumper sticker reference, not really," I answered. "I mean it looks familiar..." I paused, letting my words trail off as I reached out and with my finger traced a portion of the pattern in the air over the top of the photo. "The crosshatching and all seems to ring a bell, but I just may be thinking of a Valentine's Day card I've seen or something like that."

"Well, don't know if this makes any difference," Ben offered. "But Doc Sanders thinks these marks were done post-mortem whereas the others on his back weren't. She's waitin' on some lab results to verify that, but she's pretty sure."

"That's odd," I muttered.

"Tell me 'bout it," he grunted.

"They don't look as precise as the others," Felicity stated. "It's as if they were done out of rage."

"Or maybe the killer's just got a bad case of peekawhosits," my friend replied, his tone almost joking. "Got all worked up and went to slicin'."

"Maybe it wasn't anger," I speculated aloud. "If these cuts were made post mortem then maybe it was haste."

Ben gave a hearty nod. "Yeah, that's actually kinda what we were thinkin'. But, even so, if the killer took the time to do this before gettin' outta Dodge, then it's gotta mean somethin'."

"Well, like I said, it looks familiar," I told him. "But, I have to be honest, I can't really place a meaning on it."

"The love we feel," Felicity offered.

"Sorry?" Ben asked.

"The love we feel," she repeated. "That's one of the supposed meanings of the heart on the Leather Pride flag."

"Leather Pri... Jeezus... I don't wanna..." My friend looked at her, shaking his head, then pulled out his notebook and flipped it open before fishing in his pocket for a pen. "Okay. Go ahead. Leather Pride?"

"When I was dating Bob, we went to a couple of S&M/B&D conventions," she explained.

"Ya' mean like the one the church people were picketing a few years back?" he asked.

She nodded. "Exactly. Either way, just like Gay Pride has the rainbow, the BDSM community has the Leather Pride flag. It's black and blue horizontally striped bars top and bottom, with a white stripe dividing them across the middle. In the upper left hand corner is a heart. Many in the community say the heart is meant to symbolize 'the love we feel'."

"Black 'n blue," my friend grunted. "Go figure."

"Aye, it's not what you think. Black represents leather and blue represents denim."

Ben finished scribbling a note then stared back at my wife silently for a moment, then finally said, "You really kinda got into that whole deal, didn't ya'?"

"Yes, very much so, as long as I was the *top*," she replied. "But, I already told you I did."

He made a quick huffing noise as he closed his eyes, tightened his shoulders, and then feigned a shiver.

"What's wrong?" I asked.

He looked over to me. "This shit doesn't bother you?"

"What? The bondage stuff?"

"Well yeah."

I shrugged. "Not particularly, if it's between consenting adults."

"But..." his voice faded away and he fell silent.

"But what?" I asked.

He pointed to Felicity. "But it's her we're talkin' about here, white man. And you knew nothin' about this?"

I simply shrugged again in reply.

"I have to keep him guessing, don't I?" my wife offered. "A little mystery is good for a relationship."

He shook his head at me and then looked back to her. "Man, I'm just not sure I needed to know this shit about you, Felicity."

"Well don't dwell on it," she told him. "It will just get you all hot and bothered, then."

"Yeah, right," he snorted. "So anyway, let's get back ta' business. You're thinking maybe the killer carved a Leather Pride symbol into Wentworth?"

Felicity shrugged. "Maybe. Right now I'm merely speculating just like you. All that's really there is a heart, but if the killer was a dominatrix, it might make some sense."

"Whadda you think, Row?" he asked.

"I don't know," I replied. "Sounds like as good an explanation as any, for the moment. All I can tell you for sure is that you're right. It means *something*."

"So Wentworth's not talkin' to ya', huh?"

I knew immediately what he meant. "No. Not a word. Not yet, anyway. Why?"

"Dunno. Just got a hinky feelin' about this one."

I pointed to the pile of photographs. "So is that feeling why you came all the way out to the county to show us these?"

"Yeah, pretty much," he said with a nod. "Just can't shake the notion that there's somethin' more to this."

"Me too," I agreed. "I just don't know what it is. You know, maybe I'm rubbing off on you."

"Jeezus, I hope not."

"Aye, it could be worse," Felicity said.

"How's that?"

She shot him yet another wicked grin, but as she opened her mouth to speak, the relative quiet of the room was pierced by a sudden electronic trill that grew louder and more obnoxious with each consecutive chirp.

Ben reached beneath the table, and when his hand came back up, it was wrapped around his pager. He thumbed the device into silence then scanned the liquid crystal display.

"I'm gonna hafta make a call," he finally muttered before shoving the pager back onto his belt.

"Something important?" I asked.

"You could say that," he replied.

His demeanor had seemed to change suddenly. It had become muted and almost preoccupied. The switch seemed out of character, and I wasn't quite sure what to make of it.

"Albright?" I asked, grabbing at the first thing that came to my mind that might elicit such a reaction from him.

"No, actually it's kinda personal," he replied, his tone flat. "Listen, can I use your phone? I left my cell out in the van."

"Help yourself. There's one behind you, or if you need privacy, take your pick. You know where they all are."

When he had left the room, I looked over at my wife and raised an eyebrow. "That was weird."

"Maybe he's just tired."

"Maybe," I agreed with a nod even though I didn't really believe it. Still, I tried to let it rest and changed the subject. "So... What were you about to say to him?"

"Oh, nothing really," she replied.

"Uh-huh," I grunted. "Like I'm going to believe that. You know, you really ought to stop antagonizing him. Maybe he's not tired at all. Maybe it was you."

"But it's so much fun," she returned with exaggerated sweetness. "Besides. He deserves it."

"Yeah, well just be glad he likes you," I told her.

"Actually," she replied. "He needs to be glad that *I* like *him*."

I didn't offer a comeback. Instead, I looked down at the photograph on the table and stared at it for what seemed like a very long time. The aggravation in the back of my skull began creeping forward as my scalp tightened, and I felt the first throbbing twinges as it started the short metamorphosis into full-scale pain.

Felicity's concerned voice filtered into my ears. "Row? What's wrong?"

The first stabs of real discomfort lanced through my grey matter, and I knew then that the storm I'd sensed earlier was almost upon us. I looked back at my wife and shot her a thin smile then ignoring her question simply said, "Well, I guess you might as well get your fun in while you can then."

She frowned in return. "It's starting again, isn't it?"

I closed my eyes as I reached up to begin massaging my temple. There was no way I could hide it from her. Not anymore. Still, there was one saving grace in all of this. If she had to ask, then that meant she wasn't feeling it herself, and that told me my spell was still doing its job. That, in and of itself, made the growing pain just a little more bearable.

After a moment I opened my eyes and looked back at her troubled gaze once again. I opened my mouth to speak but was cut short by Ben as he came through the kitchen doorway.

"Listen," he said as he strode through, came to a halt at the table, and started gathering up the evidentiary photographs. "I gotta go take care of somethin'. You two gonna be around awhile?"

I had glanced up at the sound of his voice, so I looked to Felicity.

"I've got to go out for a bit," she said. "But, I can be here later if you need me to be."

I looked back to him. "I'll be here all day. Something wrong?"

"Just somethin' I gotta do," he replied, hurriedly stuffing the photos back into the envelope.

"Is there anything we can do to help, then?" my wife asked.

"No," he returned, shaking his head. "No. It's just somethin' I gotta take care of."

Ben was already heading for the front door, the seemingly anxious funk that had suddenly befallen him palpable in his wake. I set my coffee aside on the counter and headed after him with Felicity less than a half step behind me.

Our friend wasn't wasting any time. He had the front door open and was on his way through when we caught up to him.

"Listen, Ben, you're family. You know that. If there's anything we can do…" I offered.

He hesitated for a moment and looked back over his shoulder.

"Yeah, I know. Thanks," he replied, and with that he was gone, pulling the door shut behind him.

My headache ratcheted upward yet another factor, and I wondered if my friend's sudden change in demeanor had anything to do with it or if it was merely the natural progression of an unnatural pain.

"Weirder still," I finally muttered.

"Aye," Felicity voiced from behind me.

I turned back to her, and she peered into my eyes, the mask of concern still drawn across her usually soft features.

"Do you think he'll be okay?" she asked.

"I hope so," I replied. "I just wish I knew what was up."

"What about you?"

"What about me?"

"You never answered my question," she nudged. She looked to the floor then back to my face. "It is, isn't it? Happening again."

I closed my eyes and nodded. "Yeah" was all I said.

Tuesday, November 8
2:32 P.M.
Suite 1233, Concourse Suites
St. Louis, Missouri

CHAPTER 11:

Reaching out to the desk, she extracted yet another unfiltered cigarette from the rapidly depleting pack. As with each one before this, she slipped the end between her lips and then set it alight with the expiring ember of its predecessor.

Crushing out the spent butt in an overflowing ashtray, she took a drag from the fresh one then curled the end of her tongue, allowing the nicotine-laden smoke to waft slowly upward as she French inhaled. Her throat was already becoming raw, and in the back of her mind, she knew she would be paying for this.

After all, she didn't actually smoke. *She* did.

It was *her* doing the smoking, and there was nothing she could do to stop it.

And, of course, whenever *she* did anything, it was to excess. The stronger the cigarette, the better; the more cigarettes, the better; and as always, when *she* was here, things had to be done *her* way.

Following the cloudy exhale, she lifted a tumbler and took a swig of expensive rum. This, also, had been going on to excess ever since she'd returned to the room forty-five minutes ago. Considering what she'd already imbibed and how little sleep she'd had, she should be passed out where she sat. But no, as amazing as it seemed, she was sober. Stone cold sober.

She took another drink. The rum was good. It wasn't the best, but it was good nonetheless. Of course, there was still a bottle of *Barbancourt* in her luggage, but it would remain sealed for the time being. It would be a luxury now, but it was going to be an absolute necessity later.

Setting the tumbler aside, she dropped her hand down to a computer mouse and then absently slid it across the surface of the desk. With a click, she opened a window on the notebook computer's liquid crystal display. It was plain and stark, displaying as nothing more than a simple, black rectangle with a grey-white border and a cursor winking rhythmically in the upper left-hand corner.

However, as simplistic as it appeared, it was actually a somewhat sophisticated bit of code. It was, for her and the ones she accepted into her service, a hidden chat room. A private and secure slice of cyberspace, residing on an innocuous server, behind spoofed addresses and randomly forwarded routers. It was for the most part untraceable and accessible only by a chosen few.

She glanced at the clock in the corner of the screen and did a mental calculation. She had paged him quite some time ago, and she was beginning to grow impatient.

Logically, she knew the wait was to be expected. It was the middle of the day, in the middle of the week, and surely he was at work, which was probably why he had not answered yet. He was, after all, a cop, albeit a cop with a fetish for leggy, dominant women and stiletto heels.

It was too bad for him that his wife had insisted on a divorce because of it. She knew the whole story. Those in her service never failed to confess what brought them to her in the first place, and he had been no different. Imagine, after years together, finally getting up the courage to confess your kink to the woman you love, and to have her crush you like that. It had been painful for him.

She felt the tickle begin to rise in her belly even as she thought about it. What delicious pain it must have been. Not for him, of course, but for his wife. To have him broken and groveling before her like that, she had to have relished it. How could she not?

That was the only explanation that made sense. All she had to do was loosen up a bit, and it would have saved their marriage. But, she didn't take that path. No, that must not have been what she knew would fulfill her. How she must have truly gotten off by destroying his world that way!

She must have.

She would have.

The tickle continued to grow, and she closed her eyes as she imagined the scene. Her earlier anger was gone, and even her fleeting remorse over her personal servitude to a greater power was a distant memory. *She* was in control now, and that was all that mattered.

A soft "ding" emitted from the computer's speakers, and she opened her eyes, looking upward across the screen to the formerly blank chat window. The cursor was continuing to blink at her from the darkness but was now positioned below a short string of text. The glowing words reading simply, "Sorry i am late, Mistress."

He had taken great care not to capitalize the pronoun describing himself, as he understood his station beneath her.

Leaning forward, she carefully tapped out a reply on the keyboard. "You will need to be punished for that, little man."

A third line of text instantly appeared. "Yes, Mistress Miranda."

She began typing again. "What is your fondest dream, slave?"

"To serve you, Mistress" the words appeared.

"To serve me how?"

"How, Mistress?"

"As mere words on a screen, or…" She left the rest untyped but for the periods of the ellipsis.

"IRL, Mistress."

She knew the abbreviated jargon well. IRL: in real life. She'd seen it more than once and from every slave with whom she chatted. And, in this case, it was exactly what she sought.

She paused a moment before typing her reply. A wave of delightful anticipation rolling through her stomach as she gently caressed the keyboard.

She had to wonder what he must have been feeling when he read the words, "Tonight your dream comes true."

Tuesday, November 8
11:27 P.M.
St. Louis, Missouri

CHAPTER 12:

A mong my least favorite feelings was that of déjà vu, yet it seemed like a constant in my life no matter how hard I tried to deny it. Like right now.

I was just beginning to drift off when a noise struck my ears. In that netherworld between sleep and wakefulness, it seemed like a megaphone was pressed up against the side of my head. I felt myself jump as my muscles tensed, and of course, that immediately brought the headache I'd been trying to forget right back into the forefront.

I was lucid enough to realize that the noise was actually Felicity's voice, but I hadn't caught enough of it to decipher what she had said, so I grunted, "Huh?"

"I said, how's your head?" she repeated.

"Still there," I mumbled.

"What? Your head or the pain?"

"Both."

"Ha, ha" came her humorless reply. "I'm serious."

"So am I."

Unlike the morning's supernaturally propelled romp, this time we were in bed solely for the purpose of sleep. Or, at least that is what I thought we had intended. We'd been lying here for better than an hour now, and neither of us had been enjoying much success in that department. Until recently, that is, when I had finally managed to relax enough to begin nodding off. Obviously, the same had not been true for my wife.

I was exhausted, and I suspected she was too. Considering the early wake-up call along with the various extracurricular activities, there was no way to avoid it. Of course, after she had finished with her errands for the afternoon, she had taken a nap. I suppose I should have done the same.

Still, the reality was that we'd probably have gotten to bed earlier had it not been for the fact that we were both worried about Ben. Before his harried departure, he had made it a point to ask if we would be available later. Felicity had been gone less than four hours, and I hadn't left at all, making sure to hang loose in anticipation of his return or at the very least, his call.

However, later came and went without so much as a word from him, and in our minds that was troublesome.

After what I considered to be a reasonable wait, I had tried contacting him myself—several times in fact. I had alternated between his cell, his apartment, and his work number. From the cellular, I was greeted only with a full voice mailbox, which wasn't a big surprise considering his disdain for all things computerized. To be honest, I was still amazed he even had the mailbox set up at all.

His work number at the homicide division had shifted almost immediately to voice mail itself, and his home phone hadn't been any better. There, the answering machine had provided a terse, recorded demand to "leave a freakin' message if ya' feel like ya' gotta." At least neither of them told me they were full, and after a number of aborted attempts, I did as they instructed, leaving messages in both places. It was pretty much all that I could do.

I'm sure that the worry over our friend combined with the overtiredness hadn't been helping matters for either of us. And of course, in my case I still had the nagging throb inside my skull to contend with as well. Still, I'd finally managed to ignore it for just long enough to actually feel sleep coming my way. That is, until Felicity put a halt to that idea.

Since there didn't seem to be a follow up question forthcoming, I tried to relax again and let my mind drift. Unfortunately, like it had earlier, it kept coming back around to the crime scene, the heart shape, and then the pain. I flashed on a memory of watching a program about neurosurgery, probably all because of that unrelenting thud inside my head. It had been some years back on one of the educational cable channels, and I recalled that something was mentioned about the grey matter itself not feeling pain.

I considered the memory for a moment then decided that while it may well be true, you certainly weren't going to be able to convince me of the fact. Not right now, anyway.

As if reading my thoughts, Felicity broke the dark silence once again. "Is it getting worse?"

I was still awake enough to catch it on the first go around.

"Not yet," I told her.

"Did you take anything for it?"

"It's not that kind of headache. You know that."

"That's not what I asked," she pressed.

"Yeah," I murmured. "I took something."

She paused for a long while, and once again, thinking the impromptu interrogation was over, I started trying to relax.

My wife, however, decided to prove my assumption wrong again and suddenly asked, "What did you take?"

I grumbled, "Does it really matter?"

"No. Not really I guess."

"Okay then."

"So?"

"So what?"

"So, what did you take?"

I sighed heavily then rolled to the side and fumbled for the switch on the reading lamp next to the bed. After a quick grope, I located the thumbwheel and flicked it on then rolled the opposite direction to face the redheaded chatterbox curled up next to me.

"Okay, what's up?" I asked.

She twisted beneath the covers and snuggled in close. "I can't sleep."

"No kidding," I replied with exaggerated sarcasm. "So I guess if you can't sleep, nobody else is going to either?"

"You weren't asleep," she told me.

"I almost was."

"No, you weren't."

"Sure I was."

"No. You weren't."

"How do you know?"

"When you're asleep you snore. You weren't snoring."

"You didn't give me a chance."

"Aye, what's it matter? You're awake now."

"Uh-huh."

"So... Do you think Ben is all right?" she asked.

"Probably," I told her, not wanting to let on that I was probably even more worried than she. "He's a big boy. And besides, he's got a gun."

"He just seemed a bit..." She hesitated. "I don't know... Scattered, when he left."

"Yeah," I agreed then added, "But he did say it was something personal."

"I hope nothing's wrong, then," she said.

"Me too," I replied.

"You don't think something happened to Ben Junior, do you?" she asked with a mild urgency suddenly overtaking her voice.

"I doubt it," I returned. "He would have told us if it was something like that."

"Aye, I suppose he would have."

She grew quiet again, and I contemplated her spate of concern over our friend. Considering how calm she usually remained, with the exception of her occasional display of stereotypical Irish temper, I found her change in demeanor to be somewhat out of character. The more I dwelled on it, the more I wondered why.

"You're awfully concerned about Ben all of a sudden," I stated.

"Shouldn't I be?"

"I don't know," I replied. "Just doesn't seem like you."

"What's that supposed to mean, then?"

"Just making an observation."

"Are you jealous?"

"Do I need to be?"

"Of course not."

"Then you answered your own question, didn't you?"

"I'm just worried," she said after a moment. "That's all."

Something in the back of my head told me that while I knew she had a genuine concern for Ben's well being, vocalizing it was just a smokescreen. It was a surrogate for what was truly worrying her. And, I was pretty sure I knew what it was that had her in its grip. While it was something she'd never had a problem talking about before, the fact that she was hiding from it told me her concern had grown and now went even deeper than it ever had in the past.

I took a chance that I was correct and slipped my arm around her as I said, "It's okay, Felicity. I'm going to be okay."

I felt her shoulders fall as she slowly let out a heavy breath, confirming my suspicion.

"How did you know?" she finally asked.

"What? That I'm the one you're really worried about, you mean?"

"Aye."

"Just a feeling."

She sighed heavily again and then snuggled in even closer. "I don't want this to start again, Row."

"I don't want it to either, but I don't really think we have a choice, honey."

"Maybe we should move," she offered.

"Where?" I asked.

"I don't know," she told me. "Away from here."

"That won't change anything, Felicity," I said softly. "What you're trying to run away from isn't just here. It's part of me... Part of us... This is who we are."

"I'm not so sure I want to be us then."

"Yes, you do."

She didn't reply right away. She simply remained still, curled against me, her face buried against my chest. I gently stroked her hair and listened to her breathe as I closed my eyes, trying to relax once again myself. Unfortunately, my brain would have none of it. My mind was racing, and sleep wasn't going to come anytime soon.

"I need a drink," Felicity finally said.

"Now?"

I felt her nod slightly. "Aye. Maybe it will help me relax."

"Maybe so," I agreed.

"What about you?"

"What about me?"

She was already unfolding herself from the cuddle and tossing back the sheet and comforter. "A drink might help you too."

I rolled back, pushed myself up on my elbows, and paused before answering. "Maybe just some more aspirin I think."

"Sit with me then?" The tone in her voice was almost pleading.

I had already figured out that she was more disturbed about this than she'd ever been before, but from the sound of her words, it became apparent that it went even deeper than I had realized. The two-year hiatus had led us both into complacency, but she had obviously harbored a real hope that my connection with the dead was over. I, on the other hand, had always known it would never be done. Not until I myself joined their ranks, and then, who knew? It may not even be over then.

"Yeah," I told her with a nod. "I'll be in there in a minute."

She finished wrapping herself in a thick bathrobe and headed off to the kitchen. I made my way into the bathroom and fumbled through the medicine cabinet until I found a bottle of aspirin then popped the cap and poured a couple into my hand.

I gazed down at the white tablets in my palm and even though I knew full well that they weren't going to help, poured another pair out to join them before snapping the cap back on the bottle. I popped the pills into my mouth and then bent down over the sink to get a mouthful of water.

When I stood back upright, I felt a sharp stab behind my eyes, and a sudden rush of dizziness overcame me. I grabbed the basin and steadied myself, giving my head a shake then looking up to the mirror.

A flash of brightness filled my eyes, and as it faded I saw the afterimage of a heart-shaped outline floating in the air before me. Protruding from it was a thin dagger with a simple handle. There seemed to be something streaming outward from the apparition or perhaps even floating behind it.

I blinked rapidly, trying to focus on the image, but I only caught intermittent flashes of bright red as the outline faded quickly away.

I shook my head again, feeling the dizziness ebb and my sight return to normal. After a moment I let go of the basin then retrieved my own bathrobe from the back of the door and slipped into it.

I trudged through the dark house on automatic pilot, almost tripping over our English setter who had elected to sleep in the middle of the hallway. After skirting around him, I hooked through the living room, then the dining room, and into the illuminated kitchen.

I shaded my eyes against the brightness, waiting for them to adjust as I slid into a seat opposite my wife at the breakfast nook.

I heard the ice tinkling in her glass as she tilted it up and took a drink then brought it back down to the table. Even after resting it there, however, she never took her dainty hand from the tumbler.

"You okay?" I asked.

"Aye," she returned simply as she picked up a bottle and refilled the glass.

My eyes were beginning to adjust, and I looked up at her sullen features. I wasn't entirely sure that alcohol was the best thing for her, given the circumstances, especially if she had already downed one and was starting a second, but at least she wasn't sitting here drinking alone.

"So something just happened back…" I started.

Before I could complete the sentence, however, something caught my eye. The bottle she had just set back on the table between us was of a different shape than I had expected it to be. I was used to my petite wife drowning her sorrows in Irish whisky, but that definitely wasn't what she was drinking at the moment.

I reached out and turned the bottle to face me. Since I wasn't wearing my glasses, I pulled it close so that I could read the label. Even though the word only had three letters, I read it twice just to make sure I had it correct and then looked up at her with a puzzled expression.

"You were saying?" Felicity urged.

I ignored her question, replying instead with "Rum?"

"I don't know." She shook her head to indicate she didn't understand either. "I've been craving it all day."

"But you don't even like rum."

"I know," she mumbled then took another drink. She looked down at the table and then back up at me with a mix of puzzlement, and even what might have been fear, in her eyes before adding, "I don't smoke either."

"Well yeah. You've never smoked," I replied. "So what?"

She nodded. "Aye. But right now I'm dying for a cigarette."

CHAPTER 13:

I stared back at my wife without saying a word, my brain desperately trying to process the contradictory information it has just been fed.

"I must not be awake," I finally told her with a shake of my head. "I could have sworn you just said you were dying for a cigarette."

"I did," she replied with a shallow nod.

"How could you possibly... I mean... Come on..." I stuttered. "You've never even smoked one."

"Well... I did once. In college. Sort of."

"How did you 'sort of' smoke a cigarette?"

"I was at a party. I'd had too much to drink and, well, I just took a puff from a friend's cigarette. Then I coughed myself silly and almost threw up."

"One puff, and it made you sick," I echoed. "That still makes my point. If you've only ever had just one puff, and that made you sick, then how could you possibly be craving one?"

She shrugged, the curious fear still in her eyes. "I don't know. All I can say is that I'm pretty sure I want a cigarette. That's what keeps going through my mind, anyway."

The concern that had plagued me earlier in the day now returned full force.

Up until this morning, I'd had every indication that the sphere of protection I had placed around Felicity was doing its job, or so I thought. But now, I was starting to see some pretty hard evidence that maybe it wasn't. She was quite obviously being affected by something preternatural; there was absolutely no denying it. I mean, first the sexual aggression, and now here she was, sitting at the kitchen table in the middle of the night swilling rum as if it were water.

Of course, I wasn't entirely sure just how much of an issue the drinking was in and of itself. As petite as she was, she could drink virtually anyone under the table. She'd done it to both Ben and me on more than one occasion. Still, the fact that she was actually craving alcohol wasn't good, and her choice of liquor was certainly a red flag as well. She didn't care for rum at all. In fact, the one time I'd seen her take a drink of it—before this moment that is—she had literally spit it back out.

And now, to be telling me she wanted a cigarette—this coming from a woman who didn't allow smoking in our house and could even be more militant about it than a reformed smoker?

No, something was definitely wrong with this picture. It wasn't just blurry around the edges; it was completely out of focus.

Adding yet another flaw to the already screwed up family portrait was the fact that my ethereal headache was maintaining its rhythmic thud in the back of my skull. Thankfully, for the moment it didn't seem to be getting any worse, but I was already starting to "see" things, as evidenced by the episode in the bathroom. I knew that could only mean that an escalation was a mere step or two down the road.

Whatever was happening, it was a good bet that it was all connected. Unfortunately, I was desperately afraid I knew what at least part of it meant.

"I think maybe I need to call Ben," I announced.

Felicity gave her head a quick shake as she furrowed her brow. "What makes you think he'll know?"

I cocked my head and gave her a suspicious look. "Know what?"

"About Wentworth's habits," she replied. "You're wanting to find out if Hammond Wentworth was a smoker and a rum drinker, aren't you?"

"Yeah," I replied.

"I was already thinking the same thing myself," she offered. "You think I'm channeling him, don't you?"

"Actually, that's what I'm hoping for, but I don't know if we'll be that lucky."

"Aye, what do you mean lucky?" she asked incredulously. "I don't want to go through this again. It was bad enough before…"

I countered with my own query. "Well let me ask you this: Can you think of another explanation for these sudden cravings you're having?"

"Well… No… Not really," she replied hesitantly. "But, Gods…"

"Well, actually I can, and I think you'd like it even less."

"What is it then?"

The old adage "open mouth, insert foot" suddenly came to mind. I knew for certain that the name resting on the tip of my tongue was one she never wanted to hear again. I couldn't say that I was all that excited about it myself, but it was there nonetheless.

Realizing immediately that I had started down a path I should have avoided, verbally at least, I tried to backpedal as best I could. "I'd rather not say right now."

"No you don't," she returned, arching an eyebrow and stabbing her finger at me. "You don't announce something like that then just leave me hanging. What is it you're thinking?"

"Felicity, really…"

"Damn your eyes, Rowan Linden Gant, tell me!"

"All right then," I replied, hesitation now obvious in my own voice. "Do you remember when *I* started smoking again, right out of the blue?"

"Aye, I do. But that was when…"

Her voice trailed off slowly, and her already naturally pale complexion became even more pallid as any semblance of color drained instantly from her face. Her mouth curled downward into a hard frown and she spat, "When you were channeling *him*."

"Yeah," I muttered. "Exactly."

I couldn't blame her for the reaction. The *him* to whom she was referring wasn't on her short list of favorite people. He wasn't on the long list either, for that matter. The hard and cold fact about him was that he was a serial rapist who had ended up murdering two women—one of them a college cheerleader.

But, as bad as that was, it wasn't the thing that made Felicity's skin crawl the most. That was another matter entirely. You see, what set his crimes apart was that they were all by-products of a lurid fantasy he had built directly around her. In some ways, the effects of his actions still plagued her to this day.

As for me, well, channeling the sorry bastard had been one of the worst experiences of my life. It had even brought me dangerously close to committing murder myself.

I watched my wife carefully as she continued to brood in silence.

I sighed heavily and wondered about the logic of having let her press me this far. But, there was nothing I could do about it now. "So... I think you know where I'm headed here..."

The hard frown continued to crease her features, but I could also see the light behind her eyes that told me she had already turned to the same page as me.

I continued. "Put it all together with the violent sex and..."

"Do you really think that I'm channeling the killer?" she asked, cutting me off mid-sentence.

"I hope not," I told her. "But I'm really afraid you might be. Especially if the killer actually *is* female."

"Gods..." she muttered then took another drink of the rum.

"Yeah," I mumbled in return. "All of them."

After a moment of the two of us sitting and staring at one another in the nervous silence, Felicity spoke up again. "So... Is that what you were going to tell me?"

"Huh?"

"Earlier, when you started to say something happened."

"Oh, that." I shook my head absently, still mulling over the ramifications of what we'd just discussed. "No, it was something else."

"Okay, so what happened?" she pressed.

"It was kind of strange," I replied. "When I was in the bathroom I started getting dizzy, like maybe I was going to 'zone out', and then I saw this flash. It was an outline of a heart, and it kind of looked like something was floating behind it."

"You mean like what was carved into Wentworth?"

"Well, kind of, but not exactly." I shook my head again. "I suppose the stuff I thought was behind it could have been the same. But, it also had a dagger piercing it."

She summed up the imagery. "A heart with a dagger piercing it? Sounds a lot like a tattoo to me then."

"Yeah, that kind of makes sense," I agreed. "Maybe the killer has a tattoo similar to it."

"I could call Duane tomorrow... Ummm, I mean later this morning I guess," she offered, referring to the tattoo artist who had done her own pieces of body art. "We could go down to his shop, and you could look through the books."

"That might be a good idea," I mused. "If nothing else, it might trigger something if I run across a similar design."

"So..." she started again. "Are you still going to call Ben?"

I reached up to rub my eyes and let out a sigh. Not only was my head still throbbing, but the exhaustion was working on me too.

"I don't know," I replied. "It's after midnight. I'm beat. It's nothing that can't wait till morning I don't guess. What about you?"

"Aye, what *about* me?"

"Are you going to keep boozing or have you had enough?"

She twisted the now empty tumbler in her hand and gave the bottle a long stare before reaching out and picking it up. She unscrewed the lid and tipped it toward the glass.

"I don't even feel a tingle yet," she mused aloud. "You'd think I would get at least that."

I shot her a glance and quipped, "At this rate maybe we should be signing you up for AA."

She simply frowned back at me and continued pouring a healthy measure of the alcohol into the tumbler. After twisting the cap back onto the bottle, she shot me an annoyed glare and thumped it down on the table in such a way as to tell me my comment was unappreciated. Without a word she began sipping the rum, not even bothering to refresh the ice cubes that by this point in time had all but disappeared.

Before I could offer up an apology, the ringer on the phone pealed into the room. I slid out of my seat and started toward the wall where it hung.

"Maybe that's Ben," Felicity said.

"Yeah, maybe," I replied as I stepped across the room. Leaning in I squinted to read the block letters on the liquid crystal display of the caller ID box. What I saw actually made my heart skip upward into my throat.

I snatched the handset from the base and fought to keep the panic out of my voice as I spoke. "Helen? What's wrong?"

"Rowan," Ben's sister replied, her own voice tense. "Is Benjamin with you? It is very important."

CHAPTER 14:

My friend's older sister was the last person I would have expected to call at this hour of the night, and the very fact that she was on the other end of the line told me something was seriously amiss. The addition of the semi-controlled tension in her voice simply bolstered that feeling even more.

I'd never known Helen to be overly emotional. In fact, she was just the opposite. Not frigid by any means but calm and even tempered to a fault. She was, after all, not only a psychiatrist but also a trained and practicing psychotherapist, and she definitely had the temperament for it.

To be honest, it was because of this that we had first met. She had seen me through some very hard times dealing with what could only be termed as post-traumatic stress after nearly being killed by a raging sociopath, not to mention helping me come to terms with my curse of hearing the dead speak. She had even been there for Felicity in the wake of her own brush with those vile stresses. However, while our initial contact had been on a professional level, we had become good friends over the past few years, and I knew her current demeanor was out of character.

"We haven't seen him since early this afternoon," I said. "Helen, what's wrong?"

Her reply followed a perceptible hesitation. "I'm at the hospital now, and I am afraid that our father has taken a turn for the worse."

"Your who?" I blurted without thinking.

"Our father, Rowan," she replied, emotion cracking in her voice. "He's in the hospital. Did Benjamin not tell you?"

"No, he didn't."

What I couldn't bring myself to voice was the fact that I was under the impression that their father had died long ago. At least, that is what Ben had led me to believe ever since I'd known him.

"I can't say that I am surprised," she sighed.

"You said he took a turn for the worse. Is it very serious?" I asked. I suspected that I already knew the answer but didn't want to make blind assumptions.

She hesitated again. The pause gave me an instant mental picture of her weighing her words before speaking, just as I'd seen her do many times before. When she finally spoke, the matter of fact delivery was a weak barrier against the flood of emotion she was obviously trying to contain.

"He is dying, Rowan."

Out of reflex I said, "Helen... I'm so sorry..."

"Thank you," she replied.

Felicity was out of her seat now and was giving me a questioning stare as she touched my arm. I cupped my hand over the mouthpiece and whispered, "It's Helen Storm looking for Ben. Their father is dying."

"Their father?" she asked quietly, just as puzzled as I. "You mean Ben's father? But, I thought..."

I gave her a quick shrug and shake of my head then returned my attention to the phone. "Helen, is there anything we can do?"

"No," she returned. "No, but thank you. It is simply his time. It is just that... Just that Benjamin needs to be here."

"I understand," I told her. "Like I said though, the last time we saw him was early this afternoon here at the house. He got paged, made a call, and then left in a bit of a rush."

"That would have been me," she replied. "I paged him, and he did come to the hospital this afternoon, but I am afraid it didn't go very well."

I didn't ask what she meant. I was capable of doing the math, and it really wasn't all that hard to solve this particular equation with the values I already had in hand.

"So, do you think they can..." I started a question then thought better of it and stopped myself short.

"Reconcile?" she finished for me. "I don't know, but I must try."

"I understand," I said. "So, this is probably a stupid question, but I take it you've tried his cell and his pager again?"

"Yes. Several times. I have called his office, his apartment, and even Allison," she told me, referring to her former sister-in-law. "I'm afraid I don't have Constance's number, but I was hoping you might."

"He won't be there," I told her. "She's out of town right now."

Helen's list was the same one I had tried earlier, with the exception of Allison. However, hearing it recited by her made me realize that it was incomplete, especially now that I knew my friend was most likely looking for a place to hide.

"Can I reach you on your cell phone?" I asked suddenly.

"Yes," she replied. "Why?"

"I'm not sure, but I think I might have an idea where he is," I told her.

"Where?"

"*The Third Place.*"

"Excuse me?"

"It's a cigar shop downtown," I explained. "If he was in a foul mood when he left the hospital, I'm willing to bet that's where he went to cool off."

"But, would they not be closed at this hour?" Helen objected.

"To the public, yes," I agreed. "But, he knows the owner."

"Can we call there?" she pressed. "What is the number?"

"I doubt if anyone will answer the phone this time of night," I replied. "I'll try, but if I can't get hold of anyone, I'll go down there."

"I'm sorry, what?..." Helen's voice came across the line a hollow echo, as if the phone were pulled away from her mouth. I could hear several other muffled voices in the background along with nondescript commotion. Her voice grew louder as she suddenly came back on the line and said, "Hold on for a moment, Rowan..."

"Sure," I replied, not certain if she was even there to hear me.

I listened to the frantic noises going on in the hospital room at the other end of the line. Whatever was happening, it didn't sound any better than it felt. I let out a heavy breath and forced myself to ground and center. As much as I empathized with Helen, I had more than enough on my plate at the moment and that included helping her to find Ben. The last thing I needed to do right now was to tap into her plummeting emotions because if I did, I was going to be useless to her.

Felicity had disappeared almost as soon as I had finished uttering the name of the cigar shop Ben and I frequented, and she now returned to the kitchen, dressed in denim jeans and a sweatshirt. Stepping over to the table, she deftly tossed back the remains of her rum then began gathering her hair and twisting it into a loose Gibson girl.

"What are you doing?" I asked.

"Going with you, then," she replied without missing a beat. "What does it look like?"

"I might just be making a phone call," I told her.

"You won't get an answer. You know that."

"Yeah, well it would probably be a good idea for you to come along anyway, so I can keep an eye on you," I returned, glancing over at the bottle of liquor, then added quickly, "But, the booze stays here."

"Aye, I'll leave the bottle," she quipped. "I'll just fill a flask."

I didn't get a chance to retort as Helen suddenly came back on the line. "Rowan?"

"Yes, Helen, I'm here."

"Please hurry," she said, her voice revealing a new level of distress well beyond what it had earlier contained. "Benjamin needs to make his peace with our father, and there is precious little time left."

"I will."

"Thank you."

As soon as I hung up with Helen, I began stabbing the number of *The Third Place* into the phone, but as I had suspected and my wife had so matter-of-factly stated, the call went unanswered. After that first try, I quickly got dressed while filling Felicity in on the specifics of the rest of the conversation then hurried out to my truck with her close on my heels.

"You didn't really fill a flask, did you?" I asked as I began backing out of the garage.

She didn't answer, so when I came to a halt and levered the truck out of reverse, I looked over at her. The reason for her muteness was readily apparent when I caught her screwing the lid back on the stainless steel vessel.

"Felicity…" I moaned.

"This place has cigarettes, right?" she asked.

I simply sighed as the pain in my skull ratcheted up yet another notch. I was starting to feel like I was caught in the middle of a three-way collision between Ben, Felicity, and a yet to be identified supernatural force.

I just didn't know which one of them was going to crash into me first.

Before we were even halfway there, we had made three more attempts to reach the cigar shop using my cell, all with the same result. We finally gave up on the calls but pressed on and arrived at the storefront less than fifteen minutes after leaving the house. Now, standing on a deserted downtown sidewalk, I was just about to rap my knuckles hard on the glass for a third time. However, as I raised my hand, I saw motion in the back of the store and hesitated. Eventually, a figure moved forward from the shadows.

Though not quite Ben's stature, Patrick Owen was a large man, standing a head taller than me and possessing a healthy girth that bespoke of an appetite for good food and drink. His boyish features and brightly smiling eyes went a long way toward hiding his true age; however, even they were visibly betrayed by greying hair and a full beard that was almost completely ash white.

As usual, he was clad in a dark shirt and paisley vest. A gold chain dipped down across his round abdomen and back up to disappear into a watch pocket. He smiled back at me from the opposite side of the glass as he thumbed through a set of keys before finally settling on one, twisting it in the lock, and pushing the door open.

"What brings you out in the middle of the night, Rowan? Run out of MX-Two's?" he asked with a chuckle as he mentioned my preferred cigar. His voice was smooth and drawled slightly at the end of the sentence, affected by a mild accent reminiscent of middle Tennessee.

The man was a bit of an enigma. We knew little about him other than the fact that he was intelligent and filled with facts about virtually any subject. Also, if he didn't happen to know the answer, he was quite capable of making up a convincing line of bull on the fly; though he would purposely out himself before it went too far.

I can't say that I had ever seen him tired or worn down, no matter what the hour, and tonight was no exception. If I didn't know better, I would assume that he simply never slept nor even had the need.

"Nothing quite so innocuous, Patrick," I replied as we entered, and he began locking the door behind us. "We're looking for Ben. Is he here by any chance?"

The aroma of fine tobaccos mingled with the rich tang of spices, filling the atmosphere of the store with what I considered a heady aroma. Whether or not it was this incense, I couldn't say, but there was just something about this place that made me feel immediately comfortable. Even given the current situation, I felt myself relax simply upon stepping across the threshold. Ben had mentioned to me before that it had the same effect for him, so it made sense to me that this is where he would seek an escape.

"Why, yes he is," Patrick replied. "So, I take it that was you calling."

"Yeah." I nodded. "It was us."

"I suppose I should have answered the phone."

"That would have made things a little easier," I agreed.

He turned his attention to Felicity. "And, I take it this is the Missus?"

I nodded then rushed through an introduction. "Felicity, Patrick. Patrick, Felicity."

"My dear, the photograph your husband carries doesn't begin to do you justice," he told her with a smile and slight bow.

"Thank you," Felicity returned.

"You are quite welcome." He gave her a nod then extracted the pocket watch from his vest and thumbed it open. "Given the late or shall I say early hour, I assume that you are here on a task of some import."

"Yeah," I answered. "It's pretty important."

"Come along then," he told us as he stowed the watch and began ambling through the narrow store, giving us a wave to follow. "The constable is upstairs."

We trekked past the walk-in humidor, which was to our left. On our right was a display case counter with a cash register. Behind that, floor-to-ceiling shelves held various imported cigarettes, chocolates, teas, and other curiosities. At the back of the store, we went through an open doorway, continued through a small storeroom, and then made our way up a long flight of aging wooden stairs.

I had been up here countless times before. It was the "smoking room" and in some ways what made *The Third Place* what it was to many of us. It was a place where Patrick's friends and close acquaintances could sit and relax, smoke a cigar or pipe, play chess, chat, enjoy a glass of aged port, or even all of the above.

At the top of the stairs, Patrick opened a door and ushered us through. I could hear the hum of the air cleaner running, but the room still smelled of both fresh and stale smoke. While that didn't bother me at all, I noticed Felicity wrinkling her nose.

"You okay?" I asked quietly.

She nodded and then whispered, "Aye. It stinks, but I'll be fine."

"Still want a cigarette?" I chided.

She simply shot me a glance and rolled her eyes.

The brick-walled expanse we now entered was the same width as the retail space below but seemed somewhat larger since it didn't need to house the walk-in humidor. Sections of the plank floor were covered by oriental throw rugs in various states of wear. A mismatched pair of small sofas rested at opposing ends of the room, with the one at the front positioned beneath an arched window. On the left was a small bar and on the right, a trio of bookshelves fully stocked with reading material.

Basically, it was a throwback to gentlemen's clubs of days gone by, except that the overall theme was one of "post-modern fraternity house." In short, it was a patchwork décor spanning what amounted to probably three decades and a dozen differing styles.

Positioned both solitary and in pairs throughout the expanse were a handful of equally incompatible recliners; one of which was presently occupied by Ben.

As we proceeded inward, Patrick calmly proclaimed, "Benjamin... You have visitors."

"Who?" my friend said, leaning forward and peering around him. "Oh, Row, it's you... And Firehair too? Okay, well, you've both already heard this one, but I'm almost done... So, anyway, Patrick, where was I? Oh yeah... So my partner swings around the other side of the stage, and all of a sudden this asshole we're chasin' comes runnin' outta the shadows right at me. He's buck fuckin' naked and holdin' a goddamn flagpole like a spear or somethin'. He's screamin' at the top of his lungs and..."

"Ben," I interrupted. "Can this wait a minute? I really need to talk to you."

"Wassup, white man?" he asked. "You do the *Twilight Zone* thing or somethin'?"

"No, but you already knew that." I shook my head. "I'm sure you know why we're here."

"Nope. Got no idea," he replied.

I searched his face, and even though his tone was almost convincing, I knew he was lying.

"Get serious, Ben. Felicity and I just showed up here in the middle of the night and all you said was 'Oh, it's you'."

"Yeah, so?"

"Yeah, so, Helen has been trying to reach you for hours. So have we."

He stared back at me with a blank expression then took a deliberate puff on the cigar that was hooked beneath his index finger. Finally letting a cloud of smoke curl slowly from his mouth, he reached up to smooth his hair back then allowed his hand to fall down to his neck and begin working at the muscles.

After a moment he asked, "She okay?"

"She's distraught," I told him. "But given the circumstances I think that's to be expected."

"Yeah, well," he mumbled. "She made the choice."

"You should be there, Ben."

"No. No I shouldn't."

"Damn you, Benjamin Storm!" Felicity spat, unable to contain herself. "Your father is dying."

"Yeah, well, it's about fuckin' time" was his only reply.

CHAPTER 15:

"**Y**ou don't mean that," I told him.

"Hell if I don't," he spat.

"Look, Ben, I don't know what went on between you two…"

He didn't let me finish. "That's right, Row, you don't, so just stay the fuck out of it."

Felicity brushed past me and stepped toward him while exclaiming, "He's your father!"

"Not as far as I'm concerned he ain't!" he shot back.

Our friend started forward as if to stand then huffed out an angry sigh and fell back in the chair. He went silent; shaking his head as he grimaced, he then reached up to massage his temple. After a moment, he focused back on us and held up his hand. "Listen, I understand what you two are tryin' ta' do here, but you've got no clue what's goin' on. Ta' be honest, it's none of your business, and Helen never shoulda gotten ya' involved."

"That may be true, but she did," I told him.

"Well, I'm un-involvin' ya'."

"Aye, it's not as easy as all that," Felicity replied.

"Yeah it is."

"*Monar!*" she spat. "He's your father!"

Ben didn't even bother to ask for a translation of the Gaelic epithet. He simply shook his head at her and said, "Yeah, whatever. Just trust me, Felicity, let it go."

"Let it go?" she barked as she started toward him.

I reached out and took hold of her arm, stopping her dead in her tracks. She whipped her head to the side, looked down at my hand with absolute contempt, and then locked on to me with an incendiary stare. I knew immediately that I had just joined Ben as an object of her ire, but I didn't let go. Instead, I simply held her fast and shook my head.

"Back off, hon."

"Why?" she grumbled. "Someone needs to wake his sorry arse up to reality."

"Awww, Jeezus fuckin'…" Ben groaned at her comment.

"Why don't you let me talk to him," I told her.

"Aye, what if maybe you hold him, and I'll beat some sense into him then," she countered then shot her glare his direction.

Still holding her arm, I turned to face Patrick who had remained perfectly silent through the entire exchange. "Do you still have some of that imported chocolate you were telling me about?"

"Yes, Rowan, as a matter of fact I do," he replied without hesitation.

"I think Felicity would really like to try some if you don't mind."

"Not at all," he replied with a knowing tilt of his head. "Dear lady, if you would like to accompany me downstairs."

"Chocolate? *Fek! Damnú ort*, Rowan! What are you?…" my wife sputtered angrily. "I don't want any goddamned chocolate!"

"Yes, Felicity, you do," I told her sternly.

"No, I don't!" she argued.

"Felicity, please…" I appealed. "Let me handle this."

"Why don'tcha' both go have some," Ben chided.

"Rowan…" Felicity widened her eyes at me as she almost snarled her protest.

"Please…" I repeated. "Just let me handle it."

We were all tired, time was short, and I simply couldn't afford to let Felicity continue to go off on a tear right now. I wasn't sure if it was the rum finally affecting her or a combination of it all, but somehow Ben's disdain for his father had struck a serious nerve with her. My wife's legendary temper was fully alight, and she simply wasn't going to help the current situation at all.

She drew her lips into a thin frown and remained silent. The fact that her glare hadn't softened in the least was more than enough to tell me there was going to be some form of retribution in my near future. However, that was something I would have to deal with when the time came.

I just hoped Patrick was correct, and the chocolate really was *that* good.

Felicity jerked her arm from my grasp and brushed past me, starting out the door ahead of Patrick. He gave me a quick nod and followed along behind, drawing the door shut in his wake.

"You're in trouble, white man," Ben announced as I stepped farther into the room.

"Uh-huh," I agreed with a sigh. "And not the good kind I'm afraid."

"Yeah, well, ya' brought it on yourself for nothin'," he told me. "I already told ya' I'm not goin' ta' see 'im.'"

"Okay," I replied as I found a recliner opposite my friend and perched myself on the edge of the seat.

He shot me a puzzled look. "Okay? That's it? Ya' mean you're not gonna try and convince me I should go?"

I shrugged. "Seems pretty futile."

"Yeah, well I told ya' that before."

"Yes, you did."

"Okay, so what'd'ja step in the shit with Firehair for then?"

"Just saving you from an ass beating at her hands is all."

"Yeah, right..." he chuckled.

"Seemed like the thing to do at the time," I offered.

"Yeah, maybe so, but man... She's pissed."

"Yeah, she is, but it's my problem now." I leaned back in the chair but continued watching him. "You have to admit, the tension level is quite a bit lower now."

"In here," he nodded. "But I sure'as shit wouldn't trade places with ya' later."

"Yeah, well, she'll calm down. I hope."

I remained silent after that, trying to find a segue into what I was really here to do. My attempt at defusing the situation had worked, for the most part anyway. He had actually chuckled at my comment about Felicity, and the tension truly had moved down the scale perceptibly. Unfortunately, now it was my turn to dial it back up. If nothing else, the call from Helen had impressed upon me the urgency of the situation, and it was weighing on me along with everything else. I didn't have the luxury of leading him down the garden path to an enlightened realization. I needed to take a shortcut straight through the thorny hedgerow, and I suspected it wasn't going to be pretty.

As long as Ben and I had been friends, I had made it a point not to press him when he didn't want to talk. If he wanted me to know something, he would tell me, sooner or later. It was a rare occasion when I would break that unspoken rule, but now was just going to have to be one of those times.

"So. You want to talk about it?" I finally said.

"No. Not really."

"Why don't you do it anyway?"

"What? Now you're gonna start after all? What happened to 'okay'?"

"I'm not pushing you to go see him. Just tell me why you won't."

"Because I don't fuckin' wanna, okay?!" he barked.

"It might help."

"Goddammit Rowan! What did..." He shouted the curse then let his voice trail off quickly as he gave me a suspicious look. Raising an eyebrow, he gave his head a quick shake then harrumphed out a half-chuckle. "Yeah. Nice try, white man, but don't play psychologist with me. My sis's already got that base covered."

"I'm not," I replied then shrugged again and amended the statement. "Okay, well, maybe a little."

He grunted, "Uh-huh."

"Okay, so that didn't work."

"Nope." He shook his head. "Got anything else?"

I lied. "Not really."

"Then, why don'tcha grab a cigar and kick back for a bit?"

"As much as I'd like to, I'm going to need to dig myself out of this hole with Felicity, and I doubt that would help much."

"You're prob'ly right."

"Yeah. Guess I'd better head downstairs."

"Yeah. Guess you'd better."

"Well, just so you know," I offered, "Helen says he's in bad shape."

"Yeah," he mumbled then took a drag on the cigar and allowed the smoke to billow around him. "He was in bad shape this afternoon too."

"Apparently now he's worse."

"Good."

"He probably won't make it through the night."

"Even better."

While I was used to my friend's occasional bursts of brutal honesty with regard to his feelings, I was wholly unaccustomed to seeing anyone with this level of animosity toward a parent. Whatever had happened between the two of them went deeper than I wanted to imagine. On top of that, it was obvious from his comment that he and Helen had gone into it more than once, and if she was unable to pull him from the depths, I seriously doubted there was anything I could say that would make a difference.

We sat staring at one another for enough heartbeats that I eventually lost count. He quietly puffed on his cigar, once taking a moment to knock down the ash before returning it to the corner of his mouth. The look in his dark eyes was one of unabashed hatred. The scariest part was that it was not born of an emotional rage; it was cold and brooding, deep and without limit. The feeling was so palpable in the air between us that given my hypersensitivity to emotions, it made me physically ache.

I knew full well that it wasn't directed toward me, but I fell within its dark swath, and it was a place I knew I simply couldn't remain for long.

I took a deep breath and cleared my throat. I don't know

exactly why, since I clearly had his full attention, but it seemed like the thing to do, especially since I was preparing to play the hold card I'd lied about. I was about to blindside my friend, and I wasn't feeling good about it. Unfortunately, I didn't seem to have any other choice.

"I'm not going to press you on this," I finally said.

"Smart man," he replied.

"I do, however, think that you should consider Helen in all of this."

"Don't ya' think I have, Rowan? She made her decision."

I stood and pushed my hands into the pockets of my jacket then regarded him for another moment. "I believe that you think you have."

"Whaddaya mean by that?"

I sighed and pressed forward with my plan. "Family is important, Ben. Felicity and I consider you an important part of ours. I want you to know that."

He nodded. "Yeah. Same here."

I continued. "I'm serious, Ben. You're a rare kind of friend. The kind of friend that either one of us would walk through fire for; and, I know you would do the same for either of us."

"Yeah, I would. That goes without sayin'," he replied in a confused but serious tone. "So?"

"So, you have other family, my friend. Blood family…"

I pulled my hand out of my pocket and in it was my cell phone.

"Jeezus… Fuck me… Rowan, don't…"

I had flipped it open and thumbed the speed dial for Helen's cell while it was still concealed, so I put the device up to my ear. Her strained voice was already coming across the line.

"Rowan? Rowan, are you there?"

"Hold on a second, Helen," I replied.

I took the couple of short steps toward Ben and laid the phone on the end table next to his chair then looked him in the eyes once again.

I gave him a shallow nod then as I turned to walk out, I said, "I think maybe it's time you walked through some of that fire for your sister."

Before I even hit the bottom of the stairs, I could hear that Felicity and Patrick were engaged in an animated conversation. From what I could make out, I had to assume that it was about Gaelic history. I suppose that shouldn't have been a surprise.

When I came out of the back room, my wife shot me a quick glance over her shoulder.

"Did you convince him to go see his father, then?" she asked, her Celtic brogue heavily underscoring the sentence. I knew she had to be just as exhausted as me, and it wasn't out of the question that the rum could be playing a part as well. It was hard to say at this point, and the dull throb that was still residing in my own skull wasn't helping me to reach any conclusions.

"We'll see," I replied. "He's on my cell with Helen right now. Or at least I hope he is."

"You hope he is?"

"Yeah. Long story."

"Okay, so what should we do now?" she asked.

"Go home."

"You don't want to wait?"

"He'll either go or he won't." I shrugged. "We've done all we can do, and I can get my phone back later."

She considered me in silence for a moment then asked, "How's your headache?"

"Still there," I replied. "How's your drinking problem?"

"Still there." She echoed my answer.

Without missing a beat, Patrick interjected, "Somehow I don't think I want to know what the two of you are talking about."

"You don't," we replied almost in unison.

Felicity shook her head and turned back to me. "Aye, let's just go home. I'll beat you after I've had some sleep."

CHAPTER 16:

I awakened to the sensation of something soft tickling my cheek, and out of reflex I brushed at it without even opening my eyes. I had no idea how long I'd been lying in the bed. It felt like it had only been a few minutes, but I really couldn't be certain. The truth was, I barely remembered crawling beneath the covers. I was simply so exhausted at that point in time that I had been operating on autopilot.

Whether it had been a few minutes or a few hours, however, what I did know for sure was that my head remained filled with the same ache that had plagued it when I first shut my eyes.

The softness brushed against my face a second time, and again I automatically dragged the back of my hand across my cheek. But, no sooner had I done it than the light tickle returned. The annoyance suddenly disappeared of its own accord only to just as quickly reappear. It was at about this time that I realized there was a weight on my chest.

I opened my eyes and found myself staring into the grizzled face of our geriatric calico cat, Emily. She was pushing seventeen years old and still going strong, although she was moving a bit slower these days. Presently, she was perched on my chest, almost up to my throat, her nose mere inches from mine and one paw resting on my cheek. The moment she saw my eyes open, she let out a pathetic "mew" directly into my face.

I was instantly blasted with the feline equivalent of morning breath.

I scrunched up my nose, and figuring that mine probably wasn't any better, I blew my own return volley at her. She didn't seem particularly impressed by the force of my retaliation and remained unfazed; she simply patted my cheek with her paw and "mewed" again. I reached up and gently nudged her off my chest then rolled over on my side; hooking my arm around Felicity's mid-section, I nuzzled in close and closed my eyes.

Unfortunately, I didn't even get a chance to settle in before the doorbell rang and the dogs began barking. This developing theme of people getting me out of bed with phones and doorbells was really starting to wear on my nerves.

"Gods, I must have pissed someone off in a past life," I mumbled.

"Hmmm?" Felicity moaned.

"Nothing," I returned. "What time is it?"

"Aye, I don't know. Look at the clock, then," she instructed sleepily, following her words with an audible yawn. I took notice that not only the normal lilting accent still ran through her voice, but the heavy brogue was still intact, a good sign that she hadn't really rested.

With a sigh I disentangled myself from my wife and rolled back toward the nightstand so that I could peer at the clock. It read 11:45. Felicity kept it set ahead, however, so I did the calculation and mumbled, "Eleven thirty."

My wife immediately pushed herself upward and asked with a mild note of panic, "*Cac*! Eleven-thirty? What day is it?"

"Hopefully Wednesday," I replied.

"*Cac*!" she spat again, tossing back the blankets and swinging her legs over the side.

"What's wrong?"

"I'm supposed to have a lunch meeting with a new client today," she replied as she pulled on her robe.

"When?"

"In half an hour."

"Ouch. Not good."

"Aye, tell me about it," she grumbled.

I had rolled out of the bed a few seconds after her, so I was already up and pulling on a pair of pants when the doorbell rang again, sending the dogs into another round of barking.

"You get the door," she ordered as she came around to my side of the bed and snatched up the telephone. "I've got to make a call to see if I can re-schedule."

"Yeah, okay," I said as I finished pulling a t-shirt over my head. "What are you going to say?"

"I'll think of something," she told me then gave me a shove. "Go on, then."

"You can blame me if it will help," I told her.

"I probably will," she replied. "It would be the truth."

"How do you figure," I asked as I started around the end of the bed.

She suddenly exclaimed, "Dammit!"

"What?!" I asked, surprised by the outburst.

"I don't have their number in here," she returned. "After you get the door, bring me my PDA. Make it quick."

"Yeah, okay," I replied then added a sarcastic, "Will there be anything else, your Highness?"

"Watch it. Don't even think I've forgotten about last night."

"Of course not," I mumbled as I headed out the door.

"You look like hell, Rowan," FBI Special Agent Constance Mandalay said as she stepped across the threshold.

I knew that her observation was dead on. I'd had personal experience with the reflection that greeted me every morning, and it was far from pretty.

Agent Drew, with whom we'd had the run-in at the Wentworth crime scene, followed her into the house. He gave me a nod but remained silent. I returned the mute gesture.

I didn't say it out loud, but I was thankful that I'd let the dogs out the back door before answering the front because I doubted that they would like him any more than I did.

Mandalay was petite, with a thick crop of shoulder-length brunette hair that was usually neatly styled but now appeared slightly unkempt. On any other day, her soft features would have made her look several years younger than her actual age, not that she was necessarily what you would call old to begin with. Today, however, there were obvious dark semi-circles beneath her eyes, and her face sagged like a deflating balloon. Even her stylish trench coat was rumpled and appeared like it could use a rest.

Despite her playfully sarcastic greeting, amid the obvious exhaustion, she was still carrying herself in a businesslike posture and wearing a serious mask.

In contrast, Agent Drew didn't appear to have changed at all, still looking much like he had a few nights ago. In fact, unless I missed my guess, he was wearing exactly the same outfit he had been then—the stereotypical neatly pressed, dark-suited look that visually screamed government agent. I couldn't help but wonder if he took that whole persona a bit too seriously.

"Thanks, Constance," I replied, turning back to her. "But, you might want to check a mirror. You look a bit worn around the edges yourself."

"Actually, I am. I haven't slept yet," she told me with a shake of her head. "In fact I just got into Saint Louis a few hours ago on a redeye and hit the ground running. I don't think I've stopped since six a.m. yesterday."

"So Ben called you then," I said with an understanding nod.

"Ben?" she replied in a mildly puzzled tone. "Oh, do you mean Detective Storm?"

My first thought was to ask her what she had been smoking, but my brain was still too sluggish to connect the words with my mouth, so I stuttered, "Well, I don't... I mean I just figured that since you're here..."

She shook her head and gave me a confused frown as she rolled her eyes in the direction of Agent Drew. "Rowan, what are you babbling about?"

It suddenly dawned on me that her and Ben's relationship was not really one for public record, especially when it came to other law enforcement personnel. Not that they had been able to keep their personal involvement a complete secret, far from it in fact. Still, broadcasting it certainly wasn't a good idea.

I shook my head and played along. "I'm sorry, I'm still half asleep. I was up late last night. I just assumed that since you were here you had been called."

She shrugged. "About what?"

"It might not really be my place to get into it," I replied.

"Is it something important? Something to do with a current investigation?" she pressed.

Unfortunately, I had managed to not only pique her curiosity, but I could feel a tangible sense of worry starting to seep outward from her. If she wasn't careful, she was going to reveal the closeness of the relationship herself.

I sighed and shook my head. I was really beginning to excel at letting my mouth get me into trouble, and now I was dragging someone else along for the ride. If I kept it up, I could probably turn pro. Seeing no reasonable way out, I simply blurted, "Ben's father is in the hospital."

She creased her brow and cocked her head to the side. "His who? But Ben's father…"

I opened my mouth and started to cover for her, but before I could get a word out, Agent Drew unceremoniously interrupted us both.

"Look, Mandalay, I already know you're dating Detective Storm. Hell, everyone knows," he said with a flat, matter-of-fact tone. "You and Mister Gant can knock off the charades."

Mandalay shot an annoyed glance over her shoulder then turned back to me and began allowing her concern to show through. "Did I hear you correctly?"

"Yeah. His father," I told her with a nod. "See, that's why I wanted to let him tell you."

"But I thought…" She stopped herself. "Never mind. So, is it serious? Is he going to be okay?"

"Actually, when I talked to Helen last night, they weren't expecting him to see morning."

"Okay," she replied, her outward expression telling me that she was trying to process what I had just said, treating it as simple fact and nothing more. "So, what about Ben?" she asked. "How's he handling it?"

I shook my head again. "That's a whole different story, Constance. But, we should probably talk about it later."

She glanced over at Agent Drew then back to me and nodded. "Okay. Later."

"My turn," I declared. "If that's not what this is about, then what are you doing here? Ben said you weren't coming back until the end of the week."

"I'm back early because of the Wentworth case," she replied. "The Saint Louis field office is short-staffed because of the flu epidemic, just like everyone else. They wanted more warm bodies on this, and I was pretty much finished in DC anyway."

"I thought the Major Case Squad had jurisdiction on that case," I mused aloud.

"Yes and no," she explained. "They definitely have jurisdiction, and they are exercising it to the fullest. But, Wentworth was still a federal judge, so the FBI is launching its own concurrent investigation. At least until we've ruled out a professional hit, then who knows."

My brain was starting to wake up and began making various associations between this new data and the old. Normally that would be a good thing. However, in this case those connections were only producing a new question. "Okay, so why are you standing in MY doorway?"

"From what I understand, Felicity acted as an interim crime scene photographer because of the flue epidemic. This is true?"

I nodded. "Yeah, that's right. Actually, we were both there."

She fell instantly back into the no-nonsense attitude. "Does she have copies of the crime scene photos?"

"No. Not that I'm aware of," I told her. "Why?"

"Have the flash memory cards Miz O'Brien handed over to Detective Storm been returned yet?" Agent Drew asked.

I shrugged. "I don't think so, but I couldn't say for sure. Ben did stop by yesterday morning with some of the printed photos to get our opinion, but I don't remember seeing the cards. What's this about?"

"He wanted your opinion?" he pressed, ignoring my question.

"I've been known to consult for the..." I started to explain.

"I'm well aware of your history, Mister Gant," he cut me off. "Why did the detective need your opinion?"

"Back off, Drew," Mandalay snapped over her shoulder then looked back to me with a questioning gaze. "Rowan, are you saying there is an occult element to the murder?"

"Whoa, slow down," I objected. "I'm not saying anything of the sort. He just wanted us to look at something we had noticed while we were on the scene."

"And what was that?" Drew interjected again.

"Some markings," I replied. "A post mortem mutilation that formed a pattern."

"What kind of pattern?"

"Haven't you looked at any of the evidence?" I asked, befuddled by the line of questioning.

"What kind of pattern?" Mandalay echoed his question, an astringent quality overtaking her voice.

I held up my hands and shook my head. "Okay, stop. Time out. Back up. This is really starting to come off like an interrogation, and I've got to be honest, I'm not comfortable with it. Constance, I'm asking you as a friend... Is there some reason I might need to call my attorney?"

She let out a tired sigh as she closed her eyes and gave me a sorrowful nod. "You're right, Rowan. I apologize for all of this. And, no... You don't need your attorney."

"Okay then, so what's going on?"

"Like I said," she replied. "Major Case is maintaining that the Wentworth homicide is their jurisdiction, and we aren't getting the level of cooperation we'd like."

"So you're asking about the crime scene photos because..."

"We haven't even seen them yet," she finished for me. "That's right."

"Didn't you get any of your own?" I asked, directing the question at Agent Drew.

"No." His one word answer was laced with chagrin.

"Well, either way, this doesn't sound like the MCS," I mused. "They're usually pretty cooperative, aren't they?"

"Usually," Mandalay agreed. "Depending on who is running the particular investigation. And with that in mind, this particular directive is apparently coming from higher up."

That was all she had to say for me to fit the pieces together.

"Albright," I muttered, contempt in my voice.

She nodded. "What is it you and Storm always say? Give the man a cigar."

"Well, Ben told me she was going to end up in the middle of it. I guess he was right."

"So, now that you understand, would you be willing to fill us in?" Mandalay asked.

"Not that I really know all that much about it, but sure." I gave her a nod. "Let me just..."

"Rowan!" Felicity's demanding voice came from the bedroom, cutting me off before I could finish.

I reached up and rubbed my throbbing forehead then motioned for the two of them to come farther into the room and swung the front door closed in their wake.

I pointed back down the hallway and finished my prematurely truncated thought. "...Go take care of that. Why don't you two have a seat in the kitchen, and we'll be right there."

CHAPTER 17:

F elicity had taken the opportunity to freshen up while she was
waiting and was standing in front of her closet debating what to
wear when I entered the room.

"Here's your PDA," I said as I handed over the device.

She took it from me absently and didn't even bother to utter a
thank you. After a moment she glanced at me and asked, "So, who was
at the door?"

Her tone made the question sound like a regal demand.

"Constance and Agent Drew."

The name got her attention, and she turned toward me.
"Constance?"

I nodded. "Yeah, she's back in town. Look, they need to talk to
us about the Wentworth crime scene."

"Why us?"

I gave her a quick rundown of what I'd been told thus far, and
as I expected she closely mimicked my own reaction.

"I told them we'd try to help," I confessed.

"Well, I don't have the flash cards back yet," she told me as
she made a decision and snagged an outfit from the closet. Tossing it
onto the bed, she flipped open her PDA and began tapping the stylus
across it as she strode toward the phone.

"We can at least fill them in on what we saw."

She nodded. "Let me see how long I can delay this lunch
meeting. The account is too big to blow off."

"I understand," I replied. "Maybe we can set something up
with Constance for later."

"That would probably be good."

"Okay, we'll be in the kitchen."

"Go tell them I'll be there in a minute," she ordered.

"Are you feeling okay?" I asked.

"Fine. Why?"

"The attitude."

"What attitude?"

"Look," I started. "I know you're angry about last night, but this barking orders at me is starting to get a bit old. I'm not your servant."

She looked up at me and pressed her thumb against the off-hook button on the phone midway through dialing.

"I'm doing it, aren't I?" she asked.

"Pissing me off? Yes."

She let out a heavy breath, and I could see that she was forcing herself to ground. "No. Channeling," she offered. "The whole domination thing. I've actually been getting off on being a bitch to you."

"Damn," I mumbled. "I guess I'm too out of it myself. That hadn't even dawned on me. You know, between my headache and your libido, we're a hell of a mismatch at the moment."

"I'm sorry, Row," she told me.

"I'll get over it," I replied. "But, you might want to consider hematite jewelry to accessorize. It might help you stay grounded."

"Good idea."

"Okay. I'll be in the kitchen," I said as I turned to go.

"Row?"

"Yeah?"

"I *am* still mad about last night though."

"I figured," I replied with a nod. "If you're still mad later, you can beat me then."

"I'll take you up on that," she offered. "But, you should know that I just might enjoy it way too much."

"Well, that makes one of us."

"Maybe I'm slow," I said as I poured water into the coffee maker. "But it just now dawned on me why you're here."

"What do you mean?" Constance asked.

"Our friendship," I replied. "You can't tell me your boss isn't hoping to get somewhere by playing that card."

"It was mentioned," she admitted with a shrug. "But the idea to send me didn't come from my SAC."

"Really? Who then?"

"Me."

"You?" I asked, somewhat taken aback.

"Yes, me," she affirmed. "Actually, you should probably thank me."

"Why is that?"

"I had to do some fast talking to get him to go for it. After I got the call yesterday wanting to know the best way to approach Felicity…"

"And what did you say?" my wife interrupted, appearing in the doorway, her attention divided between the conversation and the task of applying her makeup with the help of the mirror in our dining room.

She was actually going to be leaving soon, but Constance had decided to pick up as much from me as she could, then check back with her later.

"Full riot gear and a prayer," Mandalay replied.

"You didn't…" I said.

"No, but I thought it," she offered with a tired smile.

"Smart woman," Felicity called through the doorway.

"Anyway," Mandalay continued. "What I did say was that it would be best to let me do it… And then I spent thirty minutes convincing him I was right."

"Why?" I asked. "Did you have to convince him, I mean."

"Because of the fact that we're friends," she explained.

"So he thought you were too close to us to be objective," I concluded.

"Which is why Agent Drew came along for the ride," she added with a nod.

"What if you hadn't been able to convince him?" I asked, curiosity getting the better of me.

"Truthfully? The approach could have been a bit more hostile."

"Why?"

"Because the assumption was that due to your history your loyalties would lie with the MCS."

"With Ben, yes," I asserted. "Maybe a few others as well, but with Albright calling the shots? No way in hell."

"That's what I told him."

"And?"

She shrugged. "He's new in town, Rowan. He doesn't know the whole history, just what's on paper. And, to be honest, we didn't know if you knew about Albright yet—which apparently you didn't... Let's just say it's a good thing I convinced him to let me handle this."

"Are you two finished?" Agent Drew asked, something akin to impatience trilling in his voice.

"Chill out," Mandalay told him.

"We're here to get information," he replied. "Not for a friendly chat."

Mandalay turned to him, and even though from my present angle I couldn't see her face, the look in his eyes told me I was glad the glare was directed at him and not me. After a moment of thick silence, she said, "You smoke, right?"

"What's that got to do with..." he started to ask.

"Why don't you go ahead outside, Agent Drew. Have a cigarette and wait for me. I'll finish up here."

"Simpson said we were both..."

"I said," she interrupted him again, the coldness of her tone unmistakable as she slowly over-enunciated the sentence. "Wait... out... side."

The ringer on the phone suddenly pealed through the room, dissipating the uncomfortable aura surrounding the standoff between the two of them.

"If that's Judy from Winzer-Lockhart, tell her I'm on my way," Felicity called out.

I stepped across the room and snatched up the handset without even taking time to check the caller ID.

"Hello?" I said as I tucked it up to my ear.

I was greeted only with silence.

"Hello?" I repeated.

The quiet continued to be my only greeting, but as I listened I was certain I could hear the sound of someone breathing at the other end. I looked over at the caller ID box and saw that it was displaying nothing but a series of dashes. The number had been blocked.

I dropped the phone back onto the hook and let out a sigh. This wasn't new. In fact, I had even been expecting it to start up again. I just hoped that my expectations and resignation to the fact hadn't been what manifested its untimely return.

"Wrong number?" Constance asked.

"Not exactly," I returned.

"The breather?" she prodded.

She knew about the calls, as did Ben. They'd both tried to help me trace them, but all they were ever able to establish was that they had come from random payphones, widely scattered through the metropolitan area.

"Yeah." I nodded.

The phone rang again, and out of reflex I reached out to pick it up then caught myself and hesitated long enough to glance at the caller ID. This time the dashes were replaced by a number I easily recognized, so I lifted the receiver and placed it to my ear once again.

"Hello."

"What're ya' doin'?" Ben's gruff voice issued from the speaker almost as a demand, sans any sort of pleasantries.

"Talking to Constance," I replied.

Mandalay looked at me and mouthed, "Is that Storm."

I simply nodded in reply.

"You didn't call her 'bout my old man, did'ja?" my friend asked, both suspicion and anger welling in his voice.

"No. Actually she just showed up at the door, and she's sitting in my kitchen right now."

"She's what? She's here? She's in Saint Louis?"

"Long story, but yeah, she and Agent Drew are here," I replied.

"You got two Feebs at your house?" he half asked, a note of understanding seeping into his voice as he picked up the hint.

"Yes."

"They pumpin' you for info on the Wentworth case?"

"Something like that."

"Jeezus... They would pull a stunt like that... Shit... Can't blame 'em I don't guess. What with fuckin' Albright closin' the door in their face," he muttered. "I told ya', didn't I?"

"Yeah, you did."

"Fuck me," he grumbled.

There was a lull at the other end, and since he had opened the door, I nudged the conversation through it. "So, how is your father anyway?"

"Dead."

"I'm sorry, Ben."

"Don't be," he huffed. "Best fuckin' thing for both of us."

"How's Helen?"

"Handlin' it. I promised I'd help 'er with the arrangements later, but listen, that's not why I called. You and Firehair free for a bit?"

"Actually, Felicity has a lunch meeting with a client."

"Can she get out of it?"

"I don't know but probably not. She's already had to reschedule."

My wife poked her head around the corner and shook her head vigorously, indicating the negative. Apparently, my reply had been enough to let her guess what he had asked.

"I just got a confirmation on that no," I told him.

"Okay, so what about you?"

"Well, I haven't even had a shower yet."

"You can do that later. I need ya' ta' look at somethin' right now."

"What about Constance and Agent Drew?"

"Bring 'em with ya'."

"Bring them with me where?"

"The Gateway Motel out on Lindbergh."

"What's going on, Ben?"

"That's what I want you ta' tell me."

Ben was adamant that we needed to leave immediately if not sooner, but after hanging up I had still taken enough time for an encounter with my toothbrush and a comb. Then I changed into something a bit more suitable for going out in public. I had done my best to make myself as presentable as I possibly could, but I'd still felt like I desperately needed to run myself through the shower.

The image that had peered back at me from the mirror had a thick crop of stubble shadowing his face, and evidence of the dull ache in his head was obvious through the creases in his otherwise flat expression. His goatee could have used a trim and even seemed to be revealing to the world a fresh spate of grey.

This definitely hadn't been the man whom I'd seen reflected here only a few days before, but there he was, and he was looking pretty ragged. As much as I wanted to do so, however, there was no denying that we were one and the same. And, to be honest, I really shouldn't have been surprised because the reflection simply looked exactly like I felt. Unfortunately for me, it seemed the physical tolls being exacted by my connection with the other side were hastening. Or, perhaps it was the two year reprieve from such things that was now making it all appear just that much more drastic.

Either way, I couldn't say that I really cared for the results.

Felicity had headed out for her lunch meeting at the same time I was leaving with Constance and Agent Drew. She wasn't expecting to be free for at least two hours, maybe longer, but she took down the address of the motel just in case. In case of what, however, we had no idea.

Whatever his reasons, Ben hadn't been forthcoming about why he wanted us there. All he would say was that we should check in with the first uniform we saw carrying a clipboard and ask for him. That, in and of itself, was enough to tell me that we were talking about a crime scene, but that much I had already suspected. Telling me to bring Mandalay and Drew said in its own way that this was probably something connected with Wentworth's murder, or at least that was the conclusion I reached. Therefore, having read between the lines, I wasn't a bit surprised by the bustle of activity greeting us when we arrived at the Gateway Motel.

I was riding with the two FBI agents for no other reason than convenience, and no sooner had we pulled onto the lot than they were flashing their ID's. We were directed to a parking space and told that someone would go inform Ben of our arrival. Thus far, I hadn't needed to utter a word. I can't say that I minded that a bit, however, because very suddenly I wasn't feeling well at all.

By the time we climbed out of the car, my headache was already ramping up uncontrollably, and I felt a violent churn in my stomach. My back was beginning to ache, alternating between severe cramps deep within my muscles and sudden stinging sensations across my skin. For the first time in a very long while, I found myself struggling to ground and center simply to keep from slipping under in an ethereal whirlpool.

I knew that I had never completely lost connection with the other side, but for two years now, it had been just so much background noise. Living with it had been akin to the tinny speaker of a cheap television with the volume turned down almost as far as it would go. It had become nothing more than an almost ignorable noise with only an occasionally recognizable string of verbiage.

In an instant, however, the volume was turned to full. My shunt through the veil was open wide, and the quiet static was now a deafening roar filling my ears to drown out the physical world around me.

The ethereal drought was over. What had only been whispers of the dead for so very long were now the anguished screams of tortured souls welcoming me back to my own personal hell.

I just wish they'd given me a gentler homecoming than the sight of the pavement rushing up toward my face.

CHAPTER 18:

I think I might have called out to Constance, but I couldn't be sure. All I knew was that I stumbled forward as I tried to recover from the sudden preternatural burst and subsequently began to fall. Unfortunately, there was nothing I could do about it. My brain appeared to have taken a hiatus from communicating with my body, and at the moment my motor reflexes didn't seem to be responding to commands, conscious or otherwise.

Physical pain bit simultaneously into my right knee and both my shoulders as I continued downward, and I somehow managed to squeeze my eyes shut. I felt weak and faint as tightness grew in my chest, and I wasn't entirely sure that I was even breathing any longer.

Logic dictated that in a split second an agony similar to that which was now piercing my knee should be ripping through my face as it married itself to the asphalt. With that front and center in my mind, I tried to brace myself for the impact.

More pain tore through my upper back and shoulders as I waited for what I assumed to be the inevitable but was taking forever to come. Then, instead of feeling my face against the surface of the parking lot, I noted the sensation of backward motion as I was jerked up by my armpits.

My head lolled to the side of its own accord, and through the banshee wails filling my ears, I almost swore I could hear a familiar voice echoing in the background as it called my name. I tried to seize on the voice, searching it out through the warbling din, but it was gone. It crossed my tortured mind that I may simply have imagined it, and I was about to give up when it came again, sharper, clearer, and even more forceful than before.

"Rowan?!... Rowan?!... Talk to me!" Mandalay urged.

"Jeezus, white man!" Ben's exclamation followed a half beat behind.

I felt myself being brought fully upright and then leaned back against something. The queasiness that earlier welled in my stomach was creeping up my throat, and I felt my mouth begin to water as nausea fought to overtake me. Out of nowhere an arc of pain shot through my jaw, and the desire to vomit was joined by the unlikely taste of apples and blood.

"ROWAN!" Ben's voice pierced my ears again, this time followed by a hard sting against my cheek.

Why it worked, I still cannot say. If the sudden pain through my knee hadn't snapped me out of the downward spiral, why the sharpness of my friend striking my cheek did so is beyond me. Still, mystery or no, it had the desired effect.

I sputtered as I involuntarily jerked forward and sucked in a cool breath. My question about breathing was instantly answered. I hadn't been.

The screaming in my ears rapidly faded, and though it didn't completely disappear, it lowered enough to become an almost manageable ring far in the background.

Slowly pitching farther forward, I placed my hands on my knees and let out a groan as I huffed in another lungful of fresh air.

"Rowan? Are you okay?" Mandalay's voice seemed loud as my hearing struggled to adjust to the violent changes it had just undergone.

"Yeah," I sputtered. "Yeah... Thanks."

"Didn't hit ya' too hard, did I?" Ben asked. He didn't sound particularly apologetic.

I hesitated for a moment as I brought my breathing under control and then carefully stood upright to look at him and said, "Between you and Felicity abusing me, I'm not sure I'm going to survive this."

"You're gonna hafta take that up with Firehair," he returned, his voice still humorless.

"What?" came Mandalay's puzzled query. "What are you talking about?"

"Trust me, you don't wanna know," Ben spat.

"More like you don't want her to know," I returned.

"Cut me some slack," he said.

Agent Drew, who had been dutifully silent up until this point, suddenly blurted. "What was that just now?"

I turned my head in the direction of his voice and saw that he was still hanging on to my right arm. Based on their positions around me, apparently he and Constance had been the ones responsible for catching me before I splattered completely onto the pavement.

Looking around I noticed that in addition to the three of them, we'd gathered a small crowd of uniformed officers and crime scene technicians. I was used to having a jaundiced eye cast my way whenever I arrived at a crime scene, but what I was seeing in their faces was far from the normal bitterness. In fact, they actually looked angry.

"*Twilight Zone*," Ben announced before I could say anything. "Row just blew past the fuckin' sign post, right, Kemosabe?"

"Yeah," I replied with a nod, breaking my attention away from the stolid frowns of the onlookers. "Something like that, Tonto."

"The what?"

"The signpost," Ben returned, voice still edgy. "You know, there's a signpost up ahead blah blah blah…"

I was beginning to wonder if my friend had gotten any sleep yet or if perhaps his father's death was truly weighing on him even though he was unwilling to admit to it. The gruff attitude he had been putting forth ever since the initial phone call was a good indication that something was definitely bothering him. Unfortunately, trying to rationalize his behavior just made my head hurt even worse.

"I still don't follow you," Agent Drew replied.

Ben gave him a wide-eyed shake of his head as if he couldn't believe what he'd just heard then finally said, "Jeezus! How fuckin' young are you anyway? It was a goddamn TV show… The monologue went…" He sputtered as he stopped himself from continuing the explanation, then snarled "Awww, fuck me, I don't have time for this. Just forget it..."

"This is what Rowan does, Drew," Mandalay interjected, trying to help.

He verbally balked. "You mean to tell me that was the psychic bullshit I've heard about?"

"Agent Drew!" she snapped.

"Don't worry about it," I told her, waving my hand in a dismissive gesture. "It doesn't matter what he believes."

Ben cocked his head to the side then gave me a short nod as he rerouted the conversation. "Guess it's been awhile, hasn't it?"

"That's an understatement," I replied.

"Well, I gotta ask," he said, shooting me a questioning gaze. "You see anything while you were off in la-la land?"

"No," I replied, giving my own head a shake and regretting it immediately as the pounding inside my skull continued to rage. "I didn't see anything. But..."

A sharp stab of intense pain lanced through my throat, and I let the rest of the sentence go unspoken. I swallowed hard then forced myself to bolster my earthly ground. I closed my eyes and tried to visualize the connection as I struggled to dissipate the negatively charged energy that was flowing relentlessly through my body.

"You okay, Row?" my friend asked.

"Not really," I managed to reply, dropping my forehead into my hand.

"Should we get you away from here, Rowan?" Constance asked.

"No," I told her without looking up. "It'll be fine. I just have to settle down."

"Give me a break," Agent Drew spouted. "You've got to be kidding. This is just..."

"Can it, Skippy," Ben barked in his direction.

As usual, my towering friend was intimidating enough to get his way, and the younger man snorted quietly but kept his mouth shut.

"You sure, white man?" Ben asked, focusing back on me.

"Yeah. It's all good."

"Okay, so what were you about ta' say?" he queried.

I sighed and looked up at him slowly as I stated, "I take it you want me to see something in that room over there."

"Well yeah, what was your first clue?"

"I think the yellow tape had something to do with it," I replied with a return volley of sarcasm. "Anyhow... Would there happen to be anything in there that would explain why I have the taste of apples and blood in my mouth?"

My friend looked back at me and frowned then reached up to smoothed back his hair before shaking his head and muttering, "Jeezus H Christ, white man... Look out folks, he's baaaacccckkkk..."

The first thing to strike me before we even entered room seven was just that very fact—it was room seven. Different motel, different side of town, but the same room number as the one where Wentworth's body had been found. Something told me that it was far from a coincidence.

The second thing was the overwhelming odor of watermelon wafting from the doorway. I wasn't sure what it meant, but given the fact that it was the very same odor that had clouded the Wentworth crime scene, it became hash mark number two on the imaginary tote board of interconnections between the crimes.

My headache had settled somewhat, dropping a notch or so below a blinding migraine. The queasiness was still there as well, but it was manageable. Of course, the sickly-sweet pungency that was already enveloping us wasn't helping in that arena. I tried to keep my breathing shallow and ignore the smell as best I could, consciously beating down the tickle that would occasionally rise in the back of my throat. Thus far, my coffee was staying put, and that was a good thing.

It had been so long since I'd dealt with such a direct assault from the realm of the dead that I had forgotten just how physically trying it could be. Still, for the moment I was managing to keep myself grounded, and that was the most important thing I could do. As long as I could accomplish that, I felt I could keep the symptoms at bay, and that would at least allow me to function.

I hoped.

"What's that stench?" Mandalay asked as we stood outside the room, signing in on the crime scene log.

"Fuck me gel," Ben replied in a matter-of-fact tone. "Watermelon flavor accordin' to the label."

"There was..." Agent Drew started.

"Yeah," Ben cut him off. "There was a tube just like it at the Wentworth scene."

"So that's why you told Rowan to bring us along?" Mandalay asked, grabbing at the dangled carrot.

"That and a few other things, yeah," he replied.

"You think the homicides are connected?" Drew asked.

"Let's just say I'm not rulin' it out."

I finished scrawling my name on the log and looked up at my friend. "Watermelons and apples are a far cry from one another, Ben."

"Oh, don't worry," he replied as he offered us each a pair of latex gloves. "There's an apple in there too. Ya' can't fuckin' miss it."

"I'll take your word for it," I returned as I fought to force my hand into one of the rubber sheaths. My palms were sweating and clammy, making it a struggle. I stood there fumbling like a nervous rookie, and I could feel the eyes of the other cops drilling into me. I was beginning to feel like this was all a completely new experience for me—the ethereal connection, the crime scene... Everything. Of course, given the unceremonious return of what some call my "gift," I suppose in a way it actually was.

I finally managed to get the glove onto my hand and began a similar altercation with the other as I continued my questions, "So, what about the victim? High profile?"

"Not really," he told me. "Actually, he was a copper."

I stopped and looked up at my friend's face. The sharpness of his attitude and the reserved anger in the faces of the officers working the scene suddenly made perfect sense. What I had originally thought to be annoyance directed at me was in fact fury at the loss of one of their own. This wasn't just another homicide; it was a cop killing.

"Do you know if he had a connection with Wentworth?" Mandalay asked.

"It's bein' checked out," he replied. "But nothin' obvious says he did."

"What about the homicide itself?" Agent Drew asked. "Same execution style murder?"

"Jeez, I almost wish it was," Ben huffed. "Then maybe it'd make more sense."

"What do you mean?" Mandalay asked.

"Well, it's…" he stammered then shook his head and replied simply, "You'll see when ya' go in. You good, Row?"

I suddenly realized that everyone was still waiting on me to finish struggling into the surgical gloves. I redoubled my effort and managed to get the covering to slip over my hand, albeit not without uncomfortably pinching my skin in several places. "Yeah," I said with a nod. "I'm ready."

I followed my friend up the pair of steps then across the threshold with Mandalay and Drew close behind. As I cleared the doorframe, I automatically looked up and toward the center of the room.

What I saw lying on the bed immediately nullified my previous statement about "being ready."

CHAPTER 19:

The room was fairly large considering that this was just a small motel, however, that was probably because it was a corner unit. Still, while touting inexpensive lodging, this place was definitely far more upscale than the place where Wentworth had seen his end.

We were barely through the doorway when an explosion of light burst forth from a camera flash unit, illuminating the space like a fleeting bolt of lightning. The brilliance fell in a wide swath across the king-size bed, which was positioned against the far back wall.

In that one hot second, the tableau before us adopted an unearthly contrast. Color blanched for an instant, and the harsh shadows demanded my full attention. In the end I was left with a stark image fading slowly from my retinas. Still, even as the color bled back into the artificially washed out picture, the horrific outline remained indelibly imprinted on my brain, and I knew for a fact that it would inhabit my nightmares for a long time to come.

"Awww, Jeez..." Ben exclaimed. "I thought I asked ya' ta' cover 'im up."

"We aren't finished with the pictures yet," the photographer replied without bothering to look away from the viewfinder.

"Well... Shit... Can ya'... Well just..." my friend stuttered.

The photographer finally pulled the camera away from his eye and regarded Ben with a flat expression. I'd seen him around other crime scenes and knew he was with the CSU, so apparently the need for freelancers had passed. I took a personal comfort in that assumption, especially considering Felicity's current imbalance between the worlds.

It immediately occurred to me that it was pure luck that she wasn't here. While in the past she had always been constant, staying unshakably grounded and centered at all times, that had obviously not been the case as of late. In fact, ever since the incident with her friend, she had suffered the same problem that continually plagued me since my first foray to the other side. That being the ability to fully maintain an earthly connection.

While I still fought with the issue myself, I was getting better at overcoming it. She, however, had yet to achieve that goal. Considering that I had already slipped once since we'd arrived, I couldn't imagine her doing any better.

"You want me to come back later?" the photographer asked.

"Jeez… Marty… Awww, crap, just get finished, will ya'."

"Okay. Give me about ten minutes, and I can probably have it wrapped up."

I was hearing the words, but the meanings weren't fully registering because the bulk of my attention was focused on the centerpiece of this scene. Their banter had simply become background noise as my brain shifted into high gear, trying desperately to wrap itself around the enormity of this unexpected sensory input.

I was already feeling like I had gone into overload as I tried to process the whole of what lay before me in a single pass. I blinked slowly then opened my eyes. Then, I did it again. But even after reopening my eyes the second time, nothing had changed. Out of respect for my sanity, I tried to force myself to focus on a single aspect at a time. I didn't have much luck as my eyes continued to roam while I mentally ticked off the facts.

The victim was an African-American male, roughly in his mid to late forties as near as I could tell. They hadn't yet told me his age, so this was merely a guess on my part. Considering the deeply contorted mix of pain and fear frozen on his face, I could have been way off.

It was impossible to ignore that he was all but completely nude, the only exception to that fact being what was probably a small fortune in leather gear. Of course, none of it really covered much since it primarily took the form of harnesses and restraints. It also couldn't escape notice that all of these items had been well put to their intended uses.

The victim was bound securely to the bed, spread eagle and on his back. From my present angle, I could see what appeared to be a taut nylon rope looping through a metal D-ring on one of the ankle cuffs. I would later find out that this is exactly what it was and that it had been criss-crossed beneath and through the bed frame before being threaded into similar rings on the other ankle cuff and both wrist restraints. It had been pulled tight enough to place visible stress on the man's muscles, almost to the point of overextension.

Whoever had done this was obviously well versed in extreme bondage techniques. Just as important, in my mind at least, was that the victim had either been unconscious or had allowed this to be done to him voluntarily. Given the nature of the restraints, I think we were all betting on the latter.

I forced my wandering gaze to return to his twisted face and tried desperately to ward myself against reliving his pain. I could feel it pressing against me, and I wanted no part of it.

Standing out amid his pained features was the apple. As Ben had emphasized earlier, it couldn't be missed, primarily because it was protruding from the corpse's mouth. Even at first glance, it was obvious that the fruit had been jammed well into his oral cavity, so far in fact that I doubted it could be removed in one piece without first dislocating his jaw.

I absently reached up and massaged that same joint on my own face. It was still throbbing with a dull ache from the earlier episode, and I suspected that I now knew why.

Below that, the man's neck and chest were bathed in his own blood; some of it was still damp enough to glisten in the incandescent light of the overhead fixture. A spatter of arterial spray left a telltale pattern across the headboard and wall. The source of the rusting crimson was the puckered wound that sliced deeply into his throat, literally from ear to ear.

For some reason there was a pillow shoved beneath the back of his head. I doubted that it was intended for his comfort, but I couldn't be sure for what purpose it had been tucked there. I had a feeling, however, that something deeper and far more selfish was behind its placement.

Had I not known better, I would have sworn I was standing on the set of a horror movie and that the dead body in front of me was an incredible endeavor in special effects makeup. I might have been able to convince myself of it if it weren't for the intensity of the fear that still lingered within these walls and was desperately trying to reach its gelid tendrils through my defenses.

The sharp noise of a blaring horn out on Lindbergh Boulevard briefly snapped me from my trance, and I noticed that a stunned hush had fallen over us all. Be it the feeling of fear or simply the visual horror, we were each being deeply affected by the scene. I continued to stare, not knowing what else to do. I struggled to understand the full magnitude of what had happened here, and as each moment passed, yet another disturbing layer of the crime revealed itself to me.

The flash unit strobed again, and this time the photographer lowered the camera and shuddered as he nodded toward the corpse. "You know, I hurt just thinking about it, much less taking pictures of it."

I followed his nod toward what was most likely the object of my friend's frustrated embarrassment. It was something I knew I had noticed initially, but somehow my subconscious had kicked in, forcing me to avoid seeing again until now.

Among the restraints gracing the dead man's body was a device that appeared to be constructed of metal rings held together by some type of adjustable straps. Had I seen it lying on a table instead of where it was currently attached, I probably wouldn't have had any idea what it was. However, since it ensconced his penis, the purpose of the apparatus was painfully clear. In fact, the severe constriction of its design and the almost tourniquet-like firmness with which it was applied was in all likelihood why the organ had not fallen completely flaccid even after the victim had taken his final breath.

However, as disconcerting a sight as it was, a far more horrifying vision lay just below, near the base of the torture implement. In fact, it was so downright obscene that I had to blink once again just to make sure it wasn't my imagination.

It wasn't.

A ragged flap of bloody flesh hung loosely between his legs. Dried blood was smeared across his inner thighs, and a large crimson stain on the dingy linens was rusting into darker shades.

He had been castrated.

My mind flashed on something I had happened to notice upon first entering the room. While I had wondered about it briefly at the time, the imagery of the scene was so intense that I had mentally set it aside. Now, a sickening thought forced me to bring my gaze to bear on it once again.

There it was, just as I remembered, sitting on the side table near the headboard. A blood smeared drinking glass. And, even at this distance, it was quite obvious that this was where the victim's testicles now resided.

It also didn't escape my notice that the glass had been positioned well within his field of vision. The deliberate placement along with the amount of blood staining the sheets between his legs told me that he had most likely been alive when the castration had been performed. I suspected he had been conscious as well because it appeared to me that they were being displayed to him in order to increase his personal horror.

I closed my eyes and winced with sympathetic pain. "Damn" was all I could manage to say, and even that came out as a low mumble.

Apparently, it only took one of us to break the silence. I heard Constance gasp behind me as she finally allowed herself to breathe.

A split second later she whispered, "Oh my God..."

Agent Drew followed immediately with his own "Holy Mary, Mother of God."

"Yeah," Ben added. "Un-fucking-believable, ain't it?"

What the three of them couldn't know, however, was that there was something more than just the physical spectacle driving my own quiet exclamation. If what my eyes were seeing weren't enough, I was also faced with the bane of being aware—the inescapable burden of feeling the emotions that were still running rampant throughout the room. And, what I was feeling now was frightening, in and of itself.

The charge in the atmosphere was the same as it had been in the room where Wentworth was murdered. In actuality, it was even stronger here than it had been there.

Sex.

Arousal.

Animal passion.

The carnal intensity that had recently filled the room was still so thick in the air that it was almost as cloying as the sweet watermelon aroma sharing its space. In fact, so fervid was the aura that it sought to overpower everything else to the point that it even managed to ignite more than just a tickle deep within my own body.

Moreover, the feeling was distinctly feminine.

But, this rapturous energy wasn't all. Through it, beneath it, and around it ran a thread of abject fear. And that emotion, I knew without a doubt, had come directly from the victim.

What I also knew, simply by standing in this room and fending off this ethereal squall, was that the killer had fed on that fear. It was what enabled her, drove her, and ultimately gratified her.

Knowing that the tickle I was now feeling had been born of and fueled by the victim's torture made my stomach continue to churn. But, even that wasn't enough to stop it.

I let out a small sigh as I felt these conflicting forces begin to take root within me, and the deep tickle started to grow. A rush of indescribable pleasure ran through my body, and every nerve ending I possessed suddenly flared into a delightful itch. In that instant I understood why Felicity had given herself over to these energies so easily.

"What's up, Row?" Ben's voice filtered into my ears. "You goin' la-la again?"

Ben's voice pierced the rush that had begun in my ears, and I was nudged back across the line. My conscious brain instantly realized what was happening, and I reinforced my ground. Swallowing hard, I pushed back the arousal before the blissful narcotic haze could take me fully into its fold.

The churning stomach was another story entirely, but I still managed to keep it at bay. In a way I was comforted that it remained.

"Yo... Ground control to Rowan," Ben called again.

I snapped to and realized I was still standing exactly where I had stopped, just a few steps inside the door. My body was rigid, and I was staring at the bizarre tableau with unearthly intensity.

At some point, Agent Drew had pushed past me and was now motionless himself, though I am sure for the more obvious reasons.

"No... Yes..." I murmured after a moment and then followed with, "Not anymore."

"Sorry," my friend apologized. "Guess I shouldn't've disturbed ya'."

"No," I told him. "This time, you should have. Thanks."

"Yeah, no problem," he replied in a puzzled tone. "So ya' gettin' somethin'?"

"It's the same," I answered.

"The same what?" Mandalay asked.

"The same as Wentworth."

Agent Drew now turned toward me and objected. "Wentworth was shot in the head. Execution style." He swept his arm out toward the bed as he continued. "This is... Well this is just sick."

I couldn't argue with him there. What we were looking at was definitely within the scope of unfathomable deviance, even for a brutal crime scene. Words such as intriguing, obscene, and even ironic came instantly to mind. You could take your pick because it was any and all of them.

"Yes, it is," I agreed. "But the feeling is still the same."

"You aren't talking about that WitchCraft BS again, are you?" he snapped.

I shook my head. "Actually, no. WitchCraft would imply the working of Magick, Agent Drew."

"Okay, then what are you talking about?" he demanded.

I answered with a shrug. "This is just plain empathic sensitivity."

"Empathic sensitivity? What's that, some kind of psychic crap?"

"Yeah," I gave him a nod, unwilling to argue. "It's psychic crap."

"Okay, Houdini," he spat. "Then why don't you look into your crystal ball and tell us who killed this guy."

"Houdini was a fuckin' escape artist," Ben growled before I could open my mouth. "Even I know that, ya' friggin' idiot."

Drew aimed himself at my friend. "Back off, Detective."

"Or what, Skippy?"

Agent Drew tensed and started forward as if he were going to take a shot at him. Ben instantly braced himself, and I saw his fist begin to clench as his shoulder started to rotate back. Fortunately, I wasn't the only one who noticed.

"Both of you back off!" Mandalay barked as she quickly nudged me to the side and interposed herself between the two men.

They both stood their ground and exchanged hot stares over the top of Mandalay's petite form but didn't say another word.

"Storm," she continued, looking up at Ben. "Put the testosterone on hold and stop insulting my agent at every turn."

Agent Drew screwed his face into a smirk and let out a snort. Constance immediately wheeled around to face him then literally stabbed her index finger into his chest. "As for you, can it. Right now. You've had an attitude ever since you picked me up at the airport, and I'm not impressed. Like it or not, you are the junior agent here, and I'm calling the shots, not you.

"Now, believe me, you don't want another letter of censure in your file." She stared him down for a moment, and while he kept his mouth shut, it was obvious from his expression that she had hit a nerve. "Yes," she added with a curt nod. "Simpson filled me in on you, and right now I haven't had enough sleep to even consider being nice about it."

A lone clapping sound echoed in the room, and I looked over Mandalay's shoulder to see one of the crime scene technicians slapping his hands slowly together. The photographer and two others were simply staring at us.

"Are you all done now?" the applauder asked with more than a hint of bitter sarcasm.

Ben and Drew both looked away from them with somewhat chagrined expressions.

"By the way, Agent Drew," I said calmly. "I'll tell you the same thing I seem to have to tell everyone else. Psychic impressions don't work like that. I don't just see a killer and say there he is."

"Yeah, whatever," he mumbled.

"So, just what are ya' feelin', Row?" Ben asked, a purposeful sort of curiosity tainting his voice.

"Nothing helpful I'm afraid, although, I will say that the energy here seems to confirm the suspicion that the killer is a woman. It also leaves me with the distinct impression that she truly enjoys it. In fact, she does it because she becomes sexually aroused by inflicting the torture and then eventually taking the life."

"Female sexual predators are almost unheard of when it comes to homicides, Rowan," Mandalay offered. "Especially if you are implying that this is a serial crime."

I nodded. "Oh yeah, something tells me this isn't her first kill. At the very least there have been two because I'm betting she's the same person who killed Judge Wentworth. But, there may have been more leading up to that."

"You got all that from a feeling?" Agent Drew asked; each word was liberally coated in sarcasm.

"Yeah. A feeling."

"You'll forgive me if I *feel* like you're full of crap."

"Agent Drew," Mandalay growled under her breath.

"Don't worry about it, Constance," I said, waving her off before she could ignite. "He's right. I just might be full of it."

"Like that's ever happened," she replied. "But let me ask you this. Are you certain about the female aspect? Could you be mixing it up? Could it be homosexual in nature?"

"You aren't actually buying into this, are you?" Drew asked her.

She quickly shot him an icy glance but didn't verbally reply.

"Actually, Ben already asked that question about Wentworth. And, the answer is no, the killer is definitely a woman," I told her with a shake of my head. "Of that much I'm certain. So is Felicity. This scene is the same. The only male energy is the one exhibiting the fear and pain."

"Okay, then I guess Wuornos just got some competition," she assented.

"Wuornos?" I questioned. "Why does that sound familiar?"

"Aileen Wuornos. Killed at least seven men in Florida." She recited the details almost mechanically. "Executed by lethal injection October ninth, two thousand two. Pronounced dead at 9:47 a.m., six minutes after the injections were started. To date she is the only female serial killer to be officially classified as a sexual predator."

"There she goes," Ben mumbled. "You're worse than Rowan with all the crap you carry around in your head."

"You should be used to it by now," she replied.

"Yeah, right," he grunted.

I couldn't help but notice that Agent Drew was staring at all of us in disbelief. I turned fully to him and shook my head. "Look, maybe I'm right, maybe I'm wrong. But, let's see if the evidence bears me out."

"And, what if the evidence isn't sufficient to make that determination?" he asked.

"Try talking to one of your profilers, and see what they have to say, I guess."

"Trust me, we will."

"I've got news for you. They'll agree with Rowan," Mandalay told him.

"How can you be sure?" he challenged.

She replied simply, "Because they always do."

CHAPTER 20:

It dawned on me as we stood there that Ben had been inordinately quiet ever since making his comment to Mandalay about her memory for facts and statistics. I looked over to find him staring blankly in my direction as he slowly massaged his neck. His face was creased with an unmistakable look of consternation, and his eyes seemed unfocused as he stared into space. I couldn't tell for certain if he was looking at me, past me, or through me, and for a moment I wondered if he had even been paying attention. Of course, I knew better. He didn't miss much, and his next words were a testament to that fact.

"So we're lookin' for some kinda seriously sick psycho-bitch who just became a serial killer," he mumbled before I could say a word; his dark eyes were still glazed and unblinking. "Given what she did to 'im, that's kinda obvious though. Ya' got anything else, Row? Anything at all?"

"No, Ben," I replied. "Sorry. I know it's not much help."

"Yeah, well, doesn't matter. That ain't what I asked you ta' come here for anyway."

"Why then?"

"There's somethin' else I want ya' to look at."

"What?"

"Remember that design that was carved into Wentworth?" he asked.

"You mean the heart shape?" I asked. "Yeah. As a matter of fact, Felicity and I had a theory about that. We were thinking maybe it's a tattoo of some sort."

"That a *Twilight Zone* thing?"

"Yes and no. I did have a quick flash of a similar symbol, but actually the tattoo idea is just a mundane theory."

"Yeah, well I think you might be able to mark that one off the list. Let's see what you make of this," my friend said, then finally blinked, turned his head slightly and called out, "Yo, Marty, you done with the table?"

"Yeah," the photographer replied. "Just be careful, it's touchy."

Ben turned his gaze back on me then pointed across the room. I followed his finger to a round table positioned in the corner. The horrific centerpiece on the bed had been the immediate focal point upon entering the room, and I hadn't even noticed the table until just now when he pointed it out.

Two straight-backed chairs, one of which was still neatly tucked beneath, flanked the piece of furniture. The other seat, however, was pulled out as if someone had been sitting there. A glowing swag lamp was suspended only a few feet above the center of the table's surface to cast illumination downward on that specific section of the room. It wasn't the brightest light in the place by any means, but it was more than enough to highlight a yellowish substance that appeared to have been poured onto the table.

"Go have a look," my friend instructed. "Just don't touch it."

I turned and gave him a puzzled glance then walked the twenty or so feet across to the corner. Agent Drew was already well ahead of me.

After only a pair of steps, what had at first appeared to be a random spill began to reveal a pattern. After another few steps, that pattern looked deliberate. A short moment later when I found myself standing next to the table, I was staring down at a tangle of yellow lines that were clearly so intricate as to be considered artful.

More than that, however, what the lines formed was eerily familiar.

On one third of the table had been drawn a cross. It wasn't your typical cross however, instead being a pair of intersecting lines that were exactly the same length. At each of the vertices formed by the four ninety-degree angles of the intersection were scribed smaller crosses. At each end of the vertical line resided yet another cross.

These, however, were encompassed in small circles. Starbursts adorned the ends of the horizontal bar, flanked inwardly by ornate, leaf-like designs. A complex filigree of both thick and thin lines slashed across the arms of the cross in both perpendicular and diagonal swaths then sprouted outward, through, and around the base design.

Positioned near the center of the artwork was a cigar—judging from the size, a petit corona. The band, however, told a more intriguing story. If the words could be believed, the stogie was contraband—a real-deal Cuban cigar.

Opposite the roll of tobacco was a bone that appeared like it might have once belonged to a chicken drumstick. At least that is the animal I suspected it had come from, even though it had obviously been stripped, bleached and well dried. Still, considering that I had seen this symbol before and knew what it was meant to represent, I was fairly confident that my identification was correct.

Gracing the next third of the table, next to the cross, was another complex drawing. The basis for this one instantly struck a nerve, as it was a heart pierced by a dagger. Within the confines of the outline, carefully spaced and curved gridlines created an almost three-dimensional quilted look to the heart itself. Around the outside, an intricate frill decorated the border, and splaying out from it was yet another purposefully twisting filigree.

Planned within the branching design were two blank patches. One of which held a filterless cigarette. The other, a glass filled with a translucent, brown liquid, which I had an inkling would prove to be rum.

By sight, this second drawing was as equally familiar as the first, if not more so considering my recent vision. Unfortunately, that was where my experience with it ended, and I did not know its inherent meaning. However, I knew all too well the significance of the cross, and that just told me that I now knew where to look in order to find the other.

And, it wasn't in a tattoo artist's design book.

Below the two symbols, filling the last third of the surface was an even more recognizable depiction of a circle divided into thirds by curving lines. It too was intricately filigreed but still obvious in its design. Positioned within its borders was what appeared to be a tube of lipstick and a small bottle of perfume.

"I don't believe this," I muttered under my breath.

Apparently, Ben could still hear me because he replied with, "Yeah, fuckin' weird, huh? The bone is what made me call ya'. That, and the heart, obviously. Either way, when I saw the bone the frickin' hair on my neck stood up."

"What?..." I shook my head for a second before what he said registered then I began to stammer, "Oh, yeah... Yeah, that's... And..." I finally stopped myself before I could look any more the fool and asked, "Does anyone know where the victim is originally from?"

"Why?"

"Because this doesn't make any sense."

"So it's just crap?" he asked hopefully. "It's not what I was thinkin' it might be?"

I shook my head vigorously. "That depends on what you were thinking."

"What is it?" Constance asked.

I shot her a quick glance. "Do you remember a little while ago asking me if there was an occult element to Wentworth's murder?"

"Yes," she replied. "You never really gave me a firm answer on that."

"Well I am now."

"Jeezus... Fuck me..." Ben muttered. "I just knew you were gonna say that. I just knew it."

"Well, it's why you wanted me to come here, isn't it?"

"Fuck no," he spat. "What I wanted was for ya' ta' come in here and say 'what the hell is that?' then get mad at me for draggin' your ass down here. What I *didn't* want was for you ta' actually tell me it's some kinda hocus-pocus shit."

"Why are you getting so wound up about it?" I asked.

"'Cause the last time you told me the crap was the real deal it got way too weird."

"Well, I'm sorry, but I'm afraid this is the real thing," I told him. "Most of it, anyway."

"Whaddaya mean most of it?"

"Well, it has all the elements, but given the scene it's definitely been bastardized to fit an agenda." I pointed to the table and moved my finger slowly about. "These designs are what's called *veve*. They're ritual symbols used to represent godlike spirits known as *Lwa*. This one..."

"So, you're saying this is some kind of WitchCraft?" Agent Drew interrupted, his tone still overtly skeptical but somewhat less confrontational than before.

"No, not WitchCraft, it's..."

"What then?" he demanded, once again cutting me off before I could complete the sentence.

"Stop interrupting the man, Agent Drew," Mandalay ordered.

"...Voodoo," I finished. "Or like I was saying, a bastardized form of it."

"Come on," he groaned. "Voodoo isn't real. It's all just a bunch of Hollywood crap."

"No, Agent Drew, it's very real," I replied. "Whether you want to believe it or not. Don't they teach you anything about alternative religions at the FBI academy?"

"They teach us about cults."

"Well, this isn't a cult. It's an actual religion."

"Yeah, okay, whatever."

I ignored his rebuke and pointed to the designs on the table once again, indicating toward the ornate cross with my index finger. "This *veve* here I've seen before. It represents *Papa Legba*. He's what you would pretty much call the head *Lwa*. He stands at the crossroads between the material world and the spiritual world and facilitates communication between the living and the dead.

"The cigar and chicken bone are offerings to him… Gifts given in order to persuade him to open the gate between the worlds so that the practitioner can speak to the spirit of a departed loved one, or even another *Lwa*."

"Well, whatever the reason, whoever did this is a hell of an artist," Mandalay observed.

"That's actually part of what marks this as real," I told her. "The ability to properly and accurately draw *veve* is a basic but very important part of the religious practice."

"You're trying to tell us Voodoo is a religion?" Drew piped up.

"What did you think it was?" I asked.

"Like I said, bullshit," he replied.

"Yeah, well, ya' learn somethin' new every day, don'tcha'," Ben jibed.

"These had to take quite a bit of time," Mandalay murmured as she continued scanning the tabletop with her eyes.

"Probably less than you would think for a skilled practitioner," I offered. "But, yeah, they still took a little bit of time to make."

"What is that? Sand?" she asked.

"Crime scene guys took a sample for the lab," Ben offered.

"I think they'll probably tell you it's just plain cornmeal," I explained. "That's what is commonly used for this."

"Cornmeal," my friend repeated then paused.

I looked over and noticed that he was taking notes.

"Sometimes flour, ashes, chalk or some other such thing," I added. "But, this definitely looks like cornmeal."

"Okay," he said, looking up from his notebook and nodding toward the table. "Does that mean anything?"

"It's just another indicator that this was at least done by someone who is either a practitioner or has deeply studied Voodoo."

"Okay, so you say the top one is for Poppa Whosits. What about the other two?"

"*Papa Legba*," I corrected him then shrugged and pointed to the circle that had been divided into thirds. "This one looks for all the world like a triskele, which is a Celtic symbol that is commonly used in various forms of WitchCraft. But, given the nature of the ritual done here, I would guess that's not what it's meant to be. The other one, I don't know. But, it definitely makes the connection with Wentworth."

"Okay, so whaddaya mean, you don't know?"

"I mean exactly that. I don't know. We'll have to look it up."

"Why don't you know it?" Drew asked, a hint of smugness returning to his voice. "I thought you were some kind of expert."

"I never claimed to be an expert, and I'm also not a Voodoo practitioner. I've just read up on it a bit." I replied. "Look, I'm perfectly willing to admit that I don't know everything."

"Okay, so then how do you know that you're right about the other one?" he pressed.

"Because I've actually seen it pictured in a ritual context before. Like I said, I've read up on it some."

"Apparently not enough."

Mandalay opened her mouth to admonish him, and I immediately laid my hand on her forearm and shook my head.

"You're Catholic, correct, Agent Drew?" I asked.

He cast a suspicious eye toward me. "Yeah, how did you know?"

"Nothing particularly esoteric on my part," I replied. "Just your exclamation earlier, '*Holy Mary Mother of God*'. I've only heard that from Catholics."

He relaxed noticeably then gave me a curt nod. "Yeah, okay. So what's that got to do with anything?"

"I assume you went to a Catholic school?"

"Yeah."

I continued. "Attended your religion classes like you were supposed to?"

"I still don't see what this has to do with anything."

"I'm just establishing that you are well educated in your faith."

"Okay. So?"

"So, can you name the original seven archangels for me?"

"Michael, Gabriel, Raphael..." he began confidently but almost immediately tapered off into silence.

I waited a moment then finished the list for him. "Anael, Samael, Sachiel, and Caffiel."

"Yeah." He nodded in agreement. "It's been awhile. So, how do *you* know them?"

"I've studied Judeo-Christian practices a little deeper than some other religions. In particular, Catholicism."

"Why?"

"Self-preservation... Anyway, back to the archangels. I suppose that asking you to draw their sigils for me would be out of the question?"

"Their what?"

"The symbols that represent each of them," I said then pointed at the table. "Like the *veve* for the *Lwa*."

"Okay, fine," he conceded. "I think I get your point."

"If you wanna win an argument with Row, pick somethin' he doesn't know anything about," Ben offered, taking pity on the younger man.

"I get it." Drew nodded. "Don't argue religion with Gant."

"I'm still not claiming to be an expert," I reminded them. "Voodoo definitely isn't my area."

"But, you're sure this is Voodoo?" Ben asked, turning his attention to me and ignoring his own advice. "I mean, shouldn't there be a doll with some pins in it or somethin'?"

"No. That would be a poppet, and then we'd be talking WitchCraft not Voodoo."

"Fuck me," he muttered as he shook his head. "I thought... No... Forget it... I don't even wanna know."

An urgent but muffled trill began warbling up the audible scale, and we all looked at one another out of reflex.

"Not mine," Constance offered.

Ben's voice fell in behind hers, "Me neither."

The escalating tune ended on a high note, only to start anew a good measure louder.

"It sounds like mine," I said aloud.

Out of reflex I reached into my jacket pocket at just about the same instant Agent Drew was announcing that it wasn't his either; however, I found that the pocket was empty. At that moment the trilling tones started anew and were far louder.

"Crap," Ben muttered, stuffing his hands into his pockets. "I've still got your phone."

Pulling out one cell and glancing at it quickly, he shook his head; he reached back in and withdrew another and then handed it to me. I instantly thumbed the annoying gadget to life and placed it to my ear as I said a quick hello.

Instead of a similar salutation, I was greeted immediately by my wife's stilted voice—her audible annoyance reigned in only by a forced, but obviously wavering, patience. "Rowan, would you please have Ben come outside and tell this young officer that I am supposed to be here."

CHAPTER 21:

Felicity's call was one of the last things I expected to happen. I stole a quick glance at my watch and did some mental ciphering with the numbers. The result was that by my calculations she was still supposed to be at her lunch meeting. So, either I needed a crash course in math, or there was a new variable in play.

Without thinking, I blurted, "Felicity's outside, and they won't let her in."

"I'll go take care of it," Ben replied with a nod as he started to turn toward the door.

Instantly realizing my mistake, I vigorously shook my head at him and waved my hand quickly as I spoke into the phone. "Hold on a second, hon."

I pulled the cell away from my face and buried the mouthpiece against my palm.

"What?" Ben asked, giving me a confused look.

"I don't want her in here," I insisted in a half whisper. "Not now. Not yet anyway."

"C'mon, Row," he replied with a nod toward the bed. "She's seen worse than this."

"It's not that," I explained. "Just trust me, she doesn't need to experience this scene right now."

"You mean…" He did a small jig through the air with his hand and let out a quavering whistle before adding, "*Twilight Zone?*"

I gave him a nod. "Right."

He raised his eyebrows. "La-la land, like you did?"

"Or maybe like yesterday morning."

"Yesterday morning?" he repeated with a knowing tone.

"Exactly. Maybe worse."

"Friggin' wunnerful."

Much to my amazement, Agent Drew held his tongue.

Mandalay, however, had her curiosity piqued and asked, "What are you two talking about?"

"I'll tell ya' later," Ben said then focused on me with a thoughtful stare once again.

"Detective Storm?" A voice interrupted from the doorway.

He turned and addressed the uniformed officer to whom it belonged, "Yeah?"

"There's a civilian out here claiming that she's supposed to be allowed on the scene."

"Yeah," Ben acknowledged as he held his hand out at mid-chest height with the palm down. "Redhead, 'bout so tall?"

"That would be her," the officer said.

He jerked his head toward me. "Yeah, she's on the phone with him right now."

The officer cast a quick glance over his shoulder then replied, "Not anymore, and, well, she's starting to get belligerent."

I immediately uncapped the mouthpiece and put the cell back up to my ear. "Felicity?"

I was met with nothing but silence. I pulled the phone away and checked the status LCD. The call had been terminated.

"He's right," I announced. "She hung up."

"You Rowan?" the officer asked me.

"Yeah, why?"

"Well, she had some choice words for you when you put her on hold."

"She's not grounding," I said to Ben.

"I'll take care of it," Ben told the officer. "I'll be out in a sec."

"Better make it quick, Golden has already threatened to cuff her."

"Yeah," my friend sighed. "Been there myself. Doesn't do any good, believe me."

"Yeah, not surprised by that," the cop returned then glanced over to me again. "Sucks to be you." He started to recede from the doorway then quickly stepped back in and added, "Oh, by the way,

Captain Albright is about fifteen minutes out. She just called. You said you wanted us to let you know."

"Just keeps gettin' better an' better," Ben replied. "How 'bout the circus. They here yet?"

The cop nodded. "Media? Oh yeah, all three rings."

There is a tired old adage that says when it rains, it pours. As exhausted and cliché as those words were, they came out of Ben's mouth right on cue, albeit with a few expletives mixed in for emphasis.

Still shaking his head, he turned back toward me. With a grimace on his face, he reached up and smoothed his hair once again before lamenting, "Anything else, white man?"

"Anything else?" I repeated, my mind now preoccupied with thoughts of what trouble Felicity was getting herself into.

"Mojo, hocus-pocus, whatever," he detailed, wagging his finger at the table.

"No, I'm afraid not," I replied with a shake of my head.

"Okay, sixty-four thousand dollar question. You think this stuff actually has anything to do with the murders?"

"I'd have to say, yes. But, that's kind of obvious."

"I mean besides just some kinda weird callin' card?"

"I'd still say yes, but I'm not sure what."

"Okay, well unless you've got somethin' more than that, better go ahead and get outta here so we can do some police work."

I was a little taken aback by the abrupt dismissal, and my tone of voice said as much. "You're welcome."

"Look, Row…"

"Hey, you called me, remember?"

"Yes, I did, and I appreciate you comin' all the way down here, but you know how these things work."

"I thought I did."

"Okay, listen. Do you really think this Voodoo stuff is somethin' I need ta' know about to solve the case?"

I shrugged. "Honestly, I don't know yet."

"Yeah, well there ya' go," he huffed.

"Sorry," I told him in a less than sincere tone.

"I didn't mean it like that," he backpedaled as he checked his watch. "Listen, I just got too much shit hittin' the fan all at once, and Albright ain't gonna be pleased to see your smilin' face. Look, just to make life a bit easier, why don't ya' grab Firehair and get outta Dodge before she gets here."

"You're sure?" I pressed. "I'm not afraid of Albright."

"I know that, but like I said, I got enough on my plate without you and her gettin' into it too. So listen, you got enough info to do some diggin' on the hocus-pocus stuff?"

"Pretty much. Some copies of the crime scene photos couldn't hurt."

"The Bureau would like a set as well," Mandalay added quickly.

"Yeah, well you just heard the same thing I did. With Bible Barb in the mix I wouldn't be countin' on it."

"You should know that we're already working on a subpoena for the Wentworth photos," Agent Drew interjected.

"More power to ya'," my friend replied. "But you need to threaten her with it, not me. I'm tellin' ya' it's outta my hands."

The voice of the uniformed officer came from the doorway again, "Detective Storm?"

"Yeah?"

"Now would really be a good time to come collect your civilian."

"Oh, man," Ben moaned. "Is she cuffed?"

"Not yet, but she's going to be in about thirty seconds."

"Jeezus, Row... What's up with her all of a sudden?"

"This place, probably," I offered. "Like I said, she's not grounding. See why I didn't want her in here?"

"Fuck me... You two are a piece a' work... Man... Go. Go get your wife, and get 'er outta here before she ends up gettin' herself arrested."

"Yeah," I agreed as I started for the door.

"I'll get ahold of ya' later," he called after me.

I was already heading through the door as his words reached me, but I didn't waste time to acknowledge them. Across the parking lot, the petite redhead standing toe to toe with a grim-faced cop had instantly become the focus of my full attention.

"I still don't see why we had to leave," Felicity announced.

"How about, because I don't have enough bail money with me," I returned, having grown tired of trying to calmly explain the downfalls of her behavior to her.

I had barely managed to extract my wife from the confrontation in time to avoid her seeing the world from the back seat of a squad car. After a somewhat embarrassing moment or two, I got her into the passenger seat of her Jeep, and we were on our way. That had been better than ten minutes ago, and she still hadn't stopped complaining. In fact, she had only gotten worse.

"He wouldn't have dared arrest me," she shot back with a haughty air.

"Yeah? Well, I wouldn't count on it. If I had been him, I would have seriously considered the use of excessive force."

"Bullshit."

I ignored the blatant curse, although I thought it odd that she didn't use Gaelic, as that was her normal language for swearing. Even so, she did occasionally let loose with an American obscenity, so I allowed the curiosity at her choice of words to die on the vine.

"Besides, Albright was going to be there at any minute," I added.

I knew that even if the officer she was tangling with were willing to forgive and forget, Albright would jump at the chance to toss my wife into a cell. Considering some of their past altercations, I almost believed she hated Felicity even more than she did me.

"Screw that bitch," she spat in a dismissive tone.

That was epithet number two she had spoken without resorting to her Celtic tongue. The curiosity was suddenly resurrected.

"He was enjoying it almost as much as I was," she continued. "Then, you had to interrupt."

"Excuse me?"

"He was getting off," she stated in no uncertain terms. "So was I. You ruined my fun."

Now I noticed something else that was peculiar. Even at her most rested and lucid, Felicity had a mild lilt in her voice that betrayed her Irish heritage. But, at this moment in time, that lilt was completely gone, and in fact had been usurped by a slight, but still noticeable, Southern affectation. On top of that, the tone itself had changed; enough so that if I'd been blindfolded, I wouldn't identify the voice as my wife's.

"You need to ground," I instructed. "Right now."

"I'm grounded."

"No you aren't."

"Hmph." She tossed her head and shot me a flat gaze. "And just how do you know that I'm not?"

"Easy," I replied. "You aren't even you right now."

"Of course I am."

"No. No you aren't. Listen to yourself."

"Listen to myself what?"

"Your voice," I insisted. "It's changed. It's not even yours."

"All right. Then who am I?"

"That's what I'd like to know. So would the police."

"And why would the police care?"

"Because, I think that right now you are the ethereal reflection of a very sick individual who's killed at least two men, and I'm sure they'd be all about stopping you... Her... Whatever."

"Or, maybe this is just a side of me you've never seen."

"No." I shook my head. "Even if you could explain away everything else, my wife wouldn't consider it a turn on to argue with a cop."

"Maybe I would and you just don't know it."

"Maybe, but I doubt it."

"All men want to be dominated by a woman, even you," she continued unfazed. "It's the ultimate fantasy of your gender and you know it. It's as it should be."

"Role playing is one thing," I replied. "You're taking it past that line."

"That's because I'm not playing," she retorted. "I'm serious."

"I know. That's another thing that tells me you aren't yourself at the moment."

"Like I said, then who am I?"

"You tell me."

"Guess."

"We don't have time for this, Felicity."

"Wrong."

"Wrong what?"

"Felicity. Wrong. Not my name."

"Okay, so I'm correct. You're channeling someone."

"Wouldn't you like to know," she teased.

"Felicity, stop it right now! Ground and center, please."

"Oh, okay, you're right. I'm not myself right now. Would you really like to know who I am?"

"Yes."

"You, little man, may call me, Mistress," she replied. "Go ahead, say it. Yes, Mistress."

I didn't reply.

Everything caught up with me all at once. My head still hadn't stopped aching, Agent Drew had been a major annoyance, even Ben was moodier than ever, and those were just for starters. Now, on top of it all, my wife was being driven by an unnatural connection with an insane individual, and she was using me for a practice dummy.

A hard sting suddenly ripped through my jaw as the back of Felicity's hand struck my face.

"I told you to say 'yes mistress', little man. Now do it!"

In that single moment, I'd had my fill.

I looked to the right and noticed a convenience store on the opposite corner of the intersection we were approaching. Instead of continuing through toward home, I immediately downshifted the vehicle and hooked it into the parking lot. The turn was so abrupt that the tires screeched as they skidded against the pavement, and Felicity was pitched sideways against the safety harness.

"What the hell are you doing!" she demanded.

I didn't respond; instead, I jammed the shift lever hard into gear and gunned the engine. We shot across the paved expanse and came to a halt between the worn lines of a parking space at the front of the building. I shut off the engine and climbed quickly out of the vehicle.

"You answer me dammit!" Felicity barked once again, the Southern drawl becoming thicker by the moment.

I slammed the door and stalked around the front of the Jeep to the passenger side then yanked her door open. Reaching in, I popped the catch on her seatbelt and pulled it free.

"Get out," I told her.

"I said answer me!" she ordered yet again.

I remained silent, my features set with grim determination. I wasn't certain how I was going to handle this, but something told me I needed to get her physically in touch with something earthbound, and the Jeep wasn't it.

"Get out," I said again, trying to remain calm.

"I will not!" she retorted.

At this rate things were going to turn ugly very fast. I sighed then reached in, taking her by the wrist and forming an instant connection. If she wasn't going to get out then I would just use myself as a conduit. The moment I touched her, I could feel a hot surge of energy coursing through her body. Its tendrils began to reach into me almost immediately. I seized on them and started to force every ounce I could through to the ground beneath my feet.

In a flash the open palm of Felicity's free hand swung toward my face once again. Fortunately, I saw the motion from the corner of my eye, and I reached up to catch her hand mid-flight. I stood there for a moment, locked in a staring contest with her as I struggled to ground out whatever she was channeling.

The look that filled her jade green eyes was at once foreign and familiar to me. The obvious contempt that burned deeply behind them was something I had never experienced from her before. The almost involuntary droop of her eyelids, however, was something I had seen before, and I knew exactly what it signaled. She was cycling through an ever-heightening state of arousal, and it was being fed by her own high-handedness.

As quickly as the entity had attempted to invade my body, it began to recede, curling back into my wife and assuming what I could only describe as a defensive posture. Whether it was the energy or Felicity herself doing it, I couldn't be sure; but one or both of them knew exactly what I was trying to do, and I was now being shut out.

I tried to reach into her, to renew the connection, but it wasn't long before I realized that as hard as I was trying to ground, she was trying to resist. It was almost as if she had become addicted to the stimulation, and she was unwilling to give it up.

I was going to need some help.

I raced through ideas as quickly as I could, discarding each as I hit upon reasons they wouldn't work. When I was almost certain I had exhausted my options, I stumbled on to a thought. I was going to have to come at this from the inside, and I thought I just might know how to do it. I just needed to go into the store and get a couple of things first.

I considered leaving Felicity in the vehicle but something told me that wasn't the best idea.

"Come on," I told her. "We need to go inside and get something."

"What thing?" she demanded.

"Some thing," I repeated with split emphasis on the syllables.

She stared at me for a moment as if she were trying to read my mind. If the look on her face was any indication, she just may have succeeded.

"No," she snapped.

"Yes."

"I said, NO," she replied coolly then followed with, "Now, get back in the car and drive me home this instant, and maybe, just maybe I'll take that into consideration when I punish you."

If it weren't for the fact that I could tell she was deadly serious, her comment would have been comical. What was worse, her rampant arousal was beginning to affect me as well. Whatever it was that she was giving off—energy, pheromones, or something else that I'd yet to figure out, she was actually getting to me. I could feel a rush of excitement welling in me, and for a moment I found myself considering the idea of obeying her without question.

Fortunately, I was still in control of my faculties. I managed to shake off the feeling then bolstered my shields against the onslaught and jerked her from the seat. Taking hold of her upper arm, I guided her out of the way and swung the door shut. I then thumbed the key fob to lock the vehicle and with a moderate nudge aimed her toward the entrance. She stumbled for a moment then dug in and resisted.

"Dammit," she growled. "Just what do you think you're doing?!"

"Taming the shrew," I spat. "Now be quiet and try not to make a scene for a change."

"You need to learn who is in charge here!"

"Right now? Me."

"Fuck you."

I pulled hard and set her into motion once again. "No thanks. Believe me, I'm feeling sufficiently screwed right now as it is."

I guided the still fuming redhead through the door and down the aisles toward the wall of drink coolers. We had already attracted some unwanted attention, but luckily the store was sparsely occupied with only a single visible clerk and a pair of patrons, so it pretty much amounted to hateful glances cast in my direction. Of course, if they only knew the reality then maybe they would be aiming them at her, but right now I didn't care. I just wanted my wife back.

I continued to hold her arm as we strolled along the cooler aisle, my eyes searching. I finally spied what I was after, and we came to a halt in front of the second door from the end. I tugged it open, reached in and retrieved a bottle of water.

Whoever was in control of Felicity seized that moment to shove the door hard against my shoulder and knock me off balance. While I didn't fall, I did stumble momentarily and lost my grip on her arm. Instead of running, however, she planted herself firmly, and as I twisted back to her, she brought her knee up toward my crotch. I managed to react quickly enough to continue my turn and sidestep her by a scant few inches, removing the intended target from harm's way. Still, I wasn't completely out of her aim, and she landed her knee hard against my thigh. The force of the blow caused me to stumble back again. Apparently dissatisfied with the result, she jacked her leg back and thrust it forward again, connecting the toe of her shoe against my kneecap with a resounding pop. The joint buckled, and I went down into a kneeling position, yelping as the pain bit into my leg a second time.

I gritted my teeth and scrambled up to my feet as I turned toward her. Stepping back, I pushed the door the rest of the way shut then fixed her with a hard gaze and sighed as I mentally reminded myself that someone else was controlling her actions.

She cocked herself into a defiant pose and placed her hands on her hips then stared back at me with a much more than contented smile on her lips. Giving her head an imperious toss, she leveled her gaze back on me and purred, "I really enjoyed that, how about you?"

"Not so much," I retorted then limped forward to take hold of her arm and pulled her toward the checkout, stopping briefly at the snack counter where stainless steel bins of condiments resided. I set the bottle on the counter momentarily, snatched up a handful of salt packets and shoved them into my pocket, then grabbed the bottle and continued on to the checkout.

The young girl behind the counter frowned and gave me a hard stare then looked over at Felicity and said, "Is everything okay, ma'am?"

My wife smiled sweetly and drawled, "Oh, don't worry, honey. He's being a little unruly, but I'll be punishing him for it soon enough."

I didn't comment. I set the water in front of the register and withdrew my wallet, then tossed a five onto the counter. Quickly stuffing the billfold back into my pocket, I took the water and tugged Felicity toward the exit.

"Don't you want your change?" the clerk asked.

"Keep it," I snapped without looking back.

Before the door could swing shut, I was certain I heard her call me an asshole.

CHAPTER 22:

I wasn't at all certain that what I was about to try would even come close to working. The fact was that since my grand plan was an arbitrarily chosen bit of Magick from an unrelated ritual, it probably stood a good chance of falling flat. While I wasn't unfamiliar with SpellCraft, by any means, the truth was that this sort of thing was really Felicity's area of expertise, not mine. Given what had transpired over the last several minutes, however, I figured it was a safe bet that she wasn't going to be giving me any help. Since this was all that I could think of at the moment, it would simply have to do. At least the components and intent were both aimed at grounding and cleansing, so at the very least it couldn't do any harm.

So far I had been unsuccessful in discovering who, or what, possessed my wife, and that wasn't going to help my plight. I had originally thought that she was simply channeling the killer, and while that might in fact still be the case to some extent, she had escalated well beyond simply being a conveyance of ethereal spirit. She had, for all intents and purposes, become one with it, and the woman I knew as Felicity O'Brien was now little more than an amalgam of two opposing personalities. Unfortunately, the darker of the pair was in full control and obviously intended to stay that way. With each passing moment, my wife was allowing her own spirit to become a mere undertone. In fact, I doubted that her psyche was even aware of what was happening to it at this point.

I had only seen her channel to this extent twice before, and in both instances the ethereal presences had been those of friends—first, one who was dead and then, another who was living. That last time, like this one, the spirit that was still rooted on this side of the veil had assumed almost complete control of Felicity's corporeal self.

I knew that giving herself over so fully to an ethereal force wouldn't be a conscious decision on her part. Not unless she believed it would make a difference in saving a life, and I knew that wasn't the case at this point. Under these circumstances she would fight it, just as I had seen her do before; of that I was certain. However, I also knew that there was an extenuating circumstance. Taking into account what she had done the day before, the sexual energy I had felt at the crime scene, and the aura she was exuding at this very moment, it wasn't hard to figure out exactly what that circumstance was.

I unlocked the Jeep and pulled the door open then guided her toward the passenger seat. She was starting to breath heavily, and since I was gripping her wrist, I could easily feel her pulse quickening.

As she climbed in through the open door, she turned toward me then pitched slightly forward as if she'd slipped. Out of reflex I moved in to steady her. As I came in close, I heard her giggle but didn't realize my mistake until her open palm met the side of my face with a resounding smack. I immediately cursed myself for letting her sandbag me, but I was still stunned enough that she managed to get in a second hard slap before I could backpedal out of her reach.

"Get back here," she ordered. "I'm not finished with you yet, little man."

"Maybe not," I muttered as I broke the seal on the water bottle and twisted off the cap. "But I'm sure as hell finished with you, whoever you are."

With a turn of my wrist, I poured out some of the water onto the ground to make some headspace in the bottle then reached into my pocket and withdrew a handful of salt packets. I fumbled the crimped edges of the paper together and gave them a quick flick before tearing them crosswise and pouring their contents into the open mouth of the plastic container. Out of the half dozen or so that were in my hand, I managed to get the equivalent of maybe two into the vessel. I had to hope that would be enough.

"I don't know what you think you're doing," Felicity snipped, her voice now thick with the Southern affectation.

I replaced the cap and gave the water bottle several vigorous shakes as I replied, "Mixing you something to drink."

"I'm not drinking that," she spat.

"Yes, you are."

"No, I am not."

"We'll see."

Still shaking the container, I moved toward her. She immediately reached for the door, but before she could pull it shut, I stepped in and caught it with my upper arm.

Falling back into the seat, she twisted and kicked her legs out toward me. I sidestepped the first thrust but caught a hard jab from the second as her pointed heel dug into my thigh. My leg was still throbbing from her earlier attack, and this didn't help matters at all.

I twisted to the side as she kicked again. This time when she connected it was only a glancing blow and not enough to slow me down. I managed to slip in between the door and her as she fell back against the console, and I used my weight to pin her legs on the seat. I insinuated myself almost directly over her as she continued taking short swings at me, actually landing more than one blow against my ribs.

If I hadn't been sure about the salt water before, I was now. Her violent resistance was more than enough to tell me that I had hit upon something that frightened the entity she had become.

"No!" she screamed, wildly twisting her face away from me.

My determination was renewed by my revelation, so I slipped an arm in and managed to twine my fingers into her hair at the back of her head. I didn't want to hurt her, but my options were even less than limited, and she certainly wasn't about to offer me any new avenues to take.

"You... Obey... Me... Damn... You..." she growled defiantly through her clenched jaw as I held her fast and used my teeth to pull the cap from the bottle of still-swirling salt water.

I tightened my grip on her hair and pulled her head back as I put the bottle up to her mouth. She twisted and bucked against me, trying to turn her face away while keeping her lips tightly sealed. I leaned farther in, trying to position myself better and lowered my elbow across her left arm, pinning it against the console. Her right, however, was still free, and she grabbed onto my ponytail then yanked hard to the side, pulling me off balance and wrenching my neck.

"Dammit, Felicity!" I yelped. "Just take a drink!"

Her only reply was a nasal whine of rage as she kept her lips tightly sealed.

She brought the sharp heel of her shoe hard against the back of my calf and drove it downward as she struggled. Continuing to kick, she then pulled hard on my hair again while twisting her other arm from beneath mine. In a flash her fingernails dug deeply into my cheek and raked across my face. I gritted my teeth as I actually felt the warm blood beginning to run down my face. I jerked upward, splashing water all across the interior of the Jeep as I tried to escape her claws.

My mind was racing, trying to figure a way out of this corner. In retrospect I knew I should have waited until we arrived home before trying to deal with this, but then, we all know what they say about hindsight. With everything that had been going on the past few days, it was obvious that my own judgment had become severely impaired. Of course, whenever it came to my wife's safety and well-being, impaired thinking seemed to be my constant downfall.

In a moment of lucidity, I decided to cut my losses and back down before any more damage could be done, and more importantly, before I accidentally hurt Felicity. I started to push myself up, but my wife still had me by the ponytail and wasn't letting go.

"All right," I told her as I struggled to turn my face enough to make eye contact with her. "You win. Let go of my hair."

"Beg me," she instructed, but her eyes seemed to be focused elsewhere.

"Dammit, Felicity," I groaned. "Let go."

I kept watching her face and realized that by her continuing to hold my head to the side, she was able to see past me to some extent. Unfortunately, I was blind to what she was staring at. I could, however, hear a car engine running behind me, and it suddenly dawned on me that the scene we were creating must not look good at all. Embarrassment now became another factor in this fiasco of my own making, as if I needed any more.

Of course, being a participant and not a spectator, what hadn't seeped in was exactly how bad it truly looked; or, more importantly, that the clerk witnessing it from behind the windows of the store had chosen this particular moment in time to be a good Samaritan and get involved.

"POLICE!" A commanding male voice struck my ears. "Turn around slowly and face me with your hands clasped behind your head!"

I stopped pulling against Felicity and froze in place, afraid to make any sudden move. Even so, she still hadn't released my ponytail, so I wasn't exactly able to comply with the instruction.

"Let me go," I told her again.

She didn't reply.

"Felicity," I insisted. "Let me go before this gets any worse."

"NOW!" the voice demanded again.

My wife rolled her face toward me, bringing her eyes to meet mine.

"You're right," she said as her mouth spread into a wicked smirk. "I win."

For a brief instant I saw what I could only describe as a purely evil sparkle behind her jade green irises. Then, with only that smug grin as warning, she let out a terrified scream.

A split second later my world stopped making any sense at all, and pain racked me to the core. The water bottle flew upward, emptying itself across the console as well as both of us. Every muscle in my body simultaneously convulsed, and I stiffened for a moment then fell forward.

As I lay there across Felicity, unable to move, my brain was desperately trying to understand what was happening to me. My senses were muddled, and I seized on the first thing I could; that turned out to be the rhythmic thumping of my own heart. However, behind the slowing cadence there was another beat, much more frantic and uncontrolled, and it seemed to be coming from beneath me.

A fleeting instant of clarity dashed through my brain, and I realized that the racing flutter was Felicity's heartbeat. As other sounds began to flood in, joining the pair of heartbeats was a high-pitched whimper and behind it, the sound of choking sobs. In that moment I feared that my actions must have truly terrified my wife. I tried to call out her name but couldn't get my mouth to even move, much less form a word.

I suddenly felt my arms being wrenched behind my back, and I was pulled backward then unceremoniously placed face down on the cool asphalt. I could feel a knee in my back as my other senses started to haphazardly return in no particular order. Cold metal bit into my wrists amid the ratcheting sound of handcuffs being applied and tightened.

I was positioned such that I was facing the open door of the Jeep, and I watched as an officer helped Felicity from the vehicle. She stood shakily, leaning back to steady herself against the doorframe. From my present angle, I could only see her from the mid-chest down, and though she was certainly disheveled, she didn't appear any worse for wear. Her actions, however, didn't prove that out as fact.

While I was able to see what was going on, I still couldn't get my muscles to execute the functions my brain wanted from them. Based on the various sensations that were now reporting in, I suspected that I had been shot with a Taser. A random memory of a story Ben had told me about the devices flitted through my grey matter, and it reminded me that it would most likely be at least a few more minutes before my nervous system fully recovered. How that got past the disorientation, I will never know. However, since there was nothing else I could do, I simply watched and listened.

Staticky radios blurped in the foreground, all underscored by the sounds of traffic out on the street and the rumbling of the police cruiser's engine a few feet away. Through it all I could hear Felicity continuing to sob. As if punctuating her staccato of whimpers, I heard her say "Why, Rowan, why?"

I finally allowed myself to relax.

She was using my name. Maybe the shock of what had just happened had been enough to interrupt the ethereal connection that was in possession of her. If she settled down, then she could tell them that I wasn't trying to hurt her, and then maybe we could put this behind us quickly. The sooner we could get home, the sooner we could regroup and figure out how to handle what was happening.

"Are you okay, ma'am?" the officer asked.

"No," she sobbed.

"Are you injured?"

I didn't even get a chance to blink. In a flash my wife stepped toward me and kicked me hard in the ribs while screaming, "You bastard!"

The cops reacted quickly and pulled her back before she could strike again, but it really didn't matter. The physical pain she had just inflicted was nothing compared to the mental torment that set in the moment I realized nothing had changed.

I felt my jaw moving in random patterns as I tried to talk, but heard no sound come from my own mouth. All I could hear was my wife continuing to sob as she fell against the officer in a grateful hug and blubbered, "Thank you... Thank you... I... I thought he was going to kill me this time..."

I still couldn't see her face, but I was willing to bet that somewhere behind that Oscar-winning performance, even if just on the inside, she was still wearing that wicked grin.

CHAPTER 23:

"Jeezus, Rowan, you look like shit."

It was Ben Storm's voice that split the relative silence of the sparse room. I had lost track of how long I had been staring at the wall. At first it had simply been an exercise to keep calm, but as the passing minutes accumulated, it eventually became nothing more than a method of surrender. So, by now, my state was almost one of a self-induced catatonia. I wasn't sure, but I fully suspected that Felicity was already hell and gone from the police station. Something told me she probably didn't head for home, but if she did she wouldn't be there for very long.

I finally blinked then broke off my empty gaze and turned to find my friend staring at me through the bars of the holding cell. At least one of us was on the outside.

"What time is it?" I asked quietly.

He gave me a confused glance but looked at his watch and answered the question. "It's a few minutes after six."

I did the math and came to the conclusion that I had been sitting here for the better part of three hours. I guess that wasn't too bad when you considered the fact that I didn't think they had even listened when I had repeatedly asked them to call Ben.

With a sigh I rocked forward and stood up from the bench then hobbled on aching legs over to where he was standing.

I'm sure his observation was correct, but I was also certain that my appearance couldn't come anywhere near the way I actually felt. My shoulders were killing me from the constant strain, and I could already feel the raw spots on my wrists where the handcuffs were still biting into my flesh. The rest of my body wasn't any better either. I hadn't fully recovered from the muscle spasms brought on by the Taser stun—nor the beating I had taken at the hands, and feet, of my wife.

The side of my face was stinging from the gashes her fingernails had left, and I was limping on what I imagined were severely bruised legs. I just hadn't had the opportunity to check. It was also a good bet that her last kick, when I was prone on the parking lot, had cracked a rib or two. At least, that is how it felt.

To top it all off, I had a headache the size of Rhode Island, and it was being fed by very insistent sources unknown but most assuredly not of this plane of existence. I just had no idea what they were trying to tell me. I now found myself wishing I would just seize up, channel someone, and be done with it. Then maybe the pounding in my skull would subside, even if just for a while.

On the bright side—if you could call it that—I was the only one in the cell at the moment, so I was able to brood in relative peace. Of course, I suppose this was all really just about on par for my life. It seemed like every time I got involved in a murder investigation, I ended up getting the crap beat out of me.

It just wasn't usually by someone I knew.

"Thanks," I finally said with an overt lack of emotion. "And, trust me, I don't feel any better than I look. So… Obviously someone actually called you. I was beginning to wonder. They didn't act like they were going to."

"Yeah, well, guess it was a good thing ya' had a get-outta-jail-free card."

He held up his hand and the object of reference was tucked between his fingers. It was his official police department business card, worn and tattered, but with a still-readable handwritten series of numbers and note on the back requesting that he be called immediately if it was presented. Years ago he had given them to both Felicity and me with the caveat that they were only for emergencies.

When I was placed under arrest and they didn't seem to care much what I had to say, I considered it just that, an emergency. I was just glad that the thing had still been in my wallet and moreover, that I had remembered it was there. Still, when I had pointed it out to the officer while I was being processed, he hadn't acted as if he cared in the least. I guess that was how the game was played, especially in the smaller municipalities.

My friend shoved the card into his jacket pocket then gave me another once over and furrowed his brow. Cocking his head to the side, he looked at my arms and asked, "You still cuffed?"

I nodded. "Yeah. They put them back on me as soon as they were finished with the fingerprinting."

"Jeezus H..." he spat then gave his head an angry shake. He quickly thrust his chin toward me as he reached into his pocket and withdrew his key ring. "Turn around and back up to the bars."

I did as he said, and a moment later the hard metal restraints loosened then fell away. I heard them clinking as he presumably stowed them in a pocket and then put away his keys.

"Guess I shouldn't be surprised," he mused aloud. "A lotta coppers aren't too keen on wife beaters."

I turned around and stared back at him while rubbing my wrists. "Is that what she told them?"

He raised an eyebrow. "Felicity? Yeah, that's pretty much the story I got. They said they've got a fuckin' novel out there that she dictated to 'em when she filed the charges. Outlines a pattern of spousal abuse that goes back several years. They don't think very highly of you around here ta' say the least."

"What about you? Do you believe that?"

He harrumphed and gave me a nonplussed glance. "Fuck no. But, she must be a hell of an actress 'cause like I said, they're buyin' it retail."

"She was putting on a performance, that's for sure," I agreed.

"Still, I gotta tell ya'. I just don't understand why she'd say all that shit if it ain't true."

"It isn't."

"I know. I'm just tryin' ta' understand why she's doin' it."

"She's not herself at the moment," I replied.

"Yeah, gotta say she didn't look like it when I saw her."

"Is she still here?" I asked hopefully.

"She was when I came in," he said with a nod.

I let out a heavy sigh of relief. "Good. I figured she had already left."

My concern for my wife instantly took a personal turn as my thoughts flashed on what had transpired on the convenience store parking lot. "So, how was she doing? I mean other than the performance. She's not hurt is she?"

"Dunno. I didn't talk to her. Just saw her through the window of the interview room. Looked okay, but she seemed like she was actin' kinda weird. Can't say for sure what... Just the way she moved or somethin'. Didn't seem hurt, but she didn't seem like Firehair to me."

"She's not."

"Well, you two have apparently been through a lot since I last saw ya'," he offered up an excuse.

"Yeah, well as long as she stays put, we should be fine," I said. "We definitely don't need her running off by herself right now."

"Well she ain't the one under arrest, Kemosabe. You are."

"I'm serious, Ben. She can't leave."

"Well, I think she's still workin' on the complaint against ya', so she'll probably be here for a bit yet. I dunno for sure," he offered.

I seized on an idea and voiced it. "Would it help to keep her here if I filed a counter complaint?"

"Maybe, but she's got witnesses sayin' you were the aggressor so it would probably be awhile before they weren't 'too busy to take your statement', if you know what I mean."

"Do I look like I attacked her?"

He cocked his head and looked at my face. "All that coulda happened while she was defending herself against you, Row."

"That's not how it was," I spat.

He splayed out his hands in mock surrender. "Hey, I'm on your side. I'm just tellin' ya' how it looks. So, anyway, just outta curiosity, what were ya' doin' that made 'er go all psycho bitch on ya'?"

"I was trying to get her to take a drink of water."

"Maybe she wasn't thirsty."

"Actually, it was salt water."

"Salt wa... No. I don't wanna know."

"Yeah, you do."

"Fuck me."

"My feelings exactly."

"Okay, so why salt water?"

"I was trying to force her to cleanse and ground."

"I was right. I don't wanna know. And, just FYI, 'force her' is a really bad phrase to use under the circumstances."

I sighed and shook my head.

"Okay, then, so who does she have as a witness," I asked, changing the subject. "The store clerk?"

"Yeah, her, and the two cops who responded to the call."

"What did the cops witness?"

"The high points? You holding 'er down... You not responding to an order from a police officer... Her screaming at the top of 'er lungs..."

"Gods, what a mess," I mumbled to no one in particular then addressed my friend directly. "Just promise me you won't let her out of here without one of us with her."

"I'll try, but it prob'ly ain't gonna be you," he huffed. "They're workin' on gettin' her an emergency TRS on your ass right now."

"A restraining order? You must be joking."

"Wish I was."

"Fuck me."

"Now you're startin' to sound like me," he replied. "And, yeah, that's pretty much what she's doin'. Fuckin' ya' over, that is."

"Well, then you're going to have to keep an eye on her."

"Thanks a lot. So listen, maybe what she needs is ta' talk with Helen or somethin'."

I shook my head. "I think your sister has enough on her plate right now. Besides, this is way out of her area of expertise."

"No. I'd just finished talkin' to her when I got the call ta' come down here. She'd pretty much wrapped stuff up and there's not much else she can do about the funeral this late anyway," he replied, ignoring the last half of my comment.

"Even so, she can't fix this."

"We could give it a try. I'm sure she'd come down here if I gave her a call. Especially for you 'n Felicity."

"No, Ben," I explained, shaking my head again. "What I'm trying to tell you is that this isn't something Helen can psychoanalyze away. When I say Felicity is not herself, I mean it literally. She's not even Felicity right now."

"Okay, so who is she? Friggin' Sybil? That's the kinda shit Helen deals with all the time."

Since I'd had ample time to sit here staring at the wall, a good part of it had been spent thinking about what was happening. Unfortunately, none of the conclusions I reached were particularly pleasant. Since Ben wasn't giving up on the therapy idea, I tossed out the most frightening of the scenarios, knowing full well it would stop him cold. Unfortunately, in a very real sense, I feared it wasn't far from the truth.

"Actually, right now, she just might be the killer you're looking for," I said in a matter-of-fact tone.

The words had their intended effect. He'd already had his mouth open to speak, but instead of hitting me with his pre-formed objection, he levered his jaw slowly shut without a word. He frowned hard and the lines in his forehead grew deeper. Giving me a one-eyed stare, he asked, "Are you tellin' me Firehair murdered Wentworth and Hobbes?"

I shook my head. "No. No. Not that. Well, not exactly. What I'm telling you is that for some reason she's possessed by an ethereal connection to the killer."

His face relaxed and he gave me a shrug. "Okay, so she's doin' the *Twilight Zone* thing. It's not like that's somethin' new for either of ya'. Jeezus, Row, you had me scared there for a sec."

"I'm afraid it goes way beyond that, and you should be scared. I am."

"Whaddaya mean? How's it get any farther out there than *Twilight Zone*?"

"I mean I don't think she's just channeling. Like I said, I believe that, in some way, shape, or form, she's possessed."

"She don't really look like Linda Blair to me, Row."

"This isn't a joke, Ben!" I snapped.

"Okay, okay, calm down. Cop humor. Sorry. So, what makes you think she's quote-quote possessed?" He said the word twice as was his habit while making imaginary symbols in the air with his fingers to punctuate the query.

"For one thing, she pretty much admitted to it."

"She told you she was possessed?"

"Not in so many words..."

"What words then?"

"She wouldn't tell me her name."

"She wouldn't tell you her name," he repeated, more as a comment than a question.

"I know it..."

He held up a hand to cut me off, and I fell silent. He continued staring at me for a long moment then shook his head. "Did one of the coppers crack you in the head with a baton?"

Exasperation filled my voice as I started to object, "Ben, listen to..."

He didn't let me finish. "Hey, I just dunno, Rowan. I've learned not to be skeptical about a lotta shit where you two are concerned, but possessed? I mean, come on."

"Look, whether you subscribe to the religion or not, in Voodoo there are such things as spirit possessions. The *Lwa*... The *Gédé*... It's actually considered normal."

"Okay. Whoa. Time out. Felicity's into Voodoo now?" he asked.

"No, I'm trying to explain..."

"Slow down," he cut me off again. "Let me ask you something. You didn't talk about this to the other cops when they arrested you, did ya'?"

I gave him a confused look. "No, why?"

"Because right now even I'm not sure that I believe you, and I've seen the shit you do. I can pretty much guarantee ya' that they'd think you're a friggin' fruit loop."

"Yeah, well I've kind of gotten used to that."

"Yeah... Uh-huh... So, anyway, you're tellin' me Firehair is possessed by some kinda Voodoo God spirit thingawhatsits."

"Not exactly."

He sighed heavily. "You ain't makin' sense, Row."

"Look, I've already admitted that I'm a bit rusty on the whole Voodoo thing. But, I do recall a little bit about it from some things I've read. The problem is that from what I can remember there are some issues. First, *Lwa* possess their followers, not random individuals off the street. Second, they take possession during rituals. Third, it is usually sudden and always complete. And, fourth, as I understand it the *Lwa* don't commit crimes or purposely cause physical harm to others during a possession."

"Okay, so you wanna boil that down into English?"

"Okay. Look at me."

"Look at you what?"

I waved my hand about to indicate the scratches on my cheek.

"Your face? So she scratched you," he said with a shrug. "According to the report, the two of you were struggling with each other when the officers arrived. Not a big surprise."

I turned slightly and pulled up my shirt to reveal a red welt on my ribcage that was already shifting into darker shades.

"Yeah," he nodded. "Report also says she kicked ya' when you were on the ground cuffed. All that does is prove she's got a temper and we already knew that, possessed or not."

"You need more?" I started to roll up my pant leg.

"Row, listen, it sounds to me like you just told me all the reasons why she ain't possessed. I gotta tell ya', you wouldn't make a very good lawyer."

"No…" I grumbled as I stopped fumbling with the leg of my trousers. "Listen to me. What I'm saying is that she might not actually be possessed by *Lwa*."

He gestured back and forth in front of himself with pointed index fingers. "You know, I think that's what I'm saying I just said you said."

I closed my eyes and dropped my forehead into my hand for a moment. Then, as I looked up, I thumped the heel of my fist against the metal bars in front of him. "Dammit, Ben, will you just listen to me!"

"Calm down, Row," he instructed as he nodded toward the corner of the room. "You're on freakin' candid camera and actin' like this ain't gonna help your case."

I took a deep breath then let it out slowly. "Just listen to me while I try to explain what I'm talking about."

"Okay. Cut to the chase."

"We know the person who killed the cop, ummm…"

"Hobbes."

"Hobbes. Anyway, Hobbes' killer performed a Voodoo ritual, the purpose of which I won't know until I either look up those other two *veve* or we find someone more knowledgeable about the religion than me. However, what I'm thinking is that during that ritual she may have become possessed."

"Assuming the killer is a she, yeah, okay." He nodded. "That's still speculation on your part."

"She is," I told him flatly. "Trust me. Now, Felicity, for some reason I can't fathom, has some type of connection to this killer. Whether it's some kind of subconscious conduit because of the fact that she's not grounding very well, I don't know, but there's no denying that the connection is there.

"I can tell you that she's already had a couple of instances where she channeled the killer. You heard about that yesterday when she got into the whole S&M fetish..."

"Yeah, yeah," he held up his hands. "We can skip that part. Go on."

"Anyway, she showed up at the crime scene today, and in a very short period of time, her personality started doing a one-eighty."

"She was arguin' with a copper. You know, we *are* talkin' about Felicity here."

"Yes, but she was going overboard."

"True."

"And, when we got into the Jeep, she told me she was getting off on it."

"You mean like, 'getting off' getting off? As in..." He allowed the question to dangle unfinished.

"Exactly. It was almost like it was foreplay to her or something. Anyway, by the time we got as far as that convenience store, she had become an entirely different person. She had taken on the persona of a dominatrix with a very violent streak."

"Yeah, well, from what she said it sounded like that was somethin' she was into anyway," Ben offered.

"Apparently she is, but just for play. Not to actually maim or kill."

"How do you know?"

"I just do."

"Yeah, okay, so maybe she was just tryin' to get you to play."

"Believe me, she wasn't playing. She was serious."

"So, you really think she wanted to kill you?"

"Maybe. I don't know," I replied. "But, I know she wanted to hurt me. Badly. And, apparently just the thought of causing me physical harm was getting her seriously aroused all over again."

"Again, I'd appreciate it if you'd skip that part."

"I wish."

"Well, you're right about one thing," he said with a sigh. "This sure's fuck's way out there past regular old *Twilight Zone* shit."

"Yeah," I said quietly. "The best I can figure is that it is some kind of 'collateral possession' or something of that sort."

Ben looked down at the floor and shook his head.

After a lethargic moment I asked, "So, do you believe me now?"

His hand slowly went up to smooth his hair then slid back and came to rest on his neck as his fingers carefully worked the muscles. "Jeezus, Row..." he finally muttered. "I still dunno."

"Okay," I said, suddenly remembering something I had left out. "Why don't you go talk to her."

"About what?"

"Doesn't matter," I replied quickly. "I just want you to hear her voice."

He looked up from the floor and furrowed his brow then pointed an index finger at me. "Is she doin' the accent?"

"She has *an* accent but not the one you're thinking."

"Southern?"

"Yeah, how'd you know?"

He nodded. "Uh-huh. Okay. So that guy wasn't an idiot after all."

"What guy? What are you talking about?"

"Desk jockey out front," he replied. "Told me Felicity had the sweetest Southern accent he'd ever heard. I argued with him for damn near five minutes tryin' ta' tell 'im it was Irish. He just looked at me like I'd lost my friggin' mind."

We stood silently staring at one another for a moment, then I said, "Ben, your killer originates from the Southern United States, and she's still out there. On top of that, right now her personality, or some aspect of it, has taken control of my wife."

"So all this is why you wanted her to drink the salt water?"

"Pretty much."

"And that'd fix 'er?"

"I don't know. It was just an idea, but I do know that the personality in control of her knew exactly what I was doing and refused to take a drink, so I must have been on to something."

"Sheesh… I ever told ya' that you two are a coupl'a freaks?"

"Yes. Several times in fact."

"Well, I'm tellin' ya' again."

"Duly noted."

"Okay, sit tight, I'll be right back."

"Where are you going?" I called to him as he turned to go.

He tossed the reply over his shoulder as he pulled open the door. "First, to check on your wife, and second, to see if I can get your happy ass outta here."

CHAPTER 24:

"**D**ammit, Ben, I told you not to let her get out of here without one of us with her!" I almost shouted the words as I chastised him through the bars.

"Hey," he spat back. "I was in here talkin' to you, remember?"

"How long ago did she leave?"

He looked away and didn't answer me.

"Ben," I pressed. "How long?"

He swiped his hand quickly across the lower half of his face and shook his head. "Man, if I tell ya', you're gonna be pissed."

"No, don't..." I allowed my voice to trail off at the implication.

"Yeah." He gave me a nod. "About two friggin' minutes after I walked in here earlier."

"Gods! Why didn't you come back here and tell me right away?"

"And you would've done what? Exactly what you're doin' right now?"

"Well what the hell were *you* doing?"

"Gettin' a cup of coffee... What the fuck do ya' think I was doin'? I was lookin' for 'er. As soon as I knew she was gone, I started makin' some calls. Now get off my ass and chill."

"But, she's got at least a half-hour head start. Maybe more."

"About forty minutes accordin' ta' my watch, but since when did this turn into a friggin' race?"

"Dammit! Get me out of here, Ben!"

"Calm down. I'm workin' on it. Somebody's comin'."

"I can't calm down, Ben! She's out there!"

"Yeah, she is, and I couldn't have done anything to stop her even if I'd been out front when she left. She's not under arrest and she's not charged with anything. She was free to go."

"You could have stayed with her. Didn't you listen to what I told you earlier?"

"Yeah, she's all *Twilight Zone* extreme."

"Well, don't you get it?"

"Yeah, Row," he barked. "I get it. Now for the last time, calm the fuck down. The hysterics aren't getting you anywhere."

"I don't think you do," I spat. "If we don't get to her first, she might get herself killed."

"Yeah, or maybe even do the killin' herself. I know," he returned. "Don't ya' think I've already thought of all that, Rowan? Look, I'm on it. They're gonna get an alert out with her description, vehicle make, model, tag numbers... The whole nine. We'll find 'er."

I shut my eyes for a moment and willed myself to remain calm. Ben was correct. I needed to get on even footing, or I wasn't going to do myself any good, much less Felicity. Still, that realization didn't make it any easier. After a few deep breaths, I found some tiny bit of control to which I could cling. I can't say that it was an overwhelming success, but when I spoke again, at least my voice was back down to an even tenor.

"Okay, so, what did you tell them?"

"About Firehair? I told 'em she's got multiple personality disorder and that she's been off her meds for a while."

"Where did you come up with that?"

"Helps to pay attention when you have a sister who's a shrink, and besides, it was all I could think of at the time."

"So, they believed that?"

"Yeah. Actually, they were already startin' ta' wonder about 'er. The cop taking her statement said she was actin' a bit flaky. Thought it was stress at first, but she just kept gettin' more 'n more out there."

"Flaky how?"

"You ready for this? She was flirting with him. He blew it off up until she came right out and propositioned him."

"Damn."

"Yeah, well don't worry, he turned her down."

"I almost wish he hadn't," I muttered. "Then she might still be here."

"Well, she really freaked 'im when she wanted to know if he'd like to let her play with his handcuffs and baton later."

"That wasn't really her saying that, it was the killer."

"Yeah, I know. I believe ya', but I couldn't exactly tell them that."

"She must be on the prowl for a new victim," I said with a resigned sigh.

"Yeah, well, considerin' what she said she wanted to do to him with the baton..."

"And he didn't arrest her for threatening a police officer or something?"

"Apparently, she didn't say it like a threat," he explained. "And she didn't ask for money, so it wasn't solicitation, it was just... Well... brazen, I guess. Either way, that's what must have been goin' on when I saw her through the glass 'cause right after that he left the room for a minute to get the watch commander and she bolted."

Upon hearing this, my impatience kicked instantly back into gear and overrode my fight to remain grounded. Looking up to the ceiling I shouted, "Gods! I can't believe this!"

"Makes two of us," Ben agreed.

"Are they sending someone to our house?" I demanded. "I don't think she'll go there, but..."

"Slow down. Got it covered," he returned with a vigorous nod. "Briarwood is gonna send a unit by, but just ta' be on the safe side I called Constance. She's on 'er way right now."

"Did you fill her in?"

"Kinda. She knows you're in custody and that I'm working on gettin' you out. And, I told 'er that Felicity ain't Felicity right now, but that's about it. I didn't try ta' get real deep with the explanation, especially since I had to get 'er outta bed for this."

"She needs to be careful," I insisted. "I don't know how Felicity might react."

"She knows, white man. She's a Feeb," he acknowledged, then in an attempt to lighten my mood added, "Ya'know, that's almost like bein' a real copper."

"Don't let her hear you say that."

"She'd get over it."

"Dammit!" I exclaimed, craning my neck to look around my friend at the door. "What the hell are they waiting for?!"

"Listen," he admonished. "I'm serious. You better just chill out, or you ain't gonna get out. They weren't all that keen on releasin' ya' to begin with, and it won't take much to make 'em change their minds."

"I thought you said they were already suspicious of how Felicity was acting?"

"They are, but that doesn't automatically clear you. As far as they're concerned, you're still a wife beater with a complaint filed on ya'. Not only that, now they also think you're an asshole for smackin' around someone with a mental handicap."

I just shook my head and sighed. It didn't seem to matter what was said, or by whom. It all just kept pushing me deeper into a hole from which I wasn't sure I'd be able to escape. And, all the while, as I was trying desperately to scale its walls, my wife's corporeal self was literally being spirited into the night.

I was just about to let loose with another impatient expletive when the door behind Ben swung open. A uniformed officer bearing sergeant's insignias on his sleeves entered and approached the holding cell door. I could tell by the way he was looking at me that this wasn't going to be quick and easy.

After staring at me for several heartbeats, he let out a sigh and shook his head. "You know, Detective Storm here says you're a pretty good guy. I honestly don't see it."

I started to open my mouth but caught a motion from my friend out of the corner of my eye as he quickly shook his head "no". As usual, he was correct and I needed to keep my opinions to myself. The simple fact of the matter was that I was going to have to stand here and take a dose of medicine I didn't really need, and that certainly wasn't bolstering my patience. Still, I shut my mouth and simply stood there.

"I don't care much for guys who beat up their wives, girlfriends, women in general..." he told me, allowing his voice to trail off, then suddenly asked, "You don't have any children do you, Mister Gant?"

"No sir," I replied, struggling to keep the annoyance out of my voice and failing miserably.

"Good," he said with a nod. "Because if there's one thing I hate worse that a wife beater, it's a child abuser."

That last implication was more than I was willing to take. Calling me a wife beater was bad enough, but as far as I was concerned, he had just stepped over the line. Discarding my better judgment, I replied. Of course, I'd never been much good at keeping my mouth shut anyway, so there was really no reason that now should be any different.

"Listen, Sergeant..." I glanced at his nametag. "Ruddle. That comment was uncalled for. I know you think you have me pegged, but there are some things going on here you simply wouldn't understand."

"Oh, I've got you pegged all right," he told me with a nod. "And, yeah, I've heard all of the excuses, so don't even try that crap with me."

"Well, I doubt you've ever heard this one," I offered.

"What? Are you going to tell me it's some kind of Witch thing?" he replied.

I'm sure there was a look of surprise on my face, and he wasted no time addressing it. "Yeah, I know who you are. I read the papers. I also think it's all a crock. And, just because you've gotten lucky and somehow helped Major Case solve a couple of murders, that doesn't mean you're a great guy and an upstanding citizen."

"Maybe not," I replied. "But, whether you choose to believe me or not, all I can tell you is that I did NOT assault my wife, and whatever she told you is a fabrication. Detective Storm explained..."

"...That she has MPD and hasn't been taking her medication, yeah, I know. That still doesn't explain what the responding officers witnessed when they arrived."

"Yeah, well don't believe anything you hear and only half of what you see. But, I guess you'll just have to believe what you want to believe, and nothing I can say is going to change that."

"You're right about that."

He continued to stare at me without another word. I allowed the intimidation tactic to play out for several moments before I had simply had more than enough to top off my disaster of a day.

"So," I said with a shrug. "Is that it? Lecture over? Can I go now?"

"Yeah, I was right."

"About what?"

"I took one look at you on the security monitor, and I could tell right away that you'd be a smartass."

I barely managed to refrain from an urge to offer him a congratulatory cigar, but I knew that sarcasm definitely wouldn't play right now.

After another hard stare, the sergeant turned and stepped back out the door. A moment later there was a loud buzzing coupled with a heavy metallic thunk. Ben immediately reached out and slid the door open.

"C'mon, let's get your stuff and go find Felicity before she hurts someone."

For the first time I could remember, I wasn't frightened by Ben's almost maniacal approach to driving. If anything, I was urging him on through red lights, stop signs, and intersections alike.

Flickering red splashes were playing down across the windshield from the magnetic bubble light my friend had literally slapped onto the roof of the van. As we raced up the off ramp from the highway, the cold November night air was whistling through the crack where the emergency light's cigarette lighter cord was keeping the window from fully closing.

Without slowing, he urged the vehicle through the yellow light and cranked the steering wheel into a hard left turn. The van fishtailed with a screech of tires then straightened and shot down the two-lane street, actually straddling the white line for several yards before edging over into the proper lane. We were now less than five minutes from my house, and we had been on the road for no more than ten as it was. Still, it seemed like forever had passed since I'd walked out of that holding cell.

Originally, I didn't think that Felicity would be at our home or that she would have even gone there in the first place. However, it was still a possibility, and given that we had no clue where she was going, it was as good a place as any to start.

The reason we were in such a rush now was that we had been unable to raise Constance on her cell phone, and that seriously concerned us both.

"Maybe she has it turned off," I offered, not really believing it myself.

At that moment Ben leaned hard on the brakes, and I was forced to thrust my arm out in front of me in order to brace myself against the dash.

He whipped the van around a slower vehicle that hadn't bothered to move off to the side and then careened to the right before glancing over at me and replying, "We're talkin' about Constance here, Row. She never turns the fuckin' thing off."

"Then maybe the battery died," I tried again. "Or maybe she left it in her car."

"Yeah, well I hope you're right, but I wouldn't lay money on it."

"Yeah, me too."

My friend withdrew his own cell phone from his pocket and flipped it open. After a pair of aborted attempts, he tossed it over into my lap.

"Friggin' little ass buttons," he complained. "Try 'er again. She's three."

I peered at the backlit screen and thumbed the button to backspace out of the several numbers he'd managed to fumble into the device with his oversized digits. Once cleared, I stabbed three and hit the send button.

The phone at the other end rang a trio of times and was followed by a click and Constance's digitally recorded greeting as it switched over to voice mail. I thumbed the end button and began stabbing in Felicity's cell number.

"Still just voice mail," I announced as I tucked the device back up to my ear.

My wife's phone mimicked Mandalay's in that it switched almost immediately to the pre-recorded voice mail announcement.

I ended the call without leaving a message then folded the cell back on itself and placed it on the console between us.

"Same thing with Felicity's," I said aloud.

"We're almost there anyway," he replied.

He slowed a bit as we approached the intersection at the head of my street then veered into a shallow turn, clipping the curb and barely missing the stop sign. As he aimed the vehicle along the pavement, I looked up through the windshield, and my heart skipped into the pit of my stomach. In the distance were two sets of flickering light bars atop what were most likely Briarwood patrol cars. Even though we were still almost a block away, I knew immediately that they weren't there on a routine traffic stop.

By the time we came to a halt behind them and in front of my house, there was a new set of frantic lights coming toward us from the opposite end of the street. I looked quickly up to my front porch, where an officer stood speaking into his radio, then back down to the rapidly approaching emergency lights.

I could tell by their configuration that they belonged to either an ambulance or a life support vehicle.

CHAPTER 25:

Agent Mandalay's sedan was parked on the street in front of the house with one of the Briarwood squad cars positioned immediately behind it. The other patrol vehicle was occupying a space against the curb across the street from them. I shot a glance up the driveway, searching for any sign of Felicity's Jeep but found none. Of course, it was entirely possible that she had pulled completely behind the house—or into the garage for that matter. While I hadn't thought she would come here, the present level of activity was more than enough to tell me that maybe I had been wrong.

Even from the street, the entire scene felt strange. There was a tickle in the center of my brain that sent a cold shiver shooting down my spine. It continued to repeat until a ripple of gooseflesh marched across the back of my neck, and even then it didn't totally subside.

I could only describe what I was feeling as an overall sense of violation, and I knew that it was coming from the ethereal wards I had placed around the house, just like any other Witch would do. Now, those preternatural shields were howling out an alarm that only I could hear, and what they were telling me was that someone uninvited had intruded upon my space.

The feeling wasn't one of just any intrusion either, so I was fairly certain that it wasn't the police officers I was being warned about. I was, however, firmly convinced that whoever it was that Felicity had now become was in large part responsible for the uncomfortable prickling sensation.

I looked up and saw that the life support vehicle was only a half-block away now, but I didn't intend to wait for it. I slammed the passenger door on the van and started toward the house only a half step ahead of Ben.

I tried not to pay attention to the gawking neighbors as we ran across the yard and up the front steps, but I couldn't help feeling their stares. This was far from the first time we'd had the front of our house painted with the multi-hued lights from emergency vehicles. In fact, Felicity and I had actually become somewhat well known on our block because of incidents such as this, though that celebrity was really more infamy than fame. Owing to that, I figured the nearby residents would all be used to this sort of thing by now.

Still, it had been a couple of years since the last episode, and a lull of that length was bound to allow some of their curiosity to return. I suppose that was the reason why several of them were now peering at the show from behind the fogged glass of their storm doors. In fact, there were even a few onlookers, who apparently lived on a side street, who were braving the chilly night just to come up the block and watch from the corner.

As we hit the porch, Ben flashed his badge and identified himself then gave the officer a cursory explanation that I was the homeowner. The cop gave him a nod then pulled open the door and called out to the officer inside as he ushered us in.

The first thing I noticed as we entered the house was the sweet odor of Felicity's favorite perfume. It was strong, almost to the point of cloying; the scent lingered on the air even heavier than it did whenever she first sprayed it on. The problem was I still didn't see her anywhere.

The second thing was a muffled ruckus coming from both of the dogs barking and whining. Their boisterous clamor was coupled with the hard scrape of frenzied pawing somewhere deeper into the house.

"Is my wife here?" I asked immediately. "Is she okay?"

"Your wife would be a Ms. Felicity O'Brien?" the officer waiting inside the door asked.

"Yes. Where is she?"

"Calm down sir," the officer replied. "She wasn't here when we arrived."

"Do you know if she was here at all?" Ben asked.

"Oh yeah," a weak female voice came from the dining room. "She was here all right."

Ben and I both turned toward the source of the words.

Agent Mandalay was sitting in the dining room looking at us. If ever there was an expression that said "splitting headache", it was the one glued to her face at this very moment.

She was leaning forward with one elbow resting on the surface of the table and her forehead clasped in her hand. The other hand was occupied with holding a dishtowel to the side of her head, just above and behind her ear. Even so, she couldn't hide the blood that stained both her hand and neck.

"Jeezus!" Ben exclaimed as he rushed toward her with me close on his heels.

"Glad you two could join the party," she quipped, voice still thready.

"What the hell happened?" Ben appealed.

Before my friend had even finished the question, I heard the storm door open and heavy footsteps entering the house.

"Over here," the police officer's voice sounded behind us.

A second later a new voice entered the mix. "Excuse me. Coming through."

An ordered commotion broke out around us as two paramedics entered the dining room and elbowed us out of the way to close in around Constance. One of them was already donning latex gloves as he asked her what had happened.

I didn't hear her answer as her low voice was drowned out by the polite but firm words of the other paramedic addressing Ben and me. "We're going to need for you to give us some space."

Ben pulled me to the side as he reluctantly stepped out of the way himself, but he remained on the periphery watching silently with deep concern behind his dark eyes.

"This way sir," the Briarwood police officer said as she took me by the arm and guided me back toward the living room.

Now, not only was I feeling like an intruder had been in my

home, I was feeling like one myself. My frustration level was rapidly climbing. I still didn't know where my wife was; Constance had been injured somehow, probably by Felicity; and to top it off the dull ache in my head had chosen this moment to ratchet up the scale yet again.

Sensory overload was kicking in, and I was losing ground very quickly. So quickly, in fact, that I wasn't entirely sure that I shouldn't just surrender and give myself over to it.

Having little choice but to follow the officer's lead, I turned away from the activity behind me and looked toward the living room. Now that I was focusing in that direction, I noticed that the area seemed more dimly lit than usual, and I looked upward. The overhead lights were on full and reflecting down from the vaulted ceiling. I caught a quick glimpse of Dickens and Salinger, who were safely perched on the exposed rafters, peering down at the goings on with curious eyes while their tails twitched nervously. Emily, our calico, was far too skittish for such activities and was probably hiding someplace upstairs as usual.

I looked back down at the room, and it still seemed dark to me. For a moment I thought it might simply be the ethereal pounding in my skull, especially considering the fact that my ears were buzzing and colors were starting to flare and bloom as my sight shifted in and out of focus.

I closed my eyes and drew in a deep breath, trying to find a decent ground. It hadn't been that long ago that I was wishing to slip across the veil as I'd done so many times before, but now I found myself fighting against it.

When I eventually opened my eyes, the flares of color had faded, but nothing else had changed. The lighting in the room still wasn't right. As I continued to stare, however, a far more mundane reason for the dimness became apparent. The torchiere lamp that normally stood next to the front doorway was no longer there. I allowed my gaze to pivot farther downward, and I saw that it was now scattered across the hardwood floor where it had fallen and shattered into countless pieces.

Intermixed with it was the base of a small antique end table, which had apparently been toppled over as well. Its marble top was now broken into two distinct pieces. Completing the jumbled mess were the remnants of something I couldn't readily identify but looked vaguely familiar.

"Excuse me, sir," a voice filtered into my ears.

I didn't respond. I simply stared at the shattered pieces of the unidentified object, trying to get a handle on where I'd seen them before. In my head I treated them as a jigsaw puzzle, mentally flipping them over and shoving them together in different ways until I formed an image that made sense. The exercise actually had a side benefit in that it gave me something on which to concentrate; that helped me remain grounded in this plane, for the time being at least.

After a moment it finally dawned on me that the ivory-colored chunks were the remains of a good-sized, ceramic faerie statuette that had once graced a recessed shelf on the wall of our dining room.

"Excuse me, sir," the voice came again. It was still calm but this time much more insistent.

I blinked and looked up to find the officer looking at me questioningly. "Sir, are you okay?"

"Yeah," I nodded. "Yeah, I'm fine."

"I'd like to ask you a few questions if I may?"

"Where are the dogs?" I asked absently, seizing on the fact that I could still hear them barking and growling somewhere in the house.

She pointed. "They've been pawing at the first door down the hallway over there."

"That's the basement. Did you put them down there?"

"No sir, that's where they were when we arrived," she replied.

I started toward the hallway to head for the basement door, and she took hold of my arm once again. "Leave them where they are, sir. They'll be fine for now."

"But…"

"Trust me, sir. It's for their safety as well as ours. They'll be fine."

I turned my attention back to her and nodded as I said, "Okay." "Do you think you can answer some questions for me?"

"Sure. I'll try."

"Are there any friends or relatives that Miz O'Brien might attempt to contact?"

"Her parents, I guess," I said with a shrug. "We have quite a few friends too, but I don't think she would contact any of them. Her parents either... She's not exactly herself right now."

"Can you give us a list of names and phone numbers anyway, sir?"

"I suppose. I'll have to look them up."

"All right," she told me with a nod then continued. "Other than friends or relatives, do you have any idea where she might go?"

"At the moment, no."

"I don't need to go to the hospital!" Mandalay's voice raised a pair of notches to be heard over everything else.

I turned away from the officer who was questioning me, so I could see what was happening.

Constance was still sitting in a chair at the table but now had a wad of gauze affixed to the side of her head. A paramedic was looking into her eyes as he flashed a penlight to and fro.

"Listen to 'em, Connie," Ben ordered.

"I'm fine," she spat in return. "And, don't call me Connie. You know better."

"Detective," one of the paramedics addressed Ben. "Please. You aren't helping."

"Agent Mandalay." The other medic was talking directly to Constance. "You've sustained a serious blow to the head. You most likely have a concussion and you really need..."

"...Sir? Sir? Mister Gant?" The officer was prodding for my attention.

I turned back to her. "What?"

"I need for you to focus, sir, and answer some more questions."

"Yeah, okay," I said with an impatient shake of my head.

"Now, is Miz O'Brien a substance abuser? Alcohol? Drugs?"

"No," I said, shaking my head again as I screwed up my face. "Not at all. I mean, she has a few drinks every now and then, but…"

"Has she been drinking today?"

"Not that I'm aware of."

"Sir, we were informed that Miz O'Brien is suffering from a mental disorder. Is she currently taking, or is she prescribed any anti-psychotic medications?"

"No. She's not on any medication. What you were told… Well…" I stuttered. "That's not… It's… Well, it's not entirely accurate."

"Not entirely accurate how, sir?"

"She doesn't have any mental disorders," I replied, knowing full well that in one sense I was telling the truth, but in another I was lying through my teeth.

She looked back at me with a flat expression then continued into the next query. "Have you been having any marital problems?"

"No."

"You're certain? Everything is okay here at home as far as you know?"

"Yes."

"Does Miz O'Brien have a previous history of violent behavior?"

"No," I replied with a puzzled shake of my head.

"How about yourself, sir?"

"What? No," I snapped.

"We could really use your cooperation here, sir."

I didn't know quite how to reply. There was no way for me to tell her the whole truth and not look like I was in need of medication myself. Why I hadn't simply played along with Ben's story I don't know. Maybe it was an inherent need to protect Felicity from a social stigma or perhaps even the fact that I was still feeling overwhelmed by everything that had happened in such a short span of time. Whatever it was, I got the feeling I hadn't done myself, nor my wife, any favors.

I looked back at the cop, and I could tell by the expression on her face that she had already decided that I was lying to her. After a moment she looked down and scribbled a quick note then sighed and paused before looking back up at me. It didn't take long for me to realize that she wasn't looking at me straight on, but instead she was silently inspecting the obvious fingernail scratches on my cheek. Out of reflex I reached up and brushed my fingertips across them and let out a sigh of my own.

"Mister Gant, do you have any reason to believe that your wife would want to hurt or even try to kill you?" she asked in a flat tone.

"Officer," I appealed. "I understand your concerns here, believe me, but I think you might be reading something into this that you shouldn't."

"Mister Gant," she replied. "The only thing I am reading into this right now are the facts, and those are the following. One, your wife assaulted a federal officer. Two, she secured said officer's sidearm. Three, she fled the scene and is now considered an armed fugitive."

CHAPTER 26:

I had always considered the comment "worrying yourself sick" to be nothing more than an exaggerated metaphor. But tonight, in a closely linked pair of painful moments, I changed my mind about that turn of phrase.

The first came, of course, when the final point ticked off by the police officer struck me like a solid punch directly to the abdomen. Apparently, the Gods had decided that it wasn't enough that I had already been agonizing over Felicity and what was now happening to her to the point where I couldn't concentrate on anything else. As was their penchant for doing, they wanted to see just how far they could push me.

My stomach had been churning ever since I discovered that my wife had ducked out of the police station, so I was on the edge as it was. I knew that she stood a real possibility of inadvertently coming face to face with the killer due to what I suspected was their shared possession, and I couldn't imagine that such a clash would be without some level of violence.

On top of that, and just as bad, was the fact that she seemed likely to act out one of the killer's fantasies and actually murder someone. After what she had apparently done with the officer while filing the complaint against me, this scenario seemed almost to be a given.

That is, of course, unless we were able to stop her first.

But, as I said, that simply wasn't enough strife for whichever deity happened to be pushing me around the cosmic chessboard on this particular day. Now, a whole new bolus of foreboding had been mainlined directly into my bloodstream, and that fear was of an overzealous cop shooting my wife because she was now considered an armed fugitive.

The column of bile that this sent rising up my throat came startlingly close to being heaved out onto the floor right where I stood. Fortunately, I managed to contain it; how, I can only assume by pure luck. All I knew was that in the end, it had taken me a good five minutes just to bring myself under enough control to even think about functioning.

Of course, this was right about the time the second moment of the fateful pair elected to reveal itself. I was just regaining my composure when I glanced toward the dining room only to see Constance being helped onto an ambulance gurney. Ben was staunchly remaining by her side, as well he should. The problem was that they were the two people whom I knew I could count on to believe me in all of this, and they were now wrapped up in their own concerns.

A panic attack tried to set up residence in my chest as I realized exactly how alone in all of this I truly felt. And then, I knew that I truly was worried sick.

The paramedics had finished strapping Mandalay onto the gurney while I was sitting on the arm of a chair in the living room. They had the head of the folding rig propped upward in a partial sitting position in order to keep her torso elevated, so I could see that she was still conscious and alert.

She had made it clear that she wasn't happy about the trip to the hospital but had agreed to at least go and get x-rayed. Not that it mattered, however, because I had the feeling that whether she agreed or not, Ben was going to see to it that she went. Judging from the bleeding she had done, I suspected some stitches would be in order as well.

They were ready to wheel her out, but she had insisted on talking to me first. Considering how isolated I had been feeling only a few moments before, her demand gave me a renewed hope.

"Okay, Rowan..." Constance said with a thin smile. "Explain to me why I shouldn't kick Felicity's ass the next time I see her."

I sighed and shook my head. It was obvious that she was making a small attempt at humor in the face of everything that had happened. I shouldn't have been surprised because I'd met only a very few members of the law enforcement community who didn't do that sort of thing. There was no reason for her to be any different.

But, I was also betting that, even with the dry humor, there was more than just a hint of seriousness in the words.

I couldn't say that I blamed her.

According to her recounting, the physical entity that was my wife had invited her in as if nothing was wrong but then immediately blindsided her as she came through the door. She had struck her hard enough with a ceramic statuette to be able to overpower her and then restrain her with her own handcuffs. Considering that Constance was a trained FBI agent, I could only speculate that it had been a lucky shot.

But, in that vein, I was also betting that it had been somewhat humiliating for Constance to identify herself as an FBI agent after being found that way by the responding officers.

Were I in her position, I would be more than a little miffed myself.

On the other hand, whoever was possessing Felicity could just as easily have killed her, and she didn't. That, in and of itself, said something about the motivation of the entity in control of my wife's body. At least, to me it did.

"Listen, I know it sounds unbelievable, Constance," I finally replied. "But, all I can say is that it wasn't really Felicity who attacked you."

She laid her head back on the pillow and closed her eyes for a moment, letting out her own sigh before quietly assuring me, "I know, Rowan. I got that distinct feeling when she was standing over me. The look in her eyes was... it was just odd."

"I know," I replied.

"Ben said you thought it had something to do with the crime scene this afternoon."

I looked over at my friend and he shook his head. "I told ya' I couldn't really explain it."

"It definitely has something to do with the ritual that was performed there," I told her. "I just still need to do some research."

"It was like she was a completely different person," she repeated. "I couldn't believe it."

"That was only her body. I think the person you know as Felicity is most likely drifting out there somewhere in the ether waiting to return."

"The *gwo-bon-anj*," one of the paramedics mumbled.

I hadn't paid much attention to either of them earlier, but now I focused directly on the man who had spoken. He was African-American, roughly in his late twenties to early thirties, and his voice was edged with what might have been a faint Creole accent. I raised an eyebrow and said, "What was that?"

"*Gwo-bon-anj*," he repeated, somewhat louder and much more clearly this time. "The great good angel. It's the part of your spirit which holds your personality and experiences."

"Where does that come from?"

"It's a religious concept," he offered, acting as if he wished he'd never opened his mouth."

"It wouldn't happen to be *Vodoun* would it?"

He looked back at me with a hint of surprise in his face. "Yeah. Actually it is."

"Do you know much about Voodoo practices?"

He shrugged. "I grew up around it, so yeah, I know some."

"What can you tell me about spirit possessions?" I pressed, urgency seeping into my voice.

"Believers say the *Lwa* will possess their followers," he replied.

"Have you ever seen it happen?"

"Whoa, hold on a second," he objected. "I said I grew up around it. That doesn't mean I actually believe in it."

"But have you ever seen it happen?"

"No."

"Okay then, have you ever seen anyone claiming to be possessed by a *Lwa*?"

"Look, I really shouldn't have…"

"Just answer me. It's important!"

"Yeah. A couple of times," he said with a dismissive shake of his head. "Look, like I was saying, I shouldn't have said anything, and I'd rather not talk about it."

"Okay, fine, but just answer me this then. *Veve*. A heart with a crosshatched pattern and a dagger piercing it. Do you know who that is a symbol for?"

"With a dagger would be *Ezili Dantó*. She's the *Petro* aspect of the *Lwa* of love."

"*Petro* aspect?"

"Negative. You know, like the opposite."

"You know quite a bit for someone who doesn't believe in it," Constance remarked.

He shrugged again but remained silent.

"Come on, Emile," the other paramedic interjected. "We need to roll."

"You. Shut up," Mandalay barked at the paramedic over her head then looked back to the foot of the gurney and said, "You. Answer the man's questions."

"Button it, Constance," Ben told her then glanced over at me and declared, "She needs to go to the hospital, Rowan."

"No, I don't," she objected.

"Stay out of it. You're goin'," he retorted without taking his eyes off me. After a second he huffed, "Make it quick."

I turned back to the paramedic and quickly asked, "What purpose would *Ezili Dantó* have in a ritual?"

"I don't really know, sir," he replied, kicking off the brake and starting to maneuver the gurney out of the room. "Like I told you, I shouldn't have said anything. I'm sorry."

"No. This is important!"

"Look, all I know is that she represents heartbreak, jealousy, and vengeance. That's about it."

"Hold on. Please. Just one last question," I pleaded, insinuating myself between them and the exit. "A round circle with three curved lines radiating out from the center and a single dot in each third. Whose *veve* is that?"

He scrunched up his face and then shook his head. "I don't know."

"Are you certain? Think."

"Yeah, I'm sure. I've never seen that one. I can tell you it's definitely not one of the greater *Lwa*, but maybe it belongs to a lesser or an ancestral spirit."

"Okay, Rowan, that's enough. Get outta the way," Ben ordered.

I stepped back and they continued rolling the gurney toward the front door.

I had hoped for more information from the young man, but what he had given me was definitely beyond what I'd had before. I didn't know that it was going to help find Felicity though.

Ben was still following along with them, wearing an expression of intense concern. He hadn't said much of anything for the past several minutes, except the terse orders he'd barked at Constance and me. I wasn't sure if it was simply his disquiet over her condition, or if he was angry.

Given the circumstances, I suppose he had plenty to be irritated about, not the least of which was me.

"I'll be right back," he grunted as he brushed past.

A second later, as they approached the front door, Constance called out, "Rowan?"

I stepped quickly over to her even as they continued to muscle the gurney out into the night air.

"Yeah, Constance?"

"I'm sorry," she said, reaching out to touch my arm.

"Whoa, hold on a second," I said to the paramedics, motioning for them to stop. Then I looked back to her. "Sorry about what?"

"I had to tell them about my weapon," she replied. "They had to know for…"

I cut her off, shaking my head vigorously as I spoke. "I understand. It's not your fault. Don't worry about it right now. You didn't have any choice. Now, let them take you to the hospital."

I stepped back again, and they continued out the door. I certainly hadn't expected the apology from Constance, and to be honest I almost wished she hadn't made it. The mere mention of the sidearm brought my fear oozing back to the surface, and I felt my stomach somersault yet again.

As the storm door swung shut, I looked around and realized that in a very real sense this time, I was suddenly very alone. The Briarwood officers were out in the front yard talking to one another and occasionally looking toward the house. I knew that the female officer who had been questioning me had still been inside when Mandalay and I started discussing the reason behind Felicity's actions. How much she had heard, I couldn't say, but I was guessing that it was a big part of the conversation going on right now.

At this point, however, I didn't care what they thought of me. I needed to figure out where my wife was likely to go and find her before this got any worse than it already was.

The problem at the moment was that I had no idea how I was going to do that.

CHAPTER 27:

O nce it was safe to do so, I had let the dogs out of the basement and shuffled them out the back door after some half-hearted strokes of reassurance for them both. I hated that they'd been traumatized this way. Simply ushering them into the back yard wasn't much better, but I had more than enough to worry about right now. Unfortunately, they were going to have to wait in line.

I had given the Briarwood police officers a list of the pertinent individuals from our address book along with contact information as they had requested. While I could tell there was still a bit of suspicion regarding my cooperation, after only a few more questions they had headed back outside.

Nothing had been mentioned about the conversation with Mandalay and the paramedic, or at least not directly to me. I did, however, happen to be staring blankly out the door when both of the cops went over to Ben and said something to him while nodding back toward the house. Eventually the officers went to their cars, and the one across the street left almost immediately. The officer parked directly in front of the house, however, didn't seem to be in a hurry to go anywhere. My guess was that I was going to be watched. Given the earlier questions, I could only assume that it was for my safety.

At the moment I felt like every nerve in my body was sparking, and there was a hollowness in my chest that I had only felt twice before. And, both of those times had been when there was an undeniably palpable threat to Felicity's life, just as there was right now. I wanted to go out looking for her, but I got the feeling that there might be some resistance to that idea from the cop parked outside. It also didn't help that I had no real idea of where to start, so driving aimlessly about the city wasn't going to be any more productive than waiting here at the house.

Of course, that was logic, and at the moment I was being driven by emotion.

It wasn't long before my subconscious coping mechanisms kicked in, and I found myself mindlessly straightening up the room just to keep myself from toppling over the precipice into hysteria.

Even though I didn't remember doing it, I had righted the remains of the lamp and end table then picked up the larger pieces of the glass and ceramic and tossed them into the trash. By the time Ben came back into the house, I was occupying myself by cleaning up the rest of the mess with the vacuum. I looked up as he stepped through the door, closing it behind him. I turned my gaze downward and took another pair of swipes across the throw rug before switching off the device and turning back to him. I didn't say anything; I just stood there waiting expectantly. He was still wearing the same expression that had been screwed onto his face when he went outside. In fact, it might even have been a bit worse than before.

I suppose I appeared somewhat surprised by the fact that he was still here, and to be honest, I was. Since it had been several minutes since the life support vehicle had left the scene, I simply assumed that he had gone ahead to the hospital.

"You gonna puke or somethin'?" my friend finally asked after a long period of uncomfortable silence.

"No. I just didn't expect you to still be here is all," I said.

"I told ya' I'd be right back."

"Well, I just figured you'd be going to the hospital with Constance."

"No" was his one word reply.

"Why not?"

"'Cause someone's gotta stay here 'n keep you outta trouble. And, since she's hurt, I lost the coin toss."

"Thanks. I think."

"Don't mention it."

"So, what makes you…"

"Save it, Rowan," he cut me off. "We both know ya' too well. You ain't gonna sit around waitin' for someone else ta' find Felicity."

"You're probably right."

"Ain't no prob'ly to it... Been down that road with ya' twice already. So listen, we need to talk."

"About what?" I said as I reached down and took hold of the power cord for the vacuum then jerked it out of the wall and retracted it in relative silence.

"This situation."

I didn't answer right away. I picked up the cleaning appliance and carried it down the hall then stowed it in the linen closet. When I returned to the living room, I bypassed his intentions for the conversation and asked, "So, what was that all about outside?"

"What was *what* all about?"

"The cops. They said something to you and kind of gave a nod this way."

"Oh that," he replied. "Well, she thinks you're in denial about Felicity and wanted ta' know if you were gonna be gettin' any help."

"Doesn't surprise me," I said with a nod. "I got that impression from her earlier."

"Yeah, well, she's the nice one. The other copper just thinks you're a flake."

"Figures."

He paused and sighed then said, "Well, I'm not so sure I don't agree with both of 'em."

I wasn't a huge fan of Shakespeare, but a single, very common quote fit the current situation so well that I simply couldn't stop myself from uttering it. "*Et tu, Brute?*"

"Yeah, me too," he returned without missing a beat. "Maybe... I dunno... Ya' see that's kinda what we need ta' talk about."

"Why?"

"Look, Rowan," he said as he stood there at the door massaging his neck. For the most part, he hadn't really moved since he'd come back into the house. After another anxious pause, he clucked his tongue and said, "Look, this whole possessed thing just goes way beyond the pale, man."

"Yeah, well you said something like that several years ago when I started having those precognitive visions."

"Yeah, I know."

"And then again when Eldon Porter started…"

"I got the picture, Row. You don't hafta take me down memory lane."

"Apparently I do if you think I'm crazy."

"Maybe not so much crazy as the denial part."

"Denial about what, Ben?"

"Let me ask you this," he said, hesitating before obviously having to force himself to proceed. "Where was Felicity when Hobbes was murdered?"

"Why?" I asked then realized where the conversation was headed and spat, "Wait… You mean… Dammit, Ben, I can't believe you just asked me that!"

"Me neither," he returned but asked me again. "So, where was she?"

"Fuck you, Ben."

"Yeah, fine. Be pissed if you wanna, but just humor me, okay?"

"She sure as hell wasn't with him."

"That's not an answer, Rowan."

"Okay, fine. I guess it depends. Did the medical examiner fix a time of death?"

"Sometime early this morning. After midnight but before ten a.m. is best guess."

"Well, we were with you at around two if you remember."

"Uh-huh. But, what about after that?"

"We were here. We came home and went to bed."

"Okay. What were you doing?"

"Like I said, we went to bed. We were both exhausted, so we went straight to sleep."

"So you were asleep?"

"Didn't I just say that?"

"Did you wake up at any time?"

"A little after eleven this morning when Constance and Agent Drew showed up."

"Did you wake up before that?"

"Not that I remember."

"So you can't say for certain that Felicity was actually in the bed with you the whole time."

"You've got to be kidding me." I waved my hands at him in an angry gesture of dismissal.

"How about when Wentworth was popped."

"What?!"

"You heard me."

"Don't you think you're the one getting a little far fetched now?"

"Maybe, maybe not, I dunno," he huffed then stared off into the dining room for a moment before looking back at me and pointing toward the chair behind me. "Sit down."

"I don't want to sit down."

"Sit your ass down, or I'm gonna do it for ya'," he ordered, and I knew he wasn't joking.

I looked over my shoulder, took a step back and perched myself on the arm of the chair then snipped, "Okay, I'm sitting. Happy?"

He didn't respond to my sarcasm. Instead, he smoothed back his hair and began massaging his neck again. I watched him, my anger with what he had just implied still percolating deep inside me. But, as I stared at my friend, I noticed that the look on his face was one of the most intensely disturbed expressions I had ever seen him wear in all the time I had known him. It wasn't one of malice but more of deep uneasiness.

At that moment, the hollowness in my chest started to grow.

Ben finally took in a deep breath and let it out in a loud huff then locked his gaze with mine. "Listen to me, Rowan. I didn't come back in right away because I got a phone call from Ackman."

I knew the name. He was one of the detectives with whom Ben worked on the Major Case Squad, and upon hearing the words, my first thought was that we were too late. Fear started to run rampant in my chest as I imagined the things my wife may have done without even knowing it.

"Gods!" I sputtered. "What happened? Did they find her?"

"No, not yet. Now, hold on, it's not what you're thinkin', but it sure as hell ain't good."

"What?" I asked, calming only slightly.

"Listen, I gotta tell ya' some stuff you ain't gonna wanna hear. They got the preliminaries back on the post from Officer Hobbes. Seems the M.E. found some foreign hairs on the body, and CSU found some that matched in the shower drain."

I knew immediately where he was heading with this, and I shot back, "Well, they aren't Felicity's if that's what you are trying to say."

"Rowan, they were red, and they were long," he replied.

"She's not the only redhead in the world, Ben," I snapped.

"I know that, Rowan. But they found some on Wentworth too."

"She was there taking the damn crime scene photos, Ben."

"Yeah, that was the thought at first. But, now, with Hobbes... She wasn't in that room. At least not with us... Today..."

"You're just jumping to conclusions."

"Yeah, you're right, I kinda am," he said with a nod. "But, listen, you told me yourself that you're afraid she's gonna hurt someone. Maybe even kill 'em."

"Yes, I did," I replied. "Now that she's under the influence of this collateral possession, that's a possibility. Which is one of the primary reasons we need to be out there looking for her right now."

"Believe me, there are plenty of people lookin' for 'er. You have no idea."

"Yeah. People with guns who think she's an armed fugitive."

He shook his head. "Got news for ya', Row. She is."

"That's not my point," I snapped. "We need to…"

He held up his hand to stop me. "Let's get back to what I was sayin'. Now, let's say I believe you on this whole possessed thing. What's to say she wasn't all *Twilight Zoned* out last night, waited for you to go to sleep, then out the door she went?"

"That's ridiculous," I objected. "Even if she snuck out of the house, which she didn't, how do you figure she would have even connected with Hobbes in such a short period of time?"

"Maybe she knew him already."

"How?"

"I dunno, Rowan. You tell me. He had her business card in his wallet."

"She's a freelance photographer, Ben. Her business card is sitting on the counter of every camera store in a fifty mile radius."

"Yeah, true." He nodded. "Or maybe she gave it to 'im when they met somewhere."

"So you're trying to tell me that my wife has been having an illicit affair?"

"Look, all I know is that they found her card in his wallet. Ackman also did some askin' around and found out Hobbes was leading a bit of a secret life," he explained. "He was really into the whole kinky sex thing. By Felicity's own admission, she was too."

"Operative word there, Ben. *Was*."

"I dunno. I got the impression she was still up for it, Row."

"Maybe so, but if it was something she wanted to get back into, I think she would have said something to me."

"Maybe not."

My retort came out as a growl. "I don't have to listen to this crap!"

"Okay, okay. Calm down. So maybe he did get her card from the camera store. They coulda hooked up another way. He was apparently a regular at a nightclub over on the east side that caters to the whole domination fetish crowd. East side's only a twenty-minute drive from here... Even less at that time of night. So maybe she cruised over..."

"Come on, Ben..."

"Look, I told ya' you weren't gonna wanna hear this."

"Let me get this straight. First you're telling me that my wife is running around on me. Now you're trying to get me to believe that she waited for me to go to sleep, slipped out, went over to a fetish bar on the east side, picked up a guy, brought him back across the river to a motel, played extreme bondage games with him, and finally she killed him. Then, after all of that, she comes home, crawls back into bed with me, and in the morning it's like nothing ever happened."

"Yeah, I know, Rowan. It sounds out there to me too."

"That's because it is," I replied. "Out there."

"Where was she when Wentworth bought it?"

"I'm not listening to any more of this crap."

"Look, I'm not sayin' this is what happened."

"That's what it sounds like to me."

"Listen, Row, I'd much rather believe your version."

"So, why even bring all this up?"

"Because it's a theory that's been advanced to the MCS."

"By who?" I demanded then held up my hand to stop him from answering. "No, wait. Don't tell me. Albright."

"Yeah," he replied with a nod.

"Bitch."

"Yeah."

"What's she even involved for?"

"The possible connection with Wentworth," he replied. "Told ya' she'd be all over it."

"So, why go to the east side?" I suddenly appealed.

"Whaddaya mean?"

"Why didn't Felicity just torture and kill me instead? I was right here. Why go to the trouble of sneaking out and going to the east side?"

"Maybe she loves ya' too much to actually kill ya'."

"Why would whatever or whoever is possessing her give a..." I let the rest of the sentence go unspoken, switching instantly from a question to an accusation. "You don't actually believe she's possessed."

"Listen, Row..." he started then blew out a heavy sigh. "Like you just figured out. It's not what I believe that's important right now. There are a lot of other people involved in this investigation, and Bible Barb has their ears."

"Felicity did NOT kill Officer Hobbes, Ben. Wentworth either."

"I believe ya', Rowan."

"And, she *is* under the influence of some type of spirit possession."

"Like I said, I believe ya'."

"Well, you'll have to excuse me, but I'm beginning to wonder."

"I'm still a cop, Row," he offered apologetically. "It was either gonna be me or someone else askin' the questions. I wanted it ta' be me. First anyway, because trust me, they'll get asked again, and not nearly as nice."

"I guess I should say thank you," I said without much conviction.

"Thank me later. I just need ya' ta' know that after everything that's happened today, Felicity's gonna be real high on the list of suspects. Especially after what happened here."

"Then let's go find her before one of them does."

"Okay, where do you want to look first?"

"I wish I knew."

"Yeah. It's a good idea on paper," he said with a nod then mumbled, "Jeezus. Déjà fuckin' vu."

"About what?" I asked.

"Your goddamned wife," he grunted. "Last time she got all la-la on us, she ran off ta' chase ghosts in a friggin' park in the middle of the night. At least that time she left us a map."

He was referring to the kidnapping and homicide case we'd worked two years ago. The first and only time, until now, that Felicity had been so in tune with the other side of the veil. And, the very reason I'd buried the poppet in the back yard, not that it seemed to be doing its job at present.

"Yeah," I replied with a nod. "But, when she did that it was a conscious decision on her part. This time it isn't. There's someone else in control of her body."

"I hate to break the bad news to ya', Rowan, but the coppers out there are lookin' for Felicity O'Brien. Not Zuli Dano, or whatever her name is."

"*Ezili Dantó*. And, something tells me she's not the *Lwa* who's doing this. I'm betting it's the one we haven't identified yet."

"Yeah, whatever, but what I'm sayin' is Firehair's the one up to her neck in shit. Not a nameless pile of cornmeal on a motel room table."

"I know."

"I don't think I hafta tell ya' that this is a fuckin' mess, right?"

"Right."

"Yeah, well, I'm gonna tell ya' anyway. This is a fuckin' mess."

Wednesday, November 9
8:46 P.M.
Suite 1233, Concourse Suites
St. Louis, Missouri

CHAPTER 28:

S he had just finished undressing and drawing a bath when the feeling came on her once again. Now, she found herself lying back on the large bed, her nude body flushed with warmth even though the air in the hotel room was crisp, almost to the point of being cold. She closed her eyes as she tried to relax.

Relax.

What a laugh. Like that was really going to happen.

She could never relax when she had been rewarded well, and last night her gift had been the sweetest yet. It wasn't unusual for her to keep reliving the moments of pleasure until the tickle finally faded away; she knew that from her past experiences. But this time the feeling went far beyond any of those that had come before. In fact, she wasn't entirely sure how much more of this she could stand.

Still the tickle blossomed, even as it had this morning and the night before. It was getting late, and she was aching with soreness. Nevertheless, she knew she would have to meet its demands.

She had been at this off and on for the entire day, whenever she could that was. There had been an unproductive business luncheon that kept her from tending to her desires, and that time had been no less than maddening. Then, there had been that annoying little man who took up her afternoon. Maybe she should have gotten his name and put him on her list. He certainly deserved a good beating.

But now she was sequestered here alone, and there was nothing to get in her way. It was a relief to finally be back here in her room.

She heard her stomach growl, and she remembered that she had not even taken time to eat. It was something she knew she desperately needed to do, especially with all of the rum she had been drinking. Maybe she should order room service? No, maybe not. She didn't really have an appetite even though her stomach audibly told her she should.

Right now, however, the nagging itch inside her belly was the greater force. And, as had been the rule of the day, it was insisting that it be scratched.

It didn't matter. There would be time for eating when she got home. At the moment, there was a different hunger that needed to be fed.

She heeded the call and her hand slipped down yet again to begin attending to its needs. She knew it wouldn't take much. Just a light tease and her recent memories would be more than enough to feed its wants.

She felt herself smile as the scene started to replay. Behind her closed eyes, she watched as the events of the previous night unfolded in vivid remembrance.

His humiliation and servitude were the appetizers, tickling her deep within.

As he crawled about on all fours, snuffling like a pig...

As he snorted while she sat astride his back and rode him like an animal...

As he licked the shiny patent leather of her shoes and hungrily kissed her feet...

His torture was the dinner salad, making her shudder with delight.

As she pulled hard on the leash with her knee in his back, listening to him gurgle and gag...

As she viciously lashed his body with a leather belt until he bled...

As she ground out burning cigarettes against his back, savoring the sickly sweet odor of burnt flesh...

His fear was a delectable morsel, making her heart race.

As he finally understood that his safe word was falling on deaf ears and meant nothing to her...
As he gagged on the washcloth and apple she shoved so deeply into his throat...
As he finally realized that, to her, this was no game, it was real and forever...

His pain was a savory main course, taking her to the brink and holding her there.

As she placed the cold steel against his genitals...
As she castrated him like the farm animal he had become...
As she held open his eyes so that he was sure to see the bloody jewels she was displaying for his benefit...

And finally, his soul... Oh yes, his soul had been dessert, filling her with heavenly pleasure.

As she sat astride the black pig and told him that they loved him...
As his eyes begged her to let him live...
As she drew the knife across his throat and offered him to Ezili...

She could still taste the sweetness on the back of her tongue, and she wanted to savor it forever. She let out an involuntary whimper as the latest orgasm took hold, and she shuddered as it drove through her abdomen and up her spine.

After a few moments passed, the wave of pleasure began to subside, and she sucked in a deep breath then let it out in a contented sigh. The tickle was still there but no longer pushing her toward the brink, as it had been earlier. Still, she had a distinct feeling that she wasn't finished with it yet. She just hoped that it would at least be a little while before the next demanding itch made itself known.

She pulled herself upright and trudged naked through the room, stopping only to pour a measure of rum into a tumbler. Picking up the drink, she took a sip as she wandered into the bathroom, then she perched the glass on the edge of the tub.

Standing before the mirror, she gathered her waist-length, fiery auburn hair atop her head and carefully pinned it in place. Once the loose Gibson-girlish coif was secure, she grabbed a towel and rolled it into a cylinder as she stepped over to the tub. She gently lowered herself into the milky water then adjusted the force of the whirlpool jets to suit her liking.

She took another sip of the rum and tried again to relax.

Yes, now *Ezili* should be pacified.

She had sacrificed a black pig just as she had been asked.

Of course, *Ezili* had no tongue and therefore, no voice, so it had actually been *Miranda* who told her of the demand. It wasn't unusual for *Miranda* to speak for *Ezili*. That was how it had always been.

She let out a resigned sigh.

She wasn't stupid. She knew full well that *Miranda* wanted the sacrifice as much as *Ezili*. Probably even more. *Miranda* always wanted a sacrifice, she just wasn't usually picky.

But then, *Miranda* always gave the sweetest rewards in return.

She bent her knees slightly and slid lower into the tub, letting the water climb over her chest as she slipped the rolled bath towel behind her neck. She closed her eyes and tried to relax again, but this time a perplexing thought crossed her mind.

It was something, much like the tickle, that had been nagging her all afternoon.

The pig's public name had been Calvin Hobbes. She knew this beyond any doubt.

She just couldn't figure out why the name Rowan kept running through her brain.

Wednesday, November 9
9:53 P.M.

CHAPTER 29:

The speakers in Ben's van were vibrating with the instrumental interlude of Del Shannon's *Runaway* as we cruised across the Poplar Street Bridge into Illinois. In just a moment, Del was going to be wondering why she ran away and where she would stay. I suppose the music was apropos because I was finding myself wondering the same thing about Felicity. The part about where she would stay, at least.

As I had suspected would be the case, the Briarwood officer stationed outside my house hadn't been particularly excited about me leaving. But, since I wasn't actually under arrest, there wasn't much she could do other than verbally object—which she did, strenuously and repeatedly. Of course, I suppose there would have been quite a bit more intimidation aimed my way had it not been for the fact that I was accompanied by a better than six-foot-tall Native American who also happened to be a cop. Yet another reason that having Ben on my side was a good thing.

My friend veered onto the off ramp without slowing and literally leaned his van through the loop then took us onto Route 3 toward the small city of Bridge, Illinois. After a short discussion, he had made a few calls then suggested that we start looking for Felicity at the club where Officer Hobbes had been known to frequent. He assured me that this wasn't because he believed Albright's theory, but that if Felicity was truly possessed by the killer in some way, and if that was where the killer had connected with Hobbes, then it stood to reason that she might return there. Given the present lack of tangible leads, I was willing to accept the logic even if I was still somewhat suspicious.

It was for that reason that I now found myself smack in the middle of what Saint Louisans commonly referred to as the "east side". While that moniker easily encompassed many points immediately east of downtown Saint Louis proper, it had actually taken on an almost slang-like meaning. In fact, for most locals the term was almost exclusively used to describe the handful of clubs that dotted the landscape over a several mile radius and specialized in adult entertainment.

The nightclubs were exactly what their subtitles of "show palace", "cabaret" and the like implied. They were the kind of place you took your buddy for his bachelor party if you really wanted to get him into trouble with his bride. Or, where businessmen went to blow their expense accounts on "lap dances" from scantily clad young women. Twenty bucks for a quick bump and grind to fuel their one-handed fantasies, if they even made it that far.

No matter how upscale and polished the names were that they placed on the marquee, most of them were little more than dimly lit strip joints, which were permeated with sickly sweet odors and had a so-called restaurant attached.

Having had what I personally considered to be the misfortune of being goaded into "entertaining" very insistent but important prospective clients at some of them from time to time, I was more familiar with their lunch fare than I would have liked. While I usually managed to smile and land the account, I also ended up pushing my meal selection around on the plate for some thirty-odd minutes and then making an excuse about not really being hungry.

Without fail, those particular business meetings would end with me grabbing something at a local diner when I was closer to home.

Of course, I certainly harbored no ill will toward the east side establishments nor their clientele. They simply weren't my kind of place and their food... Well, that was just something I didn't even want to think about.

Of course, we hadn't come over here for entertainment or dinner.

Our destination this evening was actually somewhat of an anomaly among the gentleman's cabarets, in that this one was a semiprivate club catering to the bondage and domination fetish crowd. In fact, it was the only one of its kind in the area. Most everyone knew about it, but if it wasn't your kink, it certainly wasn't where you went. Still, they did more than enough business to keep the doors open, and had done so for several years now.

"I talked to one of the coppers who was over to this place earlier today," Ben told me as we continued northward on Route 3. "He said they got a fuckin' real life dungeon thing goin' on in the basement. Got all kinds of torture shit down there almost like right outta the middle ages."

"That's what does it for some people," I replied.

"Too weird for me," he answered.

"Don't tell me you've never had any fantasies."

"Not that kinda shit," he said immediately then paused before asking, "You haven't have you... About this kinda crap, I mean?"

Were the situation different, I would have told him "yes" just to see what kind of reaction I could get, but my heart just wasn't in it tonight. All I wanted to do was find my wife, but for some reason, I found myself unable to get worked up about that either. It certainly wasn't that I didn't care. I was still worried and that hadn't changed. However, my brain had apparently settled into a subdued state. It seemed that even adrenalin had abandoned me at this point.

My head was still pounding with the loitering ethereal ache that couldn't make up its mind, but at the same time, a bizarre sense of calm had settled over me. I didn't know why I felt this way, but even concentrating on my earlier rampant fears couldn't usurp it. I shifted my attention toward maintaining my earthly ground, worried that I had allowed myself to slip between the planes, but even that didn't make a difference.

"Not really," I finally replied. "But, I've got an open mind."

"But it's weird."

"Consenting adults, Ben."

"So doesn't it freak you out that Firehair was all about this stuff?"

"No," I said with a shake of my head, and it was the truth.

"Not even just a little?"

"No," I said again.

"So, like, what if she wanted to tie you up and do shit to ya'?"

"I guess I'd let her."

"Yo, white man, are you feelin' okay?"

"Yeah, why?"

"'Cause that didn't sound like you at all. And, you're actin' a little weird. You ain't goin' *Twilight Zone*, are ya'?"

"Maybe."

"Maybe, like you're gettin' ready ta' zone out on me, or maybe you're not sure?"

"Maybe like I'm not sure," I said then pointed at a sign in the distance. "That's your turn right up here."

"How d'you know that?"

I shrugged. "I don't know. I just do."

"Jeezus, you ain't gettin' ready ta' do cornmeal art or somethin' are ya'?"

"No," I replied, screwing up my face. "Why would you think that?"

"Look, Kemosabe, somethin' ain't right with you. Maybe you're all la-la'd with that *Zili* thing too."

"I know I'm not right, Ben, but it's something else," I returned, not bothering to correct him. "I just don't know what yet. Now don't miss your turn."

"Dammit. You tell me if you're gonna go all freakazoid or somethin'. Okay?"

"I'll try."

As he made the turn, he shot me a glance and muttered, "Jeezus H…"

I couldn't give him the answer he wanted, and he knew that. But, as always, knowing that fact didn't stop him from asking me anyway. I could feel him staring at me off and on, but he didn't utter another syllable after the mumbled complaint.

We continued wordlessly for the next few minutes, the only sound being that of the engine competing with the radio, which was set to low volume and serenading us with yet another tune from the sixties. A little over five blocks and a single left hand turn later, we arrived at our destination.

We were at the end of a cul-de-sac where a large building sat back from the street. Near the curb, a lighted marquee sat atop a substantial signpost. Across it was emblazoned the name of the establishment—*The Whine Cellar*. Beyond the curb was a large gravel parking lot.

Ben pulled the van in through the entrance and slowly urged it along the rows of vehicles. The expanse was fairly well lit overall, and we both scanned either side of the aisle for Felicity's Jeep. We had just made a turn at the end and were coming back up the other side when my friend broke his silence.

"What's that up there?"

I abandoned my own search and looked over to where he was pointing. A few spaces from the end of the row sat a familiar looking boxy shape.

"Yeah. Could be," I agreed.

My friend sped up slightly and came to a halt behind the black Jeep Wrangler. I didn't even need to see the license plate. The pentacle on the spare tire cover and the "Magick Happens" bumper sticker told me all that I needed to know.

For the first time since we'd left the house, I felt like I was breaking out of the calm daze. My heart jumped in my chest, and I let out a relieved breath.

"It's hers," I said aloud.

"I'm gonna call this in," Ben announced as he reached into a pocket and withdrew his cell phone.

I objected immediately, snatching up the device out of his hand before he even flipped it open. "No, don't!"

"What the! Whaddaya mean don't?"

"Let's just go in and get her."

"Wake up, Rowan, she might be packin'."

"I doubt it."

"Hey, no offense, but Constance said she took her sidearm. I gotta take that into account. There're civilians in there and we don't need anyone gettin' hurt. You, me, her, or them. Now gimme my phone."

"Let's try it my way first," I pressed. "I don't want a bunch of trigger happy cops shooting my wife."

"You been watchin' too much TV again," he returned and reached for the phone in my hand.

I jerked it out of the way and replied, "I've been watching the news."

Ben snorted angrily and made another grab for me as he barked, "Gimme the goddamned phone, Rowan!"

He had long arms, but I'd been expecting him to do exactly this, and I already had my hand on the door handle. I popped the release and rolled out of the vehicle narrowly escaping his lunge. I backpedaled away from the van then turned and started walking as briskly as I could toward the entrance.

Behind me I heard the sound of gravel spitting as Ben gunned the engine and spun the tires. The angry sound was followed immediately by the thump of the passenger door as the effect of Newton's third law caused it to pivot in the opposite direction and slam shut. I picked up the pace, but a moment later he swung the van around the opposite end of the aisle and barreled toward me.

For a split second, I thought he was going to run me down, and I ducked quickly between two vehicles. I looked back and saw him suddenly brake then whip the Chevy hard to the left and pull it into an empty parking space. I told myself I needed to keep moving, but for some reason my legs wouldn't respond. I simply stood there and waited.

The vehicle's lights went out, and the engine sputtered as he switched it off. His own door was already creaking open before the last cough from the exhaust had died away. I heard my friend slam his door hard then watched as he stomped around and re-secured the passenger side which had not completely shut. That done, he turned around and simply stared at me across the top of the parked cars, then after a heartbeat or two, he shook his head and walked purposefully toward where I was standing.

Still, I didn't move. I simply waited. I knew I couldn't outrun him at this point even with a head start. I did, however, slip the cell phone into my jacket and zip the pocket shut.

When Ben came to a halt in front of me, he didn't look happy. The harsh shadows from the overhead light weren't helping, that was for sure, but I knew he was definitely pissed off. He sighed then opened his mouth and thrust his index finger at me. Whatever he was about to say apparently stuck somewhere between his brain and his throat, so he just closed his mouth and shook his head again.

Finally, he muttered, "Fuckit," and started toward the entrance. As he walked he called over his shoulder to me, "Just keep your damn mouth shut and let me handle this."

CHAPTER 30:

"There a problem here?" the man asked.

We hadn't even made it through the front door of the establishment before we were stopped. In fact, by the time we hit the bottom of the stairs, the bald meatloaf, clad in a faded military jacket, was waiting for us on the landing. He had positioned himself between the door and us, and it was obvious that we were going to need to run his gauntlet before gaining entry.

Under different circumstances I'm sure Ben would have simply used his size and badge to bully his way past a bouncer, but it was clear that this guy wouldn't be easy to intimidate. He looked to be only a few inches shorter than my friend, and that put him well over six feet himself. But, more importantly, what he lacked in height he made up for in muscle mass; at least, that is how he appeared; and I wasn't interested in trying to disprove it. I got the feeling that Ben wasn't either.

I had to say that security here was better than some airports I'd been in.

"No problem," my friend returned.

"Really."

"Yeah, really."

The human barricade nodded in the direction of the van then looked back to Ben. "Then what was the show all about?"

"Minor disagreement," he returned. "Mind if we go in now? It's kinda cold out here."

"What are you two doing here?"

"Whaddaya mean?"

"Did I stutter?" The man followed his question with a cold stare, sizing us both up with his eyes.

"It's the east side. What does anyone do here?"

"I think you gentlemen should leave now," he stated simply.

"We'd like to have a drink first," Ben offered up as an objection.

"This is a private club," the man returned. "And, I don't recognize either of you as members."

"Okay, so where do we sign up?"

"I already told you nicely, I think you need to leave. I don't want to have to tell you again."

"Listen, buddy, I really didn't wanna get into it with ya'," Ben said as he played the cop card, pulling open his jacket to reveal the gold shield clipped to his belt.

The bouncer glanced at the badge then back to my friend's face without ever changing his expression. "Uh-huh, I've got one of those too. Gotta love the internet."

"Yeah, asshole?" Ben snipped, finally losing his patience as he pulled out his formal ID and displayed it. "Thing is, mine's real."

The man took the identification and inspected it closely before handing it back to him then said with a shake of his head. "Okay, so? You think being a cop automatically gets you in the door?"

I had been keeping my mouth shut just like I had been told, but the pissing match between the two of them was becoming too much for me. The wave of calm that had overtaken me earlier had now faded into the background, and I was getting edgier by the second. At the rate these two were going, we could be standing here all night, and I simply wasn't interested in waiting.

"We're here looking for my wife," I blurted.

"Keep outta this, Row," Ben snapped.

The man turned his attention to me. "So, you think your wife is in there?"

"I know she is."

"Yeah, well listen, buddy, you aren't the first guy to have second thoughts about the cuckold husband game. Just go on home like a good little subby and wait. She'll be there when she's done."

"It's not what you're thinking," I replied.

"Uh-huh," he grunted with a heavy note of sarcasm. "You think I haven't heard that before? Look, I'm sorry you got cold feet, but this isn't the place to work out your marital issues, and we sure as hell don't need a domestic disturbance."

"Look," Ben interjected. "I don't know what you're rattlin' about, but here's the deal. You see that Jeep over there?"

My friend twisted and pointed back toward Felicity's vehicle.

"Yeah, what about it?"

"It belongs to this guy's wife," my friend continued as he turned back to the bouncer. "And, as it happens, his wife is currently wanted for questioning in a murder investigation. Since I have a reason to believe she's in there..." He pointed toward the door. "...I intend to go in and have a look. Now, I wanted to do this nice and quiet like, but apparently, you're wantin' to make it into a big production."

"You have a warrant?"

"I don't need one."

"Yes, you do."

"You ever heard the terms reasonable suspicion and probable cause? No, I don't need a fuckin' warrant."

"You're a Saint Louis cop." The man tried a fresh objection. "You're out of your jurisdiction."

"I'm currently assigned to Major Case. Jurisdiction ain't an issue. Now, you gonna let us in, or do I hafta arrest you for interfering with an ongoing police investigation?"

The man stared back at Ben. He didn't seem like he was particularly shaken, but he also didn't appear anywhere near as cocky or confident as he had earlier. After a moment, he gave my friend a shallow nod and said, "Wait here. I'll get the owner."

He turned and disappeared through the door, leaving us out on the wide landing by ourselves.

"Who's been watching TV now?" I asked.

"Hey," he returned defensively. "Everything I said was the real deal."

"Still sounded like a cop show."

"Yeah, well sometimes they get lucky and get it right," he huffed. "I thought I told you ta' keep your mouth shut."

"I did. For a while anyway."

"Yeah, about two minutes."

"I got tired of waiting."

"Uh-huh."

"Shouldn't we go on ahead in?"

"You heard 'im. He's gettin' the owner."

"Yeah, so," I said as I started toward the door.

"Yeah, so I'd like ta' do this peaceably," he replied as he grabbed my arm and pulled me back. "Look, if she's in there, she ain't goin' anywhere."

"I just want this over with, Ben," I complained.

"Yeah, me too," he replied as he reached up to rub his neck. After a good thirty seconds of silence, he glanced over at me and asked, "Hey, so what's a cuckold?"

"It's a word."

"No shit. What's it s'posed to mean?"

"It's a word used to describe a man married to an unfaithful wife."

"Then why'd that meatlump call it a game?"

"It is, to some extent. In the arena of female domination, the woman will sometimes humiliate her husband by being blatantly unfaithful to him. Often, right in front of him or by telling him about it in great detail. It's a fetish that some submissive men are into."

"Jeezus, I don't even wanna know how you know that."

"Don't worry," I reassured him. "The word was an answer in a crossword puzzle, and I had to look it up. I found the stuff about the fetish by following a couple of internet links out of curiosity."

"Okay, at least I know you're not that kinda weird then. Cuckold, huh? Sounds like a friggin' old clock."

"Actually, you aren't far off. The word is derived from cuckoo because with some varieties of the bird, the female lays her eggs in other birds' nests and leaves them to be taken care of by those birds. Thereby, she gains a reputation for unfaithfulness. Cuckoo. Cuckold."

"Jeez... You 'n Constance oughta go on a game show together," he told me. "Between the two of ya', you'd clean up, and we could all retire."

"Yeah, I doubt it," I returned. "By the way, thanks."

"For what?"

"For trying to keep my mind off this mess."

"Was it that obvious?"

"No, but I know you pretty well."

"So, is it workin'?"

"Not really."

"Well, stop worryin' on it anyway," he offered. "We're gonna work it out... I don't know how, but somehow."

"I hope you're right."

He didn't get a chance to respond. The door swung open and a far less than petite woman strode out. At least, she appeared to be a woman. Her blonde hair was a short bob that framed an angular face that could easily have gone either direction as far as gender. Her shoulders were broad, and with the platform shoes she was wearing, she actually stood taller than Ben. Trailing along behind her was a shorter individual who was more easily identifiable as male.

"Excuse you," she barked at us, and her husky falsetto voice did little to solve the gender mystery.

We both stepped out of the way, and she continued past us, tugging hard on a leash that was attached to a collar around the man's neck. While she was wrapped in a leather coat, he was bare from the waist up. Since the temperature had dipped into the low forties, I could only imagine that he was freezing. But then, I suppose that was part of their game. We both automatically turned, watching them as they went down the stairs then out across the parking lot.

"Tim tells me you're a cop," a more distinctly female voice came from behind us.

We turned back to find a somewhat shorter individual staring at us. She was roughly my height, so she was looking upward toward Ben as most people ended up doing. Her face was wide with large eyes and pronounced lips, all surrounded by a shoulder-length flip of dark hair. She was wrapped in a full-length fur coat that hid her figure, but unlike the person preceding her, by all outward appearances she was actually a real female. Even so, she did carry herself with a typically male posture which I could only assume was intended to intimidate.

"Yeah, Detective Ben Storm, Major Case Squad," my friend replied. "You are?"

"Vee Ostuni," she replied coolly. "I'm the owner. You may call me Lady Vee."

"Miz Ostuni…" Ben started.

"Lady Vee," she corrected.

"Yeah. Okay. So listen, Miz Ostuni," he began again, a little more forcefully.

She held out her hand in an abrupt flourish. "May I see some ID?"

Ben displayed his impatience with a loud huff but produced the wallet and badge once again, standing by as she inspected the credentials. She made a great show of holding up the ID to the light and glancing back and forth between the picture and my friend's face. After what seemed like a solid trio of minutes, she closed the wallet and handed it back over to him.

"Satisfied?" my friend asked.

"Satisfied? No, you quite rudely interrupted that," she quipped. "Oh, but I'm sure you meant the ID. Well, I suppose I don't doubt you are who you say you are. Now, what is it that you want?"

"We'd like to come in and look around."

"For what?"

"My wife," I piped up.

She glanced past Ben at me. "And she would be the murder suspect, correct."

"Incorrect," I spat. "She's…"

"She's a person of interest," Ben interjected.

"That is just another way of saying suspect," she retorted.

"Or witness," he stressed.

"Which is she then?" She blinked and raised her eyebrows in a mocking expression. "Suspect or witness?"

"Like I said," my friend spoke with forced clarity. "She is a person of interest."

"Yes, I figured as much. If you're going to lie, pick one and stick to it," she replied haughtily then turned on her heel and started toward the door. "Good evening, gentlemen, now go away."

Ben reached out quickly and took hold of her arm, spinning her back around to face us but not releasing his grip.

"Listen, I've had about enough of this crap outta you wingnuts!" he barked. "Now either we come in with your blessing, or I slap cuffs on you, make a couple of calls, and shut you down for a while."

"Ooohh, Detective," she purred. "So forceful. I am sorry, but I'm a *top*, not a *switch*. I can, however, introduce you to some submissive women if you'd like. Or would you prefer a male slave?"

"Jeezus!" he spat, quickly releasing her arm as if he thought he was touching something repugnant.

"Lady Vee," I appealed, trying to defuse the situation. "I understand your reluctance, but all we want to do is go inside and get my wife."

I was usually the one being reined in by Ben, so this was a bit of a change for me. Given the way I was feeling at the moment, I was surprising myself with my own calm.

"I really don't need a domestic disturbance in my club," she replied.

"There won't be."

"I find that hard to believe," she remarked flatly. "If she is inside and you have had to come looking for her, obviously there is an issue."

"There is," I agreed. "She's not answering her cell phone."

"And perhaps she has a good reason."

"She does, but not one you would understand."

"I'm sorry, gentlemen," she announced. "But, I don't want you in my club. If you think you need to make calls, Detective, feel free. I'll make one myself, to my attorney."

She turned and started toward the door once again, and Ben immediately reached beneath the folds of his coat. A second later I heard the clink of his handcuffs as he extracted them from his belt.

"Hold on," I said, laying my hand on his arm then I directed myself toward the club owner. "Lady Vee, wait..."

She stopped and turned back toward me as she impatiently snipped, "What is it?"

"If the issue is that you don't want an incident in your club, how about if you send her out here?"

"And what reason should I give her for sending her out?" she asked.

"Don't tell me you've never kicked anyone out before," Ben said. "I'm sure you can think of somethin'."

She stood there with her hand on the door handle, staring back at us. After a brief moment, she released the door and stepped back over to us. "All right. Do you have a picture, so I know who I am looking for?"

I quickly dug in my pocket and extracted my wallet, peeling open the Velcro tab and flipping through the pictures. Landing on the most recent photo of my wife, I turned the billfold around and handed it to her.

She glanced at the image of Felicity for a second then handed the wallet back to me.

"I'm sorry, but I'm afraid I can't send her out."

"Why not?" I couldn't keep the pleading tone out of my voice.

"Because she isn't here."

"Bullshit," Ben snapped as he jerked his thumb over his shoulder. "Her fuckin' Jeep is parked right over there."

"Be that as it may," she replied. "She is not inside my club. She left about thirty or forty minutes ago."

"Left?"

"Yes, left," she said, waving her hand out in a sweeping gesture. "As in went away, said goodbye, took her leave…"

"Was anyone with her?" I asked.

"Yes. Mat."

"Matt who?" Ben asked, reaching for his notebook.

"Not Matt who," she replied with a shake of her head. "Door Mat. He's a regular here."

"Door Mat? Jeezus… So, what's his real name?"

"I have no idea."

"You don't know his real name?"

"No, Detective, I'm afraid I don't."

"You gotta be kiddin' me? He's a regular and you don't know his real name?"

"I've already told you no twice. This makes three."

"What about someone else inside? One of your staff? One of the other 'nameless regulars' then?"

"I wouldn't know. We respect our clientele here."

"Oh yeah? Ya' coulda fooled me."

"Privacy, Detective. Their privacy."

"Yeah. Whatever."

CHAPTER 31:

Ben spent nearly fifteen minutes trying to convince the owner of
The Whine Cellar that it would not only be in her best interest,
but Door Mat's as well, if she would allow us to ask those present a
few questions. The more information we could gather, the better, but if
we at least knew his real name and got a basic description of him, it
would be a start. She kept insisting that they wouldn't have what we
were looking for other than the description she had already given us,
but eventually she assented to his appeals.

It was obvious that she wasn't happy about the situation when
she ushered us through the door; what we hadn't expected was that she
wasn't going to give in without some type of retaliation. Upon entering
the club, she instantly launched into a swell of histrionics, essentially
making a show of stopping the evening's performance mid-stream.

Since the entertainment was apparently the semi-public
flogging of various submissive members of the clientele, the
interruption didn't go over very well with the crowd. Still, with her
barking orders, it didn't take long to clear the centrally located,
circular stage. It did, however, take a minute or two for her to quell the
catcalls, the loudest of which seemed to be coming from the victims of
the whippings. But, I got the impression that she wasn't really trying
that hard.

And still, even after she had everyone's unfettered attention,
she wasn't finished with her melodramatic display. With a wholly
unnecessary flourish, she introduced both of us, immediately tagging
Ben as a cop and me as the "submissive husband" of the redhead who
had been with Door Mat.

Several voices in the group instantly called out the name
"Mistress Miranda", intermixed with commentaries ranging from
"lucky S.O.B." to "you poor bastard". Even so, none of them stepped
up to take credit for the tidbit of knowledge. Lady Vee had then

followed up by asking that anyone with any information on the individual known as Door Mat please come forward.

Just as she had said would happen, the only data coming our way was in the form of blank stares.

Ben and I both went so far as to appeal to the crowd ourselves, reviving the multiple personality disorder and skipped meds story he had concocted earlier. However, even after telling them that Mistress Miranda may very well seriously hurt their friend because of her current psychosis, not a single person was willing to help.

Whether it was because they weren't about to talk to a cop because Lady Vee had some sort of control over them, or simply that they truly didn't know anything, I couldn't say for sure. Still, it seemed odd, even to me, that not one individual in the entire club knew his real name, especially if he had been a regular.

After a smug and very public "I told you so" from Lady Vee, we were summarily escorted to the door and asked to leave post haste, though not in such polite terms. Since there wasn't really anything we could do to force the information out of them, we complied. Well, partially anyway. Felicity's Jeep was still here, and Ben wanted to search it. Fortunately for us, I had had the presence of mind to bring my set of keys for the Wrangler along with me. I didn't normally carry them, but for some reason, this time I had stuffed them into my pocket.

We had only been at the task a little more than five minutes when my growing impatience with the situation got the better of me.

"Shouldn't we be out looking for Felicity?" I asked with an almost angry edge to my voice.

"Where?" Ben called across to me without looking up and continued rifling through the front half of the vehicle.

He was kneeling on the driver's side with his head cocked over as he carefully played the beam of a flashlight beneath the seat. I was on the passenger side, doing much the same but without the aid of additional light and with much less fervor. I seriously doubted that we would find anything that would point us to where my wife had gone, and I had already said as much several times. To be perfectly honest, I didn't think my friend was expecting to either. His focus at the moment actually seemed directed more toward recovering Agent Mandalay's sidearm.

"I don't know, wherever," I spat.

"'Zactly."

"Exactly what?"

"Exactly you don't have any friggin' idea where to start, and neither do I."

"Maybe so, but we aren't getting anywhere by staying here."

"Uh-huh, just keep lookin'," he grunted absently then spoke up. "So, I hate ta' even ask this, but, how long?"

"How long what?" I replied as I gave up trying to see anything and simply slid my arm beneath the passenger seat. After feeling about, I wrapped my hand around something hard and withdrew it, only to find myself holding a collapsible umbrella. Waving it in the air, I added, "Nothing here."

"Be careful!" he barked, having noticed how blindly I had groped about. "Why don't you just back off and let me do this."

"Fine," I returned, standing and taking a half-step back then holding my hands up in plain sight. "Suit yourself. I don't know why finding the damn gun is so important right this minute anyway."

He glanced up at me without a word. There was more than enough overhead light for me to see the look on his face, and it told me I had just said something incredibly stupid. At least, that was obviously his take on my comment.

"I've already been through the console," he said, not bothering to explain his motivation. "Why don't you check to see if I missed anything that'll help us know where ta' start lookin'."

"Yeah, okay. Fine."

I puffed my cheeks as I blew a frustrated breath out in a frosty stream then leaned inside the vehicle and began going through the clutter in the center console.

"Look, I'm sorry. I just don't want anyone gettin' shot. Me, you, her, or another copper. If she ditched the gun, then I know we're probably safe, from that at least."

"Okay, I get it," I replied without conviction.

"Good."

"So, how long what?" I asked after searching in silence for another minute or two.

He continued his quest without interruption but spoke again in an almost apologetic tone. "So anyway, what I was askin' is how long do ya' think we have before she kills this guy?"

The query struck me in the chest with no less emotional intensity than if he had simply doubled up his fist and physically thrown the punch. I stopped moving and simply allowed my head to hang.

I couldn't blame him for asking. It was a valid question, and I would be lying if I said it hadn't already crossed my mind more than once. I had just been making it a point to try not to think about it.

When I didn't answer him right away, he called my name, "Row?"

The beam from the flashlight flickered in front of me, and I slowly raised my head. I'm certain the harsh light didn't help what was most likely a horribly pained expression on my face.

"Shit... Sorry, white man..." my friend mumbled. "Didn't think... I'm just kinda in cop mode right now. And, I'm not used ta' one of my friends bein'..."

"It's okay," I replied then swallowed hard as his question continued to bounce around inside my skull. I finally said, "I honestly don't know. It was pretty obvious at the other crime scenes that the killer apparently likes to torture the victims for a while. Given the nature of the abuse, I suspect it probably starts out as a consensual fetish game. How quickly it escalates from there, I have no idea."

"What about the Voodoo stuff? Think she'll do that?"

"Maybe."

"So that could buy some time."

I shook my head uncertainly. "Again, maybe. I don't know enough to be able to say how long the ritual would take."

"Okay. So, any chance Felicity could... I dunno... Win?"

"Win?"

"You know, like... I dunno... Stop herself."

"You mean her spirit?"

"Yeah, whatever... I mean like could she be fighting against this thing right now. Groundin' or whatever hocus-pocus it is you two are always doin'. You know, maybe tryin' ta' make herself snap out of it before it's too late?"

"Right now, I suspect Felicity isn't even aware that she needs to snap out of it, so she's probably not able to do anything at all. Her body has become what the *Lwa* refer to as a 'horse'. It's literally being used to take the departed spirit from one place to another and allow it to do things in the physical world."

"I thought you just said you didn't know that much about this shit?"

"I don't, really. Just a handful of relatively useless facts," I said with a shrug. "While you were making some calls back at the house, I skimmed through a couple of books we had on the shelf, but I didn't get much more than I already knew." I stopped and harrumphed thoughtfully. "I guess that's probably because I got what I knew from those books to begin with. Either way, basically, this is pretty unfamiliar ground for me. I know enough to know that I don't really have a clue."

"That doesn't inspire confidence, Row."

"Yeah, I know."

"So, I don't suppose there was a chapter in one of those books on how to make the spirit go away, was there?"

"No. Apparently, it's actually an honor to be a horse for a *Lwa,* so a follower really wouldn't want the spirit to go away."

"Prob'ly cause they haven't hung out with this one."

"I can agree with that because there's something more to this spirit, Ben. The descriptions of possessions in the books seemed adamant about *Lwa* not inflicting intentional harm."

"Maybe they need ta' write a new book."

"All I can say is that this *Lwa*, if that's what it really is, isn't normal."

"Normal ain't a word I'd use for any of this, Row," he huffed.

"Yeah, I know. Believe me, based on what I read, the spirituality here seems rooted in traditional Voodoo practices, but that's where the similarity ends. It's like it's being misinterpreted to fit a sick agenda."

"Yeah, well we've seen that kinda shit happen before, haven't we?"

I knew the rhetorical question was a reference to the first case I'd ever worked with him. WitchCraft had been the focus that time, but like now, it had been twisted into something it wasn't to fulfill the killer's psychopathic fantasy.

"Don't remind me."

"So, even knowin' all that, you still think…"

"That Felicity is acting under a spirit possession?" I replied, finishing the thought for him. "Absolutely. I refuse to believe she's a killer, Ben. I just can't. Can you?"

"As a friend, I sure as hell don't want to. As a cop…"

I interrupted him again. "Just don't…"

"I'm just tryin' ta' say…"

"No, Ben. Don't say anything else. At least let me pretend you're on my side."

"I am, Row. Believe it or not."

"There's something else I read," I told him, not exactly changing the subject but shunting it into a different direction. "Possessions are known to spontaneously end."

"So this could just all of a sudden stop?"

"Yes. In fact, more than likely it will do exactly that."

He raised an eyebrow. "So if it's gonna do that, then you're sayin' maybe we just wait it out?"

"I doubt it. The problem is that it usually happens after the spirit has accomplished what it set out to do when it took over the body to begin with."

"Fuckin' wunnerful," he grumbled then stood up. "Okay. Nothin' over here either. Let's check the back."

I backed out and closed the passenger door then stepped around the Jeep, meeting my friend behind it. I reached in and unlatched the spare tire frame, swung it to the side, then unlocked the back window on the hard shell top. Ben pointed the flashlight through the tinted glass, moving it back and forth for a moment, and then carefully lifted the hatch open.

I followed the beam of the *Mag-lite* to where it pooled in the back of the vehicle. There, partially draped across Felicity's gym bag was the pinstripe business suit she'd been wearing earlier in the day. At first I thought it might simply have been the blazer, but upon closer inspection I saw what appeared to be the waistband of the slacks, as well as the strap of her bra.

"That looks like what she was wearin' this afternoon," Ben said aloud.

"It is."

"Well, unless she left outta here naked, she musta changed clothes or somethin'."

The ensemble was haphazardly strewn across the rear cargo space, and positioned on top of it was one of her smaller, hard-sided camera cases with the hinged lid propped open. A pair of empty holes gaped back at us from the foam insert.

"It looks like there's a camera and a flash unit missing," I announced.

"Jeezus fuckin' Christ," Ben muttered. "Don't tell me she's gonna take pictures."

He continued to play the beam of the flashlight around the interior of the back of the Jeep, pausing here and there as something would catch his eye. After a moment he reached in and carefully moved the camera case then started lifting the pile of clothing to check beneath.

That was when my heart somersaulted in my chest.

"Whoa! Wait!" I insisted, reaching for his arm, but he had already stopped because he had seen the same thing that caught my eye.

Felicity's white blouse, which had been sandwiched between the blazer and slacks, was now revealed. However, it was no longer stark white, as across the left breast a bright crimson spatter stained the otherwise pristine silk.

"Gods!" I exclaimed.

"Calm down, Row," Ben urged. "That probably came from Constance when she hit 'er. She was bleedin' pretty good."

"What if it's not?!" I appealed.

"Whether it is or not, panicking ain't gonna help," he returned.

My panic ramped upward suddenly, but for a completely different reason as a voice hissed from behind us, "Hey."

At the same moment the word struck my ears, out of the corner of my eye I saw shadowy movement, followed by a hand reaching between us toward my friend's arm. I immediately jumped, startled by the intrusion, and succeeded in banging my head against the hatch strut.

Ben's reflexes, however, kicked into high gear, and he clamped his own hand onto the person's wrist then whipped around in a blur of motion. Before I knew it, he had the owner of the voice pressed face first against the side of the Jeep. In retrospect I suppose the action was overkill, but at that particular moment, our level of tension was already approaching the red zone. The truth is, he had probably showed great restraint by simply subduing the individual.

I rubbed the side of my head where it had impacted the support then stepped around to see what was happening. The voice, and hand, apparently were the property of a buzz cut young man we had seen in the club. He was decked out in leather bondage gear, including a wide dog collar complete with a silver ID tag that glinted in the dim shower of luminance from the overhead lights.

"What the fuck do you think you're doin'?" Ben almost screamed as he held him in place against the vehicle, keeping one arm twisted up behind his back.

"I just wanted to talk to you!" the young man said frantically.

"You don't sneak up on a cop unless you wanna get hurt, you goddammed moron!"

"Whoa! Hold on! I wasn't sneaking up on you. I'm trying to help!"

"Help what?" Ben barked.

The young man did his best to look in my direction, and I stared back at him wordlessly.

"Did *she* do that to you?" he asked.

"Did who do what to me?" I asked with a mix of confusion and annoyance in my voice.

"Your cheek. Did Mistress Miranda do that to you?"

"That's not her name," I spat.

"Look, that's all I know her as."

"Okay, fine," I replied. I wasn't about to tell him her real name. "Yes, she did this to me."

"Man, she's a vicious bitch."

"Is that all you came out here for?" Ben asked, pressing him harder against the Jeep.

"No, Mistress Gwen sent me out."

"What the hell for?" my friend demanded.

The young man tried to look at me again. "Are you really her husband?"

"Yeah." I gave him a short nod. "I'm her husband, why?"

"Mistress Gwen thinks she's dangerous."

"Right now, she is," I agreed. "We tried to tell everyone that inside."

"Mistress Gwen wants to know if you think she might really hurt Mat."

"I thought that's what you freaks were all about," Ben interjected with a mix of disdain and sarcasm.

"No, she means really injure him. Like something serious or permanent."

"Yeah, she might," I told him.

Ben pulled the young man away from the Jeep and shoved him in the direction of the building. The kid stumbled but caught himself and turned around to face us.

"Look, asshole, if that's all you wanted, then go tell your playmate what she wanted to hear and leave us alone. We're tryin' ta' do police work here."

"You don't get it, do you?"

"Get what?"

"I'm trying to help you."

"How?"

"Mat's a friend of mine."

"Oh yeah? Do you know his real name?" Ben demanded.

"Sure. Name, address, phone number. I can even tell you what kind of car he drives."

"Why the hell didn't you say something earlier?" I demanded with a swell of anger and stepped toward him.

He took a step back but didn't bolt.

Then, for the second time this evening, someone looked at me like I had just displayed an utter lack of intelligence by asking the stupidest of all known questions.

He shook his head and replied, "Because my Mistress didn't give me permission to speak until just now."

Ben looked at him then over to me. "I'm gonna be needin' my phone back, Row."

CHAPTER 32:

"Yeah, first name Brad, last name Lewis, L-E-W-I-S," Ben said into the cell phone as he urged the van along Highway 40 and back across the Poplar Street Bridge into Missouri. "Uh-huh... Yeah, according to the witness it's a white Ford Focus... No, don't know the plates, but his address is..."

I tuned out the rest of what he was saying. I had already heard it all once out of the young man from the club, and it had etched itself into my memory as he spoke each word. I doubted I would be forgetting it anytime soon.

Of course, that wasn't the only reason for tuning my friend out. I was having a hard time dealing with the fact that he was, for all intents and purposes, releasing the hounds on my wife. While I understood that reporting the information was something he simply had no choice but to do, it didn't make me feel any better about pointing the manhunt in Felicity's direction.

I suppose there was still one saving grace, however, and that was the fact that the handful of data Ben was handing over probably wasn't going to get anyone else any closer to finding her than we were.

Not that we were particularly close.

I just knew that I needed to find her first. Unfortunately, I was beginning to realize that this need was as much for my peace of mind as for her safety. A nagging doubt had crept into my thoughts, and it was treating my fear like a buffet line, feeding on it in a near frenzy. I was trying very hard to ignore it because the feeling it produced in the pit of my stomach made me want to vomit.

Still, even if I discounted the growing incertitude, I knew that I needed to be at the head of the pack no matter what. The thing was, right now it wasn't looking like I was going to make it. That fact, in and of itself, was bringing its own churn to my insides.

My emotions had been running hot and cold all evening as it was—bouncing up and down the scale with each passing moment. I simply wasn't used to this roller coaster. Given the circumstances, I figured I should be completely on edge right now, but that just wasn't the case.

Granted, I had started out with anger when the young man finally admitted to knowing the details about the individual with whom my wife had left the club. In fact, Ben had actually ended up needing to step between us as I started after him in a sudden rage. I don't think the beating I intended to inflict would have been the kind he was looking for either.

But, that infuriation was all too brief, and it had quickly morphed through to quiet frustration. Following that equally hasty encounter, I slipped into a moment of something close to elation before finally sweeping right back past anger and falling directly into the cold arms of depression. In the end, the entire course of emotions took less than five minutes to complete.

Now, as we cruised over the PSB, I found that I was still firmly planted in that state of melancholy. I knew that part of it came from the conscious knowledge of how futile our search had become. It seemed that we were falling further behind at every turn, and I'm sure that went a long way toward setting my current mood. And, of course, the bizarre tingle in the back of my head wasn't helping either. But, I also knew that the relentless doubt that had so recently set up residence in my thoughts was the worst of the trio of culprits. Even when things came in threes, there had to be a leader.

At the moment I was sitting slumped down in the passenger seat, gazing out the windshield with an unfocused stare. The darkness beyond the glass had morphed into a surreal landscape as we drove, and I was simply allowing myself to melt into it.

I watched wordlessly as the reflection of the Saint Louis skyline rippled in the dark waters of the Mississippi River, shortening to an abstract flicker of light as we advanced across the bridge. Ben merged to the left and continued along the highway, bypassing downtown as he pressed on toward the county.

I remained mesmerized, as yellowish-white pinpoints of light continued appearing in the distance, growing larger, then streaking past us on the left. Dusky red flickers brightened and dimmed with their out of sync rhythms on the right. Setting the pace and bisecting it all was the on-again off-again flutter of the lane markers as they came and went all at once.

On one level I knew exactly what I was seeing, but on another the familiar sights had taken on a whole new meaning. My head ached, and my brain simply didn't seem to be interested in processing reality any longer. It had become too harsh, and my subconscious was frantically seeking an escape. Turning the visual sensory input into a hypnotic kaleidoscope for its own entertainment was apparently the path of least resistance.

Given the alternative, I didn't know that I really minded a bit. In fact, I was seriously considering allowing myself to succumb to it in total when my friend decided it would be a good time to interrupt.

"Hey, Row..." Ben's voice joined a sharp jab against my shoulder.

"Yeah," I said, reluctantly surfacing from the trancelike stare.

"You gonna answer your phone?" he asked.

"What?"

"Your phone," he repeated with a mild urgency. "Answer it."

I took in a deep breath and forced my grey matter to wrap around the sentence and mull it over. It seemed like several minutes passed before the words fully registered, but apparently, time wasn't flowing in quite the same fashion for me as for the rest of the world. When I reached into my pocket and withdrew my cell phone, it was just starting into another cycle of its warbling ring tone, and that told me that only a few seconds could have actually elapsed.

My brain objected, but still it followed orders and started shifting into a higher gear, so I held the device up to my face and inspected the backlit LCD. Even with the minor fog that lingered over my cognitive abilities, however, I recognized the number instantly. My only comment was a heavy sigh before shoving the device back into my pocket.

"Who is it?" Ben asked.

"It's my father-in-law," I replied flatly.

"Aren't ya' gonna answer it?"

"No."

"Why not?"

"I'm not in the mood for it right now."

"You should answer it," he urged.

"He's already left a voice mail. He can leave another one."

"You mean he called before? When?"

"While you were still talking to the kid back at the club."

"That why you disappeared?"

"No," I replied. "I disappeared because I didn't think I could handle hearing any more."

"About what she…"

"Yeah."

"Yeah," he echoed then after a moment he added, "Ya'know, your father-in-law might be callin' about 'er."

"I'm sure he is," I agreed. "She was the subject of his first obnoxious message."

"But, what if she contacted 'im?"

"I doubt it, besides, he wouldn't be calling me if she did."

"Don't sell the man short, Row."

"Have you ever met him, Ben?"

"No, not actually."

"Okay then. Just trust me, I'm the last person Shamus O'Brien would call if he knew where she was."

"How can you know that?"

"It comes with the territory."

"One of those Witch things?"

"Kind of," I harrumphed. "Me Witch, him good Christian."

"But surely he would…"

"No, he wouldn't," I cut him off. "He's just calling to scream at me for corrupting his daughter and to blame me for whatever trouble she's in right now."

"But I thought you two still got along."

"Yeah, well, that was awhile ago. He used to just not care for me, but over the past few years that's pretty much turned into hate."

"Yeah, but even so, I don't see how he can blame you for this."

"He'll find a way."

"Jeezus."

"Yeah, him too."

"Well, you still oughta answer it."

"Too late," I said. "It's not ringing anymore."

"Then you should call 'im back."

"I'd rather not."

"You should work it out, white man."

I looked across at my friend, and I know the expression on my face had to be a mix of surprise and disbelief. He shot a glance my way then did a double take as I continued to stare at him mutely.

"What?" he finally asked.

"Just getting a good look at the hypocrite behind the wheel is all," I replied.

"Do what?"

"You," I continued. "I can't believe that you of all people are telling me how to handle my personal relationships."

He caught on immediately to my inference. "That's different. You don't know the whole story."

"And neither do you."

"Fine. Fuckit," he spat. "So don't talk to 'im."

"I don't plan to."

"I was just sayin' it might have somethin' ta' do with Firehair."

I didn't respond. Getting into an argument with him wasn't going to help the current situation, and besides, I simply didn't feel like it. The earlier funk hadn't fled; in fact, in light of the conversation, it seemed like it might even be getting worse. It was rattling around inside my head as if waiting patiently for me to return to its fold. I tried to tell myself to run from it, but to be honest I didn't see any chance of escape.

And, of course, the more I fought it, the sicker I felt.

"What happens now?" I finally asked.

"I guess we burn a lotta gas," my friend replied. "Unless I can talk ya' into waitin' at home until we hear somethin'."

"I don't know," I mumbled. "Maybe."

"Did you just say maybe?"

"Yeah. I did."

"Okay, so now I know somethin's fucked up," he returned. "You aren't seriously sayin' you'd be willin' ta' go home and wait, are ya'?"

"I don't know, Ben," I replied. "I just don't know anymore."

"What gives, Row?"

"I'm tired."

"Me too, white man," he said. "But, somethin' ain't right with you, and it's not because you're tired."

The nagging doubt bubbled to the surface, and I found suddenly that I could no longer contain it. "What if I'm wrong?" I blurted.

"Wrong about what?"

"About Felicity."

"You're not."

"You're the one who questioned me about where she was…"

"I'm the one who repeated something because I had no choice, Rowan," he snapped. "Don't read anything into it."

"But you said you weren't so sure you didn't agree with them."

"So I fucked up," he replied. "I didn't mean it."

"But…"

"But nothin'," he returned. "Is that what's botherin' you? You're doubtin' yourself?"

I didn't reply.

"Answer me!"

"Yes, dammit!" I spat. "Obviously, I'm not as in tune as I used to be. Maybe I've lost it. Maybe I'm wrong about all of this!"

"That shit at the crime scene was Voodoo stuff. You're sure about that, right?"

"Yes."

"Firehair was talkin' with a Southern accent, right?"

"Yes, but…"

"Shut up! She's not actin' like herself at all, right?"

"Yes."

"You ain't wrong then."

"I just don't know anymore, Ben," I appealed.

"You got a headache?"

"Why?"

"Just fuckin' answer me. You got a headache?"

"Yes."

"Is it one of those la-la headaches?"

"I think so."

"There ya' go."

"There I go what?"

"Somethin's fuckin' with you, Row." His voice was filled with unshakable confidence. "Just like it's fuckin' with Felicity. Now don't let it win."

The first strains of the "William Tell Overture" began chirping through the cab of the van, and my hand went into my pocket out of reflex. The minute I wrapped my fingers around the cell phone, however, I started shaking my head.

"It's probably my father-in-law again," I said aloud.

"That was pretty quick for a call back," Ben replied. "Maybe it really is important."

I pulled the phone out and looked once again to the LCD, but this time I was greeted with a wholly unfamiliar number. The first thought to go through my head was that all I needed right now was a client with a software problem. I considered letting it go to voice mail but then thumbed the answer button anyway and pressed it against my ear.

"Gant," I barked into the device.

I heard shuffling at the other end followed by what might have been sobbing.

"Hello?" I spoke again.

"*Caorthann?*" Felicity's thick Celtic brogue came across the speaker in a pained whisper as she uttered my name in Gaelic.

"Felicity?!" I yelped.

"...Help me, Rowan," she whimpered again.

All I could make out through the choked sobs that followed were the words "I think I killed him."

CHAPTER 33:

The magnetic bubble light was once again laying down its flickering red glow in front of the speeding van as we headed east. As soon as we knew where we needed to go, my friend had quickly exited the highway, looped us through various mid-town side streets, then jumped onto 40 once again and pointed us back toward Illinois.

"NO!" Ben stressed the objection loudly into his cell phone. "Absolutely not... No, I don't give a fuck... I'm tellin' ya', don't call 'er... Let me handle this... Yeah..."

I tuned out his side of the conversation and focused my attention toward my own cell. Felicity was still on the line with me but hadn't said more than a dozen words in the past five minutes. Even though I continued to speak, trying to calm her, all I could get from the other end was frightened sobbing and an occasional "yes" whenever I asked her if she was still there.

"Felicity, talk to me," I appealed.

Her only audible answer came in the form of a hard sob, punctuated by a pleading whine that sounded like "What's happening to me?"

At this point, we didn't know what the full situation really was. After the initial shock of her call had subsided, I had begun questioning my wife as to her whereabouts. At first all she seemed to be able to do was sob, but I eventually got her to tell me that she was in a bathroom. The sound of her voice made me conjure images of her cowering in a corner, and that only served to make the painful hollowness return to my chest.

After much gentle urging, I had managed to coax her out of the bathroom long enough to tell me she was in what appeared to be a motel room. Ben tried having the call traced, but we only found that she was using a cell belonging to the individual with whom she had left the club. While they worked on pinpointing her location via the cell towers, I continued to do the only thing I could—talk to her.

It took me another five minutes, but I did convince her that she needed to leave the bathroom once again and look for something that would tell her the name of the motel. I found quickly that I was damning myself for putting her through it as I listened to her hyperventilate and weep while she moved through the room. Fortunately, it wasn't in vain, as she eventually came up with the needed information from the room key before audibly scrambling back into the perceived safety of the bathroom. I wasn't particularly surprised that the number she squeaked out happened to be seven.

While I suspected the numeral held a greater meaning for the killer, I had a terribly sick feeling that it was going to say something entirely different to the police investigating the killing spree. After what Ben had told me earlier, I had no choice but to believe there would be a tremendous amount of significance placed on that fact in an attempt to tie my wife to the murders.

Once we had the name of the motel, Ben had made a quick call and determined that it was a dive known for cheap hourly rates and a guest register full of Smith's and Jones'. On top of that, it was back across the river and only a mile or so from the club we had recently left. In fact, we had to have driven past it, both on the way there and back.

The only other thing I had been able to glean from the mostly one-sided conversation with my wife was that apparently, Brad Lewis was in the room with her. At least, that was our assumption. All I could ever really make out was that someone was there, that she believed "he" was dead; and moreover, that she had been responsible for his death. I was hoping that she was wrong, but the fact that she probably still had Constance's sidearm was making my stomach twist into a knot. While I had relayed the information to Ben, he hadn't let it go any further. I didn't know why he was keeping it to himself, but I appreciated the discretion.

All in all, I counted us lucky to have gotten as much as we did. Felicity seemed on the verge of absolute hysterics at one moment, only to shift into quiet sobbing the next. It was painfully obvious that she was completely disoriented, not to mention scared out of her wits. I couldn't truly imagine what she must be going through at the moment, but my brain was definitely barraging me with a host of emotions that I was desperately trying to ignore.

I also didn't even want to consider imagining what she might have done. Even if I discounted the firearm, I felt little comfort, as there were many other ways to take a life.

Of course, we don't always get what we want, and unlike the song says, we don't necessarily get what we need either. Since my brain was already stuck in overdrive with the emotional attack, it began generating horrific scenarios to add to the torturous mix. And, no matter how hard I tried to discount each of them, they still played out inside my head with agonizing repetition.

Not knowing what this Lewis individual actually looked like other than a brief description, my mind's eye did the best it could with the imagery at hand. Unfortunately, what that meant was that I kept seeing Officer Hobbes' lifeless, mutilated body with my wife standing over it. And, every time I saw the flash of her face, she was wearing the wicked grin I had seen twisting her features earlier in the day. I fought hard to deny the image, but it soon became the only thing I saw each and every time I blinked.

As if the torment my psyche was doling out wasn't enough, frustration was coursing through me like a heavy static charge. The anxiety was so high that I could barely remain still in my seat. A voice in my head kept telling me that I needed to be with Felicity right now, this moment. I knew without a doubt that this time the voice was my own.

I wanted to hold my wife in my arms and protect her. I wanted to make all of this just go away. Unfortunately, the voice also kept telling me that the last half of my "want" simply wasn't going to happen. Whatever had occurred during the past few hours was going to be with us for a long time to come, probably even forever.

Whether it was a word, the Gods, or simply luck, I don't know. But, whatever the subconscious trigger was, something suddenly drew me out of my introspection and tuned me back into the conversation going on beside me.

"…Yeah," Ben said again, still talking into his cell. "Better get an ambulance… Good… No, I don't know… Yeah, guess you better call the coroner too, just in case… Yeah, we'll be there in less than five… Yeah…"

"Hold on, honey," I said into my phone. "We're almost there."

The only response I received was the sound of her nasal whimpering, but at least that told me she was still at the other end.

"What's happening?" I asked my friend as I cocked the cell away from my mouth.

"Ackman just pulled into the parking lot, and Osthoff's on 'is way," he replied, naming off two members of the MCS. "Ther're also a coupl'a uniforms on scene already."

"Don't let them hurt her," I appealed.

"Right now they're waitin' on us, Row," he replied. "I told 'em not to go in until we got there."

"You're sure they won't?"

"Right now they're just watchin' the door and waitin' for us," he tried to reassure me. "Ackman's gonna talk to the clerk and watch for the ambulance."

"Don't let them hurt her, Ben," I said again.

"Row…" he started then paused.

My voice slipped into a frightened plea. "Promise me."

My friend sighed heavily then finally said, "Yeah… I won't let 'em."

A frigid chill ran the length of my spine. I knew his clipped reply was meant only to placate me for the moment. Logically, I realized that there were still far too many unknowns at work for him to truly be able to make such a guarantee.

Emotionally, however, I just didn't care. I wanted her safe, no matter what the cost.

"She still on the line?" he asked after a long moment of silence.

"Yeah," I muttered.

"How is she?"

"Scared" was my initial reply. I followed it a split second later with "And confused."

"Yeah," he replied.

"Not dangerous," I stressed.

"Yeah, I know."

I waited in silence for what was most likely a full minute then asked, "What's going to happen, Ben?"

"I don't know yet."

"You've got to know something."

"This isn't the time, Row."

"Dammit, Ben," I said, but the words came out only as a fearful whisper. "You promised."

I put my hand against the console and stiffened my arm to brace myself as my friend whipped the van through the cloverleaf and back onto Route 3 for the third time tonight. Two impossibly drawn out minutes later, he turned into the parking lot of the aptly named Route Three Motel.

"Honey, we just pulled in," I said into my phone.

"Help me, Rowan..." she cried.

"What the..." Ben yelped suddenly as we rounded the end of the L-shaped building and came into view of the front of the motel.

What had originally been described to us as "a couple of uniforms" had drastically increased in that it now took the form of four Illinois state police vehicles and a county sheriff's patrol car. Mixed in with the marked cruisers were several plain sedans sporting emergency lights similar to Ben's. The face of the small building was lit up by an insane jumble of headlamps and flickering light bars. The chaotic luminance was enough to drive even a non-epileptic into a seizure.

The most frightening part of the tableau, however, was the bustle of activity among the individuals surrounding the wedge of vehicles. With a single glance I counted at least three shotguns and what appeared to be a sniper rifle.

"Goddammit, Ben!" I half-screamed.

"Calm down!" he barked in return. "I'm gonna handle it!"

"Felicity!" I said into my phone with a panicked urgency. "Stay right where you are! Lay down on the floor and don't move. Do you hear me? Don't move, just lay down and don't move!"

Ben pulled up to the scene and cranked the gearshift up hard, slamming the van into park even as he was applying the brakes. Before the vehicle had even stopped swaying, he swung his door open and jumped out. I was no more than two seconds behind him, but I could hear his voice already bellowing before I even made it around the front corner of the Chevy.

"What the fuck is going on here?!" he demanded.

"The locals," a sandy-haired man I recognized as Detective Ackman was replying as I came up next to my friend. "They started pulling in as soon as I got off the phone with you."

"What the hell do they think they're doin'?" Ben asked with a hard shake of his head.

"It's the Feeb's gun," Ackman replied. "They're treating this like a hostage situation."

"Goddammit!" my friend spat as he finished slipping his badge onto a heavy cord then hung it around his neck. "Why didn't you shut 'em down?"

"I tried, but there's a county sheriff on scene taking over."

"Jeezus..."

"Yeah, tell me about it."

"Didn't you tell 'im this was under a Major Case investigation?"

"Yeah, and he said he already knew that."

"Already knew... Then what the... Screw it, where the hell is he?"

Ackman pointed across the top of the squad cars. "Over there. Grey hair, blue jacket."

"Come on," Ben barked, starting around the van in the direction of the individual who had just been singled out.

I followed at a near jog, still keeping the cell phone pressed to my ear, although I couldn't hear much of anything over the noise of the bustling scene. Detective Ackman had to quicken his pace as well, just to keep up with my friend's long-legged gait.

"I better warn you, Storm," he said as he strode along with us. "This guy dropped Albright's name."

"Dropped it how?"

"Like maybe he's been in touch with her recently."

"You think she's directin' this?"

"I don't know. Maybe."

"Fuck me."

As much as my brain was screaming for me to plead with all of them to not hurt my wife, I managed to keep my mouth shut. Right now, Ben was my only hope in this and I knew it. I had to let him at least try to keep his promise, frail though it was.

My eyes were darting about, taking stock of the level of preparation. The comment I had earlier made to my friend about cops with itchy trigger fingers leapt back to the forefront of my thoughts, and it instantly made the hair on the back of my neck pivot upward. Everywhere I looked there was someone wrapped in a bulletproof vest and brandishing something lethal. In fact, the least threatening firearm I saw was a teargas gun.

When we were only a few yards away from the sheriff, Ben called out, "Hey, we need ta' talk."

The man turned toward us and immediately showed more than a simple glimmer of recognition. In fact, it appeared as though he was expecting us. Still, the look on his face became even harder in that very instant when he saw me.

I'm sure my own expression had to be no better because as it happened, I was just as familiar with him as he obviously was with me. He was just the last person I had expected to see, especially here. My heart fluttered in my throat the moment my eyes met his then thudded back down into my chest and began to pound viciously as the blood rushed in my ears.

The sheriff centered his gaze on my face as we took the last few steps then came to a halt in front of him.

Until now, I never knew what had actually happened to Detective Arthur McCann. All I could say was that my last run-in with him had been at least five years ago. After that, he had all but fallen off the face of the earth. I'd heard rumors of him retiring, and even one that he had been fired. To be honest I didn't particularly care one way or the other. Either of those options was fine by me as long as he was no longer packing a badge. Unfortunately, he quite obviously still was.

My experiences with the man had been less than pleasant but still not as bad as it had been for some other Pagans I knew. In brief, McCann was a self-proclaimed expert on the occult who had made it his mission in life to campaign against anything non-Judeo-Christian. Those personal crusades had often included the unwarranted hassling of Saint Louis area Pagans and alternative religious organizations from behind the auspices of his official shield.

While Barbara Albright had stepped in to fill the void he left, I wasn't actually sure just which one of them I would consider more dangerous. Either way, it didn't matter now because they had apparently been in touch with one another, and that was even worse. Of course, I suppose I really shouldn't have been surprised.

Planting his hands on his hips, McCann glowered at me for a moment then looked over to Ben.

"Detective Storm," he said. "I think you need to get Mister Gant out of here now, or I will have him removed myself."

CHAPTER 34:

It was taking all I had to keep myself from simply sprinting straight
for the door of room number seven. Ever since arriving on the
scene, my gut kept telling me to do it, and my head staunchly objected.
Something was telling me that I was going to end up in the back of a
squad car before this was all over; but, if that was the way it was going
to be, I wanted to at least be sure Felicity was safe first. Getting myself
locked down before she was ever out of the room wasn't going to help
me do that. Even so, all the logic in the world didn't keep the itch from
spreading.

Ben knew me well enough that he made it a point to position
himself between the motel and me. He had seen me make a mad dash
before, and it was obvious from the furtive glances he kept throwing
my direction that he was fully expecting me to do so this time.

"Gimme a break, McCann," my friend said to the sheriff as he
divided his attention between the two of us.

Ben was no stranger to this man's exploits either. In fact, he
had even been front and center when McCann had vociferously
recused himself from working with the MCS simply because of my
involvement with a case.

"I am," McCann returned. "I'm giving you a chance to get him
out of here before I arrest him for interfering with an ongoing
investigation."

"Jeezus," Ben spat. "You know that's a load of bullshit."

"Not in my county it isn't."

"You're a freakin' cartoon, you know that?"

"I can have you removed as well, Detective."

"Goddammit, Arthur, why didn't you just fuckin' stay retired?"

"There's no call for that sort of language, Detective Storm," he
replied. "Now, you've got two minutes to get Mister Gant out of here
or I have him arrested."

I instantly spoke up. "That's my wife in there!"

"Shut up, Rowan," Ben ordered as he gave me a sharp look then leveled his gaze back on McCann. "And, you, get off your high horse. You ain't arrestin' anybody, and you sure's hell ain't havin' me removed. This is a Major Case investigation, and as of now I'm taking over the scene."

"No sir, you are not," McCann replied.

"Yes sir, I am," my friend returned.

"I am the ranking officer on the scene, Detective Storm, and I will have you know that you are currently standing in the middle of my jurisdiction."

"Whupty-fuckin'-doo," my friend huffed. "Your county a participatin' agency with the MCS?"

"Yes, as a matter of fact it is."

"Good. Are you assigned ta' this case?"

"No, but…"

"Ain't no buts to it," Ben snapped. "You're not assigned to the case, so back off and let me handle it."

"I'm still the ranking officer on the scene," McCann objected.

"Maybe so, but I'm the ranking detective assigned to Major Case that's here now. So, like I said, this investigation belongs to us, and so does this scene…"

"Like hell it does," a fresh, but very familiar voice came from behind us.

I turned to see Agent Drew standing only a few paces away, and a wave of nausea swept over me. It seemed as though the situation simply wasn't finished with its downhill slide. I had thought that when we arrived here things would start to look up, but that belief had been dashed against the rocks as soon as I saw McCann. Now, with the arrival of the cocky FBI agent, I felt as though the current was pulling me under and holding me there.

"And just who are you?" McCann snarled at him.

The young man opened his ID with a practiced flip and thrust it out as he stepped forward. "Agent Drew, Federal Bureau of Investigation, and you are?"

"Arthur McCann. I'm the county sheriff."

"Well, Sheriff, I'm afraid you are both wrong. This is a federal investigation now and I am taking over the scene."

"Jeezus, Drew..." Ben started.

"Shut up, Storm," he interrupted. "You know I'm right. Federal law grants investigative jurisdiction to the FBI in cases of assault on a federal officer. I won't even go into interstate flight to avoid apprehension."

"That's not why..." I started.

"Can it, Gant," he snipped.

"Look, Agent Drew," McCann began to object. "I've already been in touch with Captain Albright, and..."

"So have we," Drew interrupted him again. "And she had little choice but to agree with us this time. Now, like I said, the Bureau is running this scene, whether you like it or not."

"I don't," McCann spat.

"I'm afraid you'll just have to get over it," Drew replied. "Now, the first thing I want you to do is have your men stand down and back off."

"But..."

"But nothing," he snapped. "Tell them it's time to quit playing army, and put the guns away before someone gets hurt. We'll handle this."

"Who is your superior?" McCann demanded with a sudden rush of anger. "I don't much care for your attitude, and I'm not moving anyone until I know for sure what is going on here."

"Sheriff McCann, I don't mind telling you that I'm not overly impressed with your attitude either," Drew chided. "However, if it will hasten your cooperation and make you dispense with the bullshit, my

SAC's name is Simpson. And, I wouldn't be a bit surprised if he is expecting your call."

"You wait right here," McCann replied, repeatedly stabbing his finger at a point on the ground. "All of you. I'll be right back."

"We'll be here," Drew said with a nod.

Sheriff McCann stalked off toward one of the unmarked cars in the distance. As he picked up his pace he shouted, "George! Get me the FBI on the phone. Right now!"

We watched him in relative silence for several paces then Ben turned his attention back toward Agent Drew. "Look, I know you got jurisdiction here, but listen to me…"

"Calm down, Storm," Drew insisted.

"I'll calm down when I'm damn good 'n ready to," my friend snapped. "But right now you need ta' listen ta' me."

"Agent Drew," I interjected in a pleading tone. "This is my wife we're talking about here."

"I'm well aware of that, Mister Gant."

"Goddammit, Skippy…"

Drew held up a finger to cut Ben off and snarled, "Stop it! Stop it right now. My name is Drew, got it? Drew, not Skippy. Not Junior. It's Drew."

"Yeah, whatever." Ben brushed him off.

"Dammit, Storm, can you just try cooperating with someone other than yourself for a change?"

"I try not ta' cooperate with people I don't trust."

"Well, you're just going to have to trust me."

"That's gonna be kinda hard."

"Yeah, well I've got faith in you. Now before you get your shorts any more in a bunch, you need to shut up and listen to *me* for a minute. I'm the best friend you've got here right now, so just calm down, back off, and let me handle this."

Ben shook his head and gave him an incredulous stare. "Oh yeah? Well, if *you're* my best friend then I'm seriously fucked."

"You won't get any argument from me there, Storm, but not for the reasons you're thinking."

"Okay, so you wanna explain it to me?"

"What, the fact that I can't stand you?"

"Feeling's mutual, but no, Agent Drew." Ben stressed his name in a mocking fashion. "I wanna know just how the hell you figure you're my best friend?"

"Because I'm getting this wound-up local off your back, for one."

"Yeah, well thanks for that," Ben gave a shallow nod as he replied, a note of chagrin in his voice. "But, you still need to let me handle the rest of this."

"I'm afraid I can't do that, and you know it."

"This isn't what you think it is," I blurted, unable to contain myself.

Drew turned his attention toward me. "Look, Mister Gant, I understand your frustration here, but the fact remains that your wife assaulted a federal officer and fled with her sidearm."

"It's not what you think," I appealed.

"Mister Gant, listen to me," he said with a sigh. "Believe it or not, I'm on your side here. I'm trying to help."

"Coulda fooled me," Ben interjected.

"That doesn't sound like it's all that tough," Drew chided.

"Uh-huh," my friend grunted. "So, how is it you're bein' so helpful then?"

"By defusing the situation, hopefully."

"Okay, so why?" Ben pressed.

"Mandalay called Simpson, and then me personally," he replied. "She wants Miz O'Brien out of this situation safely, just as much as either of you. And, don't ask me why, but she wants to see if this can be made to go away."

"You mean…"

Drew nodded. "Yeah, she's got a little pull, so if no one gets hurt then maybe there can be a deal."

Any elation I might have felt because of the news was immediately doused by the memory of my wife's pained voice saying, "I think I killed him."

I tried my best to force the thought from my head and moved forward with a question. "Did she tell you about her..."

"Being possessed?" he finished for me, raising his eyebrows questioningly. "Yeah, she did, and honestly, I think that it's a crock of shit."

"But..."

He held up a hand to stop me. "Hold on. I said I think it's a crock, but that isn't going to affect the situation. Not only does Agent Mandalay want to see this resolved peacefully, so does the Bureau."

"What about you?" I asked.

"I know I haven't made a friend of you, Mister Gant, and honestly, I don't really care if I ever do," he said with a shrug. "But, yes, I would rather not see your wife get hurt, or anyone else for that matter."

Ackman had remained quiet for the duration but now broke his self-imposed silence. "Okay, so, what is your plan?"

Drew shot him a glance. "Once I get this local asshole to back off, the three of us are going to see if we can get Miz O'Brien to come out and surrender."

"Four," I insisted.

"No sir," Drew replied. "Three. You're staying out here behind the line."

"He's right, Row," Ben agreed.

"Felicity is..."

"Felicity is gonna be fine," he snapped. "And, you're gonna do what you're told for a change."

"Dammit, Ben," I objected.

"Damn me all ya' want," he said with a shake of his head. "You're stayin' out here, Row."

I cast a glance past him toward the motel room door. My eyes searched the expanse of parking lot as I tried to estimate the distance between us and number seven. All the while my brain was calculating exactly what it was going to take for me to get there without being stopped instantly. The one thing I forgot, however, was my poker face. Apparently, I was broadcasting my intentions like a high wattage transmitter because a large hand suddenly clamped onto my shoulder and held fast.

"Don't even think about it, white man," Ben told me as he leveled a deadly serious gaze on my face.

"What?" I asked, trying unsuccessfully to feign ignorance.

"Yeah, right," he grunted but didn't let go.

During the thread of conversations, I had dropped my hand to my side and with it the cell phone. The fact that Felicity was still holding on now skittered back through my thoughts. I lifted the cell and placed it against my ear.

"Felicity?"

"Y-y-yes?" her halting voice issued from the small speaker. "Where are you?"

Her sobbing had lessened greatly, but I could still detect her whimpering as she waited for my response. It was killing me to hear her like this. She had always been so steadfast in the face of almost anything. For her to now sound like a terrified child was just too much for me to bear.

"It's almost over, honey," I told her, hoping that I could mask my own lack of conviction.

"I'm scared, *Caorthann*..." she whined. "I don't know what's happening to me..."

"I know," I soothed. "It's going to be okay. Trust me."

"Is that your wife?" Drew asked, pointing toward the phone in my hand.

I nodded. "Yes."

"Let me talk to her," he replied, motioning for me to hand the device over.

"She's in no condition to carry on a conversation with you right now, Agent Drew," I declared, twisting the mouthpiece away.

"Just what is her situation then?" he asked.

"She's frightened," I replied.

"She should be," he asserted. "What about the man she left the club with?"

"How'd you know about him?" Ben asked.

"News travels fast," he replied.

"So, is that how you knew where this was goin' down so quick?"

"We've been paying attention," Drew replied with a nod to the affirmative. "Besides, one of our agents was assaulted, and like I said, we have jurisdiction. You didn't really think the Bureau was going to leave this up to the locals, did you?"

"Looks like you let us do most of the legwork."

"Of course. It was the most efficient way to handle the situation."

"Fuckin' Feebs," Ben muttered, just loud enough for him to hear.

Without missing a beat, Drew replied, "Fuckin' cops," then turned his attention back to me. "What about Mister Lewis? It would be a really good thing if you could tell me that she is not holding him hostage."

I didn't reply. I wasn't entirely sure what to say.

"Mister Gant?" Drew pressed.

Ben reached up and started working the muscles on the back of his neck as he announced, "Look, the thing is we don't know his condition for sure."

"Condition?"

"Dammit," my friend muttered then looked up to the FBI agent and blurted, "Look, we haven't told anyone this yet, so don't go off half-cocked... Felicity told Rowan she thinks he's dead."

Drew looked at the ground and shook his head then cast a glance at the other officers on the scene. Looking back up at us, he gave Ben a nod. "Probably good you kept that to yourself, considering... So... Did she use Agent Mandalay's weapon?"

"We don't know," Ben replied. "Truth is we don't even know if he's really dead. Remember, she said she *thinks* he's dead."

"But if she shot him," Drew offered, leaving the conclusion unspoken.

"Like I said, we don't know."

"Then what makes her think he's dead?"

"Don't know."

"Have you asked her?"

"No. She's been a bit hysterical," I offered before Ben could answer.

He thrust his chin toward the phone. "Then ask her."

"I don't think..." I started.

"Mister Gant, please ask her. Trust me. I'm just trying to help."

I sighed heavily then twisted the phone back to my mouth. "Felicity?"

"Y-y-yes..."

"I need to ask you a question, sweetheart," I said, continuing my prolific use of endearments as a tool to keep her connected with me.

"I-I... I thought you were here..." she murmured. "Where are you?"

"I am, honey. Now I need you to answer something for me."

"W-w-what?"

"The man in the room..."

The moment I said the words, her whimpering increased, and I could hear her breathing become more rapid.

"Honey... Calm down..." I tried to soothe her. "I just need you to tell me something."

"W-w-what?" she whined.

I closed my eyes and tried to ground the sudden panic that was welling up from my stomach, but I knew that it was no use. My wife's emotional pain was now expanding beyond the bounds of the room, and I was caught up in its wake. After a long pause, I sighed and mumbled, "Nothing. Nothing. Just stay where you are right now."

"W-w-why? I thought you were here… Where are you?"

"I am, honey, I am… Just hold on. I'll see you soon."

"Mister Gant…" Drew began.

"Forget it," I returned with a hard shake of my head. "I'm not going to ask her. She's distraught and confused enough as it is. I know you don't believe what's happened, but I do, and I'm telling you she can't answer this question right now."

He stared back at me with a grim frown slashed across the lower half of his face. I was fully expecting him to launch into an authoritative diatribe telling me to ask her or else, but after a moment he simply nodded.

"Okay," he said. "I understand. Let me ask you this. Do you think she will come out and surrender?"

"Probably," I said with a nod of my head. "But I'm not going to ask her to do that with all this firepower pointed at her."

"I'm working on that," he replied.

"Yeah, and it looks like you won that round," Ben announced.

"What?"

My friend nodded past him and he turned. I was already looking in that direction but only now took notice that some of the cars on the parking lot were beginning to move. As I watched, it didn't escape my attention that while there were still flak-vested officers running about, the bulk of their activity involved stowing weaponry and backing off.

Arthur McCann was stomping toward us with an angry gait, his form silhouetted off and on by the flash of headlights and light bars as vehicles whipped around one another. We stood waiting for him until he came to a halt in front of us and planted his hands on his hips once again.

"Okay, Agent Drew, the scene is apparently yours," McCann spat.

"Thank you, Sheriff," Drew replied. "I appreciate your cooperation."

"Yes, well I seriously doubt that you're going to appreciate this," he shot back. "Your SAC agreed with me that Mister Gant is to be removed from the scene immediately."

"Okay," Drew said with a nod. "That's fine."

McCann fell speechless for a moment as he stared at him, obviously taken aback by the young man's unfettered agreement.

"Good," he finally said.

"Anything else?" Drew asked.

"Not that would interest you," the sheriff replied then turned his attention to Ben. "But, you might want to know, Detective Storm, that I've filed a formal complaint against you with both the Major Case Squad commander and Saint Louis City Homicide."

Ben glared back at him and shook his head as he replied, "Join the fuckin' club, McCann. Join the fuckin' club."

"Honey, I'm going to hand the phone over to Ben," I said, speaking up to be heard over the thudding echoes of the news helicopters above. They were hovering far closer than I would have liked, but there was little I could do about it other than try to ignore them.

"Okay," Felicity whimpered in return, her voice barely audible.

The contingent of officers had dutifully backed off as they had been ordered, but the tension among their ranks was still running at full bore. The fact that in a handful of heartbeats I was going to be sent back to mill about among them did little to allay my own anxiety.

"I love you," I said then listened to her faint response before I pulled the cell away from my ear.

I stood there staring at the device for a long moment before hesitantly holding it out toward Ben. I couldn't help but see what I was doing as surrendering my only physically tangible connection to my wife. In a very real sense, it made me feel as though I was abandoning her.

My friend gave me an understanding nod as he took the phone from me and placed it up to his own ear.

"Heya, Firehair," he said in as soothing a tone as he could muster under the circumstances.

After he stood listening for a moment, he spoke again, "Yeah, I know... It's all gonna be over soon... Well, that's because you've done some things that aren't so good... Yes... Yes, I'm afraid so... I know... That's why I'm here... Now, listen carefully. I need ta' tell ya' how we're gonna handle this..."

Detective Ackman took me by the arm and started leading me back toward the barrier of vehicles. I didn't resist, instead I simply trudged along on autopilot as I twisted my head and continued looking back at Ben.

"Don't worry, Mister Gant," he said to me. "We're going to take care of her."

"This has gotten completely out of hand," I managed to reply.

"Yeah, it has," he agreed. "But we're trying to fix that."

"You should just let me go in there."

"We can't do that."

"I know... But, you still should."

"Listen, Mister Gant," he began. "You need to understand that your wife is going to be arrested."

"I know that."

"I mean she is going to be arrested right now," he stressed. "When she comes out, she is going to be cuffed immediately."

"Don't hurt her."

"We don't want to."

All I could do was repeat my three-word appeal.

CHAPTER 35:

It seemed as though an entire decade passed before the door of the motel room even moved. And, when it finally did, it was barely perceptible, simply appearing as the sudden jump of a shadow across its whitewashed face. In fact, since it was so quick and wasn't followed by any other movement, I began to wonder if it was only my eyes playing tricks on me.

I went ahead and blinked. It was something I probably hadn't done for several minutes. Nothing changed, so I blinked again.

As it turned out, I hadn't been completely removed from the scene, as McCann wanted. Still, since I was now parked in the back of a squad car, I was about as far from the action as I could get. I'm not sure who was responsible for ordering me placed here, but I suspected that there hadn't been a single objection to it, not even from Ben.

I continued watching through the window, trying not to exhale against the chilled glass so as to avoid the obscuring fog. It was rapidly becoming a losing battle, and after wiping my sleeve against the frosted surface more than once, I had taken to holding my breath rather than look away.

My stomach was roiling with fear. The nagging trepidation told me that I didn't want to watch for fear of witnessing something I wouldn't be able to bear. Still, I was unable to avert my gaze; no matter how hard I tried. In fact, I had even begun telling myself that as long as I was watching, nothing bad could happen.

The police radio in the front of the patrol car burped with a blast of static, followed by voices exchanging meaningless information—well, meaningless to me, at least. All that mattered right now in my world was Felicity and her safety. Everything else was moot.

The jump of the shadow was finally followed by a slow drifting motion as the panel of muted darkness elongated and spread. It continued to become more oblique with each passing second, until it completely consumed the opening.

Detective Ackman, Agent Drew, and Ben were all positioned strategically around the room's entrance, weapons at the ready. I could somewhat understand Ackman and Drew. They didn't know Felicity. They couldn't understand what was really going on and that she posed no threat.

But, the fact that my friend's hand was also filled with a pistol made me physically ill. Deep inside I wanted to despise him for it. I just hoped that the dark feeling was something I would be able to get over.

I kept staring at the doorway, now fully open. Dim yellow light spilled outward, only to be immediately consumed by the harsh glare of the spotlights directed toward the front of the building.

A new shadow began to move in the framed opening, and I saw Felicity step forward to the threshold. Even at this distance, I could make out a wealth of detail, and I could see that her face was painted with a heavier than usual application of makeup. Considering both that and the harsh shadows, I almost wouldn't have recognized her, save for her petite build and fiery mane of auburn hair. Still, I knew the person standing there was my wife, and I could see the fear twisting her face as she trembled.

She was clad in all black, not that there was much of it mind you; it was a stark contrast against her ivory skin. Of course, the ensemble was obviously intended to be the trappings of the dominatrix persona who had possessed her, and it certainly succeeded, consisting of no more than a flared miniskirt, cropped mesh top, thigh high stockings, and stiletto heels.

I watched her, unblinking, as the blood began rushing in my ears. My heart was pumping furiously, driving against my ribcage at an ever-quickening pace. Of course, I'm sure the fact that I still hadn't taken a breath wasn't helping in the least.

Felicity moved forward slowly then hesitated. My eyes darted about, and though I couldn't hear him, I could see that Ben's lips were moving as he instructed her on what to do.

The rapid thud in my chest ramped upward, strove toward a summit, and upon reaching the peak, began to turn back in on itself. Harsh light bloomed in front of me, washing color in and out of the scene as my heartbeat became an off-balance metronome ticking along a wholly different timeline from the rest of the world.

The radio in the front of the vehicle stuttered once again, but this time it became a droning mix of unintelligible noise. The sound slid past my ears in a stream of Doppler distorted gibberish.

Felicity finally moved again, coming forward with fluid lethargy, as my world transformed into a slow motion video clip. She was now standing only a few paces in front of the doorway, and Ben's mouth began moving again as he held his Beretta pointed at her back. My gaze remained frozen on that single point as my wife's arms started floating upward through a protracted arc.

I stared hard at the pistol in my friend's hands then to the weapons held by Ackman and Drew. Bile seared up my throat and I swallowed hard.

My eyes were beginning to burn as they dried, but I forced them to stay open. I simply could not blink until this was over. If I did, I would break the spell. And, if I broke the spell, something bad would happen.

My wife's arms finally came perpendicular to the rest of her body, then they began folding inward with the same hurtful torpidity. A handful of seconds transformed into what seemed like minutes before her hands landed firmly atop her head, and she began to ooze downward onto her knees. Ben was now in motion, moving in behind her and holstering his sidearm as she knelt. With equal lethargy he brought his hand up and placed it on top of hers. In his other hand I saw the light glint from the shiny metal of the handcuffs as he slapped them against her dainty wrist.

Detective Ackman was already going through the door of the motel room, pistol stiff-armed before him as he skirted behind Ben. Agent Drew was continuing to hold his weapon pointed at my wife as my friend pulled one of her arms down behind her back, then the other, each with painfully unnatural slowness.

A discordant rhythm suddenly began to rattle around me, driving into my skull and threatening to shatter my eardrums. The tableau beyond the window shifted in that instant, making the leap from slow motion to real time, and I watched Ben placing my wife face down on the sidewalk.

Detective Ackman came back out of the door and said something to Agent Drew as they were both holstering their own sidearms. Drew looked toward the emergency vehicles and began gesturing quickly as he beckoned someone.

The crescendo continued unabated, transforming from merely discordant to horrifically painful.

Sharp agony started biting into my shoulder from nowhere, disappearing one moment, only to return the next. My hands were beginning to ache, and I was almost certain that what felt like a blow had just landed against my forehead. I had no clue from where the sudden attack was coming; I only knew that I refused to succumb. Even as the pain continued, the scene before me began fading into obscurity behind a bloom of frosty white.

The deafening noise warbled into nothingness, then returned anew, immediately on the heels of the dying sound.

It was at that moment, I realized that the pain I felt was the product of me slamming my own body against the locked door of the squad car in a futile attempt to reach Felicity.

And, the ghastly wail was none other than my own voice screaming out her name.

Thursday, November 10
8:27 A.M.
FBI Field Office
Saint Louis, Missouri

CHAPTER 36:

I thought I heard a noise, but given that it was so quiet in the room and the sound itself had been so soft, I wasn't really certain. I thought it might simply be my imagination. Since it didn't seem particularly important, I just ignored it. Instead, I continued staring at the blob of metal bits that made up the magnetic sculpture sitting on the edge of the desk in front of me, absently pondering just exactly what the current shape was meant to be.

I couldn't remember the last time I had slept, and while my body was screaming at me to allow it to shut down, I staunchly refused. Although I am sure that to the outside world I looked like I had slipped into a vegetative state, I actually had a singular mission in mind, and it required that I remain conscious.

A louder noise eventually followed the first, but I disregarded it too. Apparently, it didn't want to be ignored, so it poked me in the eardrum once again, sharper and louder. This time I had no choice but to take notice of a looming presence at my side. I broke my stare away from the desk art and turned my face upward.

Initially, I couldn't muster anything more than a questioning grunt of "Huh?"

Ben looked down at me and asked, "I said, do ya' want some more coffee?"

I glanced down at my hands and noticed that they were fiddling with a Styrofoam cup, moving deliberately but completely of their own accord. Then, I looked back up to him. "No. What I want is to see my wife."

"I've been workin' on it."

"You've been sitting here with me."

"No, I've been gone for twenty minutes, Row."

"You were?"

"Yeah."

"When?"

"Just now. I just walked in the room two seconds ago."

"What's taking so long?"

"I dunno."

"That's not a very good answer."

"Yeah, well, I prob'ly got less pull around here than you do, so gimme a break. I'm tryin'."

In all the years I had been involved with police investigations, I had never set foot inside the FBI field office. Of course, like most anyone living in Saint Louis, I had driven past it numerous times when traveling along Market Street. Still, it had never been on my top ten list of places to visit, and there was a huge difference between absently cruising past a building and occupying a chair in one of its offices for so long that you literally lose track of the passing hours.

I had to admit, however, that the seating here was vastly more comfortable than the molded plastic dinette refugees I was used to warming when sitting next to Ben's desk at city police headquarters. The coffee was far better too. I just didn't think my stomach could take any more of it, good or not.

"Got some other news," my friend offered. "Mister 'Door Mat' is conscious and talkin'."

Felicity had been wrong. Lewis hadn't been dead after all; this was a fact they quickly discovered when they finally entered the room. He had, however, been unconscious and bleeding from several wounds. Considering how bad he looked when the ambulance crew brought him out, I could easily see why my wife had thought he was deceased. To be honest, up until now I hadn't known whether he had died on the way to the hospital or if he would even recover from his injuries.

"Is he going to be okay?" I asked. As callous as it made me feel, the only reason I cared was because a good portion of my wife's impending fate hinged on his health. Other than that, I didn't give a damn one way or the other, and that was unlike me.

"He actually looked a lot worse than he really was... Not that he ain't pretty screwed up though... He's got a broken nose so mosta the blood ya' saw was from that, and some other superficial wounds...

"He's got some busted ribs, a concussion, and a buncha scrapes 'n cuts... Lotta contusions shaped oddly enough like high-heeled footprints in Firehair's size... Tons of gouges that 'pparently came from the tips of the heels... Guess that's why they call 'im Door Mat though... Go figure...

"Ackman said he's already startin' ta' turn black, blue, purple and the whole nine... Workin' on a pair of shiners that are prob'ly gonna make 'im look like a friggin' raccoon... Gonna have some serious scars too, 'cause she tore 'im up good... Real good..."

My friend finally paused at the end of the inventory, then for some odd reason, he actually let out what sounded to be a perplexed chuckle before continuing. "But yeah... Yeah... He's gonna be just fine. Physically anyway."

"What do you mean?"

"Well, you're not gonna believe this," he replied, shaking his head. "But the first thing the sick fuck wanted ta' know when he came to was where his Mistress was. Ackman said he tried to explain the situation to 'im, but all he did was ask for Mistress Miranda's number, so he could ask her what he was allowed to say. Guess you could say he was exercisin' his right ta' remain silent after bein' Mirandized."

He snickered half-heartedly at his own joke, but his flippancy faded when he noticed that I wasn't laughing. I really couldn't find much of anything funny right now, least of all a play on words when the word happened to be Miranda. I simply stayed quiet and mulled over the meat of the commentary.

Finally, I said, "I guess that means he won't be pressing assault charges against her then."

"Yeah, I really doubt if he'll be filin' a complaint... And if he won't do that, then the prosecuting attorney most likely won't file either... Wouldn't be worth the time. So, I think you're prob'ly free 'n clear on that one," he agreed. "Although, ta' be honest it wouldn't surprise me if ya' ended up filin' a restrainin' order against the friggin' wingnut if he ever finds out where ya' live. It sounds a lot like he lell in fuv with your wife."

"That wasn't my wife he fell for."

"Yeah, I know... But you know what I meant."

"We'll deal with that if it happens," I replied. "I'm just glad she didn't kill him."

"Uh-huh. For his sake or for hers?"

"Hers."

"Yeah. I figured as much."

"Sorry," I told him in a humorless tone. "When it comes to anyone besides my wife right now, I'm just not in a particularly compassionate mood."

"Don't worry 'bout it. Like I said, the sick fuck got 'zactly what he wanted, and he's already beggin' for more."

I fell silent and dropped my eyes back down to the disposable cup in my hands. I watched with a distant gaze as my hands continued moving without the benefit of conscious direction. My left was slowly spinning the Styrofoam vessel while with my right thumbnail I was making small indentations around the rim. It was already starting to crumble where I had been over the same spot repeatedly for who knew how long.

"What time is it?" I finally asked, looking back up to my friend and not bothering to check my own watch.

"Eight thirty or so, why?"

"Just wondering. Seems like we've been here quite awhile."

"Yeah. We have. You got someplace to be? You need me ta' make a call for ya' or somethin'?"

"No," I answered with a shake of my head.

"You sure?"

"No," I repeated, mainly because I wasn't really sure of anything at the moment. For all I knew I was leaving a client hanging or missing a breakfast meeting. That part of my life seemed so distant right now that it was as if it belonged to someone else.

"Well, just let me know if ya' need me to call someone."

"What about you?" I asked, purely out of reflex.

"What about me?"

"Do you have someplace to be?"

"No."

Something about the way he spoke the word sparked a reaction in my brain that made me feel that he was lying.

"No?" I echoed, my psyche still hovering in a no-man's-land somewhere between the conversation and my prison cell of introspection. "Are *you* sure?"

He sighed heavily and dropped his oversized frame into a chair next to me. "Well, funeral's not until tomorrow, not that I really wanna be there ta' begin with. I suppose I did promise Helen I'd help with some stuff today, but that can wait till later."

"Funeral?" I asked.

"Yeah, *the* funeral," he stressed bitterly.

His tone lit a wide swath through the fog of my obfuscation, and I seized on a vague memory that his father had recently crossed over. The remembrance made me feel like I wasn't being much of a friend to him; but then, like I had told him, I wasn't feeling much sympathy for the rest of the world right now anyway.

It also didn't help much that the man next to me had been pointing a gun at my wife only a few hours ago, ready to pull the trigger if he felt it warranted. I still wasn't sure that I had forgiven him for that trespass against our friendship, and I had already told him as much.

After a weighty pause he said, "You know I wasn't aiming for a kill shot, Rowan. Right?"

I knew he couldn't read my mind, but I got the distinct impression that everything I had said to him while standing on that motel parking lot was still weighing on him just as heavily as it was me. I suppose his sudden return to the subject was a verbal testament of that fact.

"I don't want to talk about it right now," I replied coldly.

"I was doin' my job, Row. I wouldn't have killed her."

"Maybe so, but did you really have to treat her the way you did?"

"Whaddaya mean?"

"Cuffing her on the ground like some kind of hardened criminal. I mean, come on… She's over a foot shorter than you and barely a hundred pounds soaking wet, Ben. Not to mention that there were three of you. She was confused and scared. She wasn't dangerous."

"She took Mandalay's weapon, Row."

"You saw what she was wearing. Where was she going to hide it?"

"That's not the point."

"She wasn't dangerous—she *isn't* dangerous, Ben."

"Tell that ta' Door Mat."

"That was different. He obviously wanted the abuse."

"Uh-huh…Yeah, well then forget him. Just grab a mirror an' look at what 'barely a hundred pounds soakin' wet' did ta' *you*."

"That was different too."

"Yeah, right. Well, I wasn't interested in wearin' her claw marks. Neither were Ackman or Drew. It was just procedure, Row."

"I don't want to talk about it."

"Coulda fooled me."

"Let's just drop it, okay?"

"Yeah. Okay. But, the point is I wouldn't have shot to kill. I just want ya' ta' know…" He ended the sentence in a mumble, allowing his voice to trail off.

A tense silence fell between us, and I re-inspected my progress on the coffee cup's disintegrating rim for a long moment while I listened to him shift uncomfortably in his seat.

"Look, if you need to go…" I offered, not looking up.

He replied without hesitation. "Like I said, it can wait. Unless, you're just tryin' ta' get me ta' leave."

"Doesn't matter to me."

"Then I'll wait."

"Well, shouldn't you call your sister then?"

"I'm bettin' she's already seen the news, Row. She'll prob'ly call me."

A faint noise fell in behind his words. Instead of ignoring it, however, this time my attention had been pulled back far enough into the here and now to realize I was hearing a door open behind us as someone entered the office. I turned to glance over my shoulder and saw Special Agent Mandalay coming through the opening.

"Shouldn't you be at the hospital?" Ben asked her as he shot a look her way then did a double take and came up from his seat even as he was turning to fully face her.

"No," she replied. "I should be right where I am."

"You positive 'bout that?"

"The doctor released me hours ago, Ben," she returned. "Lighten up."

"So, you get stitches?"

"Twelve," she said as she reached up and gently touched the gauze bandage taped behind her ear.

"You got a concussion?"

"Mild."

"'Kay then, so shouldn't ya' be resting or somethin'?"

"I need to stay awake, so I might as well be useful," she replied. "Besides, I needed to be down here to pull some strings."

"Yeah, okay," he conceded. "So how's that goin'?"

"We may have it worked out," she told him. "My SAC's got to file something, there's no way around that. But, I think I've convinced him to just turn me in for a letter of censure for temporarily misplacing my sidearm. If we can do that, and make a few calls to the local authorities regarding the actual assault, Felicity should walk away from this okay as long as nothing else changes."

Ben gave her a nod and the grim look on his face left me with the impression that they now shared a secret to which I was not going to be made privy. I assumed it had something to do with the letter of reprimand she was inviting upon herself. While my attitude toward the rest of the world still hadn't changed much, I felt I should at least apologize to her.

"I'm sorry," I blurted. "You shouldn't be taking this on yourself."

"Don't be," she answered with a smile. "It's okay."

"But how is this going to affect your career?" I asked.

She shook her head. "Don't worry about it, Rowan. I'll be fine. Let's just worry about you and Felicity right now."

I didn't press the subject. There was someone else on my mind whose importance outweighed everyone, including me, and Constance had just uttered her name.

"Have you seen her?" I asked hopefully.

She nodded. "That's why I'm here. I'm going to take you to see your wife."

I don't know how long we stood there in the tight embrace. It could have been a minute; it could have been an hour. It didn't matter to me if it was forever, as long as I could hold my wife and feel her heart beating, her warm breath against my neck, and even her hot tears dampening my shoulder.

At the moment, life was far from perfect, but it had taken immense strides from where it had been less than a day before.

We had been left alone in the interview room, Ben and Constance excusing themselves, ostensibly to get coffee. However, it was fairly obvious that the ploy was actually to give us a moment or two of privacy, for which I was appreciative. They even managed to get the agent who had been conducting the interview to join them, although I was certain that the door was still being guarded.

"Oh, *Caorthann*..." Felicity murmured through her quiet sobs as she lifted her head and gazed into my face. Concern welled in her wet eyes as she gently brushed her fingertips against the scabbed over welts along my cheek and whispered, "Gods... What happened?"

"It's nothing," I told her.

"Did *I* do this to you?" she asked.

"No," I replied. "Someone who was keeping you from me did."

She dropped her face back against my shoulder and continued to sniffle as more tears made their way onto my shirt.

"It's okay," I told her. "I'm here. It's going to be fine."

I knew my words had to sound like trite dialogue from a B-movie, but there was nothing else for me to say.

"I don't know what's happening to me, then..." she said, the Celtic brogue thick in her voice.

As much as I adored her on again-off again accent, I never could have imagined how hearing it at this moment could make me feel. Even with the heavy emotion threading through her words, its very sound was a calming melody whispering lightly in my ears.

"I know," I soothed. "I know."

"Aye," she said. "I killed him, didn't I?"

"No," I told her. "No. He's alive and he'll be fine."

I felt her shudder against me as she released a relieved sigh and tightened her grip.

"You're certain?" she whispered.

"Yes."

"I thought sure I had killed him then..." she said as she finally loosened her grip on me and pushed back.

She put her hand to her mouth and trembled as she closed her eyes, tears still rolling down her flushed cheeks. She looked far more waiflike than she had hours before. Her face had been scrubbed clean of the makeup, and her pale complexion was blotchy from her continuous weeping. She was wearing a pair of blue jeans that were a half size or so larger than her shape required and over them, a baggy sweatshirt with a faded and peeling college logo silk-screened above the left breast.

Constance had told me on our way down here that she had brought Felicity some clothing from her own wardrobe since what my wife had been wearing when she was taken into custody was being confiscated. I hadn't been told why they were taking her clothes, but I didn't really care.

It simply didn't matter what she was wearing. It was enough for me that she was safe.

Felicity took in a deep breath and let it out slowly. I could tell she was trying hard to ground herself. I could also tell she was having very little success. After repeating the breaths several times, she finally opened her eyes and looked up at me.

"Aye, what's happening to me then, Rowan?" she asked.

"Honey, we can talk about this later," I replied.

"I need to know," she came back with a pleading tone in her voice.

I looked at her and let out my own heavy sigh. I didn't think this was the time or the place, but she deserved to know. After all, it was her to whom it had happened.

"I think you underwent a possession by a *Lwa*," I stated.

"A *Lwa*? Isn't that a *Vodou* deity?" she asked, sniffling.

"Yes."

"But how? Why?"

"I don't know," I replied, shaking my head. "I wish I did. All I know is that some form of Voodoo ritual was performed at the murder scene where you showed up yesterday."

"But... But why would it affect me, then?" she stammered.

"Again, I don't know," I said with a note of apology in my voice. "I wish I did... Do you remember anything? Anything at all? Maybe that would help us figure it out."

She shook her head then hugged herself tightly as she began pacing around the room. "I remember arguing with a police officer about letting me in somewhere... I'm not really sure where, it's all fuzzy... Then I think I called you on my cell phone... But... But I'm not sure..."

"That would have been the crime scene where the ritual was done," I acknowledged. "Is that it?"

"Aye," she said with a nod then stopped pacing and dropped her eyes to the floor. "After that it was as if I was in a dreamless sleep, right up until I awoke in that room with..."

"It's okay," I told her as her voice trailed off. "You've been through enough."

"Rowan," she said, looking up at me with a startled visage. "They took some of my hair. Why?"

Constance had told me that Felicity had been filled in on her escapades with the assault, taking the firearm, and even some sketchy details about the search that had ensued. My wife's question, however, told me that they had completely left out any reference to her being a suspect in the two homicides. I wasn't sure if that was a good thing or not, but I knew for certain that I didn't want to tell her. Unfortunately, it looked like I wasn't going to have a choice.

"It isn't important right now," I said, stepping forward and reaching for her in an attempt to skirt the issue.

She backed away and cocked her head to the side, unwilling to yield to my half-hearted attempt. "No. Tell me."

I dropped my forehead into my hand and massaged it for a moment before looking back to her frightened face. "They found several long red hairs at both of the homicide crime scenes. After what happened yesterday, you're being considered a suspect."

"Gods..." she murmured, as an icy terror frosted her eyes.

"It's going to be okay, honey," I offered. "When they compare your hair with the ones from the crime scenes, you'll be cleared."

"Aye, and what if I'm not?"

"You will be."

"Rowan..." she started, then paused.

"What?"

"There *is* something else I remember then," she said quietly.

"What?"

She swallowed hard, looked to the ceiling, then back to my face. "When I woke up in the motel room, I was standing on that man's chest and stamping on his face."

I shook my head hard and waved at her with a dismissive gesture. "That's not important honey. You were under the influence of a spirit possession at the time."

"No, you don't understand," she objected. "When I came to, that was what I was doing, and I was... I was... Aroused."

"Again, that's part of..."

"Listen to me, Rowan," she interrupted. "I was VERY aroused."

"So?"

"So... So..." She closed her eyes again as she took in a deep breath then opened them and blurted, "So I kept doing it."

"You kept doing what?" I asked, even though I was afraid I already knew the answer.

"I kept stomping on him," she said, her voice cracking with a mix of fear and excitement. "I didn't stop. I just kept stomping on his body because it felt so good to do it... To be dominant... To punish him... I was enjoying it, and I kept going until... Until... Until I came to an orgasm."

I stared back at her. I truly didn't know what to say.

"Have you told anyone else about this?" I finally managed to ask.

"No."

"Don't."

"Aye, but maybe I should," she replied, her voice near a whisper. "Maybe it is me. Maybe I *am* the killer."

CHAPTER 37:

*M*aybe *I* am *the killer.*
    Those words echoed inside my skull as I stood there in the wake of my wife's fading voice. She already had more than enough people who truly believed that speculation to be fact. She certainly didn't need any more. Hell, even my own faith in her had been shaken for an instant during the night, but for her to now doubt her own sanity simply wouldn't do. She couldn't afford to let that happen right now, because the fear that came with questioning your own right-mindedness was a terror like no other, and it would consume you if you allowed it to take hold.

    Unfortunately, I could already see it swelling behind her eyes, and she was looking to me to stop it. I couldn't say that I didn't understand what she was going through inside her head, because I did, all too well. I had been suspect of my own grasp on reality more than once over the past several years.

    She and Ben had too.

    Still, that didn't give me the right to doubt hers now. In fact, it simply meant that I needed to stand by her just as she had by me, even while her certainty in my saneness was faltering.

    She kept her gaze locked with mine, eyes searching my face, and I knew she was looking for a reaction. More than that, she was seeking a lifeline, a reason to maintain hope. And, it had to come from me, no one else.

    I finally shook my head and said, "No, Felicity. You aren't the killer."

    "How do you know?"

    "I just do."

    "I wish I could be so sure."

    "You don't really believe that you killed anyone, do you?"

    "Right now, I don't know."

"Well, you didn't."

"How can you be so sure, then?" she asked, blatantly challenging me to prove my belief in her innocence.

"Simple. How did you feel when you came to?" I asked.

"I just told you," she murmured. "I was turned on."

"No, I mean other than that."

"A bit dizzy," she replied. "Disoriented for a moment, maybe. But that passed quickly."

"Sounds like a possession, or at the very least an unchecked channeling, to me."

"But you don't understand how aroused…"

"Actually, yes, I do." I cut her off, remembering the swell of internal pleasure that had accosted me at the last crime scene before I had managed to ground myself. "Believe it or not, I do. And, trust me, that doesn't make you the killer."

"I don't know, then."

"Like I said, I do," I replied.

"I appreciate your blind faith, Rowan, but it doesn't help me."

"Okay, let me ask you this: Where were you Monday night?"

"Why?"

"Just tell me where you were."

She shook her head then shrugged, and I could see by her expression that she was searching her memory for the answer. "Monday, I did a last minute product shoot for a new client and it ran late. But you know that."

"Yes, I do," I said with a nod. "But, now you need to remind yourself."

She shrugged again but began reciting facts as if she was comforted by the fact that she could actually remember them. "Well, they were better than an hour outside Saint Louis, and when I left their office it was late… I took a wrong turn getting back to the highway and got lost for a bit… It was almost two when I finally got home… And then I'd barely gotten to sleep when Ben called."

"There you go."

"There I go what?"

"You just gave me your alibi for when Hammond Wentworth was murdered."

"Perhaps, but what if I just don't remember doing it?"

"You remember the details of the photo shoot and the trip home, don't you?"

"Aye."

"Any blackouts? Time you can't account for?"

"No."

"Then you're in the clear."

"But what if it's a false memory?"

"Any seemingly false memories from last night?"

"I don't think so."

"I would think that if your psyche were going to produce false memories to account for your actions, it would have made some up to cover the ten or so hours you're missing right now."

"Aye, maybe so."

"And, I bet we can call the client and verify your story."

"All right then, but what of the other one?"

"Even simpler. I'm your alibi. That victim was killed while you and I were in bed asleep."

"But are you sure I was there?"

"Honey, what are you trying to do? Make a case for the prosecution?"

"No," she replied, frustration thick in her voice. "I just don't remember anything after we went to bed. Just like last night."

"That's because we were both completely exhausted, Felicity," I explained. "We were asleep. Hell, we *over*slept."

"But, what if I was sleepwalking?"

"You weren't."

"How do you know?"

"I just do."

"Were you awake, then? Did you sit and watch me sleeping?"

"No, but that doesn't matter."

"Of course it does!" she exclaimed. "Rowan, you channeled a killer once, remember? And, you went out roaming the city without any memory of it. Just like is happening to me. But, maybe, just maybe I went that extra step and really did murder someone!"

"That was different."

"Different how?"

"It just was."

"That's not good enough. How do you know I didn't do it?"

"Because I'm telling you that you didn't," I replied, my voice moving perceptibly up in volume.

"You can't know that!" she insisted, raising her voice as well.

"Yes, by the fucking Gods I can!" I declared harshly. "You didn't do it, Felicity!"

She stared back at me for a moment then took in a deep breath and said with strained calm, "Because I really didn't do it, or because you just refuse to believe that I did?"

"Both," I told her, my voice now barely above a whisper.

She continued to stare at me for a long moment then slowly buried her face in her hands. I watched her shoulders rise and fall as again she tried to force herself to ground and center.

"Aye," she finally said, looking back up at me. "Suppose you're right? What about last night then? What I did to that man even after I came to. Explain that."

"I already did."

"No, you didn't. I'm not talking about while I was blacked out. I'm talking about after," she appealed. "Don't you get it, Rowan? I was conscious of what I was doing, and I got off on it."

"Did you?"

"Yes," she returned. "I can't believe I'm standing here saying this, but yes. I had an absolutely incredible orgasm."

"That's not what I'm asking. I mean did you really get off on what you did to him?"

She gave her head a confused shake. "I just told you I did."

"If *you* really did, then why did *you* pick up his phone and call me?"

She stared at me a moment then said, "I was scared."

"I know."

"But..."

I stopped her before she could finish voicing her objection. "But nothing, honey. Look, I know that you're actually into the dominant role-play thing, and I'm sure that in some way that fact helped fuel what was happening to you. But tell me the truth. Have you ever seriously entertained the idea of physically hurting me and gotten aroused by it?"

"Yes."

"I mean before the other day."

"Yes," she repeated in a deadly serious tone, nodding vigorously to punctuate the word. "I've actually fantasized about dominating you."

I was slightly taken aback but not overly surprised by her candid answer. Given what I had learned about her a few days prior, I should have expected it. Still, I tried my best not to betray the fact that I was a bit ruffled. Some glimmer of an expression must have passed across my face, however, because she suddenly rushed to explain.

"Yes, I've wanted to *play*," she said. "And, I've even hinted at it a few times. I just never had the courage to come right out and ask if you would be interested in experimenting that way. I... I didn't want you to... to..."

"To what? Think you were strange?"

"No. I didn't want you to stop loving me."

"That's not going to happen."

"Promise?"

"Promise."

"So you still don't think it was all me? Even after what I just told you?"

"No, I don't, but if you still need convincing, let me re-phrase the question. You just said *play*. You even stressed the word. So, have you ever entertained the idea of taking it beyond a game? Of hurting me so badly that I ended up in the hospital?"

"No..." she said, shaking her head. "Of course not. I would never..."

"Well, that's exactly where you put that man last night."

"But, I love you," she countered. "Maybe I was capable of hurting him that badly because I don't have any feelings for him."

"Emotional attachment or not, I don't believe that the Felicity Caitlin O'Brien I married is capable of that level of malice."

"Maybe I'm not her anymore."

"Yes, you are. You weren't last night, but you are now, and I'm going to prove it."

"How?"

"I don't know yet," I said, stepping toward her again, and this time she didn't shy away. "Look, I'm nowhere near knowledgeable enough about Voodoo to tell you for sure what happened to you yesterday, or more importantly, why. What I do know, however, is that either you were possessed by someone, or you were seriously channeling someone... There's no doubt in my mind about that...

"And, just so you know, no matter how dominant you think you are, the person who was controlling your body yesterday makes Felicity O'Brien look like Little Red Riding Hood."

She allowed herself a half-hearted smile then shook her head. "I'm still scared."

"I know."

"So... What is going to happen now?"

"Constance didn't tell you?" I asked.

"Not really."

"Well, she's falling on her sword for you."

"How so?"

"She's convinced her superiors to clean your slate and give her a reprimand."

"How did she manage that?"

"I have no idea."

"Aye, but she didn't do anything wrong."

"No, she didn't."

Felicity simply sighed and fell against me once again. I slipped my arms around her as she quietly rested her head on my shoulder. She didn't resume her sobbing, and I took that as a good sign. But, I could easily feel her confusion and fear flowing into me, prickling my skin with a cold wave of gooseflesh.

I stroked her hair as I gently rocked her. After a comfortable silence I said, "If I understood Constance correctly, they should be letting you out of here soon. Then we can go home."

"And then?"

"And then I figure out what's going on and why it's happening to you."

She didn't answer me right away, but when she did her voice was a pleading whisper. "Make it stop, Rowan... Please..."

"I'm trying" was all I could think of to say.

Friday, November 18
1:27 P.M.
Saint Louis, Missouri

CHAPTER 38:

My head was killing me, and the aspirin I had taken earlier hadn't even fazed the pain. I knew full well that generally meant there was something more to it than simple brain chemistry or inflamed sinuses. However, I had been putting in far more hours than usual in front of my computer, so it was more than likely eyestrain. At least, that was what I was telling myself.

Ever since bringing Felicity back home just over a week ago, researching Voodoo, as well as its related offshoots and similar religions, had become a near obsession for me. Every waking moment I had free from my business or other daily chores, I spent reading, surfing the net, or even making calls in an attempt to track down information.

It was really all that I could do. I wasn't being brought into the investigation any longer, and the last time I had spoken to Ben had been at his father's funeral. Even then the conversation was clipped and stiff. I'd also heard nothing more about the physical evidence that had been mentioned. I wasn't sure whether to be worried about that or simply consider it a blessing.

Still, I felt I had to do something, and finding out all I could about Voodoo seemed to be the best use of my time. Maybe I could find something that would help track down the actual killer. Unfortunately, while I was now armed with far more knowledge on the subject than I had been several days prior, or had ever wanted to know for that matter, I was just becoming more and more confused.

Certain questions were answered, of course, such as the heretofore-unrealized significance behind the murder of Officer Hobbes. I didn't actually make the connection right away. Not until I read an in-depth chapter pertaining to *Ezili Dantó* in one of the many books I had obtained. I discovered that this particular *Lwa* tended to demand of her followers the sacrifice of a black pig. I also found out that such an animal was rare here in the U.S. and was native to Haiti—a bit of trivia I hadn't known. Suddenly, the choice of Officer Hobbes as a victim made sense, especially for a serial killer who was twisting the religion to fit her purpose. Granted, it was a convoluted and sick kind of sense, but it made sense all the same.

I had also managed very easily to verify my identification of the *Papa Legba veve,* as well as corroborate the sketchy information given me by the paramedic. The third *veve,* however, remained slightly elusive. I had been fruitless in my quest to pin it on any widely known *Lwa,* so I had to assume that it really did signify a personal ancestor or guiding spirit of sorts. Since the offerings left for it were perfume and lipstick, it was a good bet that said spirit was also female. I wasn't terribly surprised.

After making a sketch of the triskele-like symbol for Felicity, she had informed me that she'd seen it several times before, and she wasn't referring to the Celtic religious icon. According to her it was yet another emblem of the dom-sub bondage crowd. She explained that each third was meant to signify a facet of the subculture—D/S, B/D, S/M. Each dot residing within the thirds was also important, supposedly holding the individual meanings: safe, sane, and consensual.

Under the circumstances, I found that last set of details to be considerably ironic.

On the flip side of the coin, however, it seemed that more questions were being raised than were being answered. Just as I had suspected, while dealing with my foggy memories of what I'd read on the subject, *Lwa* didn't tend to possess non-followers. They also didn't even make a habit of taking over their followers just for something to do. And, while there were exceptions, spirit possessions did usually occur within the confines of a ritual.

That general idea certainly made sense where the killer was concerned but not necessarily where I was looking to apply it.

One of the primary questions that still remained was whether or not Felicity's preternatural incident had actually been her body being used as a *horse* by a *Lwa*, or if it was something else entirely? And, if it was something else, just exactly what was it? Moreover, why had she been the victim of it in the first place?

It was for all of those reasons, as well as a host of others, that I once again found myself making a long distance call to yet another someone I had never met, nor had any reason to believe would be willing to talk to me, much less answer my questions.

I tilted my head up and peered at my screen through the bottom half of my bifocals as I punched in the phone number listed on the web page before me. Once I entered the string of digits, I rocked back in my chair and began idly moving the mouse across the surface of my desk. I watched the pointer move about the screen in the random patterns I was creating as the phone began to ring several hundred miles away.

"Louisiana State University Department of Sociology," a woman's voice eventually drawled into my ear. "How may I direct your call?"

"Doctor Rieth's office, please," I replied.

"Please hold."

I continued watching the pointer as I nudged it around the screen. My real attention, however, remained focused on the hollow sound of the phone as I waited for the transfer to occur.

A minute or so passed before there was a dull click at the other end and a new voice issued from the handset. "Doctor Rieth's office, this is Kathy, may I help you?"

"Good afternoon, Kathy," I said as I rocked back forward and straightened my posture. "Is Doctor Rieth in by any chance?"

"No sir, I'm afraid she's gone for the holiday break. I'm her assistant, can I help you?"

It hadn't even dawned on me that Thanksgiving was less than one week away at this point. Considering that, I was probably fortunate to have reached anyone at the University at all.

"No offense, but probably not," I replied. "I'm calling from Saint Louis, and I need to speak with the doctor about something in her book, *Voodoo Practice in American Culture.*"

I glanced at the corner of my desk where the tome was resting atop a pile of other books, all with the same general subject matter, Afro-Cuban religion and mysticism.

"I'm sorry, sir, but all queries regarding Doctor Rieth's books should be made via the University Press," Kathy replied, launching into a decidedly prepared sounding spiel. "The address can be found..."

"I understand that," I spoke up, truncating her instructions. "Please understand that I'm not looking for an autograph or trying to dispute her or anything like that. I'm doing some research regarding a murder investigation here, and I think she might be able to help me."

There was no reply from the other end, but I could still hear background noise, so I knew she hadn't hung up.

"Hello?" I said.

"Yes, I'm here," the assistant replied. "I'm sorry. Where did you say you were calling from again?"

"Saint Louis, Missouri, why?"

"Just curious. Doctor Rieth received a call a year or so back from a police officer in South Carolina regarding a murder investigation."

My curiosity was immediately piqued. "Really? Do you remember any of the details?"

"No," she replied. "And, honestly, I really shouldn't have said anything."

"That's okay, I won't tell," I replied half jokingly then moved on rather than risk alienating her. "Is there any way I can reach Doctor Rieth? It's very important."

"I'm afraid not," she replied. "She is scheduled to return the Monday after the holiday however."

I wasn't excited about the wait, but it was just that time of year, so there was little I could do. I went ahead and asked, "Do you think it would be possible for me to leave a message for the doctor then?"

"Yes sir, I can certainly do that," she answered. "Which police department are you with again?"

"I'm actually an independent consultant," I explained then took the truth and wrapped it into an interwoven pretzel before relaying it to her. "I'm currently working with the Greater Saint Louis Major Case Squad."

It wasn't a complete lie, but I hoped that the doctor didn't elect to verify my story because I was betting no one would be willing to back me up. Right now I was apparently persona non grata, but even when I was actually working with them, my capacity wasn't exactly what one could call official.

I finished giving her my contact information and bid her a pleasant afternoon before hanging up and pondering what the young woman had just let slip. Hopefully, if and when Doctor Rieth returned my call, she would be willing to share a bit more about what she had consulted on in South Carolina.

I picked up a pen and jotted a quick note about it in a steno pad I had been using for keeping track of my research. I heard the dogs barking outside and wondered for a moment if they were wanting back in the house. I started to get up, but they quieted down before I could get completely out of my seat, so I figured it must be a taunting squirrel or simply a passerby. When I settled back into the chair, however, a familiar prickling sensation crawled across the back of my neck as I felt my hair pivoting at the roots.

I reached up and rubbed the offending spot as I looked around the room. I couldn't imagine a reason for the brief attack of shivers. It faded quickly so I tried to put it out of my mind.

Returning to the materials I had at hand, I shuffled through the stack of books on my desk and withdrew another one, heavily laden with bookmarks protruding from the end, and flipped it open to the copyright page. I was just about to begin typing in the publisher's website address in search of contact information for the author when I heard the doorbell ring.

Now I had my answer as to why the dogs had been barking.

I knew Felicity was downstairs in her darkroom and probably wouldn't be able to answer it. In reality, most of her work these days was digital and didn't require the somewhat antiquated processes of chemicals and light sensitive papers. However, I had the impression that my wife was finding the familiarity and closeness of her analog workspace a comfort in the wake of her recent experience. Put simply, she was hiding from the world, and while I was willing to condone it for a brief period, I wasn't going to allow her to do it forever. But, at this particular moment, I wasn't going to press the issue.

I tossed the book back onto the pile and pushed away from my desk. I found that I had to skirt around Dickens, our black domestic feline, who had elected to take a nap almost immediately in front of the office door. He opened one yellow eye and regarded me silently as I stepped over him, but other than that he didn't even twitch.

I was making my way down the stairs when the doorbell pealed once again in a rapid staccato.

"Hold on!" I yelled, not that I really expected anyone outside to hear me. "I'm coming, I'm coming…"

I skipped the last couple of stairs near the bottom, making the turn at the landing and almost jogged across the living room. With a quick turn of my wrist, I unlocked the door and swung it open.

Ben Storm was standing on my front porch, along with someone else I thought I recognized as a detective with the MCS but to whom I couldn't place a name. Neither of them looked particularly happy, but I didn't need to see their expressions to know something was wrong. I had been feeling the warning signs for a while now. I had just been too absorbed, and even more unwilling, to pay attention to them.

I had pretty much forgiven my friend for the incident involving the gun pointed at my wife, but there was still a bit of tension between us. Whether it was because of something yet unresolved regarding that, or if it was simply because Felicity was still considered a suspect in the eyes of the Major Case Squad, I wasn't sure. Either way, I had no choice but to feel it flowing between us right now as our eyes met.

Ben reached out and pulled the storm door open and looked at me quietly for a heartbeat or two before saying, "Do you mind if we come in, Row?"

I definitely didn't like the sound of his voice, and my skin started prickling once again.

"That depends, Ben," I replied evenly. "Do I have any choice in the matter?"

He reached up and smoothed his hair back, looked down at the porch briefly, then back up to my face. "Actually... No."

"Do I need to call our attorney?" I asked.

He returned a shallow nod. "It'd be a good idea, Row."

Ten minutes later I was standing in the middle of my living room, a copy of an arrest warrant clenched in my fist and quiet rage boiling in my chest as my friend applied a pair of handcuffs to my wife.

As he was snapping them shut, I heard him quietly say to her, "Felicity, listen ta' me carefully, and do exactly what I tell ya'. Just acknowledge your rights, and then don't say another word. Do ya' hear me?"

"Detective Storm!" the other man said.

"Fuck off," my friend barked, shooting a hard stare at the other cop.

Thick silence filled in behind the outburst, and he turned back to Felicity. His voice slipped into an official tenor, droning through a flat monotone.

As he spoke, his words bit into my skull, raping my ears with the vile reason for their existence.

"You have the right to remain silent and refuse to answer questions. Do you understand?..."

Saturday, November 19
10:05 A.M.
Saint Louis, Missouri

EPILOGUE:

The man hadn't slept in better than twenty-four hours. Not since he had awakened early Friday morning. His eyes were bloodshot, and his face sagged with exhaustion, but sleep simply wouldn't come. Every time he closed his eyes, he saw her face.

Her face as it grew even paler than her ivory skin could possibly be...

Her eyes as she looked to him for salvation he was unable to give...

Her lips as she plead with him, calling his name even though they were beginning to tremble...

Her mask of fear as she was placed in restraints and hastily led away from him...

He sighed heavily and felt the pain well deep within once again. The sadness was overwhelming, and all he really wanted to do was sit and cry. But, he couldn't. There were no more tears left. He had already used them all.

Besides, crying wasn't going to do any good, and he knew that. He just wasn't sure what would.

Sharp sound split the silence. The phone was ringing, rattling through the house with a haunting echo. After three repetitions, there was a click, and the outgoing message from the answering machine spilled into the room.

"You have reached the Gant and O'Brien household, please leave a message..."

There was a short pause, and it was then followed by a high-pitched electronic tone. On its heels came an angry male voice affected with a harsh Irish accent. "You damn bastard!... I know you're there!... Pick up the phone!... This is all your fault, Rowan Gant! You and your Godlessness!... Damn your eyes, you bastard! Look what you've done to her! Look what you've done to my daughter!"

A heavy click came immediately behind the angry words as the phone at the calling end was slammed down. This wasn't the first message of that sort that had been left, and it was sure not to be the last.

Even so, the man ignored it just like all the rest.

He continued moving through the seemingly empty house, trudging about with no particular mission in mind. The place was an absolute wreck. Emptied drawers, upturned cushions. Visible carnage where the police had executed their search warrant, seizing everything from articles of her clothing to some of the books that he had checked out of the local library.

Through it all, a man he called his best friend stood watching, an unspoken apology obvious in his eyes.

Once again, the telephone began to peal, interrupting the man's anguish with its unwanted bid for attention. The last bell in the trio of rings ended, and the machine burped its greeting once again. This time, in the wake of the tone, a wholly different voice issued from the speaker. One that was authoritative, feminine, and possessed of a heavy Southern accent.

"I am calling for a Mister Rowan Gant," the woman announced. "I picked up a message from my office that he was trying to reach me. My name is Doctor Velvet Rieth, and I can…"

The man had the phone off the hook before she could complete the sentence.

It can only get worse before it gets better,
and Rowan Gant knows that more than anyone…

ALL ACTS OF PLEASURE
A ROWAN GANT INVESTIGATION

Novel number seven
in the bestselling
RGI Series

Coming to bookstores nationwide
Autumn 2006

The Rowan Gant Investigations
Serial Killers...

MURDEROUS SATAN WORSHIPPING WITCHES

When a young woman is ritualistically murdered in her Saint Louis apartment with the primary clue being a pentacle scrawled in her own blood, police are quick to dismiss it as a cult killing. Not one for taking things at face value, city homicide detective Ben Storm calls on his long time friend, Rowan Gant—a practicing Witch—for help.

In helping his friend, Rowan discovers that the victim is one of his former pupils. Even worse, the clues that he helps to uncover show that this murder is only a prelude to even more ritualistic bloodletting for dark purposes.

As the body count starts to rise, Rowan is suddenly thrust into an investigation where not only must he help stop a sadistic serial killer, but also must fight the prejudices and suspicions of those his is working with—including his best friend.

THE RETURN OF THE BURNING TIMES

In 1484, then Pope Innocent VIII issued a papal bull—a decree giving the endorsement of the church to the inquisitors of the day who hunted, tortured, tried and ultimately murdered those accused of heresy—especially the practice of WitchCraft. Modern day Witches refer to this dark period of history as "The Burning Times."

Rowan Gant returns to face a nightmare long thought to be a distant memory. A killer armed with gross misinterpretations of the *Holy Bible* and a 15th century Witch hunting manual known as the *Malleus Maleficarum* has resurrected the Inquisition and the members of the Pagan community of St. Louis are his prey.

With the unspeakable horrors of "The Burning Times" being played out across the metropolitan area, Rowan is again enlisted by homicide detective Benjamin Storm and the Major Case Squad to help solve the crimes—all the while knowing full well that his religion makes him a potential target.

ISBN 096782219X / $8.95 US

PICTURE PERFECT

Rowan Gant is a Witch.
His bane is to see things that others cannot.
To feel things he wishes he could not.
To experience events through the eyes of another...
Through the eyes of victims...
Sometimes, the things he sees are evil...
Criminal...
Because of this, in the span of less than two years, Rowan has come face to face with not one, but two sadistic serial killers...
In both cases he was lucky to survive.
Still, he abides the basic rule of The Craft—Harm None.

This predator could make Rowan forget that rule...

LET THE BURNINGS BEGIN...

In February of 2001, serial killer Eldon Andrew Porter set about creating a modern day version of the 15th century inquisition and Witch trials. Following the tenets of the *Malleus Maleficarum* and his own insane interpretation of the *Holy Bible*, he tortured and subsequently murdered several innocent people.

During a showdown on the old Chain of Rocks Bridge, he narrowly escaped apprehension by the Greater St. Louis Major Case Squad.

In the process, his left arm was severely crippled by a gunshot fired at close range.

A gunshot fired by a man he was trying to kill. A man who embraced the mystical arts. A Witch. Rowan Gant.

In December of the same year, Eldon Porter's fingerprints were found at the scene of a horrific murder in Cape Girardeau, Missouri, just south of St. Louis. An eyewitness who later spotted the victim's stolen vehicle reported that it was headed north...

ISBN 0967822181 / $14.95 US

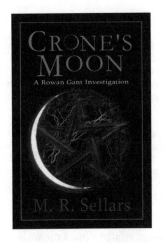

Photograph Copyright © 2004, K. J. Epps

ABOUT THE AUTHOR

M. R. Sellars has been called the "Dennis Miller of Paganism" for his quick wit and humorously deadpan observations of life within the Pagan community and beyond. However, his humor is only one facet of his personality, as evidenced by the dark thrillers he pens.

While being fast-paced, intensely entertaining reads, his books are also filled with real-life pagan dynamics and even a dash of magick! All of the current *Rowan Gant* novels have spent several consecutive weeks on numerous bookstore bestseller lists. *The Law of Three*, book #4 in the saga, received the *St. Louis Riverfront Times People's Choice award* soon after its debut.

An honorary elder of *Mystic Moon*, a teaching coven based in Kansas City, and an honorary member of *Dragon Clan Circle* in Indiana, Sellars is for the most part a solitary practitioner of an eclectic mix of Pagan paths, and has been since the late seventies. He currently resides in the Midwest with his wife, daughter, and a host of rescued felines. His schedule never seems to slow down and when not writing, researching a project, or taking time to spend with his family, he can be found on the road performing workshops and book signings nationwide.

At the time of this writing, Sellars is working on several projects, as well as traveling on promotional tour.

For more information about M. R. Sellars and his work, visit him on the World Wide Web at www.mrsellars.com.